EX LIBRIS

VINTAGE **CLASSICS**

THE MASTER AND MARGARITA

Mikhail Afanasievich Bulgakov was born in Kiev on 15 May 1891. He graduated as a doctor from Kiev University in 1916, but gave up the practice of medicine in 1920 to devote himself to literature. In 1925 he completed the satirical novel *The Heart of a Dog,* which remained unpublished in the Soviet Union until 1987. This was one of the many defeats he was to suffer at the hands of the censors. By 1930 Bulgakov had become so frustrated by the political atmosphere and the suppression of his works that he wrote to Stalin begging to be allowed to emigrate if he was not to be given the opportunity to make his living as a writer in the USSR. Stalin telephoned him personally and offered to arrange a job for him at the Moscow Arts Theatre instead. In 1938, a year before contracting a fatal illness, he completed his prose masterpiece, *The Master and Margarita.* He died in 1940. In 1966–7, thanks to the persistence of his widow, the novel made a first, incomplete, appearance in *Moskva,* and in 1973 appeared in full.

ALSO BY MIKHAIL BULGAKOV

Fiction

Diaboliad

The Heart of a Dog

The White Guard

A Country Doctor's Notebook

Black Snow

Drama

The Days of the Turbins

Zoya's Apartment

The Crimson Island

Flight

The Cabal of Hypocrites

Adam and Eve

Bliss

Ivan Vasilievich

Last Days

Batum

About Mikhail Bulgakov

Manuscripts Don't Burn: A Life in Letters and Diaries
Compiled and translated by J. A. E. Curtis

MIKHAIL BULGAKOV

The Master and Margarita

TRANSLATED FROM THE RUSSIAN BY
Michael Glenny

WITH AN INTRODUCTION BY
Will Self

VINTAGE BOOKS
London

Published by Vintage 2004

12

Copyright in the English translation © The Harvill Press and
Harper and Row Publishers 1967

First published in Great Britain in 1967 by Collins and
The Harvill Press

First published by Vintage in 2003

Vintage
Random House, 20 Vauxhall Bridge Road,
London SW1V 2SA

www.vintage-classics.info

Addresses for companies within The Random House Group Limited
can be found at: www.randomhouse.co.uk/offices.htm

The Random House Group Limited Reg. No. 954009

A CIP catalogue record for this book
is available from the British Library

ISBN 9780099540946

Penguin Random House is committed to a sustainable future for
our business, our readers and our planet. This book is made from
Forest Stewardship Council® certified paper.

Printed and bound in Great Britain by Clays Ltd, St Ives plc

INTRODUCTION

I can't recall exactly when I first read *The Master and Margarita*, but it was almost certainly in the mid-1970s. The curious thing about reading the novel at that time was that although Bulgakov had still been working on a fourth draft shortly before his death in 1940, no part of the work was published until 1966, when expurgated sections appeared in *Moscow* magazine. All the material that had been redacted was subsequently available, in Russia, in samizdat form, and an English translation appeared in the same year in a single volume. *The Master and Margarita* was thus a literary phenomenon experienced simultaneously in the Russian and the English-speaking world, while even a decade later it still had the faint – yet still discernible – penumbra that surrounds an exciting contemporary novel.

Of course, the synchrony of *The Master and Margarita* appearing on the cusp of the 1960s social and cultural revolutions was not accidental; the brief thawing of the Soviet hegemony that was to lead to the Prague Spring was underway, and while the flower-waving, guitar-strumming, and even Molotov-cocktail-mixing of Western youth is perhaps not to be confused with such a serious assault upon a serious tyranny, with the benefit of lengthening hindsight the extent to which West and East were not-much-funhouse mirror images of one another throughout the Cold War seems only to magnify.

Nevertheless, while the impact of the book in the USSR may have been broadly along the axis between the political and the satiric, in the West it was along the line stretched – mostly tendentiously – from the spiritual to the hallucinogenic. During this era a number of anti-naturalist literary works underwent a retrospective conversion to the cause of Freak Power, most notably *Alice in Wonderland*, which took on a troubling new life, when, in her trademark sing-scream,

Jefferson Airplane's Grace Slick admonished her loved-up listeners, 'And you've just had some kind of mushroom / And your mind is moving slow / Go ask Alice / I think she'll know'.

The Master and Margarita is certainly a calculated exercise in mind-bending and the stresses it provokes. Some critics have pointed to Bulgakov's own year as morphine addict for an explanation of his flamboyantly hallucinogenic prose – but I think this unlikely; opiates are not particularly perception-distorting (certainly not when compared with actual hallucinogens such as LSD and marijuana), and the writer (who at that time was labouring in the wreckage of the Russian civil war as an under-qualified doctor), seems most likely to have become accidentally addicted as a side-effect of self-medication.

Nevertheless, *The Master and Margarita* has been cited as a seminal influence on the Rolling Stones' song 'Sympathy for the Devil'[1], although not by Mick Jagger himself, who was its principal begetter. There may be an element of muddying the waters here – a refusal to acknowledge liberal borrowing; certainly the parallels between Jagger's Lucifer and Bulgakov's Woland are considerable: both are boastful about their longevity and presence at the crucial and bloody junctures of human history; both are dandyish – at once *raffinée* and dissolute. Moreover, the lines with which Jagger's Devil presents himself: 'Please allow me to introduce myself / I'm a man of wealth and taste . . .' have an obvious correspondence to Woland's opening remark to the unfortunate literary functionary, Berlioz: 'Excuse me, please . . . for permitting myself, without an introduction . . .'

But let's not get carried away by this; Bulgakov would certainly have recognised his descriptions of the diabolic as being travestied in the Rolling Stones' stage shtick of the late 1960s and early 70s – the cloaks, the sceptres, the dresses, the skulls: a festival *saison d'enfer* – but the Russian master could in no way be to blame for the way their Satanic Majesties subsequently transmogrified into a stadium rock act sponsored by an underwear manufacturer. No, in as much as *The Master*

---

[1] From the 1968 album *Beggar's Banquet*

and Margarita shared the fate of other anti-naturalist literary classics, becoming just another item on sale in the cultural bargain basement frequented by kohl-eyed Goths, so its author's very real intent – satiric, philosophic, religious – was utterly lost.

I certainly remember the impact that the novel had on me. It arrived at a vital moment during my own progression towards becoming a writer, and like a handful of other texts showed me the way ahead by imprinting on the polymorphous clay of the collective imagination a definite form: something to aim at. Subsequently, my own novel, *My Idea of Fun* (1993), featured a diabolic protagonist, The Fat Controller, who, with his mixture of carnival hocus-pocus and very real malevolence bears a strong resemblance to Woland. I even stole (and that is the correct term here, 'borrowed' would imply I intended giving it back), the entire fluid drift of Woland's arrival in Moscow, with its instances of uncanny precognition, its seeding of anarchy, and its local – yet devastating – eruptions of the supernatural into the bog-ordinary urban context.

Bulgakov's novel – as did his more succinct and pointed satire, *The Heart of a Dog* (1925) – taught me some key lessons about how to practise the darkest of the novelist's arts: suspending the reader's disbelief. This exercise in levitation is always best achieved in one of two ways: either by foregrounding that which the reader finds offensive to her commonsense with specious – yet incrementally credible – propositions; or else by letting her have it, sans phrase. An example of the former method of flying fancy might be Huxley's *Brave New World*, with its cod-science, and elaborations upon social planning; for the latter we need look no further than Kafka's *The Metamorphosis* (1915), the opening line of which, 'As Gregor Samsa awoke one morning from uneasy dreams he found himself transformed in his bed into a gigantic vermin', challenges the sceptic either to take issue – and so presumably abandon the novella at once – or else accept this 'impossibility', and having done so all that needs must follow.

The examples I cite are mine – Bulgakov had his own conjuring tutors. Almost certainly it was from Gogol that he learnt to blend the two techniques; at once assaulting the reader with the incredible, and disguising the point at which it joins with natural law deep in the shabby folds of the quotidian. That Bulgakov was an earnest student of Gogol we know: he worked long and hard on a stage adaptation of *Dead Souls*; and although neither that novel's protagonist, Chichikov, nor the hapless barber, Yakolevich – who finds the eponymous 'Nose' in his breakfast – bears any resemblance to Woland, these works are perfect examples of the two methods.

Much is made of Bulgakov – and indeed of Gogol – as a 'precursor' of Magical Realism, the school of the credibly fantastic that found its codification – if not summation – in the works of the South American novelists Gabriel Garcia Marquez, Carlos Fuentes and Isabel Allende *inter alia*. I think this a perfect nonsense – quite as wrongheaded as imagining *Tristram Shandy* or *Don Quixote* to be precursors of literary postmodernism. The truth is that almost all styles and modes of fictionalising were attempted before the crystallization of the social-realist novel in the nineteenth century; that this one mode has become a deadening – near-Stalinist – orthodoxy says much about the extent to which literature is the complaisant poodle of post-Enlightenment progressivism, and very little about the rites that may be performed at the altar of high art.

Bulgakov's Woland is, I would argue, not synonymous with the Christian Satan[2], any more than his Yeshua Ha-Notsri is identical with the Jesus Christ either of scriptural record, historical fact, or millenarian belief. One of the aspects of *The Master and Margarita* I found so liberating was that Bulgakov deposed at one and the same time the eternal gods of moral

[2] Indeed, although I've never seen it cited as an influence before, it seems to me quite probable that Woland's arrival in Moscow was, in part, formulated by Bulgakov as both a riposte and a complement to Dostoevski's *The Idiot* (1869), in which the Christ-like Myshkin returns to Petersburg and has a similarly disruptive impact.

absolutism *and* the temporal powers of physics. He understood perfectly that in a cosmos no longer governed an omniscient, omnipotent super-being, all sorts of odd sports and chimeras must exist. Hence Woland – a high-ranking demon – and his entourage of ipsissimii, minor demons such as Koroviev, Behemoth and Azazello. Woland is no more absolutely evil, than Yeshua is absolutely good – or divine. We see no godly special effects in the crucifixion sections of the novel, such as we've come to expect of the faithful's depictions – from the Pauline to the Gibsonian; and the magic tricks and japes of the Moscow tourists can – once the dust has settled – be dismissed, albeit with difficulty, as just that.

That Bulgakov chose as the object of his satire not the apex of the Soviet hierarchy but its bulging middle-to-upper section can be variously interpreted. In part, it seems to me, this was the continuation of the campaign against Russian *poshlost*[3] that Gogol had so enthusiastically promulgated. Bulgakov took aim, through the creation of the pampered society of authors, Masolit, at all those placemen and women whose accommodation with the Soviet regime ensured that their inferior products were widely distributed, while his luxury goods remained locked in the pantry. But really, by spreading his net wide, Bulgakov was able to catch all kinds of fish: a political satire, which aims only for the head, may achieve decapitation, yet still the sturgeon continues to flop about. By taking on theatre managers and essayists, Maître D's and psychiatrists, Bulgakov was ripping out the belly of Soviet society during the Terror and placing its corrupt caviar on view.

Still, let's not deceive ourselves in relation to a work that is entirely concerned with not being deceived. Bulgakov and Gogol share many attributes as writers, but also, as men – and as Ukrainians who have been co-opted to the Russian pantheon. In the Russian manner, they both seem to have retained a touching faith in the benignity of absolutism, addressing themselves to the directly to the 'little father' hidden inside the despot when their personal fate was in the balance. Thus Gogol

---

[3] An untranslatable term, but let's opt for self-satisfied bourgeois quietism

wrote to Tsar Nicholas l, cravenly thanking him for allowing *The Government Inspector* to be staged, and Bulgakov made two direct appeals to Stalin, who he addressed in ringing acclamation: 'Much esteemed Yosif Vissarionovich!'

Bulgakov tenanted the limbo of the protected – yet not endorsed – for the majority of his Moscow years: permitted to work as a jobbing-adaptor, an actor, and an occasional playwright, yet fully conscious that were he to speak or write his mind the savage suppression – and public flaying of – his *Heart of a Dog* would be extended to his very person, and that of his adored third wife, Yelena. Unlike his sometime neighbour, Osip Mandelstam, Bulgakov was not given to penning a 'sixteen line death sentence', such as the former's 'Epigram on Stalin'. Instead, Bulgakov became one of the great exponents of Orwellian doublethink: his play *The Days of the Turbins* (of which *The White Guard* was a prose-narrative counterpart), had gained Stalin's favour with its realist depiction of the impact of the civil war on a Kiev family, but the writer's imagination was really antic – and deeply romantic. The passionate affair of the Master and Margarita; her unswerving devotion to his work; their desire for a sequestration from both critical barbs and physical hardships – this was a romance within a romance, just as the story of Pilate and Ha-Notsri constitutes a novel within a novel.

Perhaps it is this: the sense the reader has of the weight of an unbearable tenderness about to collapse through the very roof of the work that gives *The Master and Margarita* its especial poignancy. Bulgakov, as befits a dramatist, has an acute sense of the spatial – its confinement and its unfolding. The tiny courtyard outside the Master's basement apartment; the dismal view from the asylum; the sky over Golgotha pregnant with lachrymose rain; Pilate's entrapment within Jerusalem's golden domes – these counterpoints of claustrophobia and expansiveness, of imprisonment and release are sensual as well as emotional: this is a sexy book, something that can be said of scarcely any other great Russian-language novel – with the exception of Bulgakov's friend Zamyatin's *We*.

The stripping of the covetous women at the Variety Theatre during Woland's 'act'; the nakedness of his vampiric witch, Hella; the demonic toilette of Margarita and her maid Natasha before their astonishing night flight over Moscow – these states of undress are all prefigurations of Woland's own dishabille, as he lounges in the darkness of the bedroom in the apartment at 302A Sadovaya Street receiving a massage. The ambivalence of Bulgakov's portrayal of his demon is in line with the ambivalence we all have towards sex itself: our passion and our revulsion. To the objection that the removal of clothes alone is a pretty facile form of taboo-busting, can be asserted this incontrovertible truth: that in our own contemporary world – in its own way quite as tightly-buttoned as the puritan Moscow of the purges – nudity just *is* sexy.

But if anymore argument were required, the entire Walpurgis Night of Woland's ball is a calculated exercise in the deployment of sensual effects; Margarita's flight is an act of coitus that spans the empyrean, complete with its foreplay of anarchic window-smashing, its long darkness of aching limbs and rigid strictures, and its eventual dreamy resolution, back at Sadovaya Street, in the arms of her true love. That the union of Mikhail and Yelena's alter-egos should be under attack by the excoriation of critical hirelings in the pay of the regime, is another strand of Bulgakov's romanticism: his passionate attachment to his chosen metier, and his transcendent belief in the universal validity of literature itself. After all, it's quite one thing to call a character modelled on the Devil 'the Master', quite another to wrest that ascription for your own. That we find nothing whatsoever absurd or overweening in this is proof positive that *The Master and Margarita* remains an example of the highest kind of literary art.

Will Self, London, 2008

'Say at last — who art thou?'
 'That Power I serve
Which wills forever evil
Yet does forever good.'

GOETHE, *Faust*

Contents

BOOK ONE

1. *Never Talk to Strangers*

At the sunset hour of one warm spring day two men were to be seen at Patriarch's Ponds. The first of them—aged about forty, dressed in a greyish summer suit—was short, dark-haired, well-fed and bald. He carried his decorous pork-pie hat by the brim and his neatly shaven face was embellished by black horn-rimmed spectacles of preternatural dimensions. The other, a broad-shouldered young man with curly reddish hair and a check cap pushed back to the nape of his neck, was wearing a tartan shirt, chewed white trousers and black sneakers.

The first was none other than Mikhail Alexandrovich Berlioz, editor of a highbrow literary magazine and chairman of the management committee of one of the biggest Moscow literary clubs, known by its abbreviation as MASSOLIT; his young companion was the poet Ivan Nikolayich Poniryov who wrote under the pseudonym of Bezdomny.

Reaching the shade of the budding lime trees, the two writers went straight to a gaily-painted kiosk labelled 'Beer and Minerals'.

There was an oddness about that terrible day in May which is worth recording: not only at the kiosk but along the whole avenue parallel to Malaya Bronnaya Street there was not a person to be seen. It was the hour of the day when people feel too exhausted to breathe, when Moscow glows in a dry haze as the sun disappears behind the Sadovaya Boulevard—yet no one had come out for a walk under the limes, no one was sitting on a bench, the avenue was empty.

'A glass of lemonade, please,' said Berlioz.

'There isn't any,' replied the woman in the kiosk. For some reason the request seemed to offend her.

'Got any beer?' enquired Bezdomny in a hoarse voice.

'Beer's being delivered later this evening,' said the woman.

'Well what have you got?' asked Berlioz.

'Apricot juice, only it's warm,' was the answer.

'All right, let's have some.'

The apricot juice produced a rich yellow froth, making the air smell like a hairdresser's. After drinking it the two writers immediately began to hiccup. They paid and sat down on a bench facing the pond, their backs to Bronnaya Street.

Then occurred the second oddness, which affected Berlioz alone. He suddenly stopped hiccuping, his heart thumped and for a moment vanished, then returned but with a blunt needle sticking into it. In addition Berlioz was seized by a fear that was groundless but so powerful that he had an immediate impulse to run away from Patriarch's Ponds without looking back.

Berlioz gazed miserably about him, unable to say what had frightened him. He went pale, wiped his forehead with his handkerchief and thought : 'What's the matter with me? This has never happened before. Heart playing tricks . . . I'm overstrained . . . I think it's time to chuck everything up and go and take the waters at Kislovodsk. . . .'

Just then the sultry air coagulated and wove itself into the shape of a man—a transparent man of the strangest appearance. On his small head was a jockey-cap and he wore a short check bum-freezer made of air. The man was seven feet tall but narrow in the shoulders, incredibly thin and with a face made for derision.

Berlioz's life was so arranged that he was not accustomed to seeing unusual phenomena. Paling even more, he stared and thought in consternation : 'It can't be!'

But alas it was, and the tall, transparent gentleman was swaying from left to right in front of him without touching the ground.

Berlioz was so overcome with horror that he shut his eyes. When he opened them he saw that it was all over, the mirage had dissolved, the chequered figure had vanished and the blunt needle had simultaneously removed itself from his heart.

' The devil ! ' exclaimed the editor. ' D'you know, Ivan, the heat nearly gave me a stroke just then ! I even saw something like a hallucination . . . ' He tried to smile but his eyes were still blinking with fear and his hands trembled. However he gradually calmed down, flapped his handkerchief and with a brave enough ' Well, now . . . ' carried on the conversation that had been interrupted by their drink of apricot juice.

They had been talking, it seemed, about Jesus Christ. The fact was that the editor had commissioned the poet to write a long anti-religious poem for one of the regular issues of his magazine. Ivan Nikolayich had written this poem in record time, but unfortunately the editor did not care for it at all. Bezdomny had drawn the chief figure in his poem, Jesus, in very black colours, yet in the editor's opinion the whole poem had to be written again. And now he was reading Bezdomny a lecture on Jesus in order to stress the poet's fundamental error.

It was hard to say exactly what had made Bezdomny write as he had—whether it was his great talent for graphic description or complete ignorance of the subject he was writing on, but his Jesus had come out, well, completely alive, a Jesus who had really existed, although admittedly a Jesus who had every possible fault.

Berlioz however wanted to prove to the poet that the main object was not who Jesus was, whether he was bad or good, but that as a person Jesus had never existed at all and that all the stories about him were mere invention, pure myth.

The editor was a well-read man and able to make skilful reference to the ancient historians, such as the famous Philo of Alexandria and the brilliantly educated Josephus Flavius, neither of whom mentioned a word of Jesus' existence. With a display of solid erudition, Mikhail Alexandrovich informed the poet that incidentally, the passage in Chapter 44 of the fifteenth book of Tacitus' *Annals*, where he describes the execution of Jesus, was nothing but a later forgery.

The poet, for whom everything the editor was saying was a novelty, listened attentively to Mikhail Alexandrovich, fixing him with his bold green eyes, occasionally hiccuping and cursing the apricot juice under his breath.

' There is not one oriental religion,' said Berlioz, ' in which an immaculate virgin does not bring a god into the world. And the Christians, lacking any originality, invented their Jesus in exactly the same way. In fact he never lived at all. That's where the stress has got to lie. . . .'

Berlioz's high tenor resounded along the empty avenue and as Mikhail Alexandrovich picked his way round the sort of historical pitfalls that can only be negotiated safely by a highly educated man, the poet learned more and more useful and instructive facts about the Egyptian god Osiris, son of Earth and Heaven, about the Phoenician god Thammuz, about Marduk and even about the fierce little-known god Vitzli-Putzli, who had once been held in great veneration by the Aztecs of Mexico. At the very moment when Mikhail Alexandrovich was telling the poet how the Aztecs used to model figurines of Vitzli-Putzli out of dough—the first man appeared in the avenue.

Afterwards, when it was frankly too late, various bodies collected their data and issued descriptions of this man. As to his teeth, he had platinum crowns on his left side and gold ones on his right. He wore an expensive grey suit and foreign shoes of the same colour as his suit. His grey beret was stuck jauntily over one ear and under his arm he carried a walking-stick with a knob in the shape of a poodle's head. He looked slightly over forty. Crooked sort of mouth. Clean-shaven. Dark hair. Right eye black, left eye for some reason green. Eyebrows black, but one higher than the other. In short—a foreigner.

As he passed the bench occupied by the editor and the poet, the foreigner gave them a sidelong glance, stopped and suddenly sat down on the next bench a couple of paces away from the two friends.

' A German,' thought Berlioz. ' An Englishman. . . . ' thought Bezdomny. ' Phew, he must be hot in those gloves ! '

The stranger glanced round the tall houses that formed a square round the pond, from which it was obvious that he was seeing this locality for the first time and that it interested him. His gaze halted on the upper storeys, whose panes threw back a blinding, fragmented reflection of the sun which was setting on Mikhail Alexandrovich for ever; he then looked downwards to where the windows were turning darker in the early evening twilight, smiled patronisingly at something, frowned, placed his hands on the knob of his cane and laid his chin on his hands.

' You see, Ivan,' said Berlioz, ' you have written a marvellously satirical description of the birth of Jesus, the son of God, but the whole joke lies in the fact that there had already been a whole series of sons of God before Jesus, such as the Phoenician Adonis, the Phrygian Attis, the Persian Mithras. Of course not one of these ever existed, including Jesus, and instead of the nativity or the arrival of the Magi you should have described the absurd rumours about their arrival. But according to your story the nativity really took place . . . ! '

Here Bezdomny made an effort to stop his torturing hiccups and held his breath, but it only made him hiccup more loudly and painfully. At that moment Berlioz interrupted his speech because the foreigner suddenly rose and approached the two writers. They stared at him in astonishment.

' Excuse me, please,' said the stranger with a foreign accent, although in correct Russian, ' for permitting myself, without an introduction . . . but the subject of your learned conversation was so interesting that . . . '

Here he politely took off his beret and the two friends had no alternative but to rise and bow.

' No, probably a Frenchman. . . . ' thought Berlioz.

' A Pole,' thought Bezdomny.

I should add that the poet had found the stranger repulsive from first sight, although Berlioz had liked the look of him, or rather not exactly liked him but, well . . . been interested by him.

' May I join you ? ' enquired the foreigner politely, and as the two friends moved somewhat unwillingly aside he adroitly placed himself between them and at once joined the conversation. ' If I'm not mistaken, you were saying that Jesus never existed, were you not ? ' he asked, turning his green left eye on Berlioz.

' No, you were not mistaken,' replied Berlioz courteously. ' I did indeed say that.'

' Ah, how interesting ! ' exclaimed the foreigner.

' What the hell does he want ? ' thought Bezdomny and frowned.

' And do you agree with your friend ? ' enquired the unknown man, turning to Bezdomny on his right.

' A hundred per cent ! ' affirmed the poet, who loved to use pretentious numerical expressions.

' Astounding ! ' cried their unbidden companion. Glancing furtively round and lowering his voice he said : ' Forgive me for being so rude, but am I right in thinking that you do not believe in God either ? ' He gave a horrified look and said : ' I swear not to tell anyone ! '

' Yes, neither of us believes in God,' answered Berlioz with a faint smile at this foreign tourist's apprehension. ' But we can talk about it with absolute freedom.'

The foreigner leaned against the backrest of the bench and asked, in a voice positively squeaking with curiosity :

' Are you . . . atheists ? '

' Yes, we're atheists,' replied Berlioz, smiling, and Bezdomny thought angrily : ' Trying to pick an argument, damn foreigner ! '

' Oh, how delightful ! ' exclaimed the astonishing foreigner and swivelled his head from side to side, staring at each of them in turn.

' In our country there's nothing surprising about atheism,' said Berlioz with diplomatic politeness. ' Most of us have long ago and quite consciously given up believing in all those fairy-tales about God.'

At this the foreigner did an extraordinary thing—he stood up and shook the astonished editor by the hand, saying as he did so :

' Allow me to thank you with all my heart ! '

'What are you thanking him for ? ' asked Bezdomny, blinking.

'For some very valuable information, which as a traveller I find extremely interesting,' said the eccentric foreigner, raising his forefinger meaningfully.

This valuable piece of information had obviously made a powerful impression on the traveller, as he gave a frightened glance at the houses as though afraid of seeing an atheist at every window.

'No, he's not an Englishman,' thought Berlioz. Bezdomny thought : 'What I'd like to know is—where did he manage to pick up such good Russian ? ' and frowned again.

'But might I enquire,' began the visitor from abroad after some worried reflection, ' how you account for the proofs of the existence of God, of which there are, as you know, five ? '

'Alas ! ' replied Berlioz regretfully. 'Not one of these proofs is valid, and mankind has long since relegated them to the archives. You must agree that rationally there can be no proof of the existence of God.'

'Bravo ! ' exclaimed the stranger. 'Bravo ! You have exactly repeated the views of the immortal Emmanuel on that subject. But here's the oddity of it : he completely demolished all five proofs and then, as though to deride his own efforts, he formulated a sixth proof of his own.'

'Kant's proof,' objected the learned editor with a thin smile, ' is also unconvincing. Not for nothing did Schiller say that Kant's reasoning on this question would only satisfy slaves, and Strauss simply laughed at his proof.'

As Berlioz spoke he thought to himself : ' But who on earth *is* he ? And how does he speak such good Russian ? '

'Kant ought to be arrested and given three years in Solovki asylum for that " proof " of his ! ' Ivan Nikolayich burst out completely unexpectedly.

'Ivan ! ' whispered Berlioz, embarrassed.

But the suggestion to pack Kant off to an asylum not only did not surprise the stranger but actually delighted him. 'Exactly, exactly ! ' he cried and his green left eye, turned on Berlioz, glittered. ' That's exactly the place for him ! I said to him myself that morning at breakfast : " If you'll forgive me, professor, your theory is no good. It may be clever but it's horribly incomprehensible. People will think you're mad." '

Berlioz's eyes bulged. ' At breakfast . . . to Kant ? What is he rambling about ? ' he thought.

' But,' went on the foreigner, unperturbed by Berlioz's amazement and turning to the poet, ' sending him to Solovki is out of the question, because for over a hundred years now he has been somewhere far away from Solovki and I assure you that it is totally impossible to bring him back.'

' What a pity ! ' said the impetuous poet.

' It is a pity,' agreed the unknown man with a glint in his eye, and went on : ' But this is the question that disturbs me—if there is no God, then who, one wonders, rules the life of man and keeps the world in order?'

' Man rules himself,' said Bezdomny angrily in answer to such an obviously absurd question.

' I beg your pardon,' retorted the stranger quietly, ' but to rule one must have a precise plan worked out for some reasonable period ahead. Allow me to enquire how man can control his own affairs when he is not only incapable of compiling a plan for some laughably short term, such as, say, a thousand years, but cannot even predict what will happen to him tomorrow ? '

' In fact,' here the stranger turned to Berlioz, ' imagine what would happen if you, for instance, were to start organising others and yourself, and you developed a taste for it—then suddenly you got . . . he, he . . . a slight heart attack . . . ' at this the foreigner smiled sweetly, as though the thought of a heart attack gave him pleasure. . . . ' Yes, a heart attack,' he repeated the word sonorously, grinning like a cat, ' and that's the end of you as an organiser ! No one's fate except your own interests you any longer. Your relations start lying to you. Sensing that something is amiss you rush to a specialist, then to a charlatan, and even perhaps to a fortune-teller. Each of them is as useless as the other, as you know perfectly well. And it all ends in tragedy : the man who thought he was in charge is suddenly reduced to lying prone and motionless in a wooden box and his fellow men, realising that there is no more sense to be had of him, incinerate him.

'Sometimes it can be even worse : a man decides to go to Kislovodsk,'—here the stranger stared at Berlioz—'a trivial matter you may think, but he cannot because for no good reason he suddenly jumps up and falls under a tram ! You're not going to tell me that he arranged to do that himself ? Wouldn't it be nearer the truth to say that someone quite different was directing his fate ? ' The stranger gave an eerie peal of laughter.

Berlioz had been following the unpleasant story about the heart attack and the tram with great attention and some uncomfortable thoughts had begun to worry him. 'He's not a foreigner . . . he's not a foreigner,' he thought, 'he's a very peculiar character . . . but I ask you, *who* is he ? . . . '

'I see you'd like to smoke,' said the stranger unexpectedly, turning to Bezdomny, ' what sort do you prefer ? '

'Do you mean you've got different sorts ? ' glumly asked the poet, who had run out of cigarettes.

'Which do you prefer ? ' repeated the mysterious stranger.

'Well, then " Our Brand ",' replied Bezdomny, irritated.

The unknown man immediately pulled a cigarette case out of his pocket and offered it to Bezdomny.

' " Our Brand " . . . '

The editor and the poet were not so much surprised by the fact that the cigarette case actually contained ' Our Brand ' as by the cigarette case itself. It was of enormous dimensions, made of solid gold and on the inside of the cover a triangle of diamonds flashed with blue and white fire.

Their reactions were different. Berlioz thought : 'No, he's a foreigner.' Bezdomny thought : ' What the hell is he . . . ? '

The poet and the owner of the case lit their cigarettes and Berlioz, who did not smoke, refused.

' I shall refute his argument by saying,' Berlioz decided to himself, ' that of course man is mortal, no one will argue with that. But the fact is that . . . '

However he was not able to pronounce the words before the stranger spoke :

'Of course man is mortal, but that's only half the problem. The trouble is that mortality sometimes comes to him so suddenly ! And he cannot even say what he will be doing this evening.'

' What a stupid way of putting the question. . . . ' thought Berlioz and objected :

' Now there you exaggerate. I know more or less exactly what I'm going to be doing this evening. Provided of course that a brick doesn't fall on my head in the street . . . '

' A brick is neither here nor there,' the stranger interrupted persuasively. ' A brick never falls on anyone's head. You in particular, I assure you, are in no danger from that. Your death will be different.'

' Perhaps you know exactly how I am going to die ? ' enquired Berlioz with understandable sarcasm at the ridiculous turn that the conversation seemed to be taking. ' Would you like to tell me ? '

' Certainly,' rejoined the stranger. He looked Berlioz up and down as though he were measuring him for a suit and muttered through his teeth something that sounded like : ' One, two . . . Mercury in the second house . . . the moon waning . . . six— accident . . . evening—seven . . . ' then announced loudly and cheerfully : ' Your head will be cut off ! '

Bezdomny turned to the stranger with a wild, furious stare and Berlioz asked with a sardonic grin :

' By whom ? Enemies ? Foreign spies ? '

' No,' replied their companion, ' by a Russian woman, a member of the Komsomol.'

' Hm,' grunted Berlioz, upset by the foreigner's little joke. ' That, if you don't mind my saying so, is most improbable.'

' I beg your pardon,' replied the foreigner, ' but it is so. Oh yes, I was going to ask you—what are you doing this evening, if it's not a secret ? '

' It's no secret. From here I'm going home, and then at ten o'clock this evening there's a meeting at the MASSOLIT and I shall be in the chair.'

' No, that is absolutely impossible,' said the stranger firmly.

' Why ? '

' Because,' replied the foreigner and frowned up at the sky where, sensing the oncoming cool of the evening, the birds were flying to roost, ' Anna has already bought the sunflower-seed oil, in fact she has not only bought it, but has already spilled it. So that meeting will not take place.'

With this, as one might imagine, there was silence beneath the lime trees.

' Excuse me,' said Berlioz after a pause with a glance at the stranger's jaunty beret, ' but what on earth has sunflower-seed oil got to do with it . . . and who is Anna ? '

' I'll tell you what sunflower-seed oil's got to do with it,' said Bezdomny suddenly, having obviously decided to declare war on their uninvited companion. ' Have you, citizen, ever had to spend any time in a mental hospital ? '

' Ivan ! ' hissed Mikhail Alexandrovich.

But the stranger was not in the least offended and gave a cheerful laugh. ' Yes, I have, I have, and more than once ! ' he exclaimed laughing, though the stare that he gave the poet was mirthless. ' Where haven't I been ! My only regret is that I didn't stay long enough to ask the professor what schizophrenia was. But you are going to find that out from him yourself, Ivan Nikolayich ! '

' How do you know my name ? '

' My dear fellow, who doesn't know you ? ' With this the foreigner pulled the previous day's issue of *The Literary Gazette* out of his pocket and Ivan Nikolayich saw his own picture on the front page above some of his own verse. Suddenly what had delighted him yesterday as proof of his fame and popularity no longer gave the poet any pleasure at all.

' I beg your pardon,' he said, his face darkening. ' Would you excuse us for a minute ? I should like a word or two with my friend.'

' Oh, with pleasure ! ' exclaimed the stranger. ' It's so delightful sitting here under the trees and I'm not in a hurry to go anywhere, as it happens.'

' Look here, Misha,' whispered the poet when he had drawn Berlioz aside. ' He's not just a foreign tourist, he's a spy. He's a Russian émigré and he's trying to catch us out. Ask him for his papers and then he'll go away . . . '

' Do you think we should ? ' whispered Berlioz anxiously, thinking to himself—' He's right, of course . . . '

' Mark my words,' the poet whispered to him. ' He's pretending to be an idiot so that he can trap us with some compromising question. You can hear how he speaks Russian,' said the poet, glancing sideways and watching to see that the stranger was not eavesdropping. ' Come on, let's arrest him and then we'll get rid of him.'

The poet led Berlioz by the arm back to the bench.

The unknown man was no longer sitting on it but standing beside it, holding a booklet in a dark grey binding, a fat envelope made of good paper and a visiting card.

' Forgive me, but in the heat of our argument I forgot to introduce myself. Here is my card, my passport and a letter inviting me to come to Moscow for consultations,' said the stranger gravely, giving both writers a piercing stare.

The two men were embarrassed. ' Hell, he overheard us . . . ' thought Berlioz, indicating with a polite gesture that there was no need for this show of documents. Whilst the stranger was offering them to the editor, the poet managed to catch sight of the visiting card. On it in foreign lettering was the word ' Professor ' and the initial letter of a surname which began with a ' W '.

' Delighted,' muttered the editor awkwardly as the foreigner put his papers back into his pocket.

Good relations having been re-established, all three sat down again on the bench.

'So you've been invited here as a consultant, have you, professor?' asked Berlioz.

'Yes, I have.'

'Are you German?' enquired Bezdomny.

'I?' rejoined the professor and thought for a moment. 'Yes, I suppose I am German. . . .' he said.

'You speak excellent Russian,' remarked Bezdomny.

'Oh, I'm something of a polyglot. I know a great number of languages,' replied the professor.

'And what is your particular field of work?' asked Berlioz.

'I specialise in black magic.'

'Like hell you do! . . .' thought Mikhail Alexandrovich.

'And . . . and you've been invited here to give advice on *that*?' he asked with a gulp.

'Yes,' the professor assured him, and went on: 'Apparently your National Library has unearthed some original manuscripts of the ninth-century necromancer Herbert Aurilachs. I have been asked to decipher them. I am the only specialist in the world.'

'Aha! So you're a historian?' asked Berlioz in a tone of considerable relief and respect.

'Yes, I am a historian,' adding with apparently complete inconsequence, 'this evening a historic event is going to take place here at Patriarch's Ponds.'

Again the editor and the poet showed signs of utter amazement, but the professor beckoned to them and when both had bent their heads towards him he whispered:

'Jesus did exist, you know.'

'Look, professor,' said Berlioz, with a forced smile, 'With all respect to you as a scholar we take a different attitude on that point.'

'It's not a question of having an attitude,' replied the strange professor. 'He existed, that's all there is to it.'

'But one must have some proof. . . .' began Berlioz.

'There's no need for any proof,' answered the professor. In a low voice, his foreign accent vanishing altogether, he began: 'It's very simple—early in the morning on the fourteenth of the spring month of Nisan the Procurator of Judaea, Pontius Pilate, in a white cloak lined with blood-red. . . .'

2. *Pontius Pilate*

Early in the morning on the fourteenth of the spring month of Nisan the Procurator of Judaea, Pontius Pilate, in a white cloak lined with blood-red, emerged with his shuffling cavalryman's walk into the arcade connecting the two wings of the palace of Herod the Great.

More than anything else in the world the Procurator hated the smell of attar of roses. The omens for the day were bad, as this scent had been haunting him since dawn.

It seemed to the Procurator that the very cypresses and palms in the garden were exuding the smell of roses, that this damned stench of roses was even mingling with the smell of leather tackle and sweat from his mounted bodyguard.

A haze of smoke was drifting towards the arcade across the upper courtyard of the garden, coming from the wing at the rear of the palace, the quarters of the first cohort of the XII Legion; known as the 'Lightning', it had been stationed in Jerusalem since the Procurator's arrival. The same oily perfume of roses was mixed with the acrid smoke that showed that the centuries' cooks had started to prepare breakfast.

' Oh gods, what are you punishing me for ? . . . No, there's no doubt, I have it again, this terrible incurable pain . . . hemicrania, when half the head aches . . . there's no cure for it, nothing helps. . . . I must try not to move my head. . . . '

A chair had already been placed on the mosaic floor by the fountain; without a glance round, the Procurator sat in it and stretched out his hand to one side. His secretary deferentially laid a piece of parchment in his hand. Unable to restrain a grimace of agony the Procurator gave a fleeting sideways look at its contents, returned the parchment to his secretary and said painfully :

' The accused comes from Galilee, does he ? Was the case sent to the tetrarch ? '

' Yes, Procurator,' replied the secretary. ' He declined to confirm the finding of the court and passed the Sanhedrin's sentence of death to you for confirmation.'

The Procurator's cheek twitched and he said quietly :

' Bring in the accused.'

At once two legionaries escorted a man of about twenty-seven from the courtyard, under the arcade and up to the balcony, where they placed him before the Procurator's chair. The man was dressed in a shabby, torn blue chiton. His head was covered with a white bandage fastened round his forehead, his hands tied behind his back. There was a large bruise under the man's left eye and a scab of dried blood in one corner of his mouth. The prisoner stared at the Procurator with anxious curiosity.

The Procurator was silent at first, then asked quietly in Aramaic :

' So you have been inciting the people to destroy the temple of Jerusalem ? '

The Procurator sat as though carved in stone, his lips barely moving as he pronounced the words. The Procurator was like stone from fear of shaking his fiendishly aching head.

The man with bound hands made a slight move forwards and began speaking :

' Good man ! Believe me . . . '

But the Procurator, immobile as before and without raising his voice, at once interrupted him :

' You call me good man ? You are making a mistake. The rumour about me in Jerusalem is that I am a raving monster and that is absolutely correct,' and he added in the same monotone : ' Send centurion Muribellum to me.'

The balcony seemed to darken when the centurion of the first century, Mark surnamed Muribellum, appeared before the Procurator. Muribellum was a head taller than the tallest soldier in the legion and so broad in the shoulders that he completely obscured the rising sun.

The Procurator said to the centurion in Latin :

' This criminal calls me " good man ". Take him away for a minute and show him the proper way to address me. But do not mutilate him.'

All except the motionless Procurator watched Mark Muribellum as he gestured to the prisoner to follow him. Because of his height people always watched Muribellum wherever he went. Those who saw him for the first time were inevitably fascinated by his disfigured face : his nose had once been smashed by a blow from a German club.

Mark's heavy boots resounded on the mosaic, the bound man followed him noiselessly. There was complete silence under the arcade except for the cooing of doves in the garden below and the water singing its seductive tune in the fountain.

The Procurator had a sudden urge to get up and put his temples under the stream of water until they were numb. But he knew that even that would not help.

Having led the prisoner out of the arcade into the garden, Muribellum took a whip from the hands of a legionary standing by the plinth of a bronze statue and with a gentle swing struck the prisoner across the shoulders. The centurion's movement was slight, almost negligent, but the bound man collapsed instantly as though his legs had been struck from under him and he gasped for air. The colour fled from his face and his eyes clouded.

With only his left hand Mark lifted the fallen man into the air as lightly as an empty sack, set him on his feet and said in broken, nasal Aramaic :

' You call a Roman Procurator " hegemon " Don't say anything else. Stand to attention. Do you understand or must I hit you again ? '

The prisoner staggered helplessly, his colour returned, he gulped and answered hoarsely :

' I understand you. Don't beat me.'

A minute later he was again standing in front of the Procurator.

The harsh, suffering voice rang out:

' Name? '

' Mine? ' enquired the prisoner hurriedly, his whole being expressing readiness to answer sensibly and to forestall any further anger.

The Procurator said quietly:

' I know my own name. Don't pretend to be stupider than you are. Your name.'

' Yeshua,' replied the prisoner hastily.

' Surname? '

' Ha-Notsri.'

' Where are you from? '

' From the town of Gamala,' replied the prisoner, nodding his head to show that far over there to his right, in the north, was the town of Gamala.

' Who are you by birth? '

' I don't know exactly,' promptly answered the prisoner, ' I don't remember my parents. I was told that my father was a Syrian. . . . '

' Where is your fixed abode? '

' I have no home,' said the prisoner shamefacedly, ' I move from town to town.'

' There is a shorter way of saying that—in a word you are a vagrant,' said the Procurator and asked: ' Have you any relations? '

' No, none. Not one in the world.'

' Can you read and write? '

' Yes.'

' Do you know any language besides Aramaic? '

' Yes. Greek.'

One swollen eyelid was raised and a pain-clouded eye stared at the prisoner. The other eye remained closed.

Pilate said in Greek:

' So you intended to destroy the temple building and incited the people to do so? '

' Never, goo . . . ' Terror flashed across the prisoner's face for having so nearly said the wrong word. ' Never in my life, hegemon, have I intended to destroy the temple. Nor have I ever tried to persuade anyone to do such a senseless thing.'

A look of amazement came over the secretary's face as he bent over a low table recording the evidence. He raised his head but immediately lowered it again over his parchment.

' People of all kinds are streaming into the city for the feast-day. Among them there are magicians, astrologers, seers and murderers,' said the Procurator in a monotone. ' There are also liars. You, for instance, are a liar. It is clearly written down : he incited people to destroy the temple. Witnesses have said so.'

' These good people,' the prisoner began, and hastily adding ' hegemon ', he went on, ' are unlearned and have confused everything I said. I am beginning to fear that this confusion will last for a very long time. And all because he untruthfully wrote down what I said.'

There was silence. Now both pain-filled eyes stared heavily at the prisoner.

' I repeat, but for the last time—stop pretending to be mad, scoundrel,' said Pilate softly and evenly. ' What has been written down about you is little enough, but it is sufficient to hang you.'

' No, no, hegemon,' said the prisoner, straining with the desire to convince. ' This man follows me everywhere with nothing but his goatskin parchment and writes incessantly. But I once caught a glimpse of that parchment and I was horrified. I had not said a word of what was written there. I begged him— please burn this parchment of yours ! But he tore it out of my hands and ran away.'

' Who was he ? ' enquired Pilate in a strained voice and put his hand to his temple.

' Matthew the Levite,' said the prisoner eagerly. ' He was a tax-collector. I first met him on the road to Bethlehem at the corner where the road skirts a fig orchard and I started talking to him. At first he was rude and even insulted me, or rather he thought he was insulting me by calling me a dog.' The prisoner laughed. ' Personally I see nothing wrong with that animal so I was not offended by the word. . . . '

The secretary stopped taking notes and glanced surreptitiously, not at the prisoner, but at the Procurator.

' However, when he had heard me out he grew milder,' went on Yeshua, ' and in the end he threw his money into the road and said that he would go travelling with me. . . . '

Pilate laughed with one cheek. Baring his yellow teeth and turning fully round to his secretary he said :

' Oh, city of Jerusalem ! What tales you have to tell ! A tax-collector, did you hear, throwing away his money ! '

Not knowing what reply was expected of him, the secretary chose to return Pilate's smile.

' And he said that henceforth he loathed his money,' said Yeshua in explanation of Matthew the Levite's strange action, adding : ' And since then he has been my companion.'

His teeth still bared in a grin, the Procurator glanced at the prisoner, then at the sun rising inexorably over the equestrian statues of the hippodrome far below to his left, and suddenly in a moment of agonising nausea it occurred to him that the simplest thing would be to dismiss this curious rascal from his balcony with no more than two words : ' Hang him. ' Dismiss the body-guard too, leave the arcade and go indoors, order the room to be darkened, fall on to his couch, send for cold water, call for his dog Banga in a pitiful voice and complain to the dog about his hemicrania. Suddenly the tempting thought of poison flashed through the Procurator's mind.

He stared dully at the prisoner for a while, trying painfully to recall why this man with the bruised face was standing in front of him in the pitiless Jerusalem morning sunshine and what further useless questions he should put to him.

' Matthew the Levite ? ' asked the suffering man in a hoarse voice, closing his eyes.

' Yes, Matthew the Levite,' came the grating, high-pitched reply.

' So you did make a speech about the temple to the crowd in the temple forecourt ? '

The voice that answered seemed to strike Pilate on the forehead, causing him inexpressible torture and it said:

' I spoke, hegemon, of how the temple of the old beliefs would fall down and the new temple of truth would be built up. I used those words to make my meaning easier to understand.'

' Why should a tramp like you upset the crowd in the bazaar by talking about truth, something of which you have no conception ? What is truth ? '

At this the Procurator thought : ' Ye gods ! This is a court of law and I am asking him an irrelevant question . . . my mind no longer obeys me. . . . ' Once more he had a vision of a goblet of dark liquid. ' Poison, I need poison. . . . '

And again he heard the voice :

' At this moment the truth is chiefly that your head is aching and aching so hard that you are having cowardly thoughts about death. Not only are you in no condition to talk to me, but it even hurts you to look at me. This makes me seem to be your torturer, which distresses me. You cannot even think and you can only long for your dog, who is clearly the only creature for whom you have any affection. But the pain will stop soon and your headache will go.'

The secretary stared at the prisoner, his note-taking abandoned.

Pilate raised his martyred eyes to the prisoner and saw how high the sun now stood above the hippodrome, how a ray had penetrated the arcade, had crept towards Yeshua's patched sandals and how the man moved aside from the sunlight. The Procurator stood up and clasped his head in his hands. Horror came over his yellowish, clean-shaven face. With an effort of will he controlled his expression and sank back into his chair.

Meanwhile the prisoner continued talking, but the secretary had stopped writing, craning his neck like a goose in the effort not to miss a single word.

'There, it has gone,' said the prisoner, with a kindly glance at Pilate. 'I am so glad. I would advise you, hegemon, to leave the palace for a while and take a walk somewhere nearby, perhaps in the gardens or on Mount Eleona. There will be thunder . . .' The prisoner turned and squinted into the sun . . . 'later, towards evening. A walk would do you a great deal of good and I should be happy to go with you. Some new thoughts have just come into my head which you might, I think, find interesting and I should like to discuss them with you, the more so as you strike me as a man of great intelligence.' The secretary turned mortally pale and dropped his scroll to the ground. 'Your trouble is,' went on the unstoppable prisoner, 'that your mind is too closed and you have finally lost your faith in human beings. You must admit that no one ought to lavish all their devotion on a dog. Your life is a cramped one, hegemon.' Here the speaker allowed himself to smile.

The only thought in the secretary's mind now was whether he could believe his ears. He had to believe them. He then tried to guess in what strange form the Procurator's fiery temper might break out at the prisoner's unheard-of insolence. Although he knew the Procurator well the secretary's imagination failed him.

Then the hoarse, broken voice of the Procurator barked out in Latin :

'Untie his hands.'

One of the legionary escorts tapped the ground with his lance, gave it to his neighbour, approached and removed the prisoner's bonds. The secretary picked up his scroll, decided to take no more notes for a while and to be astonished at nothing he might hear.

'Tell me,' said Pilate softly in Latin, 'are you a great physician ? '

'No, Procurator, I am no physician,' replied the prisoner, gratefully rubbing his twisted, swollen, purpling wrist.

Staring from beneath his eyelids, Pilate's eyes bored into the prisoner and those eyes were no longer dull. They now flashed with their familiar sparkle.

' I did not ask you,' said Pilate. ' Do you know Latin too ? '

' Yes, I do,' replied the prisoner.

The colour flowed back into Pilate's yellowed cheeks and he asked in Latin :

' How did you know that I wanted to call my dog ? '

' Quite simple,' the prisoner answered in Latin. ' You moved your hand through the air . . .' the prisoner repeated Pilate's gesture . . . ' as though to stroke something and your lips . . . '

' Yes,' said Pilate.

There was silence. Then Pilate put a question in Greek :

' So you are a physician ? '

' No, no,' was the prisoner's eager reply. ' Believe me I am not.'

' Very well, if you wish to keep it a secret, do so. It has no direct bearing on the case. So you maintain that you never incited people to tear down . . . or burn, or by any means destroy the temple ? '

' I repeat, hegemon, that I have never tried to persuade anyone to attempt any such thing. Do I look weak in the head? '

' Oh no, you do not,' replied the Procurator quietly, and smiled an ominous smile. ' Very well, swear that it is not so.'

' What would you have me swear by ? ' enquired the unbound prisoner with great urgency.

' Well, by your life,' replied the Procurator. ' It is high time to swear by it because you should know that it is hanging by a thread.'

' You do not believe, do you, hegemon, that it is you who have strung it up ? ' asked the prisoner. ' If you do you are mistaken.'

Pilate shuddered and answered through clenched teeth :

' I can cut that thread.'

' You are mistaken there too,' objected the prisoner, beaming and shading himself from the sun with his hand. ' You must agree, I think, that the thread can only be cut by the one who has suspended it ? '

' Yes, yes,' said Pilate, smiling. ' I now have no doubt that the idle gapers of Jerusalem have been pursuing you. I do not know who strung up your tongue, but he strung it well. By the way. tell me, is it true that you entered Jerusalem by the Susim Gate mounted on a donkey, accompanied by a rabble who greeted you as though you were a prophet ? ' Here the Procurator pointed to a scroll of parchment.

The prisoner stared dubiously at the Procurator.

' I have no donkey, hegemon,' he said. ' I certainly came into Jerusalem through the Susim Gate, but I came on foot alone except for Matthew the Levite and nobody shouted a word to me as no one in Jerusalem knew me then.'

' Do you happen to know,' went on Pilate without taking his eyes off the prisoner, ' anyone called Dismas ? Or Hestas ? Or a third—Bar-Abba ? '

' I do not know these good men,' replied the prisoner.

' Is that the truth ? '

' It is.'

' And now tell me why you always use that expression " good men " ? Is that what you call everybody ? '

' Yes, everybody,' answered the prisoner. ' There are no evil people on earth.'

' That is news to me,' said Pilate with a laugh. ' But perhaps I am too ignorant of life. You need take no further notes,' he said to the secretary, although the man had taken none for some time. Pilate turned back to the prisoner :

' Did you read about that in some Greek book ? '

' No, I reached that conclusion in my own mind.'

' And is that what you preach ? '

' Yes.'

' Centurion Mark Muribellum, for instance—is he good ? '

' Yes,' replied the prisoner. ' He is, it is true, an unhappy man. Since the good people disfigured him he has become harsh and callous. It would be interesting to know who mutilated him.'

' That I will gladly tell you,' rejoined Pilate, ' because I was a witness to it. These good men threw themselves at him like dogs at a bear. The Germans clung to his neck, his arms, his legs. An infantry maniple had been ambushed and had it not been for a troop of cavalry breaking through from the flank—a troop commanded by me—you, philosopher, would not have been talking to Muribellum just now. It happened at the battle of Idistavizo in the Valley of the Virgins.'

' If I were to talk to him,' the prisoner suddenly said in a reflective voice, ' I am sure that he would change greatly.'

' I suspect,' said Pilate, ' that the Legate of the Legion would not be best pleased if you took it into your head to talk to one of his officers or soldiers. Fortunately for us all any such thing is forbidden and the first person to ensure that it cannot occur would be myself.'

At that moment a swallow darted into the arcade, circled under the gilded ceiling, flew lower, almost brushed its pointed wingtip over the face of a bronze statue in a niche and disappeared behind the capital of a column, perhaps with the thought of nesting there.

As it flew an idea formed itself in the Procurator's mind, which was now bright and clear. It was thus : the hegemon had examined the case of the vagrant philosopher Yeshua, surnamed Ha-Notsri, and could not substantiate the criminal charge made against him. In particular he could not find the slightest con- nection between Yeshua's actions and the recent disorders in Jerusalem. The vagrant philosopher was mentally ill, as a result of which the sentence of death pronounced on Ha-Notsri by the Lesser Sanhedrin would not be confirmed. But in view of the danger of unrest liable to be caused by Yeshua's mad, utopian preaching, the Procurator would remove the man from Jerusalem and sentence him to imprisonment in Caesarea Stratonova on the Mediterranean—the place of the Procurator's own residence.

It only remained to dictate this to the secretary.

The swallow's wings fluttered over the hegemon's head, the bird flew towards the fountain and out into freedom. The

Procurator raised his eyes to the prisoner and saw that a column of dust had swirled up beside him.

' Is that all there is on this man ? ' Pilate asked the secretary.

' No, unfortunately,' replied the secretary unexpectedly, and handed Pilate another parchment.

' What else is there ? ' enquired Pilate and frowned.

Having read the further evidence a change came over his expression. Whether it was blood flowing back into his neck and face or from something else that occurred, his skin changed from yellow to red-brown and his eyes appeared to collapse. Probably caused by the increased blood-pressure in his temples, something happened to the Procurator's sight. He seemed to see the prisoner's head vanish and another appear in its place, bald and crowned with a spiked golden diadem. The skin of the forehead was split by a round, livid scar smeared with ointment. A sunken, toothless mouth with a capricious, pendulous lower lip. Pilate had the sensation that the pink columns of his balcony and the roofscape of Jerusalem below and beyond the garden had all vanished, drowned in the thick foliage of cypress groves. His hearing, too, was strangely affected—there was a sound as of distant trumpets, muted and threatening, and a nasal voice could clearly be heard arrogantly intoning the words: ' The law pertaining to high treason . . .'

Strange, rapid, disconnected thoughts passed through his mind. ' Dead ! ' Then : ' They have killed him ! . . .' And an absurd notion about immortality, the thought of which aroused a sense of unbearable grief.

Pilate straightened up, banished the vision, turned his gaze back to the balcony and again the prisoner's eyes met his.

' Listen, Ha-Notsri,' began the Procurator, giving Yeshua a strange look. His expression was grim but his eyes betrayed anxiety. ' Have you ever said anything about great Caesar ? Answer ! Did you say anything of the sort ? Or did you . . . not ? ' Pilate gave the word ' not ' more emphasis than was proper in a court of law and his look seemed to be trying to project a particular thought into the prisoner's mind.

' Telling the truth is easy and pleasant,' remarked the prisoner.

' I do not want to know,' replied Pilate in a voice of suppressed anger, ' whether you enjoy telling the truth or not. You are obliged to tell me the truth. But when you speak weigh every word, if you wish to avoid a painful death.'

No one knows what passed through the mind of the Procurator of Judaea, but he permitted himself to raise his hand as though shading himself from a ray of sunlight and, shielded by that hand, to throw the prisoner a glance that conveyed a hint.

' So,' he said, ' answer this question : do you know a certain Judas of Karioth and if you have ever spoken to him what did you say to him about Caesar ? '

' It happened thus,' began the prisoner readily. ' The day before yesterday, in the evening, I met a young man near the temple who called himself Judas, from the town of Karioth. He invited me to his home in the Lower City and gave me supper . . . '

' Is he a good man ? ' asked Pilate, a diabolical glitter in his eyes.

' A very good man and eager to learn,' affirmed the prisoner. ' He expressed the greatest interest in my ideas and welcomed me joyfully . . . '

' Lit the candles. . . .' said Pilate through clenched teeth to the prisoner, his eyes glittering.

' Yes,' said Yeshua, slightly astonished that the Procurator should be so well informed, and went on : ' He asked me for my views on the government. The question interested him very much.'

' And so what did you say ? ' asked Pilate. ' Or are you going to reply that you have forgotten what you said ? ' But there was already a note of hopelessness in Pilate's voice.

' Among other things I said,' continued the prisoner, ' that all power is a form of violence exercised over people and that the time will come when there will be no rule by Caesar nor any other form of rule. Man will pass into the kingdom of truth and justice where no sort of power will be needed.'

39

' Go on ! '

' There is no more to tell,' said the prisoner. ' After that some men came running in, tied me up and took me to prison.'

The secretary, straining not to miss a word, rapidly scribbled the statement on his parchment.

' There never has been, nor yet shall be a greater and more perfect government in this world than the rule of the emperor Tiberius ! ' Pilate's voice rang out harshly and painfully. The Procurator stared at his secretary and at the bodyguard with what seemed like hatred. ' And what business have you, a criminal lunatic, to discuss such matters ! ' Pilate shouted. ' Remove the guards from the balcony ! ' And turning to his secretary he added : ' Leave me alone with this criminal. This is a case of treason.'

The bodyguard raised their lances and with the measured tread of their iron-shod caligae marched from the balcony towards the garden followed by the secretary.

For a while the silence on the balcony was only disturbed bv the splashing of the fountain. Pilate watched the water splay out at the apex of the jet and drip downwards.

The prisoner was the first to speak :

' I see that there has been some trouble as a result of my conversation with that young man from Karioth. I have a presentiment, hegemon, that some misfortune will befall him and I feel very sorry for him.'

' I think,' replied the Procurator with a strange smile, ' that there is someone else in this world for whom you should feel sorrier than for Judas of Karioth and who is destined for a fate much worse than Judas' ! . . . So Mark Muribellum, a cold-blooded killer, the people who I see '—the Procurator pointed to Yeshua's disfigured face—' beat you for what you preached, the robbers Dismas and Hestas who with their confederates killed four soldiers, and finally this dirty informer Judas—are they all good men ? '

' Yes,' answered the prisoner.

' And will the kingdom of truth come ? '

' It will, hegemon,' replied Yeshua with conviction.

' It will never come ! ' Pilate suddenly shouted in a voice so terrible that Yeshua staggered back. Many years ago in the Valley of the Virgins Pilate had shouted in that same voice to his horsemen : ' Cut them down ! Cut them down ! They have caught the giant Muribellum ! ' And again he raised his parade-ground voice, barking out the words so that they would be heard in the garden : ' Criminal ! Criminal ! Criminal ! ' Then lowering his voice he asked : ' Yeshua Ha-Notsri, do you believe in any gods ? '

' God is one,' answered Yeshua. ' I believe in Him.'

' Then pray to him ! Pray hard ! However,' at this Pilate's voice fell again, ' it will do no good. Have you a wife ? ' asked Pilate with a sudden inexplicable access of depression.

' No, I am alone.'

' I hate this city,' the Procurator suddenly mumbled, hunching his shoulders as though from cold and wiping his hands as though washing them. ' If they had murdered you before your meeting with Judas of Karioth I really believe it would have been better.'

' You should let me go, hegemon,' was the prisoner's unexpected request, his voice full of anxiety. ' I see now that they want to kill me.'

A spasm distorted Pilate's face as he turned his blood-shot eyes on Yeshua and said :

' Do you imagine, you miserable creature, that a Roman Procurator could release a man who has said what you have said to me ? Oh gods, oh gods ! Or do you think I'm prepared to take your place ? I don't believe in your ideas ! And listen to me : if from this moment onward you say so much as a word or try to talk to anybody, beware ! I repeat—beware ! '

' Hegemon . . .'

' Be quiet ! ' shouted Pilate, his infuriated stare following the swallow which had flown on to the balcony again. ' Here ! ' shouted Pilate.

The secretary and the guards returned to their places and Pilate

announced that he confirmed the sentence of death pronounced
by the Lesser Sanhedrin on the accused Yeshua Ha-Notsri and the
secretary recorded Pilate's words.

A minute later centurion Mark Muribellum stood before the
Procurator. He was ordered by the Procurator to hand the felon
over to the captain of the secret service and in doing so to transmit
the Procurator's directive that Yeshua Ha-Notsri was to be
segregated from the other convicts, also that the captain of
the secret service was forbidden on pain of severe punish-
ment to talk to Yeshua or to answer any questions he might
ask.

At a signal from Mark the guard closed ranks around Yeshua
and escorted him from the balcony.

Later the Procurator received a call from a handsome man with
a blond beard, eagles' feathers in the crest of his helmet, glittering
lions' muzzles on his breastplate, a gold-studded sword belt,
triple-soled boots laced to the knee and a purple cloak thrown
over his left shoulder. He was the commanding officer, the
Legate of the Legion.

The Procurator asked him where the Sebastian cohort was
stationed. The Legate reported that the Sebastian was on cordon
duty in the square in front of the hippodrome, where the sentences
on the prisoners would be announced to the crowd.

Then the Procurator instructed the Legate to detach two
centuries from the Roman cohort. One of them, under the
command of Muribellum, was to escort the convicts, the carts
transporting the executioners' equipment and the executioners
themselves to Mount Golgotha and on arrival to cordon off the
summit area. The other was to proceed at once to Mount
Golgotha and to form a cordon immediately on arrival. To assist
in the task of guarding the hill, the Procurator asked the Legate
to despatch an auxiliary cavalry regiment, the Syrian ala.

When the Legate had left the balcony, the Procurator ordered
his secretary to summon to the palace the president of the Sanhedrin, two of its members and the captain of the Jerusalem
temple guard, but added that he wished arrangements to be

made which would allow him, before conferring with all these people, to have a private meeting with the president of the Sanhedrin.

The Procurator's orders were carried out rapidly and precisely and the sun, which had lately seemed to scorch Jerusalem with such particular vehemence, had not yet reached its zenith when the meeting took place between the Procurator and the president of the Sanhedrin, the High Priest of Judaea, Joseph Caiaphas. They met on the upper terrace of the garden between two white marble lions guarding the staircase.

It was quiet in the garden. But as he emerged from the arcade on to the sun-drenched upper terrace of the garden with its palms on their monstrous elephantine legs, the terrace from which the whole of Pilate's detested city of Jerusalem lay spread out before the Procurator with its suspension bridges, its fortresses and over it all that indescribable lump of marble with a golden dragon's scale instead of a roof—the temple of Jerusalem—the Procurator's sharp hearing detected far below, down there where a stone wall divided the lower terraces of the palace garden from the city square, a low rumbling broken now and again by faint sounds, half groans, half cries.

The Procurator realised that already there was assembling in the square a numberless crowd of the inhabitants of Jerusalem, excited by the recent disorders ; that this crowd was waiting impatiently for the pronouncement of sentence and that the water-sellers were busily shouting their wares.

The Procurator began by inviting the High Priest on to the balcony to find some shade from the pitiless heat, but Caiaphas politely excused himself, explaining that he could not do that on the eve of a feast-day.

Pilate pulled his cowl over his slightly balding head and began the conversation, which was conducted in Greek.

Pilate remarked that he had examined the case of Yeshua Ha-Notsri and had confirmed the sentence of death. Consequently those due for execution that day were the three robbers—Hestas, Dismas and Bar-Abba—and now this other man, Yeshua Ha-

Notsri. The first two, who had tried to incite the people to rebel against Caesar, had been forcibly apprehended by the Roman authorities ; they were therefore the Procurator's responsibility and there was no reason to discuss their case. The last two, however, Bar-Abba and Ha-Notsri, had been arrested by the local authorities and tried before the Sanhedrin. In accordance with law and custom, one of these two criminals should be released in honour of the imminent great feast of Passover. The Procurator therefore wished to know which of these two felons the Sanhedrin proposed to discharge—Bar-Abba or Ha-Notsri ?

Caiaphas inclined his head as a sign that he understood the question and replied :

' The Sanhedrin requests the release of Bar-Abba.'

The Procurator well knew that this would be the High Priest's reply ; his problem was to show that the request aroused his astonishment.

This Pilate did with great skill. The eyebrows rose on his proud forehead and the Procurator looked the High Priest straight in the eye with amazement.

' I confess that your reply surprises me,' began the Procurator softly. ' I fear there may have been some misunderstanding here.'

Pilate stressed that the Roman government wished to make no inroads into the prerogatives of the local priestly authority, the High Priest was well aware of that, but in this particular case an obvious error seemed to have occurred. And the Roman government naturally had an interest in correcting such an error. The crimes of Bar-Abba and Ha-Notsri were after all not comparable in gravity. If the latter, a man who was clearly insane, were guilty of making some absurd speeches in Jerusalem and various other localities, the former stood convicted of offences that were infinitely more serious. Not only had he permitted himself to make direct appeals to rebellion, but he had killed a sentry while resisting arrest. Bar-Abba was immeasurably more dangerous than Ha-Notsri. In view of all these facts, the Procurator requested the High Priest to reconsider his decision and to discharge the least dangerous of the two convicts and that one was undoubtedly Ha-Notsri . . . Therefore ?

Caiaphas said in a quiet but firm voice that the Sanhedrin had taken due cognisance of the case and repeated its intention to release Bar-Abba.

'What? Even after my intervention? The intervention of the representative of the Roman government? High Priest, say it for the third time.'

'And for the third time I say that we shall release Bar-Abba,' said Caiaphas softly.

It was over and there was no more to be discussed. Ha-Notsri had gone for ever and there was no one to heal the Procurator's terrible, savage pains ; there was no cure for them now except death. But this thought did not strike Pilate immediately. At first his whole being was seized with the same incomprehensible sense of grief which had come to him on the balcony. He at once sought for its explanation and its cause was a strange one : the Procurator was obscurely aware that he still had something to say to the prisoner and that perhaps, too, he had more to learn from him.

Pilate banished the thought and it passed as quickly as it had come. It passed, yet that grievous ache remained a mystery, for it could not be explained by another thought that had flashed in and out of his mind like lightning—'Immortality . . . immortality has come . . .' Whose immortality had come ? The Procurator could not understand it, but that puzzling thought of immortality sent a chill over him despite the sun's heat.

'Very well,' said Pilate. 'So be it.'

With that he looked round. The visible world vanished from his sight and an astonishing change occurred. The flower-laden rosebush disappeared, the cypresses fringing the upper terrace disappeared, as did the pomegranate tree, the white statue among the foliage and the foliage itself. In their place came a kind of dense purple mass in which seaweed waved and swayed and Pilate himself was swaying with it. He was seized, suffocating and burning, by the most terrible rage of all rage—the rage of impotence.

' I am suffocating,' said Pilate. ' Suffocating ! '

With a cold damp hand he tore the buckle from the collar of his cloak and it fell on to the sand.

' It is stifling today, there is a thunderstorm brewing,' said Caiaphas, his gaze fixed on the Procurator's reddening face, foreseeing all the discomfort that the weather was yet to bring. ' The month of Nisan has been terrible this year ! '

' No,' said Pilate. ' That is not why I am suffocating. I feel stifled by your presence, Caiaphas.' Narrowing his eyes Pilate added : ' Beware, High Priest ! '

The High Priest's dark eyes flashed and—no less cunningly than the Procurator—his face showed astonishment.

' What do I hear, Procurator ? ' Caiaphas answered proudly and calmly. ' Are you threatening me—when sentence has been duly pronounced and confirmed by yourself ? Can this be so ? We are accustomed to the Roman Procurator choosing his words carefully before saying anything. I trust no one can have overheard us, hegemon ? '

With lifeless eyes Pilate gazed at the High Priest and manufactured a smile.

' Come now, High Priest ! Who can overhear us here? Do you take me for a fool, like that crazy young vagrant who is to be executed today ? Am I a child, Caiaphas ? I know what I'm saying and where I'm saying it. This garden, this whole palace is so well cordoned that there's not a crack for a mouse to slip through. Not a mouse—and not even that man—what's his name . . ? That man from Karioth. You do know him, don't you, High Priest ? Yes . . . if someone like that were to get in here, he would bitterly regret it. You believe me when I say that, don't you ? I tell you, High Priest, that from henceforth you shall have no peace ! Neither you nor your people '—Pilate pointed to the right where the pinnacle of the temple flashed in the distance. ' I, Pontius Pilate, knight of the Golden Lance, tell you so ! '

' I know it ! ' fearlessly replied the bearded Caiaphas. His eyes flashed as he raised his hand to the sky and went on : ' The Jewish people knows that you hate it with a terrible hatred and that you have brought it much suffering—but you will never destroy it ! God will protect it. And *he* shall hear us—mighty Caesar shall hear us and protect us from Pilate the oppressor ! '

' Oh no ! ' rejoined Pilate, feeling more and more relieved with every word that he spoke ; there was no longer any need to dissemble, no need to pick his words : ' You have complained of me to Caesar too often and now my hour has come, Caiaphas ! Now I shall send word—but not to the viceroy in Antioch, not even to Rome but straight to Capreia, to the emperor himself, word of how you in Jerusalem are saving convicted rebels from death. And then it will not be water from Solomon's pool, as I once intended for your benefit, that I shall give Jerusalem to drink—no, it will not be water ! Remember how thanks to you I was made to remove the shields with the imperial cipher from the walls, to transfer troops, to come and take charge here myself ! Remember my words, High Priest : you are going to see more than one cohort here in Jerusalem ! Under the city walls you are going to see the Fulminata legion at full strength and Arab cavalry too. Then the weeping and lamentation will be bitter ! Then you will remember that you saved Bar-Abba and you will regret that you sent that preacher of peace to his death !

Flecks of colour spread over the High Priest's face, his eyes burned. Like the Procurator he grinned mirthlessly and replied :

' Do you really believe what you have just said, Procurator ? No, you do not ! It was not peace that this rabble-rouser brought to Jerusalem and of that, hegamon, you are well aware. You wanted to release him so that he could stir up the people, curse our faith and deliver the people to your Roman swords ! But as long as I, the High Priest of Judaea, am alive I shall not allow the faith to be defamed and I shall protect the people ! Do you hear, Pilate ? ' With this Caiaphas raised his arm threateningly : ' Take heed, Procurator ! '

Caiaphas was silent and again the Procurator heard a murmuring as of the sea, rolling up to the very walls of Herod the Great's garden. The sound flowed upwards from below until it seemed to swirl round the Procurator's legs and into his face. Behind his back, from beyond the wings of the palace, came urgent trumpet calls, the heavy crunch of hundreds of feet, the clank of metal. It told the Procurator that the Roman infantry was marching out, on his orders, to the execution parade that was to strike terror into the hearts of all thieves and rebels

' Do you hear, Procurator ? ' the High Priest quietly repeated his words. ' Surely you are not trying to tell me that all this '— here the High Priest raised both arms and his dark cowl slipped from his head—' can have been evoked by that miserable thief Bar-Abba ? '

With the back of his wrist the Procurator wiped his damp, cold forehead, stared at the ground, then frowning skywards he saw that the incandescent ball was nearly overhead, that Caiaphas' shadow had shrunk to almost nothing and he said in a calm, expressionless voice :

' The execution will be at noon. We have enjoyed this conversation, but matters must proceed.'

Excusing himself to the High Priest in a few artificial phrases, he invited him to sit down on a bench in the shade of a magnolia and to wait while he summoned the others necessary for the final short consultation and to give one more order concerning the execution.

Caiaphas bowed politely, placing his hand on his heart, and remained in the garden while Pilate returned to the balcony. There he ordered his waiting secretary to call the Legate of the Legion and the Tribune of the cohort into the garden, also the two members of the Sanhedrin and the captain of the temple guard, who were standing grouped round the fountain on the lower terrace awaiting his call. Pilate added that he would himself shortly return to join them in the garden, and disappeared inside the palace.

While the secretary convened the meeting, inside his darkened, shuttered room the Procurator spoke to a man whose face, despite the complete absence of sunlight from the room, remained half covered by a hood. The interview was very short. The Procurator whispered a few words to the man, who immediately departed. Pilate passed through the arcade into the garden.

There in the presence of all the men he had asked to see, the Procurator solemnly and curtly repeated that he confirmed the sentence of death on Yeshua Ha-Notsri and enquired officially of the Sanhedrin members as to which of the prisoners it had pleased them to release. On being told that it was Bar-Abba, the Procurator said :

' Very well,' and ordered the secretary to enter it in the minutes. He clutched the buckle which the secretary had picked up from the sand and announced solemnly : ' It is time ! '

At this all present set off down the broad marble staircase between the lines of rose bushes, exuding their stupefying aroma, down towards the palace wall, to a gate leading to the smoothly paved square at whose end could be seen the columns and statues of the Jerusalem hippodrome.

As soon as the group entered the square and began climbing up to the broad temporary wooden platform raised high above the square, Pilate assessed the situation through narrowed eyelids.

The cleared passage that he had just crossed between the palace walls and the scaffolding platform was empty, but in front of Pilate the square could no longer be seen—it had been devoured by the crowd. The mob would have poured on to the platform and the passage too if there had not been two triple rows of soldiers, one from the Sebastian cohort on Pilate's left and on his right another from the Ituraean auxiliary cohort, to keep it clear.

Pilate climbed the platform, mechanically clenching and unclenching his fist on the useless buckle and frowning hard. The Procurator was not frowning because the sun was blinding him but to somehow avoid seeing the group of prisoners which, as

49

he well knew, would shortly be led out on the platform behind him.

The moment the white cloak with the blood-red lining appeared atop the stone block at the edge of that human sea a wave of sound—' Aaahh '—struck the unseeing Pilate's ears. It began softly, far away at the hippodrome end of the square, then grew to thunderous volume and after a few seconds, began to diminish again. ' They have seen me,' thought the Procurator. The wave of sound did not recede altogether and began unexpectedly to grow again and waveringly rose to a higher pitch than the first and on top of the second surge of noise, like foam on the crest of a wave at sea, could be heard whistles and the shrieks of several women audible above the roar. ' That means they have led them out on to the platform,' thought Pilate, ' and those screams are from women who were crushed when the crowd surged forward.'

He waited for a while, knowing that nothing could silence the crowd until it had let loose its pent-up feelings and quietened of its own accord.

When that moment came the Procurator threw up his right hand and the last murmurings of the crowd expired. Then Pilate took as deep a breath as he could of the hot air and his cracked voice rang out over the thousands of heads :

' In the name of imperial Caesar ! . . .'

At once his ears were struck by a clipped, metallic chorus as the cohorts, raising lances and standards, roared out their fearful response :

' Hail, Caesar ! '

Pilate jerked his head up straight at the sun. He had a sensation of green fire piercing his eyelids, his brain seemed to burn. In hoarse Aramaic he flung his words out over the crowd :

' Four criminals, arrested in Jerusalem for murder, incitement to rebellion, contempt of the law and blasphemy, have been condemned to the most shameful form of execution—crucifixion ! Their execution will be carried out shortly on Mount Golgotha

The names of these felons are Dismas, Hestas, Bar-Abba and Ha-Notsri and there they stand before you ! '

Pilate pointed to the right, unable to see the prisoners but knowing that they were standing where they should be.

The crowd responded with a long rumble that could have been surprise or relief. When it had subsided Pilate went on :

' But only three of them are to be executed for, in accordance with law and custom, in honour of the great feast of Passover the emperor Caesar in his magnanimity will, at the choice of the Lesser Sanhedrin and with the approval of the Roman government, render back to one of these convicted men his contemptible life ! '

As Pilate rasped out his words he noticed that the rumbling had given way to a great silence. Now not a sigh, not a rustle reached his ears and there even came a moment when it seemed to Pilate that the people around him had vanished altogether. The city he so hated might have died and only he alone stood there, scorched by the vertical rays of the sun, his face craning skywards. Pilate allowed the silence to continue and then began to shout again : ' The name of the man who is about to be released before you . . .'

He paused once more, holding back the name, mentally confirming that he had said everything, because he knew that as soon as he pronounced the name of the fortunate man the lifeless city would awaken and nothing more that he might say would be audible.

' Is that everything ? ' Pilate whispered soundlessly to himself. ' Yes, it is. Now the name ! ' And rolling his ' r 's over the heads of the silent populace he roared : ' Bar-Abba ! '

It was as though the sun detonated above him and drowned his ears in fire, a fire that roared, shrieked, groaned, laughed and whistled.

Pilate turned and walked back along the platform towards the steps, glancing only at the parti-coloured wooden blocks of the steps beneath his feet to save himself from stumbling. He knew that behind his back a hail of bronze coins and dates was shower-

ing the platform, that people in the whooping crowd, elbowing
each other aside, were climbing on to shoulders to see a miracle
with their own eyes—a man already in the arms of death and
torn from their grasp! They watched the legionaries as they
untied his bonds, involuntarily causing him searing pain in his
swollen arms, watched as grimacing and complaining he nevertheless smiled an insane, senseless smile.

Pilate knew that the escort was now marching the three bound
prisoners to the side steps of the platform to lead them off on
the road westward, out of the city, towards Mount Golgotha.
Only when he stood beneath and behind the platform did Pilate
open his eyes, knowing that he was now safe—he could no
longer see the convicted men.

As the roar of the crowd began to die down the separate,
piercing voices of the heralds could be heard repeating, one in
Aramaic, the others in Greek, the announcement that the Procurator had just made from the platform. Besides that his ears
caught the approaching irregular clatter of horses' hoofs and
the sharp, bright call of a trumpet. This sound was echoed by
the piercing whistles of boys from the rooftops and by shouts of
'Look out!'

A lone soldier, standing in the space cleared in the square,
waved his standard in warning, at which the Procurator, the
Legate of the Legion and their escort halted.

A squadron of cavalry entered the square at a fast trot, cutting
across it diagonally, past a knot of people, then down a side-
street along a vine-covered stone wall in order to gallop on to
Mount Golgotha by the shortest route.

As the squadron commander, a Syrian as small as a boy and
as dark as a mulatto, trotted past Pilate he gave a high-pitched
cry and drew his sword from its scabbard. His sweating, ugly-
tempered black horse snorted and reared up on its hind legs.
Sheathing his sword the commander struck the horse's neck
with his whip, brought its forelegs down and moved off down
the side street, breaking into a gallop. Behind him in columns
of three galloped the horsemen in a haze of dust, the tips of their

bamboo lances bobbing rhythmically. They swept past the Procurator, their faces unnaturally dark in contrast with their white turbans, grinning cheerfully, teeth flashing.

Raising a cloud of dust the squadron surged down the street, the last trooper to pass Pilate carrying a glinting trumpet slung across his back.

Shielding his face from the dust with his hand and frowning with annoyance Pilate walked on, hurrying towards the gate of the palace garden followed by the Legate, the secretary and the escort.

It was about ten o'clock in the morning.

3. The Seventh Proof

' Yes, it was about ten o'clock in the morning, my dear Ivan Nikolayich,' said the professor.

The poet drew his hand across his face like a man who has just woken up and noticed that it was now evening. The water in the pond had turned black, a little boat was gliding across it and he could hear the splash of an oar and a girl's laughter in the boat. People were beginning to appear in the avenues and were sitting on the benches on all sides of the square except on the side where our friends were talking.

Over Moscow it was as if the sky had blossomed : a clear, full moon had risen, still white and not yet golden. It was much less stuffy and the voices under the lime trees now had an even-tide softness.

' Why didn't I notice what a long story he's been telling us ? ' thought Bezdomny in amazement. ' It's evening already ! Perhaps he hasn't told it at all but I simply fell asleep and dreamed it ? '

But if the professor had not told the story Berlioz must have been having the identical dream because he said, gazing attentively into the stranger's face :

' Your story is extremely interesting, professor, but it differs completely from the accounts in the gospels.'

' But surely,' replied the professor with a condescending smile, ' you of all people must realise that absolutely nothing written in the gospels actually happened. If you want to regard the gospels as a proper historical source . . .' He smiled again and Berlioz was silenced. He had just been saying exactly the same thing to Bezdomny on their walk from Bronnaya Street to Patriarch's Ponds.

' I agree,' answered Berlioz, ' but I'm afraid that no one is in a position to prove the authenticity of your version either.'

' Oh yes ! I can easily confirm it ! ' rejoined the professor with great confidence, lapsing into his foreign accent and mysteriously beckoning the two friends closer. They bent towards him from both sides and he began, this time without a trace of his accent which seemed to come and go without rhyme or reason :

' The fact is . . .' here the professor glanced round nervously and dropped his voice to a whisper, ' I was there myself. On the balcony with Pontius Pilate, in the garden when he talked to Caiaphas and on the platform, but secretly, incognito so to speak, so don't breathe a word of it to anyone and please keep it an absolute secret, sshhh . . .'

There was silence. Berlioz went pale.

' How . . . how long did you say you'd been in Moscow ? ' he asked in a shaky voice.

' I have just this minute arrived in Moscow,' replied the professor, slightly disconcerted. Only then did it occur to the two friends to look him properly in the eyes. They saw that his green left eye was completely mad, his right eye black, expressionless and dead.

' That explains it all,' thought Berlioz perplexedly. ' He's some mad German who's just arrived or else he's suddenly gone out of his mind here at Patriarch's. What an extraordinary business ! ' This really seemed to account for everything—the mysterious breakfast with the philosopher Kant, the idiotic ramblings about sunflower-seed oil and Anna, the prediction about Berlioz's head being cut off and all the rest : the professor was a lunatic.

Berlioz at once started to think what they ought to do. Leaning back on the bench he winked at Bezdomny behind the professor's back, meaning ' Humour him ! ' But the poet, now thoroughly confused, failed to understand the signal.

' Yes, yes, yes,' said Berlioz with great animation. ' It's quite possible, of course. Even probable—Pontius Pilate, the balcony, and so on. . . . Have you come here alone or with your wife?'

'Alone, alone, I am always alone,' replied the professor bitterly.

'But where is your luggage, professor?' asked Berlioz cunningly. 'At the Metropole? Where are you staying?'

'Where am I staying? Nowhere. . . .' answered the mad German, staring moodily around Patriarch's Ponds with his green eye

'What! . . . But . . . where are you going to live?'

'In your flat,' the lunatic suddenly replied casually and winked.

'I'm . . . I should be delighted . . .' stuttered Berlioz, 'but I'm afraid you wouldn't be very comfortable at my place . . . the rooms at the Metropole are excellent, it's a first-class hotel . . .'

'And the devil doesn't exist either, I suppose?' the madman suddenly enquired cheerfully of Ivan Nikolayich.

'And the devil . . .'

'Don't contradict him,' mouthed Berlioz silently, leaning back and grimacing behind the professor's back.

'There's no such thing as the devil!' Ivan Nikolayich burst out, hopelessly muddled by all this dumb show, ruining all Berlioz's plans by shouting: 'And stop playing the amateur psychologist!'

At this the lunatic gave such a laugh that it startled the sparrows out of the tree above them.

'Well now, that is interesting,' said the professor, quaking with laughter. 'Whatever I ask you about—it doesn't exist!' He suddenly stopped laughing and with a typical madman reaction he immediately went to the other extreme, shouting angrily and harshly: 'So you think the devil doesn't exist?'

'Calm down, calm down, calm down, professor,' stammered Berlioz, frightened of exciting this lunatic. 'You stay here a minute with comrade Bezdomny while I run round the corner and make a 'phone call and then we'll take you where you want to go. You don't know your way around town, after all . . . .'

Berlioz's plan was obviously right—to run to the nearest telephone box and tell the Aliens' Bureau that there was a foreign professor sitting at Patriarch's Ponds who was clearly insane. Something had to be done or there might be a nasty scene.

'Telephone? Of course, go and telephone if you want to,' agreed the lunatic sadly, and then suddenly begged with passion : ' But please—as a farewell request—at least say you believe in the devil ! I won't ask anything more of you. Don't forget that there's still the seventh proof—the soundest ! And it's just about to be demonstrated to you ! '

' All right, all right,' said Berlioz pretending to agree. With a wink to the wretched Bezdomny, who by no means relished the thought of keeping watch on this crazy German, he rushed towards the park gates at the corner of Bronnaya and Yermolayevsky Streets.

At once the professor seemed to recover his reason and good spirits.

' Mikhail Alexandrovich ! ' he shouted after Berlioz, who shuddered as he turned round and then remembered that the professor could have learned his name from a newspaper.

The professor, cupping his hands into a trumpet, shouted :

' Wouldn't you like me to send a telegram to your uncle in Kiev ? '

Another shock—how did this madman know that he had an uncle in Kiev ? Nobody had ever put *that* in any newspaper. Could Bezdomny be right about him after all ? And what about those phoney-looking documents of his ? Definitely a weird character . . . ring up, ring up the Bureau at once . . . they'll come and sort it all out in no time.

Without waiting to hear any more, Berlioz ran on.

At the park gates leading into Bronnaya Street, the identical man, whom a short while ago the editor had seen materialise out of a mirage, got up from a bench and walked toward him. This time, however, he was not made of air but of flesh and blood. In the early twilight Berlioz could clearly distinguish his feathery little moustache, his little eyes, mocking and half drunk, his check trousers pulled up so tight that his dirty white socks were showing.

Mikhail Alexandrovich stopped, but dismissed it as a ridiculous coincidence. He had in any case no time to stop and puzzle it out now.

' Are you looking for the turnstile, sir ? ' enquired the check-clad man in a quavering tenor. ' This way, please ! Straight on for the exit. How about the price of a drink for showing you the way, sir ? . . . church choirmaster out of work, sir . . . need a helping hand, sir. . . .' Bending double, the weird creature pulled off his jockey cap in a sweeping gesture.

Without stopping to listen to the choirmaster's begging and whining, Berlioz ran to the turnstile and pushed it. Having passed through he was just about to step off the pavement and cross the tramlines when a white and red light flashed in his face and the pedestrian signal lit up with the words ' Stop ! Tramway ! ' A tram rolled into view, rocking slightly along the newly-laid track that ran down Yermolayevsky Street and into Bronnaya. As it turned to join the main line it suddenly switched its inside lights on, hooted and accelerated.

Although he was standing in safety, the cautious Berlioz decided to retreat behind the railings. He put his hand on the turnstile and took a step backwards. He missed his grip and his foot slipped on the cobbles as inexorably as though on ice. As it slid towards the tramlines his other leg gave way and Berlioz was thrown across the track. Grabbing wildly, Berlioz fell prone. He struck his head violently on the cobblestones and the gilded moon flashed hazily across his vision. He just had time to turn on his back, drawing his legs up to his stomach with a frenzied movement and as he turned over he saw the woman tram-driver's face, white with horror above her red necktie, as she bore down on him with irresistible force and speed. Berlioz made no sound, but all round him the street rang with the desperate shrieks of women's voices. The driver grabbed the electric brake, the car pitched forward, jumped the rails and with a tinkling crash the glass broke in all its windows. At this moment Berlioz heard a despairing voice: ' Oh, no . . . ! ' Once more and for the last time the moon flashed before his eyes but it split into fragments and then went black.

Berlioz vanished from sight under the tramcar and a round, dark object rolled across the cobbles, over the kerbstone and bounced along the pavement.

It was a severed head.

4. The Pursuit

The women's hysterical shrieks and the sound of police whistles died away. Two ambulances drove off, one bearing the body and the decapitated head to the morgue, the other carrying the beautiful tram-driver who had been wounded by slivers of glass. Street sweepers in white overalls swept up the broken glass and poured sand on the pools of blood. Ivan Nikolayich, who had failed to reach the turnstile in time, collapsed on a bench and remained there. Several times he tried to get up, but his legs refused to obey him, stricken by a kind of paralysis.

The moment he had heard the first cry the poet had rushed towards the turnstile and seen the head bouncing on the pavement. The sight unnerved him so much that he bit his hand until it drew blood. He had naturally forgotten all about the mad German and could do nothing but wonder how one minute he could have been talking to Berlioz and the next . . . his head . . .

Excited people were running along the avenue past the poet shouting something, but Ivan Nikolayich did not hear them. Suddenly two women collided alongside him and one of them, with a pointed nose and straight hair, shouted to the other woman just above his ear :

' . . . Anna, it was our Anna ! She was coming from Sadovaya ! It's her job, you see . . . she was carrying a litre of sunflower-seed oil to the grocery and she broke her jug on the turnstile ! It went all over her skirt and ruined it and she swore and swore. . . . ! And that poor man must have slipped on the oil and fallen under the tram. . . . '

One word stuck in Ivan Nikolayich's brain—' Anna ' . . . ' Anna ? . . . Anna ? ' muttered the poet, looking round in alarm. ' Hey, what was that you said . . . ? '

The name ' Anna ' evoked the words ' sunflower-seed oil '
and ' Pontius Pilate '. Bezdomny rejected ' Pilate ' and began
linking together a chain of associations starting with ' Anna '.
Very soon the chain was complete and it led straight back to the
mad professor.

' Of course ! He said the meeting wouldn't take place because
Anna had spilled the oil. And, by God, it won't take place now !
And what's more he said Berlioz would have his head cut off by
a woman ! ! Yes—and the tram-driver was a woman ! ! ! Who
the hell is he ? '

There was no longer a grain of doubt that the mysterious
professor had foreseen every detail of Berlioz's death before it
had occurred. Two thoughts struck the poet : firstly—' he's no
madman ' and secondly—' did he arrange the whole thing himself ? '

' But how on earth could he ? We've got to look into this ! '

With a tremendous effort Ivan Nikolayich got up from the
bench and ran back to where he had been talking to the professor,
who was fortunately still there.

The lamps were already lit on Bronnaya Street and a golden
moon was shining over Patriarch's Ponds. By the light of the
moon, deceptive as it always is, it seemed to Ivan Nikolayich
that the thing under the professor's arm was not a stick but a
sword.

The ex-choirmaster was sitting on the seat occupied a short
while before by Ivan Nikolayich himself. The choirmaster had
now clipped on to his nose an obviously useless pince-nez. One
lens was missing and the other rattled in its frame. It made the
check-suited man look even more repulsive than when he had
shown Berlioz the way to the tramlines. With a chill of fear
Ivan walked up to the professor. A glance at his face convinced
him that there was not a trace of insanity in it.

' Confess—who are you ? ' asked Ivan grimly.

The stranger frowned, looked at the poet as if seeing him for
the first time, and answered disagreeably :

' No understand . . . no speak Russian . . . '

'He doesn't understand,' put in the choirmaster from his bench, although no one had asked him.

'Stop pretending!' said Ivan threateningly, a cold feeling growing in the pit of his stomach. 'Just now you spoke Russian perfectly well. You're no German and you're not a professor! You're a spy and a murderer! Show me your papers!' cried Ivan angrily.

The enigmatic professor gave his already crooked mouth a further twist and shrugged his shoulders.

'Look here, citizen,' put in the horrible choirmaster again. 'What do you mean by upsetting this foreign tourist? You'll have the police after you!'

The dubious professor put on a haughty look, turned and walked away from Ivan, who felt himself beginning to lose his head. Gasping, he turned to the choirmaster:

'Hey, you, help me arrest this criminal! It's your duty!'

The choirmaster leaped eagerly to his feet and bawled:

'What criminal? Where is he? A foreign criminal?' His eyes lit up joyfully. 'That man? If he's a criminal the first thing to do is to shout "Stop thief!" Otherwise he'll get away. Come on, let's shout together!' And the choirmaster opened his mouth wide.

The stupefied Ivan obeyed and shouted 'Stop thief!' but the choirmaster fooled him by not making a sound.

Ivan's lonely, hoarse cry was worse than useless. A couple of girls dodged him and he heard them say '... drunk.'

'So you're in league with him, are you?' shouted Ivan, helpless with anger. 'Make fun of me, would you? Out of my way!'

Ivan set off towards his right and the choirmaster did the opposite, blocking his way. Ivan moved leftward, the other to his right and the same thing happened.

'Are you trying to get in my way on purpose?' screamed Ivan, infuriated. '*You're* the one I'm going to report to the police!'

Ivan tried to grab the choirmaster by the sleeve, missed and found himself grasping nothing : it was as if the choirmaster had been swallowed up by the ground.

With a groan Ivan looked ahead and saw the hated stranger. He had already reached the exit leading on to Patriarch's Street and he was no longer alone. The weird choirmaster had managed to join him. But that was not all. The third member of the company was a cat the size of a pig, black as soot and with luxuriant cavalry officers' whiskers. The threesome was walking towards Patriarch's Street, the cat trotting along on its hind legs.

As he set off after the villains Ivan realised at once that it was going to be very hard to catch them up. In a flash the three of them were across the street and on the Spiridonovka. Ivan quickened his pace, but the distance between him and his quarry grew no less. Before the poet had realised it they had left the quiet Spiridonovka and were approaching Nikita Gate, where his difficulties increased. There was a crowd and to make matters worse the evil band had decided to use the favourite trick of bandits on the run and split up.

With great agility the choirmaster jumped on board a moving bus bound for Arbat Square and vanished. Having lost one of them, Ivan concentrated his attention on the cat and saw how the strange animal walked up to the platform of an ' A ' tram waiting at a stop, cheekily pushed off a screaming woman, grasped the handrail and offered the conductress a ten-kopeck piece.

Ivan was so amazed by the cat's behaviour that he was frozen into immobility beside a street corner grocery. He was struck with even greater amazement as he watched the reaction of the conductress. Seeing the cat board her tram, she yelled, shaking with anger :

' No cats allowed ! I'm not moving with a cat on board ! Go on—shoo ! Get off, or I'll call the police ! '

Both conductress and passengers seemed completely oblivious of the most extraordinary thing of all : not that a cat had boarded a tramcar—that was after all possible—but the fact that the animal was offering to pay its fare !

The cat proved to be not only a fare-paying but a law-abiding animal. At the first shriek from the conductress it retreated, stepped off the platform and sat down at the tram-stop, stroking its whiskers with the ten-kopeck piece. But no sooner had the conductress yanked the bell-rope and the car begun to move off, than the cat acted like anyone else who has been pushed off a tram and is still determined to get to his destination. Letting all three cars draw past it, the cat jumped on to the coupling-hook of the last car, latched its paw round a pipe sticking out of one of the windows and sailed away, having saved itself ten kopecks.

Fascinated by the odious cat, Ivan almost lost sight of the most important of the three—the professor. Luckily he had not managed to slip away. Ivan spotted his grey beret in the crowd at the top of Herzen Street. In a flash Ivan was there too, but in vain. The poet speeded up to a run and began shoving people aside, but it brought him not an inch nearer the professor.

Confused though Ivan was, he was nevertheless astounded by the supernatural speed of the pursuit. Less than twenty seconds after leaving Nikita Gate Ivan Nikolayich was dazzled by the lights of Arbat Square. A few more seconds and he was in a dark alleyway with uneven pavements where he tripped and hurt his knee. Again a well-lit main road—Kropotkin Street—another side-street, then Ostozhenka Street, then another grim, dirty and badly-lit alley. It was here that Ivan Nikolayich finally lost sight of his quarry. The professor had disappeared.

Disconcerted, but not for long, for no apparent reason Ivan Nikolayich had a sudden intuition that the professor must be in house No. 13, flat 47.

Bursting through the front door, Ivan Nikolayich flew up the stairs, found the right flat and impatiently rang the bell. He did not have to wait long. The door was opened by a little girl of about five, who silently disappeared inside again. The hall was a vast, incredibly neglected room feebly lit by a tiny electric light that dangled in one corner from a ceiling black with dirt. On the wall hung a bicycle without any tyres, beneath it a huge iron-banded trunk. On the shelf over the coat-rack was a winter fur cap, its long earflaps untied and hanging down. From behind one of the doors a man's voice could be heard booming from the radio, angrily declaiming poetry.

Not at all put out by these unfamiliar surroundings, Ivan Nikolayich made straight for the corridor, thinking to himself : ' He's obviously hiding in the bathroom.' The passage was dark. Bumping into the walls, Ivan saw a faint streak of light under a doorway. He groped for the handle and gave it a gentle turn. The door opened and Ivan found himself in luck—it was the bathroom.

However it wasn't quite the sort of luck he had hoped for. Amid the damp steam and by the light of the coals smouldering in the geyser, he made out a large basin attached to the wall and a bath streaked with black where the enamel had chipped off. There in the bath stood a naked woman, covered in soapsuds and holding a loofah. She peered short-sightedly at Ivan as he came in and obviously mistaking him for someone else in the hellish light she whispered gaily :

' Kiryushka ! Do stop fooling ! You must be crazy . . . Fyodor Ivanovich will be back any minute now. Go on—out you go ! ' And she waved her loofah at Ivan.

The mistake was plain and it was, of course, Ivan Nikolayich's fault, but rather than admit it he gave a shocked cry of ' Brazen hussy ! ' and suddenly found himself in the kitchen. It was empty. In the gloom a silent row of ten or so Primuses stood on a marble slab. A single ray of moonlight, struggling through a dirty window that had not been cleaned for years, cast a dim light into one corner where there hung a forgotten ikon, the stubs of two candles still stuck in its frame. Beneath the big ikon was another made of paper and fastened to the wall with tin-tacks.

Nobody knows what came over Ivan but before letting himself out by the back staircase he stole one of the candles and the little paper ikon. Clutching these objects he left the strange apartment, muttering, embarrassed by his recent experience in the bathroom. He could not help wondering who the shameless

Kiryushka might be and whether he was the owner of the nasty fur cap with dangling ear-flaps.

In the deserted, cheerless alleyway Bezdomny looked round for the fugitive but there was no sign of him. Ivan said firmly to himself :

' Of course ! He's on the Moscow River ! Come on ! '

Somebody should of course have asked Ivan Nikolayich why he imagined the professor would be on the Moscow River of all places, but unfortunately there was no one to ask him—the nasty little alley was completely empty.

In no time at all Ivan Nikolayich was to be seen on the granite steps of the Moscow lido. Taking off his clothes, Ivan entrusted them to a kindly old man with a beard, dressed in a torn white Russian blouse and patched, unlaced boots. Waving him aside, Ivan took a swallow-dive into the water. The water was so cold that it took his breath away and for a moment he even doubted whether he would reach the surface again. But reach it he did, and puffing and snorting, his eyes round with terror, Ivan Nikolayich began swimming in the black, oily-smelling water towards the shimmering zig-zags of the embankment lights reflected in the water.

When Ivan clambered damply up the steps at the place where he had left his clothes in the care of the bearded man, not only his clothes but their venerable guardian had apparently been spirited away. On the very spot where the heap of clothes had been there was now a pair of check underpants, a torn Russian blouse, a candle, a paper ikon and a box of matches. Shaking his fist into space with impotent rage, Ivan clambered into what was left.

As he did so two thoughts worried him. To begin with he had now lost his MASSOLIT membership card; normally he never went anywhere without it. Secondly it occurred to him that he might be arrested for walking around Moscow in this state. After all, he had practically nothing on but a pair of underpants. . . .

Ivan tore the buttons off the long underpants where they were

fastened at the ankles, in the hope that people might think they
were a pair of lightweight summer trousers. He then picked up
the ikon, the candle and matches and set off, saying to himself:

' I must go to Griboyedov! He's bound to be there.'

Ivan Nikolayich's fears were completely justified—passers-by
noticed him and turned round to stare, so he decided to leave the
main streets and make his way through the side-roads where
people were not so inquisitive, where there was less chance of
them stopping a barefoot man and badgering him with questions
about his underpants—which obstinately refused to look like
trousers.

Ivan plunged into a maze of sidestreets round the Arbat and
began to sidle along the walls, blinking fearfully, glancing round,
occasionally hiding in doorways, avoiding crossroads with
traffic lights and the elegant porticos of embassy mansions.

5. The Affair at Griboyedov

It was an old two-storied house, painted cream, that stood on the ring boulevard behind a ragged garden, fenced off from the pavement by wrought-iron railings. In winter the paved front courtyard was usually full of shovelled snow, whilst in summer, shaded by a canvas awning, it became a delightful outdoor extension to the club restaurant.

The house was called ' Griboyedov House ' because it might once have belonged to an aunt of the famous playwright Alexander Sergeyevich Griboyedov. Nobody really knows for sure whether she ever owned it or not. People even say that Griboyedov never had an aunt who owned any such property. . . . Still, that was its name. What is more, a dubious tale used to circulate in Moscow of how in the round, colonnaded salon on the second floor the famous writer had once read extracts from *Woe From Wit* to that same aunt as she reclined on a sofa. Perhaps he did ; in any case it doesn't matter.

It matters much more that this house now belonged to MASSOLIT, which until his excursion to Patriarch's Ponds was headed by the unfortunate Mikhail Alexandrovich Berlioz. No one, least of all the members of MASSOLIT, called the place ' Griboyedov House '. Everyone simply called it ' Griboyedov ' :

' I spent a couple of hours lobbying at Griboyedov yesterday.'

' Well ? '

' Wangled myself a month in Yalta.'

' Good for you ! '

Or : ' Go to Berlioz—he's seeing people from four to five this afternoon at Griboyedov . . .'—and so on.

MASSOLIT had installed itself in Griboyedov very comfortably indeed. As you entered you were first confronted with a notice-board full of announcements by the various sports clubs, then with the photographs of every individual member of MASSOLIT, who were strung up (their photographs, of course) along the walls of the staircase leading to the first floor.

On the door of the first room on the upper storey was a large notice : ' Angling and Weekend Cottages ', with a picture of a carp caught on a hook.

On the door of the second room was a slightly confusing notice : ' Writers' day-return rail warrants. Apply to M.V. Podlozhnaya.'

The next door bore a brief and completely incomprehensible legend : ' Perelygino '. From there the chance visitor's eye would be caught by countless more notices pinned to the aunt's walnut doors : ' Waiting List for Paper—Apply to Poklevkina ' ; ' Cashier's Office ' ; ' Sketch-Writers : Personal Accounts ' . . .

At the head of the longest queue, which started downstairs at the porter's desk, was a door under constant siege labelled ' Housing Problem '.

Past the housing problem hung a gorgeous poster showing a cliff, along whose summit rode a man on a chestnut horse with a rifle slung over his shoulder. Below were some palm-trees and a balcony. On it sat a shock-haired young man gazing upwards with a bold, urgent look and holding a fountain pen in his hands. The wording read : ' All-in Writing Holidays, from two weeks (short story, novella) to one year (novel, trilogy) : Yalta, Suuk-Su, Borovoye, Tsikhidziri, Makhinjauri, Leningrad (Winter Palace).' There was a queue at this door too, but not an excessively long one—only about a hundred and fifty people.

Following the erratic twists, the steps up and steps down of Griboyedov's corridors, one found other notices : ' MASSOLIT-Management ', ' Cashiers Nos. 2, 3, 4, 5,' ' Editorial Board ', ' MASSOLIT-Chairman ', ' Billiard Room ', then various subsidiary organisations and finally that colonnaded salon where the aunt had listened with such delight to the readings of his comedy by her brilliant nephew.

Every visitor to Griboyedov, unless of course he were completely insensitive, was made immediately aware of how good life was for the lucky members of MASSOLIT and he would at once be consumed with black envy. At once, too, he would curse heaven for having failed to endow him at birth with literary talent, without which, of course, no one could so much as dream of acquiring a MASSOLIT membership card—that brown card known to all Moscow, smelling of expensive leather and embellished with a wide gold border.

Who is prepared to say a word in defence of envy? It is a despicable emotion, but put yourself in the visitor's place : what he had seen on the upper floor was by no means all. The entire ground floor of the aunt's house was occupied by a restaurant—and what a restaurant ! It was rightly considered the best in Moscow. Not only because it occupied two large rooms with vaulted ceilings and lilac-painted horses with flowing manes, not only because every table had a lamp shaded with lace, not only because it was barred to the hoi polloi, but above all for the quality of its food. Griboyedov could beat any restaurant in Moscow you cared to name and its prices were extremely moderate.

There is therefore nothing odd in the conversation which the author of these lines actually overheard once outside the iron railings of Griboyedov :

' Where are you dining today, Ambrose ? '

' What a question ! Here, of course, Vanya ! Archibald Archibaldovich whispered to me this morning that there's *filets de perche au naturel* on the menu tonight. Sheer virtuosity ! '

' You do know how to live, Ambrose ! ' sighed Vanya, a thin pinched man with a carbuncle on his neck, to Ambrose, a strapping, red-lipped, golden-haired, ruddy-cheeked poet.

' It's no special talent,' countered Ambrose. ' Just a perfectly normal desire to live a decent, human existence. Now I suppose you're going to say that you can get perch at the Coliseum. So you can. But a helping of perch at the Coliseum costs thirty roubles fifty kopecks and here it costs five fifty ! Apart from that the perch at the Coliseum are three days old and what's more

70

if you go to the Coliseum there's no guarantee you won't get a
bunch of grapes thrown in your face by the first young man to
burst in from Theatre Street. No, I loathe the Coliseum,' shouted
Ambrose the gastronome at the top of his voice. ' Don't try and
talk me into liking it, Vanya ! '

' I'm not trying to talk you into it, Ambrose,' squeaked
Vanya. ' You might have been dining at home.'

' Thank you very much,' trumpeted Ambrose. ' Just imagine
your wife trying to cook *filets de perche au naturel* in a saucepan,
in the kitchen you share with half a dozen other people ! He, he,
he ! . . . *Au revoir*, Vanya ! ' And humming to himself Ambrose
hurried off to the verandah under the awning.

Ha, ha, ha ! . . . Yes, that's how it used to be ! . . . Some of us
old inhabitants of Moscow still remember the famous Griboyedov. But boiled fillets of perch was nothing, my dear Ambrose !
What about the sturgeon, sturgeon in a silver-plated pan, sturgeon
filleted and served between lobsters' tails and fresh caviar ? And
oeufs en cocotte with mushroom purée in little bowls ? And didn't
you like the thrushes' breasts ? With truffles ? The quails *alla
Genovese* ? Nine roubles fifty ! And oh, the band, the polite
waiters ! And in July when the whole family's in the country
and pressing literary business is keeping you in town—out on
the verandah, in the shade of a climbing vine, a plate of *potage
printanière* looking like a golden stain on the snow-white tablecloth ? Do you remember, Ambrose ? But of course you do—I
can see from your lips you remember. Not just your salmon or
your perch either—what about the snipe, the woodcock in
season, the quail, the grouse ? And the sparkling wines ! But I
digress, reader.

At half past ten on the evening that Berlioz died at Patriarch's
Ponds, only one upstairs room at Griboyedov was lit. In it sat
twelve weary authors, gathered for a meeting and still waiting
for Mikhail Alexandrovich. Sitting on chairs, on tables and even
on the two window ledges, the management committee of
MASSOLIT was suffering badly from the heat and stuffiness. Not
a single fresh breeze penetrated the open window. Moscow was

exuding the heat of the day accumulated in its asphalt and it was obvious that the night was not going to bring any relief. There was a smell of onion coming from the restaurant kitchen in the cellar, everybody wanted a drink, everybody was nervous and irritable.

Beskudnikov, a quiet, well-dressed essayist with eyes that were at once attentive yet shifty, took out his watch. The hands were just creeping up to eleven. Beskudnikov tapped the watch face with his finger and showed it to his neighbour, the poet Dvubratsky, who was sitting on the table, bored and swinging his feet shod in yellow rubber-soled slippers.

' Well, really . . . ' muttered Dvubratsky.

' I suppose the lad's got stuck out at Klyazma,' said Nastasya Lukinishna Nepremenova, orphaned daughter of a Moscow business man, who had turned writer and wrote naval war stories under the pseudonym of ' Bo'sun George '.

' Look here ! ' burst out Zagrivov, a writer of popular short stories. ' I don't know about you, but I'd rather be drinking tea out on the balcony right now instead of stewing in here. Was this meeting called for ten o'clock or wasn't it ? '

' It must be nice out at Klyazma now,' said Bo'sun George in a tone of calculated innocence, knowing that the writers' summer colony out at Perelygino near Klyazma was a sore point. ' I expect the nightingales are singing there now. Somehow I always seem to work better out of town, especially in the spring.'

' I've been paying my contributions for three years now to send my sick wife to that paradise but somehow nothing ever appears on the horizon,' said Hieronymus Poprikhin the novelist, with bitter venom.

' Some people are lucky and others aren't, that's all,' boomed the critic Ababkov from the window-ledge.

Bos'un George's little eyes lit up, and softening her contralto rasp she said :

' We mustn't be jealous, comrades. There are only twenty-two dachas, only seven more are being built, and there are three thousand of us in MASSOLIT.'

'Three thousand one hundred and eleven,' put in someone from a corner.

'Well, there you are,' the Bo'sun went on. 'What can one do? Naturally the dachas are allocated to those with the most talent . . .'

'They're allocated to the people at the top!' barked Glukharyov, a script writer.

Beskudnikov, yawning artificially, left the room.

'One of them has five rooms to himself at Perelygino,' Glukharyov shouted after him.

'Lavrovich has six rooms to himself,' shouted Deniskin, 'and the dining-room's panelled in oak!'

'Well, at the moment that's not the point,' boomed Ababkov. 'The point is that it's half past eleven.'

A noise began, heralding mutiny. Somebody rang up the hated Perelygino but got through to the wrong dacha, which turned out to belong to Lavrovich, where they were told that Lavrovich was out on the river. This produced utter confusion. Somebody made a wild telephone call to the Fine Arts and Literature Commission, where of course there was no reply.

'He might have rung up!' shouted Deniskin, Glukharyov and Quant.

Alas, they shouted in vain. Mikhail Alexandrovich was in no state to telephone anyone. Far, far from Griboyedov, in a vast hall lit by thousand-candle-power lamps, what had recently been Mikhail Alexandrovich was lying on three zinc-topped tables. On the first was the naked, blood-caked body with a fractured arm and smashed rib-cage, on the second the head, its front teeth knocked in, its vacant open eyes undisturbed by the blinding light, and on the third—a heap of mangled rags. Round the decapitated corpse stood the professor of forensic medicine, the pathological anatomist and his dissector, a few detectives and Mikhail Alexandrovich's deputy as chairman of MASSOLIT, the writer Zheldybin, summoned by telephone from the bedside of his sick wife.

A car had been sent for Zheldybin and had first taken him and the detectives (it was about midnight) to the dead man's flat where his papers were placed under seal, after which they all drove to the morgue.

The group round the remains of the deceased were conferring on the best course to take—should they sew the severed head back on to the neck or allow the body to lie in state in the main hall of Griboyedov covered by a black cloth as far as the chin ?

Yes, Mikhail Alexandrovich was quite incapable of telephoning and Deniskin, Glukharyov, Quant and Beskudnikov were exciting themselves for nothing. On the stroke of midnight all twelve writers left the upper storey and went down to the restaurant. There they said more unkind things about Mikhail Alexandrovich : all the tables on the verandah were full and they were obliged to dine in the beautiful but stifling indoor rooms.

On the stroke of midnight the first of these rooms suddenly woke up and leaped into life with a crash and a roar. A thin male voice gave a desperate shriek of ' Alleluia ! ! ' Music. It was the famous Griboyedov jazz band striking up. Sweat-covered faces lit up, the painted horses on the ceiling came to life, the lamps seemed to shine brighter. Suddenly, as though bursting their chains, everybody in the two rooms started dancing, followed by everybody on the verandah.

Glukharyov danced away with the poetess Tamara Polumesyatz, Quant danced, Zhukopov the novelist seized a film actress in a yellow dress and danced. They all danced—Dragunsky and Cherdakchi danced, little Deniskin danced with the gigantic Bo'sun George and the beautiful girl architect Semeikin-Hall was grabbed by a stranger in white straw-cloth trousers. Members and guests, from Moscow and from out of town, they all danced—the writer Johann from Kronstadt, a producer called Vitya Kuftik from Rostov with lilac-coloured eczema all over his face, the leading lights of the poetry section of MASSOLIT—

Pavianov, Bogokhulsky, Sladky, Shpichkin and Adelfina Buzdyak, young men of unknown occupation with cropped hair and shoulders padded with cotton wool, an old, old man with a chive sticking out of his beard danced with a thin, anaemic girl in an orange silk dress.

Pouring sweat, the waiters carried dripping mugs of beer over the dancers' heads, yelling hoarsely and venomously ' Sorry, sir ! ' Somewhere a man bellowed through a megaphone : ' Chops once ! Kebab twice ! Chicken à la King ! ' The vocalist was no longer singing—he was howling. Now and again the crash of cymbals in the band drowned the noise of dirty crockery flung down a sloping chute to the scullery. In short—hell.

At midnight there appeared a vision in this hell. On to the verandah strode a handsome, black-eyed man with a pointed beard and wearing a tail coat. With regal gaze he surveyed his domain. According to some romantics there had once been a time when this noble figure had worn not tails but a broad leather belt round his waist, stuck with pistol-butts, that his raven-black hair had been tied up in a scarlet kerchief and that his brig had sailed the Caribbean under the Jolly Roger.

But that, of course, is pure fantasy—the Caribbean doesn't exist, no desperate buccaneers sail it, no corvette ever chases them, no puffs of cannon-smoke ever roll across the waves. Pure invention. Look at that scraggy tree, look at the iron railings, the boulevard. . . . And the ice is floating in the wine-bucket and at the next table there's a man with ox-like, bloodshot eyes and it's pandemonium. . . . Oh gods—poison, I need poison ! . . .

Suddenly from one of the tables the word ' Berlioz ! ! ' flew up and exploded in the air. Instantly the band collapsed and stopped, as though someone had punched it. ' What, what, what—*what ? ! !* '

' Berlioz ! ! ! '

Everybody began rushing about and screaming.

A wave of grief surged up at the terrible news about Mikhail Alexandrovich. Someone fussed around shouting that they must all immediately, here and now, without delay compose a collective telegram and send it off.

But what telegram, you may ask ? And why send it ? Send it where ? And what use is a telegram to the man whose battered skull is being mauled by the rubber hands of a dissector, whose neck is being pierced by the professor's crooked needles ? He's dead, he doesn't want a telegram. It's all over, let's not overload the post office.

Yes, he's dead . . . but we are still alive !

The wave of grief rose, lasted for a while and then began to recede. Somebody went back to their table and—furtively to begin with, then openly—drank a glass of vodka and took a bite to eat. After all, what's the point of wasting the *côtelettes de volaille* ? What good are we going to do Mikhail Alexandrovich by going hungry ? We're still alive, aren't we ?

Naturally the piano was shut and locked, the band went home and a few journalists left for their newspaper offices to write obituaries. The news spread that Zheldybin was back from the morgue. He moved into Berlioz's upstairs office and at once a rumour started that he was going to take over from Berlioz. Zheldybin summoned all twelve members of the management committee from the restaurant and in an emergency session they began discussing such urgent questions as the preparation of the colonnaded hall, the transfer of the body from the morgue, the times at which members could attend the lying-in-state and other matters connected with the tragic event.

Downstairs in the restaurant life had returned to normal and would have continued on its usual nocturnal course until closing time at four, had not something quite abnormal occurred which shocked the diners considerably more than the news of Berlioz's death.

The first to be alarmed were the cab drivers waiting outside the gates of Griboyedov. Jerking up with a start one of them shouted :

' Hey ! Look at that ! '

A little glimmer flared up near the iron railings and started to bob towards the verandah. Some of the diners stood up, stared and saw that the flickering light was accompanied by a white apparition. As it approached the verandah trellis every diner froze, eyes bulging, sturgeon-laden forks motionless in mid-air. The club porter, who at that moment had just left the restaurant cloakroom to go outside for a smoke, stubbed out his cigarette and was just going to advance on the apparition with the aim of barring its way into the restaurant when for some reason he changed his mind, stopped and grinned stupidly.

The apparition, passing through an opening in the trellis, mounted the verandah unhindered. As it did so everyone saw that this was no apparition but the distinguished poet Ivan Nikolayich Bezdomny.

He was barefoot and wearing a torn, dirty white Russian blouse. To its front was safety-pinned a paper ikon with a picture of some unknown saint. He was wearing long white underpants with a lighted candle in his hand and his right cheek bore a fresh scratch. It would be hard to fathom the depth of the silence which reigned on the verandah. Beer poured on to the floor from a mug held sideways by one of the waiters.

The poet raised the candle above his head and said in a loud voice :

' Greetings, friends ! ' He then looked under the nearest table and exclaimed with disappointment :

' No, he's not there.'

Two voices were heard. A bass voice said pitilessly : ' An obvious case of D.Ts.'

The second, a frightened woman's voice enquired nervously :

' How did the police let him on to the streets in that state ? '

Ivan Nikolayich heard this and replied :

' They tried to arrest me twice, once in Skatertny Street and once here on Bronnaya, but I climbed over the fence and that's how I scratched my cheek ! ' Ivan Nikolayich lifted up his candle and shouted : ' Fellow artists ! ' (His squeaky voice grew stronger and more urgent.) ' Listen to me, all of you! He's come! Catch him at once or he'll do untold harm!'

' What's that? What? What did he say? Who's come?' came the questions from all sides.

' A professor,' answered Ivan, ' and it was this professor who killed Misha Berlioz this evening at Patriarch's.'

By now people were streaming on to the verandah from the indoor rooms and a crowd began milling round Ivan.

' 1 beg your pardon, would you say that again more clearly ? ' said a low, courteous voice right beside Ivan Nikolayich's ear. ' Tell me, how was he killed ? Who killed him ? '

' A foreigner—he's a professor and a spy,' replied Ivan, looking round.

' What's his name ? ' said the voice again into his ear.

' That's just the trouble! ' cried Ivan in frustration. ' If only I knew his name! I couldn't read it properly on his visiting card . . . I only remember the letter ' W '—the name began with a ' W '. What could it have been ? ' Ivan asked himself aloud, clutching his forehead with his hand. ' We, wi, wa . . . wo . . . Walter ? Wagner ? Weiner ? Wegner ? Winter ? ' The hairs on Ivan's head started to stand on end from the effort.

' Wolff ? ' shouted a woman, trying to help him.

Ivan lost his temper.

' You fool! ' he shouted, looking for the woman in the crowd. ' What's Wolff got to do with it ? He didn't do it . . . Wo, wa . . . No, I'll never remember it like this. Now look, everybody— ring up the police at once and tell them to send five motorcycles and sidecars with machine-guns to catch the professor. And don't forget to say that there are two others with him—a tall fellow in checks with a wobbly pince-nez and a great black cat. . . . Meanwhile I'm going to search Griboyedov—I can sense that he's here! '

Ivan was by now in a state of some excitement. Pushing the bystanders aside he began waving his candle about, pouring wax on himself, and started to look under the tables. Then somebody said ' Doctor! ' and a fat, kindly face, clean-shaven, smelling of drink and with horn-rimmed spectacles, appeared in front of Ivan.

'Comrade Bezdomny,' said the face solemnly, 'calm down! You're upset by the death of our beloved Mikhail Alexandrovich ... no, I mean plain Misha Berlioz. We all realise how you feel. You need rest. You'll be taken home to bed in a moment and then you can relax and forget all about it ...'

'Don't you realise,' Ivan interrupted, scowling, 'that we've got to catch the professor? And all you can do is come creeping up to me talking all this rubbish! Cretin!'

'Excuse *me*, Comrade Bezdomny!' replied the face, blushing, retreating and already wishing it had never let itself get involved in this affair.

'No, I don't care who you are—I won't excuse you,' said Ivan Nikolayich with quiet hatred.

A spasm distorted his face, he rapidly switched the candle from his right to his left hand, swung his arm and punched the sympathetic face on the ear.

Several people reached the same conclusion at once and hurled themselves at Ivan. The candle went out, the horn-rims fell off the face and were instantly smashed underfoot. Ivan let out a dreadful war-whoop audible, to everybody's embarrassment, as far as the boulevard, and began to defend himself. There came a tinkle of breaking crockery, women screamed.

While the waiters tied up the poet with dish-cloths, a conversation was in progress in the cloakroom between the porter and the captain of the brig.

'Didn't you see that he was wearing underpants?' asked the pirate coldly.

'But Archibald Archibaldovich—I'm a coward,' replied the porter, 'how could I stop him from coming in? He's a member!'

'Didn't you see that he was wearing underpants?' repeated the pirate.

'Please, Archibald Archibaldovich,—' said the porter, turning purple, 'what could I do? I know there are ladies on the verandah, but . . .'

'The ladies don't matter. They don't mind,' replied the pirate, roasting the porter with his glare. 'But the police mind! There's only one way a man can walk round Moscow in his underwear—when he's being escorted by the police on the way to a police station! And you, if you call yourself a porter, ought to know that if you see a man in that state it's your duty not to waste a moment but to start blowing your whistle! Do you hear? Can't you hear what's happening on the verandah?'

The wretched porter could hear the sounds of smashing crockery, groans and women's screams from the verandah only too well.

'Now what do you propose to do about it?' enquired the buccaneer.

The skin on the porter's face took on a leprous shade and his eyes went blank. It seemed to him that the other man's black hair, now neatly parted, was covered by a fiery silk kerchief. Starched shirtfront and tail-coat vanished, a pistol was sticking out of his leather belt. The porter saw himself dangling from the foretop yard-arm, his tongue protruding from his lifeless, drooping head. He could even hear the waves lapping against the ship's side. The porter's knees trembled. But the buccaneer took pity on him and switched off his terrifying glare.

'All right, Nikolai—but mind it never happens again! We can't have porters like you in a restaurant—you'd better go and be a verger in a church.' Having said this the captain gave a few rapid, crisp, clear orders: 'Send the barman. Police. Statement. Car. Mental hospital.' And he added: 'Whistle!'

A quarter of an hour later, to the astonishment of the people in the restaurant, on the boulevard and at the windows of the surrounding houses, the barman, the porter, a policeman, a waiter and the poet Ryukhin were to be seen emerging from the gates of Griboyedov dragging a young man trussed up like a mummy, who was weeping, spitting, lashing out at Ryukhin and shouting for the whole street to hear:

'You swine ! . . . You swine ! . . .'

A buzzing crowd collected, discussing the incredible scene. It was of course an abominable, disgusting, thrilling, revolting scandal which only ended when a lorry drove away from the gates of Griboyedov carrying the unfortunate Ivan Nikolayich, the policeman, the barman and Ryukhin.

6. Schizophrenia

At half past one in the morning a man with a pointed beard and wearing a white overall entered the reception hall of a famous psychiatric clinic recently completed in the suburbs of Moscow. Three orderlies and the poet Ryukhin stood nervously watching Ivan Nikolayich as he sat on a divan. The dish-cloths that had been used to pinion Ivan Nikolayich now lay in a heap on the same divan, leaving his arms and legs free.

As the man came in Ryukhin turned pale, coughed and said timidly :

' Good morning, doctor.'

The doctor bowed to Ryukhin but looked at Ivan Nikolayich, who was sitting completely immobile and scowling furiously. He did not even move when the doctor appeared.

' This, doctor,' began Ryukhin in a mysterious whisper, glancing anxiously at Ivan Nikolayich, ' is the famous poet Ivan Bezdomny. We're afraid he may have D.Ts.'

' Has he been drinking heavily ? ' enquired the doctor through clenched teeth.

' No, he's had a few drinks, but not enough . . .'

' Has he been trying to catch spiders, rats, little devils or dogs ? '

' No,' replied Ryukhin, shuddering. ' I saw him yesterday and this morning . . . he was perfectly well then.'

' Why is he in his underpants ? Did you have to pull him out of bed ? '

' He came into a restaurant like this, doctor.'

' Aha, aha,' said the doctor in a tone of great satisfaction. ' And why the scratches ? Has he been fighting ? '

' He fell off the fence and then he hit someone in the restaurant . . . and someone else, too . . .'

' I see, I see, I see,' said the doctor and added, turning to Ivan :
' Good morning ! '

' Hello, you quack ! ' said Ivan, loudly and viciously.

Ryukhin was so embarrassed that he dared not raise his eyes.
The courteous doctor, however, showed no signs of offence
and with a practised gesture took off his spectacles, lifted the
skirt of his overall, put them in his hip pocket and then asked
Ivan :

' How old are you ? '

' Go to hell ! ' shouted Ivan rudely and turned away.

' Why are you being so disagreeable ? Have I said anything to
upset you ? '

' I'm twenty-three,' said Ivan excitedly, ' and I'm going to
lodge a complaint against all of you—and you in particular, you
louse ! ' He spat at Ryukhin.

' What will your complaint be ? '

' That you arrested me, a perfectly healthy man, and forcibly
dragged me off to the madhouse ! ' answered Ivan in fury.

At this Ryukhin took a close look at Ivan and felt a chill down
his spine : there was not a trace of insanity in the man's eyes.
They had been slightly clouded at Griboyedov, but now they
were as clear as before.

' Godfathers ! ' thought Ryukhin in terror. ' He really is
perfectly normal ! What a ghastly business ! Why *have* we
brought him here ? There's nothing the matter with him except
a few scratches on his face . . .'

' You are not,' said the doctor calmly, sitting down on a
stool on a single chromium-plated stalk, ' in a madhouse but
in a clinic, where nobody is going to keep you if it isn't
necessary.'

Ivan gave him a suspicious scowl, but muttered :

' Thank God for that ! At last I've found one normal person
among all these idiots and the worst idiot of the lot is that
incompetent fraud Sasha ! '

' Who is this incompetent Sasha ? ' enquired the doctor.

' That's him, Ryukhin,' replied Ivan, jabbing a dirty finger in

Ryukhin's direction, who spluttered in protest. ' That's all the thanks I get,' he thought bitterly, ' for showing him some sympathy ! What a miserable swine he is ! '

' A typical kulak mentality,' said Ivan Nikolayich, who obviously felt a sudden urge to attack Ryukhin. ' And what's more he's a kulak masquerading as a proletarian. Look at his mean face and compare it with all that pompous verse he writes for May Day . . . all that stuff about "onwards and upwards" and "banners waving " ! If you could look inside him and see what he's thinking you'd be sickened ! ' And Ivan Nikolayich gave a hoot of malicious laughter.

Ryukhin, breathing heavily, turned red. There was only one thought in his mind—that he had nourished a serpent in his bosom, that he had tried to help someone who when it came to the pinch had treacherously rounded on him. The worst of it was that he could not answer back—one mustn't swear at a lunatic !

' Exactly why have they brought you here ? ' asked the doctor, who had listened to Bezdomny's outburst with great attention.

' God knows, the blockheads ! They grabbed me, tied me up with some filthy rags and dumped me in a lorry ! '

' May I ask why you came into the restaurant in nothing but your underwear ? '

' There's nothing odd about it,' answered Ivan. ' I went for a swim in the Moscow River and someone pinched my clothes and left me this junk instead ! I couldn't walk round Moscow naked, could I ? I had to put on what there was, because I was in a hurry to get to the Griboyedov restaurant.'

The doctor glanced questioningly at Ryukhin, who mumbled sulkily :

' Yes, that's the name of the restaurant.'

' Aha,' said the doctor, ' but why were you in such a hurry ? Did you have an appointment there ? '

' I had to catch the professor,' replied Ivan Nikolayich, glancing nervously round.

' What professor ? '

'Do you know Berlioz?' asked Ivan with a meaning look.

'You mean . . . the composer?'

Ivan looked puzzled. 'What composer? Oh, yes . . . no, no. The composer just happens to have the same name as Misha Berlioz.'

Ryukhin was still feeling too offended to speak, but he had to explain:

'Berlioz, the chairman of MASSOLIT, was run over by a tram this evening at Patriarch's.'

'Don't lie, you—you don't know anything about it,' Ivan burst out at Ryukhin. 'I was there, not you! He made him fall under that tram on purpose!'

'Did he push him?'

'What are you talking about?' exclaimed Ivan, irritated by his listener's failure to grasp the situation. 'He didn't have to push him! He can do things you'd never believe! He knew in advance that Berlioz was going to fall under a tram!'

'Did anybody see this professor apart from you?'

'No, that's the trouble. Only Berlioz and myself.'

'I see. What steps did you take to arrest this murderer?' At this point the doctor turned and threw a glance at a woman in a white overall sitting behind a desk.

'This is what I did: I took this candle from the kitchen . . .'

'This one?' asked the doctor, pointing to a broken candle lying on the desk beside the ikon.

'Yes, that's the one, and . . .'

'Why the ikon?'

'Well, er, the ikon. . . .' Ivan blushed. 'You see an ikon frightens them more than anything else.' He again pointed at Ryukhin. 'But the fact is that the professor is . . . well, let's be frank . . . he's in league with the powers of evil . . . and it's not so easy to catch someone like him.'

The orderlies stretched their hands down their trouser-seams and stared even harder at Ivan.

'Yes,' went on Ivan. 'He's in league with them. There's no arguing about it. He once talked to Pontius Pilate. It's no good looking at me like that, I'm telling you the truth! He saw it all —the balcony, the palm trees. He was actually with Pontius Pilate, I'll swear it.'

' Well, now . . .'

' So, as I was saying, I pinned the ikon to my chest and ran . . .'
Here the clock struck twice.

' Oh, my God! ' exclaimed Ivan and rose from the divan. ' It's two o'clock and here am I wasting time talking to you! Would you mind—where's the telephone? '

' Show him the telephone,' the doctor said to the orderlies.

As Ivan grasped the receiver the woman quietly asked Ryukhin:
' Is he married? '

' No, he's a bachelor,' replied Ryukhin, startled.

' Is he a union member? '

' Yes.'

' Police? ' shouted Ivan into the mouthpiece. ' Police? Is that the duty officer? Sergeant, please arrange to send five motor cycles with sidecars, armed with machine-guns to arrest the foreign professor. What? Take me with you, I'll show you where to go. . . . This is Bezdomny, I'm a poet, and I'm speaking from the lunatic asylum. . . . What's your address? ' Bezdomny whispered to the doctor, covering the mouthpiece with his palm, and then yelled back into the receiver: ' Are you listening? Hullo! . . . Fools! . . .' Ivan suddenly roared, hurling the receiver at the wall. Then he turned round to the doctor, offered him his hand, said a curt goodbye and started to go.

' Excuse me, but where are you proposing to go? ' said the doctor, looking Ivan in the eye. ' At this hour of night, in your underwear . . . You're not well, stay with us.'

' Come on, let me through,' said Ivan to the orderlies who had lined up to block the doorway. ' Are you going to let me go or not? ' shouted the poet in a terrible voice.

Ryukhin shuddered. The woman pressed a button on the desk; a glittering metal box and a sealed ampoule popped out on to its glass surface.

' Ah, so that's your game, is it? ' said Ivan with a wild, hunted glance around. ' All right then . . . Goodbye ! ! ' And he threw himself head first at the shuttered window.

There was a loud crash, but the glass did not even crack, and a moment later Ivan Nikolayich was struggling in the arms of the orderlies. He screamed, tried to bite, then shouted :

' Fine sort of glass you put in your windows ! Let me go ! Let me go ! '

A hypodermic syringe glittered in the doctor's hand, with one sweep the woman pushed back the tattered sleeve of Ivan's blouse and clamped his arm in a most un-feminine grip. There was a smell of ether, Ivan weakened slightly in the grasp of the four men and the doctor skilfully seized the moment to jab the needle into Ivan's arm. Ivan kept up the struggle for a few more seconds, then collapsed on to the divan.

' Bandits ! ' cried Ivan and leaped up, only to be pushed back. As soon as they let him go he jumped up again, but sat down of his own accord. He said nothing, staring wildly about him, then gave a sudden unexpected yawn and smiled malevolently :

' So you're going to lock me up after all,' he said, yawned again, lay down with his head on the cushion, his fist under his cheek like a child and muttered in a sleepy voice but without malice : ' All right, then . . . but you'll pay for it . . . I warned you, but if you want to . . . What interests me most now is Pontius Pilate . . . Pilate . . .' And with that he closed his eyes.

' Vanna, put him in No. 117 by himself and with someone to watch him.' The doctor gave his instructions and replaced his spectacles. Then Ryukhin shuddered again : a pair of white doors opened without a sound and beyond them stretched a corridor lit by a row of blue night-bulbs. Out of the corridor rolled a couch on rubber wheels. The sleeping Ivan was lifted on to it, he was pushed off down the corridor and the doors closed after him.

' Doctor,' asked the shaken Ryukhin in a whisper, ' is he really ill ? '

' Oh yes,' replied the doctor.

' Then what's the matter with him ? ' enquired Rvukhin timidly.

The exhausted doctor looked at Ryukhin and answered wearily :

' Overstimulation of the motor nerves and speech centres . . . delirious illusions. . . . Obviously a complicated case. Schizophrenia, I should think . . . touch of alcoholism, too. . . .'

Ryukhin understood nothing of this, except that Ivan Nikolayich was obviously in poor shape. He sighed and asked :

' What was that he said about some professor ? '

' I expect he saw someone who gave a shock to his disturbed imagination. Or maybe it was a hallucination. . . .'

A few minutes later a lorry was taking Ryukhin back into Moscow. Dawn was breaking and the still-lit street lamps seemed superfluous and unpleasant. The driver, annoyed at missing a night's sleep, pushed his lorry as hard as it would go, making it skid round the corners.

The woods fell away in the distance and the river wandered off in another direction. As the lorry drove on the scenery slowly changed : fences, a watchman's hut, piles of logs, dried and split telegraph poles with bobbins strung on the wires between them, heaps of stones, ditches—in short, a feeling that Moscow was about to appear round the next corner and would rise up and engulf them at any moment.

The log of wood on which Ryukhin was sitting kept wobbling and slithering about and now and again it tried to slide away from under him altogether. The restaurant dish-cloths, which the policeman and the barman had thrown on to the back of the lorry before leaving earlier by trolley-bus, were being flung about all over the back of the lorry. Ryukhin started to try and pick them up, but with a sudden burst of ill-temper he hissed : ' To hell with them ! Why should I crawl around after them ? ' He pushed them away with his foot and turned away from them.

Ryukhin was in a state of depression. It was obvious that his visit to the asylum had affected him deeply. He tried to think what it was that was disturbing him. Was it the corridor with its blue lamps, which had lodged so firmly in his memory ? Was it the thought that the worst misfortune in the world was to lose one's reason? Yes, it was that, of course—but that after all was a generalisation, it applied to everybody. There was something else, though. What was it? The insult—that was it. Yes, those insulting words that Bezdomny had flung into his face. And the agony of it was not that they were insulting but that they were true.

The poet stopped looking about him and instead stared gloomily at the dirty, shaking floor of the lorry in an agony of self-reproach.

Yes, his poetry . . . He was thirty-two! And what were his prospects? To go on writing a few poems every year. How long—until he was an old man? Yes, until he was an old man. What would these poems do for him? Make him famous? ' What rubbish! Don't fool yourself. Nobody ever gets famous from writing bad poetry. Why is it bad, though? He was right —he was telling the truth! ' said Ryukhin pitilessly to himself. I don't believe in a single word of what I've written . . . ! '

Embittered by an upsurge of neurasthenia, the poet swayed. The floor beneath had stopped shaking. Ryukhin lifted his head and saw that he was in the middle of Moscow, that day had dawned, that his lorry had stopped in a traffic-jam at a boulevard intersection and that right near him stood a metal man on a plinth, his head inclined slightly forward, staring blankly down the street.

Strange thoughts assailed the poet, who was beginning to feel ill. ' Now there's an example of pure luck . . .'—Ryukhin stood up on the lorry's platform and raised his fist in an inexplicable urge to attack the harmless cast-iron man—'. . . everything he did in life, whatever happened to him, it all went his way, everything conspired to make him famous! But what did he achieve? I've never been able to discover . . . What about that famous phrase of his that begins " A storm of mist . . ." ? What a load of rot! He was lucky, that's all, just lucky! '—Ryukhin concluded venomously, feeling the lorry start to move under him—' and just because that White officer shot at him and smashed his hip, he's famous for ever . . .'

The jam was moving. Less than two minutes later the poet, now not only ill but ageing, walked on to the Griboyedov verandah. It was nearly empty.

Ryukhin, laden with dish-cloths, was greeted warmly by Archibald Archibaldovich and immediately relieved of the horrible rags. If Ryukhin had not been so exhausted by the lorry-ride and by his experiences at the clinic, he would probably have enjoyed describing everything that had happened in the hospital and would have embellished the story with some invented details. But for the moment he was incapable. Although Ryukhin was not an observant man, now, after his agony on the lorry, for the first time he looked really hard at the pirate and realised that although the man was asking questions about Bezdomny and even exclaiming ' Oh, poor fellow ! ' he was in reality totally indifferent to Bezdomny's fate and did not feel sorry for him at all. ' Good for him ! He's right ! ' thought Ryukhin with cynical, masochistic relish and breaking off his description of the symptoms of schizophrenia, he asked :

' Archibald Archibaldovich, could I possibly have a glass of vodka . . . ? '

The pirate put on a sympathetic expression and whispered :

' Of course, I quite understand . . . right away . . .' and signalled to a waiter.

A quarter of an hour later Ryukhin was sitting in absolute solitude hunched over a dish of sardines, drinking glass after glass of vodka, understanding more and more about himself and admitting that there was nothing in his life that he could put right—he could only try to forget.

The poet had wasted his night while others had spent it enjoying themselves and now he realised that it was lost forever. He only had to lift his head up from the lamp and look at the sky to see that the night had gone beyond return. Waiters were hurriedly jerking the cloths off the tables. The cats pacing the verandah had a morning look about them. Day broke inexorably over the poet.

7. The Haunted Flat

If next day someone had said to Stepa Likhodeyev 'Stepa! If you don't get up this minute you're going to be shot,' he would have replied in a faint, languid voice : ' All right, shoot me. Do what you like to me, but I'm not getting up ! '

The worst of it was that he could not open his eyes, because when he did so there would be a flash of lightning and his head would shiver to fragments. A great bell was tolling in his head, brown spots with livid green edges were swimming around somewhere between his eyeballs and his closed lids. To cap it all he felt sick and the nausea was somehow connected with the sound of a gramophone.

Stepa tried to remember what had happened, but could only recall one thing—yesterday, somewhere, God knows where, he had been holding a table napkin and trying to kiss a woman, promising her that he would come and visit her tomorrow at the stroke of noon. She had refused, saying ' No, no, I won't be at home,' but Stepa had insisted ' I don't care—I'll come anyway ! '

Stepa had now completely forgotten who that woman had been, what the time was, what day of what month it was, and worst of all he had no idea where he was. In an effort to find out, he unstuck his gummed-up left eyelid. Something glimmered in the semi-darkness. At last Stepa recognised it as a mirror. He was lying cross-wise on the bed in his own bedroom. Then something hit him on the head and he closed his eyes and groaned.

Stepa Likhodeyev, manager of the Variety Theatre, had woken up that morning in the flat that he shared with Berlioz in a big six-storey block of flats on Sadovaya Street. This flat—No. 50— had a strange reputation. Two years before, it had been owned by the widow of a jeweller called de Fougère, Anna Frantzevna, a respectable and very business-like lady of fifty, who let three of her five rooms to lodgers. One of them was, it seems, called Belomut; the other's name has been lost.

Two years ago odd things began happening in that apartment—people started to vanish from it without trace. One Monday afternoon a policeman called, invited the second lodger (the one whose name is no longer known) into the hall and asked him to come along to the police station for a minute or two to sign a document. The lodger told Anfisa, Anna Frantzevna's devoted servant of many years, to say that if anybody rang him up he would be back in ten minutes. He then went out accompanied by the courteous policeman in white gloves. But he not only failed to come back in ten minutes; he never came back at all. Odder still, the policeman appeared to have vanished with him.

Anfisa, a devout and frankly rather a superstitious woman, informed the distraught Anna Frantzevna that it was witchcraft, that she knew perfectly well who had enticed away the lodger and the policeman, only she dared not pronounce the name at night-time.

Witchcraft once started, as we all know, is virtually unstoppable. The anonymous lodger disappeared, you will remember, on a Monday; the following Wednesday Belomut, too, vanished from the face of the earth, although admittedly in different circumstances. He was fetched as usual in the morning by the car which took him to work, but it never brought him back and never called again.

Words cannot describe the pain and distress which this caused to madame Belomut, but alas for her, she was not fated to endure even this unhappy state for long. On returning from her dacha that evening, whither she had hastily gone with Anfisa, Anna Frantzevna found no trace of madame Belomut in the flat and what was more, the doors of both rooms occupied by the Belomuts had been sealed. Two days of uncertainty and insomnia passed for Anna Frantzevna; on the third day she made another hasty visit to her dacha from whence, it need hardly be said, she never returned. Anfisa, left alone, cried her eyes out and finally went to bed at two-o'clock in the morning. Nobody knows what happened to her after that, but tenants of the neighbouring flat described having heard knocking coming from No. 50 and having seen lights burning in the windows all night. By morning Anfisa too was gone. Legends of all kinds about the mysterious flat and its vanishing lodgers circulated in the building for some time. According to one of them the devout and spinsterly Anfisa used to carry twenty-five large diamonds, belonging to Anna Frantzevna, in a chamois-leather bag between her withered breasts. It was said, too, that among other things a priceless treasure consisting of those same diamonds and a hoard of tsarist gold coins were somehow found in the coal-shed behind Anna Frantzevna's dacha. Lacking proof, of course, we shall never know how true these rumours were. However, the flat only remained empty for a week before Berlioz and his wife and Stepa and his wife moved into it. Naturally as soon as they took possession of the haunted flat the oddest things started happening to them too. Within a single month both wives had disappeared, although not without trace. Rumour had it that Berlioz's wife had been seen in Kharkov with a ballet-master, whilst Stepa's wife had apparently found her way to an orphanage where, the story went, the manager of the Variety had used his connections to get her a room on condition that she never showed her face in Sadovaya Street again. . . .

So Stepa groaned. He wanted to call his maid, Grunya, and ask her for an aspirin but he was conscious enough to realise that it would be useless because Grunya most probably had no aspirin. He tried to call for Berlioz's help and twice moaned ' Misha . . . Misha . . .', but as you will have guessed, there was no reply. There was complete silence in the flat.

Wriggling his toes, Stepa deduced that he was lying in his socks. He ran a trembling hand down his hip to test whether he had his trousers on or not and found that he had not. At last, realising that he was alone and abandoned. that there was nobody to help him, he decided to get up, whatever superhuman effort it might cost him.

Stepa prised open his eyelids and saw himself reflected in the long mirror in the shape of a man whose hair stuck out in all directions, with a puffy, stubble-grown face, with watery eyes and wearing a dirty shirt, a collar, tie, underpants and socks.

As he looked at himself in the mirror, he also noticed standing beside it a strange man dressed in a black suit and a black beret.

Stepa sat up on the bed and did his best to focus his bloodshot eyes on the stranger. The silence was broken by the unknown visitor, who said gravely, in a low voice with a foreign accent:

' Good morning, my dear Stepan Bogdanovich! '

There was a pause. Pulling himself together with fearful effort Stepa said:

' What do you want? ' He did not recognise his own voice. He had spoken the word ' what ' in a treble, ' do you ' in a bass and ' want ' had simply not emerged at all.

The stranger gave an amiable smile, pulled out a large gold watch with a diamond triangle on the cover, listened to it strike eleven times and said:

' Eleven. I have been waiting exactly an hour for you to wake up. You gave me an appointment to see you at your flat at ten so here I am! '

Stepa fumbled for his trousers on the chair beside his bed and whispered:

' Excuse me. . . .' He put on his trousers and asked hoarsely: ' Please tell me—who are you? '

He found talking difficult, as with every word someone stuck a needle into his brain, causing him infernal agony.

' What! Have you forgotten my name too? ' The stranger smiled.

' Sorry . . .' said Stepa huskily. He could feel his hangover developing a new symptom: the floor beside his bed seemed to be on the move and any moment now he was liable to take a dive head first down into hell.

' My dear Stepan Bogdanovich,' said the visitor with a shrewd

smile. ' Aspirin will do you no good. Follow a wise old rule—
the hair of the dog. The only thing that will bring you back to
life is two measures of vodka with something sharp and peppery
to eat.'

Ill though Stepa was he had enough sense to realise that since
he had been found in this state he had better tell all.

' Frankly . . .' he began, scarcely able to move his tongue, ' I
did have a bit too . . .'

' Say no more ! ' interrupted the visitor and pushed the armchair to one side.

Stepa's eyes bulged. There on a little table was a tray, laid
with slices of white bread and butter, pressed caviare in a glass
bowl, pickled mushrooms on a saucer, something in a little
saucepan and finally vodka in one of the jeweller's ornate
decanters. The decanter was so chilled that it was wet with
condensation from standing in a finger-bowl full of cracked
ice.

The stranger cut Stepa's astonishment short by deftly pouring
him out half a glass of vodka.

' What about you ? ' croaked Stepa.

' With pleasure ! '

With a shaking hand Stepa raised the glass to his lips and the
mysterious guest swallowed his at one gulp. As he munched his
caviare Stepa was able to squeeze out the words :

' Won't you have a bite to eat too ? '

' Thank you, but I never eat when I'm drinking,' replied the
stranger, pouring out a second round. He lifted the lid of the
saucepan. It contained little frankfurters in tomato sauce.

Slowly the awful green blobs in front of his eyes dissolved,
words started to form and most important of all Stepa's memory
began to come back. That was it—he had been at Khustov's
dacha at Skhodna and Khustov had driven Stepa out there by
taxi. He even remembered hailing the taxi outside the Metropole.
There had been another man with them—an actor . . . or was he
an actor ? . . . anyhow he had a portable gramophone. Yes, yes,
they had all gone to the dacha ! And the dogs, he remembered,

95

had started howling when they played the gramophone. Only the woman Stepa had tried to kiss remained a complete blank . . . who the hell was she ? . . . Didn't she work for the radio ? Or perhaps she didn't. . . .

Gradually the previous day came back into focus, but Stepa was much more interested in today and in particular in this odd stranger who had materialised in his bedroom complete with snacks and vodka. If only someone would explain it all !

'Well, now, I hope, you've remembered my name ? '

Stepa could only grin sheepishly and spread his hands.

'Well, really ! I suspect you drank port on top of vodka last night. What a way to behave ! '

'Please keep this to yourself,' said Stepa imploringly.

'Oh, of course, of course ! But naturally I can't vouch for Khustov.'

'Do you know Khustov ? '

'I saw that individual for a moment or two in your office yesterday, but one cursory glance at his face was enough to convince me that he was a scheming, quarrelsome, sycophantic swine.'

'He's absolutely right ! ' thought Stepa, amazed at such a truthful, precise and succinct description of Khustov.

The ruins of yesterday were piecing themselves together now, but the manager of the Variety still felt vaguely anxious. There was still a gaping black void in his memory. He had absolutely no recollection of having seen this stranger in his office the day before.

'Woland, professor of black magic,' said the visitor gravely, and seeing Stepa was still in difficulties he described their meeting in detail.

He had arrived in Moscow from abroad yesterday, had immediately called on Stepa and offered himself as a guest artiste at the Variety. Stepa had telephoned the Moscow District Theatrical Commission, had agreed to the proposal (Stepa turned pale and blinked) and had signed a contract with Professor Woland for seven performances (Stepa's mouth dropped open), inviting Woland to call on him at ten o'clock the next morning to conclude the details. . . . So Woland had come. When he arrived he had been met by Grunya the maid, who explained that she herself had only just arrived because she lived out, that Berlioz wasn't at home and that if the gentleman wanted to see Stepan Bogdanovich he should go into the bedroom. Stepan Bogdanovich had been sleeping so soundly that she had been unable to wake him. Seeing the condition that Stepa was in, the artiste had sent Grunya out to the nearest delicatessen for some vodka and snacks, to the chemist for some ice and . . .

'You must let me settle up with you,' moaned Stepa, thoroughly crushed, and began hunting for his wallet.

'Oh, what nonsense!' exclaimed the artiste and would hear no more of it.

So that explained the vodka and the food; but Stepa was miserably confused: he could remember absolutely nothing about a contract and he would die before admitting to having seen Woland the previous day. Khustov had been there all right, but not Woland.

'Would you mind showing me the contract?' asked Stepa gently.

'Oh, but of course. . . .'

Stepa looked at the sheet of paper and went numb. It was all there: his own bold signature, the backward-sloping signature of Rimsky, the treasurer, sanctioning the payment to Woland of a cash advance of ten thousand roubles against his total fee of thirty-five thousand roubles for seven performances. And what was more—Woland's receipt for ten thousand roubles!

'What the hell?' thought the miserable Stepa. His head began to spin. Was this one of his lapses of memory? Well, of course, now that the actual contract had been produced any further signs of disbelief would merely be rude. Stepa excused himself for a moment and ran to the telephone in the hall. On the way he shouted towards the kitchen:

'Grunya!'

There was no reply. He glanced at the door of Berlioz's study, which opened off the hall, and stopped, as they say, dumbfounded. There, tied to the door-handle, hung an enormous wax seal.

'My God!' said a voice in Stepa's head. 'If that isn't the last straw!' It would be difficult to describe Stepa's mental confusion. First this diabolical character with his black beret, the iced vodka and that incredible contract. . . . And then, if you please, a seal on the door! Who could ever imagine Berlioz getting into any sort of trouble? No one. Yet there it was—a seal. H'm.

Stepa was at once assailed by a number of uncomfortable little thoughts about an article which he had recently talked Mikhail Alexandrovich into printing in his magazine. Frankly the article had been awful—stupid, politically dubious and badly paid. Hard on the heels of his recollection of the article came a memory of a slightly equivocal conversation which had taken place, as far as he could remember, on 24th April here in the dining-room when Stepa and Berlioz had been having supper together. Of course their talk had not really been dubious (Stepa would not have joined in any such conversation) but it had been on a rather unnecessary subject. They could easily have avoided having it altogether. Before the appearance of this seal the conversation would undoubtedly have been dismissed as utterly trivial, but since the seal . . .

'Oh, Berlioz, Berlioz,' buzzed the voice in Stepa's head. 'Surely he'll never mention it!'

But there was no time for regrets. Stepa dialled the office of Rimsky, the Variety Theatre's treasurer. Stepa was in a delicate position: for one thing, the foreigner might be offended at Stepa ringing up to check on him after he had been shown the contract and for another, the treasurer was an extremely difficult man to deal with. After all he couldn't just say to him: 'Look here, did I sign a contract yesterday for thirty-five thousand roubles with a professor of black magic?' It simply wouldn't do!

'Yes?' came Rimsky's harsh, unpleasant voice in the earphone.

' Hello, Grigory Danilovich,' said Stepa gently. ' Likhodeyev speaking. It's about this . . . er . . . this fellow . . . this artiste, in my flat, called, er, Woland . . . I just wanted to ask you about this evening—is everything O.K.? '

' Oh, the black magician? ' replied Rimsky. ' The posters will be here any minute now.'

' Uhuh . . .' said Stepa weakly. ' O.K., so long . . .'

' Will you be coming over soon? ' asked Rimsky.

' In half an hour,' answered Stepa and replacing the receiver he clasped his feverish head. God, how embarrassing! What an appalling thing to forget!

As it would be rude to stay in the hall for much longer, Stepa concocted a plan. He had to use every possible means of concealing his incredible forgetfulness and begin by cunningly persuading the foreigner to tell him exactly what he proposed to do in his act at the Variety.

With this Stepan turned away from the telephone and in the hall mirror, which the lazy Grunya had not dusted for years, he clearly saw a weird-looking man, as thin as a bean-pole and wearing a pince-nez. Then the apparition vanished. Stepa peered anxiously down the hallway and immediately had another shock as a huge black cat appeared in the mirror and also vanished.

Stepa's heart gave a jump and he staggered back.

' What in God's name . . . ? ' he thought. ' Am I going out of my mind? Where are these reflections coming from? ' He gave another look round the hall and shouted in alarm:

' Grunya! What's this cat doing, sneaking in here? Where does it come from? And who's this other character? '

' Don't worry, Stepan Bogdanovich,' came a voice, though not Grunya's—it was the visitor speaking from the bedroom. ' The cat is mine. Don't be nervous. And Grunya's not here—I sent her away to her family in Voronezh. She complained that you had cheated her out of her leave.'

These words were so unexpected and so absurd that Stepa decided he had not heard them. In utter bewilderment he bounded back into the bedroom and froze on the threshold. His hair rose and a mild sweat broke out on his forehead.

The visitor was no longer alone in the bedroom. The second armchair was now occupied by the creature who had materialised in the hall. He was now to be seen quite plainly—feathery moustache, one lens of his pince-nez glittering, the other missing. But worst of all was the third invader : a black cat of revolting proportions sprawled in a nonchalant attitude on the pouffe, a glass of vodka in one paw and a fork, on which he had just speared a pickled mushroom, in the other.

Stepa felt the light in the bedroom, already weak enough, begin to fade. ' This must be what it's like to go mad . . .' he thought, clutching the doorpost.

' You seem slightly astonished, my dear Stepan Bogdanovich,' said Woland. Stepa's teeth were chattering. ' But I assure you there is nothing to be surprised at. These are my assistants.'

Here the cat drank its vodka and Stepa's hand dropped from the doorpost.

' And my assistants need a place to stay,' went on Woland, ' so it seems that there is one too many of us in this flat. That one, I rather think, is you.'

' Yes, that's them ! ' said the tall man in a goatish voice, speaking of Stepa in the plural. ' They've been behaving disgustingly lately. Getting drunk, carrying on with women, trading on their position and not doing a stroke of work—not that they could do anything even if they tried because they're completely incompetent. Pulling the wool over the boss's eyes, that's what they've been doing ! '

' Drives around in a free car ! ' said the cat slanderously, chewing a mushroom.

Then occurred the fourth and last phenomenon at which Stepa collapsed entirely, his weakened hand scraping down the doorpost as he slid to the floor.

Straight from the full-length mirror stepped a short but unusually broad-shouldered man with a bowler hat on his head.

A fang protruding from his mouth disfigured an already hideous physiognomy that was topped with fiery red hair.

'I cannot,' put in the new arrival, 'understand how he ever came to be manager'—his voice grew more and more nasal— 'he's as much a manager as I am a bishop.'

'You don't look much like a bishop, Azazello,' remarked the cat, piling sausages on his plate.

'That's what I mean,' snarled the man with red hair and turning to Woland he added in a voice of respect : 'Will you permit us, messire, to kick him out of Moscow ? '

'Shoo ! ! ' suddenly hissed the cat, its hair standing on end.

The bedroom began to spin round Stepa, he hit his head on the doorpost and as he lost consciousness he thought, 'I'm dying . . .'

But he did not die. Opening his eyes slightly he found himself sitting on something made of stone. There was a roaring sound nearby. When he opened his eyes fully he realised that the roaring was the sea ; that the waves were breaking at his feet, that he was in fact sitting on the very end of a stone pier, a shining blue sky above him and behind him a white town climbing up the mountainside.

Not knowing quite what to do in a case like this, Stepa raised himself on to his shaking legs and walked down the pier to the shore.

On the pier stood a man, smoking and spitting into the sea. He glared at Stepa and stopped spitting.

Stepa then did an odd thing—he kneeled down in front of the unknown smoker and said :

'Tell me, please, where am I ? '

'Well, I'm damned ! ' said the unsympathetic smoker.

'I'm not drunk,' said Stepa hoarsely. 'Something's happened to me, I'm ill. . . . Where am I ? What town is this ? '

'Yalta, of course. . . .'

Stepa gave a gentle sigh, collapsed and fainted as he struck his head on the warm stonework of the pier.

8. A Duel between Professor and Poet

At about half past eleven that morning, just as Stepa lost consciousness in Yalta, Ivan Nikolayich Bezdomny regained it, waking from a deep and prolonged sleep. For a while he tried to think why he was in this strange room with its white walls, its odd little bedside table made of shiny metal and its white shutters, through which the sun appeared to be shining.

Ivan shook his head to convince himself that it was not aching and remembered that he was in a hospital. This in turn reminded him of Berlioz's death, but today Ivan no longer found this very disturbing. After his long sleep Ivan Nikolayich felt calmer and able to think more clearly. After lying for a while motionless in his spotlessly clean and comfortably sprung bed, Ivan noticed a bell-push beside him. Out of a habit of fingering anything in sight, Ivan pressed it. He expected a bell to ring or a person to appear, but something quite different happened.

At the foot of Ivan's bed a frosted-glass cylinder lit up with the word 'DRINK'. After a short spell in that position, the cylinder began turning until it stopped at another word: 'NANNY'. Ivan found this clever machine slightly confusing. 'NANNY' was replaced by 'CALL THE DOCTOR'.

'H'm . . .' said Ivan, at a loss to know what the machine expected him to do. Luck came to his rescue. Ivan pressed the button at the word 'NURSE'. In reply the machine gave a faint tinkle, stopped and went out. Into the room came a kind-looking woman in a clean white overall and said to Ivan:

' Good morning ! '

Ivan did not reply, as he felt the greeting out of place in the circumstances. They had, after all, dumped a perfectly healthy man in hospital and were making it worse by pretending it was necessary! With the same kind look the woman pressed a button and raised the blind. Sunlight poured into the room through a light, wide-mesh grille that extended to the floor. Beyond the grille was a balcony, beyond that the bank of a meandering river and on the far side a cheerful pine forest.

' Bath time! ' said the woman invitingly and pushed aside a folding partition to reveal a magnificently equipped bathroom.

Although Ivan had made up his mind not to talk to the woman, when he saw a broad stream of water thundering into the bath from a glittering tap he could not help saying sarcastically :

' Look at that! Just like in the Metropole! '

' Oh, no,' replied the woman proudly. ' Much better. There's no equipment like this anywhere, even abroad. Professors and doctors come here specially to inspect our clinic. We have foreign tourists here every day.'

At the words ' foreign tourist ' Ivan at once remembered the mysterious professor of the day before. He scowled and said :

' Foreign tourists . . . why do you all think they're so wonderful ? There are some pretty odd specimens among them, I can tell you. I met one yesterday—he was a charmer! '

He was just going to start telling her about Pontius Pilate, but changed his mind. The woman would never understand and it was useless to expect any help from her.

Washed and clean, Ivan Nikolayich was immediately provided with everything a man needs after a bath—a freshly ironed shirt, underpants and socks. That was only a beginning : opening the door of a wardrobe, the woman pointed inside and asked him :

' What would you like to wear—a dressing gown or pyjamas ? '

Although he was a prisoner in his new home, Ivan found it hard to resist the woman's easy, friendly manner and he pointed to a pair of crimson flannelette pyjamas.

After that Ivan Nikolayich was led along an empty, soundless corridor into a room of vast dimensions. He had decided to treat everything in this wonderfully equipped building with sarcasm and he at once mentally christened this room 'the factory kitchen'.

And with good reason. There were cupboards and glass-fronted cabinets full of gleaming nickel-plated instruments. There were armchairs of strangely complex design, lamps with shiny, bulbous shades, a mass of phials, bunsen burners, electric cables and various totally mysterious pieces of apparatus.

Three people came into the room to see Ivan, two women and one man, all in white. They began by taking Ivan to a desk in the corner to interrogate him.

Ivan considered the situation. He had a choice of three courses. The first was extremely tempting—to hurl himself at these lamps and other ingenious gadgets and smash them all to pieces as a way of expressing his protest at being locked up for nothing. But today's Ivan was significantly different from the Ivan of yesterday and he found the first course dubious ; it would only make them more convinced that he was a dangerous lunatic, so he abandoned it. There was a second—to begin at once telling them the story about the professor and Pontius Pilate. However yesterday's experience had shown him that people either refused to believe the story or completely misunderstood it, so Ivan rejected that course too, deciding to adopt the third : he would wrap himself in proud silence.

It proved impossible to keep it up, and willy-nilly he found himself answering, albeit curtly and sulkily, a whole series of questions. They carefully extracted from Ivan everything about his past life, down to an attack of scarlet fever fifteen years before. Having filled a whole page on Ivan they turned it over and one of the women in white started questioning him about his relatives. It was a lengthy performance—who had died, when and why, did they drink, had they suffered from venereal disease and so forth. Finally they asked him to describe what had happened on the previous day at Patriarch's Ponds, but they did not pay much attention to it and the story about Pontius Pilate left them cold.

The woman then handed Ivan over to the man, who took a

different line with him, this time in silence. He took Ivan's temperature, felt his pulse and looked into his eyes while he shone a lamp into them. The other woman came to the man's assistance and they hit Ivan on the back with some instrument, though not painfully, traced some signs on the skin of his chest with the handle of a little hammer, hit him on the knees with more little hammers, making Ivan's legs jerk, pricked his finger and drew blood from it, pricked his elbow joint, wrapped rubber bracelets round his arm . . .

Ivan could only smile bitterly to himself and ponder on the absurdity of it all. He had wanted to warn them all of the danger threatening them from the mysterious professor, and had tried to catch him, yet all he had achieved was to land up in this weird laboratory just to talk a lot of rubbish about his uncle Fyodor who had died of drink in Vologda.

At last they let Ivan go. He was led back to his room where he was given a cup of coffee, two soft-boiled eggs and a slice of white bread and butter. When he had eaten his breakfast, Ivan made up his mind to wait for someone in charge of the clinic to arrive, to make him listen and to plead for justice.

The man came soon after Ivan's breakfast. The door into Ivan's room suddenly opened and in swept a crowd of people in white overalls. In front strode a man of about forty-five, with a clean-shaven, actorish face, kind but extremely piercing eyes and a courteous manner. The whole retinue showed him signs of attention and respect, which gave his entrance a certain solemnity. ' Like Pontius Pilate ! ' thought Ivan.

Yes, he was undoubtedly the man in charge. He sat down on a stool. Everybody else remained standing.

' How do you do. My name is doctor Stravinsky,' he said as he sat down, looking amiably at Ivan.

' Here you are, Alexander Nikolayich,' said a neatly bearded man and handed the chief Ivan's filled-in questionnaire.

' They've got it all sewn up,' thought Ivan. The man in charge ran a practised eye over the sheet of paper, muttered

'Mm'hh' and exchanged a few words with his colleagues in a strange language. 'And he speaks Latin too—like Pilate', mused Ivan sadly. Suddenly a word made him shudder. It was the word 'schizophrenia', which the sinister stranger had spoken at Patriarch's Ponds. Now professor Stravinsky was saying it. 'So he knew about this, too!' thought Ivan uneasily.

The chief had adopted the rule of agreeing with everybody and being pleased with whatever other people might say, expressing it by the word 'Splendid . . .'

'Splendid!' said Stravinsky, handing back the sheet of paper. He turned to Ivan.

'Are you a poet?'

'Yes, I am,' replied Ivan glumly and for the first time he suddenly felt an inexplicable revulsion to poetry. Remembering some of his own poems, they struck him as vaguely unpleasant.

Frowning, he returned Stravinsky's question by asking:

'Are you a professor?'

To this Stravinsky, with engaging courtesy, inclined his head.

'Are you in charge here?' Ivan went on.

To this, too, Stravinsky nodded.

'I must talk to you,' said Ivan Nikolayich in a significant tone.

'That's why I'm here,' answered Stravinsky.

'Well this is the situation,' Ivan began, sensing that his hour had come. 'They say I'm mad and nobody wants to listen to me!'

'Oh no, we will listen very carefully to everything you have to say,' said Stravinsky seriously and reassuringly, 'and on no account shall we allow anyone to say you're mad.'

'All right, then, listen: yesterday evening at Patriarch's Ponds I met a mysterious person, who may or may not have been a foreigner, who knew about Berlioz's death before it happened, and had met Pontius Pilate.'

The retinue listened to Ivan, silent and unmoving.

'Pilate? Is that the Pilate who lived at the time of Jesus Christ?' enquired Stravinsky, peering at Ivan.

' Yes.'

' Aha,' said Stravinsky. ' And this Berlioz is the one who died falling under a tram ? '

' Yes. I was there yesterday evening when the tram killed him, and this mysterious character was there too . . .'

' Pontius Pilate's friend ? ' asked Stravinsky, obviously a man of exceptional intelligence.

' Exactly,' said Ivan, studying Stravinsky. ' He told us, before it happened, that Anna had spilt the sunflower-seed oil . . . and that was the very spot where Berlioz slipped ! How d'you like that ? ! ' Ivan concluded, expecting his story to produce a big effect.

But it produced none. Stravinsky simply asked :

' And who is this Anna ? '

Slightly disconcerted by the question, Ivan frowned.

' Anna doesn't matter,' he said irritably. ' God knows who she is. Simply some stupid girl from Sadovaya Street. What's important, don't you see, is that he knew about the sunflower-seed oil beforehand. Do you follow me ? '

' Perfectly,' replied Stravinsky seriously. Patting the poet's knee he added : ' Relax and go on.'

' All right,' said Ivan, trying to fall into Stravinsky's tone and knowing from bitter experience that only calm would help him. ' So obviously this terrible man (he's lying, by the way—he's no professor) has some unusual power . . . For instance, if you chase him you can't catch up with him . . . and there's a couple of others with him, just as peculiar in their way : a tall fellow with broken spectacles and an enormous cat who rides on the tram by himself. What's more,' went on Ivan with great heat and conviction, ' he was on the balcony with Pontius Pilate, there's no doubt of it. What about that, eh ? He must be arrested immediately or he'll do untold harm.'

' So you think he should be arrested ? Have I understood you correctly ? ' asked Stravinsky.

' He's clever,' thought Ivan, ' I must admit there are a few bright ones among the intellectuals,' and he replied :

'Quite correct. It's obvious—he *must* be arrested! And meanwhile I'm being kept here by force while they flash lamps at me, bath me and ask me idiotic questions about uncle Fyodor! He's been dead for years! I demand to be let out at once!'

'Splendid, splendid!' cried Stravinsky. 'I see it all now. You're right—what is the use of keeping a healthy man in hospital? Very well, I'll discharge you at once if you tell me you're normal. You don't have to prove it—just say it. Well, are you normal?'

There was complete silence. The fat woman who had examined Ivan that morning glanced reverently at the professor and once again Ivan thought:

'Extremely clever!'

The professor's offer pleased him a great deal, but before replying he thought hard, frowning, until at last he announced firmly:

'I am normal.'

'Splendid,' exclaimed Stravinsky with relief. 'In that case let us reason logically. We'll begin by considering what happened to you yesterday.' Here he turned and was immediately handed Ivan's questionnaire. 'Yesterday, while in search of an unknown man, who had introduced himself as a friend of Pontius Pilate, you did the following:' Here Stravinsky began ticking off the points on his long fingers, glancing back and forth from the paper to Ivan. 'You pinned an ikon to your chest. Right?'

'Right,' Ivan agreed sulkily.

'You fell off a fence and scratched your face. Right? You appeared in a restaurant carrying a lighted candle, wearing only underpants, and you hit somebody in the restaurant. You were tied up and brought here, where you rang the police and asked them to send some machine-guns. You then attempted to throw yourself out of the window. Right? The question—is that the way to set about catching or arresting somebody? If you're normal you're bound to reply—no, it isn't. You want to leave here? Very well. But where, if you don't mind my asking, do you propose to go?'

' To the police, of course,' replied Ivan, although rather less firmly and slightly disconcerted by the professor's stare.

' Straight from here ? '

' Mm'hh.'

' Won't you go home first ? ' Stravinsky asked quickly.

' Why should I go there ? While I'm going home he might get away ! '

' I see. And what will you tell the police ? '

' I'll tell them about Pontius Pilate,' replied Ivan Nikolayich, his eyes clouding.

' Splendid ! ' exclaimed Stravinsky, defeated, and turning to the man with the beard he said : ' Fyodor Vasilievich, please arrange for citizen Bezdomny to be discharged. But don't put anybody else in this room and don't change the bedclothes. Citizen Bezdomny will be back here again in two hours. Well,' he said to the poet, ' I won't wish you success because I see no chance whatever of your succeeding. See you soon ! ' He got up and his retinue started to go.

' Why will I come back here ? ' asked Ivan anxiously.

' Because as soon as you appear at a police station dressed in your underpants and say you've met a man who knew Pontius Pilate, you'll immediately be brought back here and put in this room again.'

' Because of my underpants ? ' asked Ivan, staring distractedly about him.

' Chiefly because of Pontius Pilate. But the underpants will help. We shall have to take away your hospital clothes and give you back your own. And you came here wearing underpants. Incidentally you said nothing about going home first, despite my hint. After that you only have to start talking about Pontius Pilate . . . and you're done for.'

At this point something odd happened to Ivan Nikolayich. His will-power seemed to crumple. He felt himself weak and in need of advice.

' What should I do, then ? ' he asked, timidly this time.

' Splendid ! ' said Stravinsky. ' A most reasonable question.

Now I'll tell you what has really happened to you. Yesterday someone gave you a bad fright and upset you with this story about Pontius Pilate and other things. So you, worn out and nerve-racked, wandered round the town talking about Pontius Pilate. Quite naturally people took you for a lunatic. Your only salvation now is complete rest. And you must stay here.'

'But somebody must arrest him ! ' cried Ivan, imploringly.

'Certainly, but why should you have to do it ? Put down all your suspicions and accusations against this man on a piece of paper. Nothing could be simpler than to send your statement to the proper authorities and if, as you suspect, the man is a criminal, it will come to light soon enough. But on one condition—don't over-exert your mind and try to think a bit less about Pontius Pilate. If you harp on that story I don't think many people are going to believe you.'

'Right you are ! ' announced Ivan firmly. 'Please give me pen and paper.'

'Give him some paper and a short pencil,' said Stravinsky to the fat woman, then turning to Ivan : 'But I don't advise you to start writing today.'

'No, no, today ! I must do it today ! ' cried Ivan excitedly.

'All right. Only don't overtax your brain. If you don't get it quite right today, tomorrow will do.'

'But he'll get away ! '

'Oh no,' countered Stravinsky. 'I assure you he's not going to get away. And remember—we are here to help you in every way we can and unless we do, nothing will come of your plan. D'you hear ? ' Stravinsky suddenly asked, seizing Ivan Nikolayich by both hands. As he held them in his own he stared intently into Ivan's eyes, repeating : 'We shall help you . . . do you hear ? . . . We shall help you . . . you will be able to relax . . . it's quiet here, everything's going to be all right . . . all right . . . we shall help you . . .'

Ivan Nikolayich suddenly yawned and his expression softened.

'Yes, I see,' he said quietly.

'Splendid ! ' said Stravinsky, closing the conversation in his habitual way and getting up. 'Goodbye!' He shook Ivan by the hand and as he went out he turned to the man with the beard and said: 'Yes, and try oxygen . . . and baths.'

A few moments later Stravinsky and his retinue were gone. Through the window and the grille the gay, springtime wood gleamed brightly on the far bank and the river sparkled in the noon sunshine.

9. Koroviev's Tricks

Nikanor Ivanovich Bosoi, chairman of the tenants' association of No. 302A, Sadovaya Street, Moscow, where the late Berlioz had lived, was in trouble. It had all begun on the previous Wednesday night.

At midnight, as we already know, the police had arrived with Zheldybin, had hauled Nikanor Ivanovich out of bed, told him of Berlioz's death and followed him to flat No. 50. There they had sealed the deceased's papers and personal effects. Neither Grunya the maid, who lived out, nor the imprudent Stepan Bogdanovich were in the flat at the time. The police informed Nikanor Ivanovich that they would call later to collect Berlioz's manuscripts for sorting and examination and that his accommodation, consisting of three rooms (the jeweller's study, drawing-room and dining-room) would revert to the tenants' association for disposal. His effects were to be kept under seal until the legatees' claims were proved by the court.

The news of Berlioz's death spread through the building with supernatural speed and from seven o'clock on Thursday morning Bosoi started to get telephone calls. After that people began calling in person with written pleas of their urgent need of vacant housing space. Within the space of two hours Nikanor Ivanovich had collected thirty-two such statements.

They contained entreaties, threats, intrigue, denunciations, promises to redecorate the flat, remarks about overcrowding and the impossibility of sharing a flat with bandits. Among them was a description, shattering in its literary power, of the theft of some meat-balls from someone's jacket pocket in flat No. 31, two threats of suicide and one confession of secret pregnancy.

Nikanor Ivanovich was again and again taken aside with

a wink and assured in whispers that he would do well on the deal. . . .

This torture lasted until one o'clock, when Nikanor Ivanovich simply ran out of his flat by the main entrance, only to run away again when he found them lying in wait for him outside. Somehow contriving to throw off the people who chased him across the asphalt courtyard, Nikanor Ivanovich took refuge in staircase 6 and climbed to the fatal apartment.

Panting with exertion, the stout Nikanor Ivanovich rang the bell on the fifth-floor landing. No one opened. He rang again and again and began to swear quietly. Still no answer. Nikanor Ivanovich's patience gave way and pulling a bunch of duplicate keys from his pocket he opened the door with a masterful flourish and walked in.

' Hello, there ! ' shouted Nikanor Ivanovich in the dim hallway. ' Are you there, Grunya ? '

No reply.

Nikanor Ivanovich then took a folding ruler out of his pocket, used it to prise the seal from the study door and strode in. At least he began by striding in, but stopped in the doorway with a start of amazement.

Behind Berlioz's desk sat a tall, thin stranger in a check jacket, jockey cap and pince-nez. . . .

' And who might you be, citizen ? ' asked Nikanor Ivanovich.

' Nikanor Ivanovich ! ' cried the mysterious stranger in a quavering tenor. He leaped up and greeted the chairman with an unexpectedly powerful handshake which Nikanor Ivanovich found extremely painful.

' Pardon me,' he said suspiciously, ' but who are you ? Are you somebody official ? '

' Ah, Nikanor Ivanovich ! ' said the stranger in a man-to-man voice. ' Who is official and who is unofficial these days ? It all depends on your point of view. It's all so vague and changeable, Nikanor Ivanovich. Today I'm unofficial, tomorrow, hey presto ! I'm official ! Or maybe vice-versa—who knows ? '

None of this satisfied the chairman. By nature a suspicious

man, he decided that this voluble individual was not only unofficial but had no business to be there.

'Who are you ? What's your name ? ' said the chairman firmly,
advancing on the stranger.

'My name,' replied the man, quite unmoved by this hostile
reception, 'is . . . er . . . let's say . . . Koroviev. Wouldn't you
like a bite to eat, Nikanor Ivanovich ? As we're friends ? '

'Look here,' said Nikanor Ivanovich disagreeably, 'what the
hell do you mean—eat ? ' (Sad though it is to admit, Nikanor
Ivanovich had no manners.) 'You're not allowed to come into
a dead man's flat ! What are you doing here ? '

'Now just sit down, Nikanor Ivanovich,' said the imperturb-
able stranger in a wheedling voice, offering Nikanor Ivanovich
a chair.

Infuriated, Nikanor Ivanovich kicked the chair away and
yelled :

'Who are you ? '

'I am employed as interpreter to a foreign gentleman residing
in this flat,' said the self-styled Koroviev by way of introduction
as he clicked the heels of his dirty brown boots.

Nikanor Ivanovich's mouth fell open. A foreigner in this flat,
complete with interpreter, was a total surprise to him and he
demanded an explanation.

This the interpreter willingly supplied. Monsieur Woland, an
artiste from abroad, had been kindly invited by the manager of
the Variety Theatre, Stepan Bogdanovich Likhodeyev, to spend
his stay as a guest artiste, about a week, in his flat. Likhodeyev
had written to Nikanor Ivanovich about it yesterday, requesting
him to register the gentlemen from abroad as a temporary
resident while Likhodeyev himself was away in Yalta.

'But he hasn't written to me,' said the bewildered chairman.

'Take a look in your briefcase, Nikanor Ivanovich,' suggested
Koroviev amiably.

Shrugging his shoulders Nikanor Ivanovich opened his briefcase and found a letter from Likhodeyev.

'Now how could I have forgotten that?' mumbled Nikanor Ivanovich, gazing stupidly at the opened envelope.

'It happens to the best of us, Nikanor Ivanovich!' cackled Koroviev. 'Absent-mindedness, overstrain and high blood-pressure, my dear friend! Why, I'm horribly absent-minded. Some time over a glass or two I'll tell you a few things that have happened to me—you'll die with laughter!'

'When is Likhodeyev going to Yalta?'

'He's already gone,' cried the interpreter. 'He's on his way there. God knows where he is by now.' And the interpreter waved his arms like windmill sails.

Nikanor Ivanovich announced that he had to see the foreign gentleman in person, but this was refused. It was quite out of the question. Monsieur Woland was busy. Training his cat.

'You can see the cat if you like,' suggested Koroviev.

This Nikanor Ivanovich declined and the interpreter then made him an unexpected but most interesting proposal: since Monsieur Woland could not bear staying in hotels and was used to spacious quarters, couldn't the tenants' association lease him the whole flat for his week's stay, including the dead man's rooms?

'After all, what does he care? He's dead,' hissed Koroviev in a whisper. 'You must admit the flat's no use to him now, is it?'

In some perplexity Nikanor Ivanovich objected that foreigners were normally supposed to stay at the Metropole and not in private accommodation . . .

'I tell you he's so fussy, you'd never believe it,' whispered Koroviev. 'He simply refuses! He hates hotels! I can tell you I'm fed up with these foreign tourists,' complained Koroviev confidentially. 'They wear me out. They come here and either they go spying and snooping or they send me mad with their whims and fancies—this isn't right, that isn't just so! And there'd be plenty in it for your association, Nikanor Ivanovich. He's not short of money.' Koroviev glanced round and then whispered in the chairman's ear: 'He's a millionaire!'

The suggestion was obviously a sensible one, but there was something ridiculous about his manner, his clothes and that absurd, useless pince-nez that all combined to make Nikanor Ivanovich vaguely uneasy. However he agreed to the suggestion. The tenants' association, alas, was showing an enormous deficit. In the autumn they would have to buy oil for the steam heating plant and there was not a kopeck in the till, but with this foreigner's money they might just manage it. Nikanor Ivanovich, however, practical and cautious as ever, insisted on clearing the matter with the tourist bureau.

' Of course ! ' cried Koroviev. ' It must be done properly. There's the telephone, Nikanor Ivanovich, ring them up right away ! And don't worry about money,' he added in a whisper as he led the chairman to the telephone in the hall, ' if anyone can pay handsomely, he can. If you could see his villa in Nice ! When you go abroad next summer you must go there specially and have a look at it—you'll be amazed ! '

The matter was fixed with the tourist bureau with astonishing ease and speed. The bureau appeared to know all about Monsieur Woland's intention to stay in Likodeyev's flat and raised no objections.

' Excellent ! ' cried Koroviev.

Slightly stupefied by this man's incessant cackling, the chairman announced that the tenants' association was prepared to lease flat No. 50 to Monsieur Woland the artiste at a rent of . . . Nikanor Ivanovich stammered a little and said :

' Five hundred roubles a day.'

At this Koroviev surpassed himself. Winking conspiratorially towards the bedroom door, through which they could hear a series of soft thumps as the cat practised its leaps, he said :

' So for a week that would amount to three and a half thousand, wouldn't it ? '

Nikanor Ivanovich quite expected the man to add ' Greedy, aren't you, Nikanor Ivanovich ? ' but instead he said :

' That's not much. Ask him for five thousand, he'll pay.'

Grinning with embarrassment, Nikanor Ivanovich did not

even notice how he suddenly came to be standing beside Berlioz's desk and how Koroviev had managed with such incredible speed and dexterity to draft a contract in duplicate. This done, he flew into the bedroom and returned with the two copies signed in the stranger's florid hand. The chairman signed in turn and Koroviev asked him to make out a receipt for five . . .

' Write it out in words, Nikanor Ivanovich. " Five thousand roubles ".' Then with a flourish which seemed vaguely out of place in such a serious matter—' *Eins! zwei! drei!* '—he laid five bundles of brand-new banknotes on the table.

Nikanor Ivanovich checked them, to an accompaniment of witticisms from Koroviev of the ' better safe than sorry ' variety. Having counted the money the chairman took the stranger's passport to be stamped with his temporary residence permit, put contract, passport and money into his briefcase and asked shyly for a free ticket to the show . . .

' But of course ! ' exclaimed Koroviev. ' How many do you want, Nikanor Ivanovich—twelve, fifteen ? '

Overwhelmed, the chairman explained that he only wanted two, one for his wife Pelagea Antonovna and one for himself.

Koroviev seized a note-pad and dashed off an order to the box office for two complimentary tickets in the front row. As the interpreter handed it to Nikanor Ivanovich with his left hand, with his right he gave him a thick, crackling package. Glancing at it Nikanor Ivanovich blushed hard and started to push it away.

' It's not proper . . .'

' I won't hear any objection,' Koroviev whispered right in his ear. ' We don't do this sort of thing but foreigners do. You'll offend him, Nikanor Ivanovich, and that might be awkward. You've earned it . . .'

' It's strictly forbidden . . .' whispered the chairman in a tiny voice, with a furtive glance around.

' Where are the witnesses ? ' hissed Koroviev into his other ear. ' I ask you—where are they ? Come, now . . .'

There then happened what the chairman later described as a miracle—the package jumped into his briefcase of its own accord, after which he found himself, feeling weak and battered, on the staircase. A storm of thoughts was whirling round inside his head. Among them were the villa in Nice, the trained cat, relief that there had been no witnesses and his wife's pleasure at the complimentary tickets. Yet despite these mostly comforting thoughts, in the depths of his soul the chairman still felt the pricking of a little needle. It was the needle of unease. Suddenly, halfway down the staircase, something else occurred to him—how had that interpreter found his way into the study past a sealed door? And why on earth had he, Nikanor Ivanovich, forgotten to ask him about it? For a while the chairman stared at the steps like a sheep, then decided to forget it and not to bother himself with imaginary problems . . .

As soon as the chairman had left the flat a low voice came from the bedroom:

' I don't care for that Nikanor Ivanovich. He's a sly rogue. Why not fix it so that he doesn't come here again? '

' Messire, you only have to give the order . . .' answered Koroviev in a firm, clear voice that no longer quavered.

At once the diabolical interpreter was in the hall, had dialled a number and started to speak in a whining voice:

' Hullo! I consider it my duty to report that the chairman of our tenants' association at No. 302A Sadovaya Street, Nikanor Ivanovich Bosoi, is dealing in black-market foreign currency. He has just stuffed four hundred dollars wrapped in newspaper into the ventilation shaft of the lavatory in his flat, No. 35. My name is Timothy Kvastsov and I live in the same block, flat No. 11. But please keep my name a secret. I'm afraid of what that man may do if he finds out . . .'

And with that the scoundrel hung up.

What happened after that in No. 50 is a mystery, although what happened to Nikanor Ivanovich is common knowledge. Locking himself in the lavatory, he pulled the package out of his briefcase and found that it contained four hundred roubles. He wrapped it up in a sheet of old newspaper and pushed it into the ventilation shaft. Five minutes later he was sitting down at table in his little dining-room. From the kitchen his wife brought in a pickled herring, sliced and thickly sprinkled with raw onion. Nikanor Ivanovich poured himself a wineglassful of vodka, drank it, poured out another, drank that, speared three slices of herring on his fork . . . and then the doorbell rang. Pelagea Antonovna was just bringing in a steaming casserole, one glance at which was enough to tell you that in the midst of all that hot, thick borsch was one of the most delicious things in the world —a marrow bone.

Gulping down his running saliva, Nikanor Ivanovich snarled : ' Who the hell is that—at this hour ! They won't even allow a man to eat his supper. . . . Don't let anybody in—I'm not at home. . . . If it's about the flat tell them to stop worrying. There'll be a committee meeting about it in a week's time.'

His wife ran into the hall and Nikanor Ivanovich ladled the quivering marrow bone out of its steaming lake. At that moment three men came into the dining-room, followed by a very pale Pelagea Antonovna. At the sight of them Nikanor Ivanovich turned white and got up.

' Where's the W.C. ? ' enquired the first man urgently.

There was a crash as Nikanor Ivanovich dropped the ladle on to the oilcloth table-top.

' Here, in here,' babbled Pelagea Antonovna. The visitors turned and rushed back into the passage.

' What's going on ? ' asked Nikanor Ivanovich as he followed them. ' You can't just burst into our flat like that . . . Where's your identity card if you don't mind ? '

The first man showed Nikanor Ivanovich his identity card while the second clambered up on to a stool in the lavatory and thrust his arm into the ventilation shaft. Nikanor Ivanovich began to feel faint. They unwrapped the sheet of newspaper to find that the banknotes in the package were not roubles but some unknown foreign money—bluish-green in colour with a picture of an old man. Nikanor Ivanovich, however, saw none of it very clearly because spots were swimming in front of his eyes.

' Dollars in the ventilation shaft. . . .' said the first man thoughtfully and asked Nikanor Ivanovich politely : ' Is this your little parcel ? '

' No ! ' replied Nikanor Ivanovich in a terrified voice. ' It's been planted on me ! '

' Could be,' agreed the first man, adding as quietly as before : ' Still, you'd better give up the rest.'

' There isn't any more ! I swear to God I've never even seen any ! ' screamed the chairman in desperation. He rushed to a chest, pulled out a drawer and out of that his briefcase, shouting distractedly as he did so :

' It's all in here . . . the contract . . . that interpreter must have planted them on me . . . Koroviev, the man in the pince-nez ! '

He opened the briefcase, looked inside, thrust his hand in, turned blue in the face and dropped his briefcase into the borsch. There was nothing in it—no letter from Stepan, no contract, no passport, no money and no complimentary tickets. Nothing, in short, except a folding ruler.

' Comrades ! ' screamed the chairman frantically. ' Arrest them ! The forces of evil are in this house ! '

Something odd happened to Pelagea Antonovna at this point. Wringing her hands she cried :

' Confess, Nikanor ! They'll reduce your sentence if you do ! '

Eyes bloodshot, Nikanor Ivanovich raised his clenched fists over his wife's head and screamed :

' Aaah ! You stupid bitch ! '

Then he crumpled and fell into a chair, having obviously decided to bow to the inevitable. Meanwhile, out on the landing, Timothy Kondratievich Kvastsov was pressing first his ear then his eye to the keyhole of the chairman's front door, burning with curiosity.

Five minutes later the tenants saw the chairman led out into the courtyard by two men. Nikanor Ivanovich, so they said later, had been scarcely recognisable—staggering like a drunkard and muttering to himself.

Another hour after that a stranger appeared at flat No. 11 just when Timothy Kondratievich, gulping with pleasure, was describing to some other tenants how the chairman had been whisked away; the stranger beckoned Timothy Kondratievich out of his kitchen into the hall, said something and took him away.

10. *News from Yalta*

As disaster overtook Nikanor Ivanovich in Sadovaya Street, not far from No. 302A two men were sitting in the office of Rimsky the treasurer of the Variety Theatre: Rimsky himself and the house manager, Varenukha.

From this large office on the second floor two windows gave on to Sadovaya and another, just behind the treasurer's back as he sat at his desk, on to the Variety's garden; it was used in summer and contained several bars for serving cold drinks, a shooting gallery and an open promenade. The furniture of the room, apart from the desk, consisted of a collection of old posters hanging on the wall, a small table with a carafe of water, four chairs and a stand in one corner supporting a dusty, long-forgotten model of a stage set. Naturally the office also contained a small, battered fireproof safe standing to the left of Rimsky's desk.

Rimsky had been in a bad mood all morning. Varenukha, by contrast, was extremely cheerful and lively, if somewhat nervous. Today, however, there was no outlet for his energy.

Varenukha had just taken refuge in the treasurer's office from the complimentary ticket hounds who made his life a misery, especially on the days when there was a change of programme. And today was one of those days. As soon as the telephone started to ring Varenukha picked up the receiver and lied into it:

'Who? Varenukha? He's not here. He's left the theatre.'

'Please try and ring Likhodeyev once more,' said Rimsky testily.

'But he's not at home. I've already sent Karpov; the flat's empty.'

'I wish to God I knew what was going on!' hissed Rimsky, fidgeting with his adding machine.

The door opened and a theatre usher dragged in a thick package of newly-printed fly-posters, which announced in large red letters on a green background:

Tonight and All This Week
in the
Variety Theatre
A Special Act
PROFESSOR WOLAND
Black Magic
All Mysteries Revealed

As Varenukha stepped back from the poster, which he had propped up on the model, he admired it and ordered the usher to have all the copies posted up.

'All right—look sharp,' said Varenukha to the departing usher.

'I don't care for this project at all,' growled Rimsky disagreeably, staring at the poster through his horn-rims. 'I'm amazed that he was ever engaged.'

'No, Grigory Danilovich, don't say that! It's a very smart move. All the fun is in showing how it's done—" the mysteries revealed ".'

'I don't know, I don't know. I don't see any fun in that myself . . . just like him to dream up something of this sort. If only he'd shown us this magician. Did you see him? God knows where he's dug him up from.'

It transpired that Varenukha, like Rimsky, had not seen the magician either. Yesterday Stepa had rushed ('like a madman', in Rimsky's words) into the treasurer's office clutching a draft contract, had ordered him to countersign it and pay Woland his money. The magician had vanished and no one except Stepa himself had seen him.

Rimsky pulled out his watch, saw that it was five minutes to three and was seized with fury. Really, this was too much! Likhodeyev had rung at about eleven o'clock, had said that he would come in about half an hour and now he had not only failed to appear but had disappeared from his flat.

' It's holding up all my work,' snarled Rimsky, tapping a pile of unsigned papers.

' I suppose he hasn't fallen under a tram, like Berlioz ? ' said Varenukha, holding the receiver to his ear and hearing nothing but a continual, hopeless buzz as Stepa's telephone rang unanswered.

' It would be a damned good thing if he has . . .' said Rimsky softly between his teeth.

At that moment in came a woman in a uniform jacket, peaked cap, black skirt and sneakers. She took a square of white paper and a notebook out of a little pouch on her belt and enquired :

' Which of you is Variety ? Priority telegram for you. Sign here.'

Varenukha scrawled some hieroglyphic in the woman's notebook and as soon as the door had slammed behind her, opened the envelope. Having read the telegram he blinked and handed it to Rimsky.

The telegram read as follows : ' YALTA TO MOSCOW VARIETY STOP TODAY 1130 PSYCHIATRIC CASE NIGHTSHIRTED TROUSERED SHOELESS STAGGERED POLICE STATION ALLEGING SELF LIKHODEYEV MANAGER VARIETY WIRE YALTA POLICE WHERE LIKHODEYEV.'

' Thanks—and I'm a Dutchman ! ' exclaimed Rimsky and added : ' Another little surprise package ! '

' The False Dimitry ! ' said Varenukha and spoke into the telephone : ' Telegrams, please. On account, Variety Theatre. Priority. Ready ? " Yalta Police stop Likhodeyev Moscow Rimsky Treasurer." '

Disregarding the Pretender of Yalta, Varenukha tried again to locate Stepa by telephone and could not, of course, find him anywhere. While he was still holding the receiver in his hand and wondering where to ring next, the same woman came in again and handed Varenukha a new envelope. Hastily opening it Varenukha read the text and whistled.

' What is it now ? ' asked Rimsky, twitching nervously.

Varenukha silently passed him the telegram and the treasurer read the words :

' BEG BELIEVE TRANSPORTED YALTA WOLANDS HYPNOSIS WIRE POLICE CONFIRMATION MY IDENTITY LIKHODEYEV.'

Rimsky and Varenukha put their heads together, read the telegram again and stared at one another in silence.

' Come on, come on ! ' said the woman irritably. ' Sign here. Then you can sit and stare at it as long as you like. I've got urgent telegrams to deliver ! '

Without taking his eyes off the telegram Varenukha scribbled in her book and the woman disappeared.

' You say you spoke to him on the telephone just after eleven ? ' said the house manager in complete bewilderment.

' Yes, extraordinary as it may seem ! ' shouted Rimsky. ' But whether I did or not, he can't be in Yalta now. It's funny.'

' He's drunk . . .' said Varenukha.

' Who's drunk ? ' asked Rimsky and they stared at each other again.

There was no doubt that some lunatic or practical joker was telegraphing from Yalta. But the strange thing was—how did this wit in Yalta know about Woland, who had only arrived in Moscow the evening before ? How did he know of the connection between Likhodeyev and Woland ?

' " Hypnosis ",' muttered Varenukha, repeating one of the words in the telegram. ' How does he know about Woland ? ' He blinked and suddenly shouted firmly : ' No, of course not. It can't be ! Rubbish ! '

' Where the hell has this man Woland got to, damn him ? ' asked Rimsky.

Varenukha at once got in touch with the tourist bureau and announced to Rimsky's utter astonishment that Woland was staying in Likhodeyev's flat. Having then dialled Likhodeyev's flat yet again, Varenukha listened for a long time as the ringing tone buzzed thickly in the earpiece. In between the buzzes a distant baritone voice could be heard singing and Varenukha decided that somewhere the telephone system had got its wires crossed with the radio station.

'No reply from his flat,' said Varenukha, replacing the receiver on its rest. 'I'll try once more . . .'

Before he could finish in came the same woman and both men rose to greet her as this time she took out of her pouch not a white, but a black sheet of paper.

'This is getting interesting,' said Varenukha through gritted teeth, watching the woman as she hurried out. Rimsky was the first to look at the message.

On a dark sheet of photographic paper the following lines were clearly visible :

'As proof herewith specimen my handwriting and signature wire confirmation my identity. Have Woland secretly followed. Likhodeyev.'

In twenty years of experience in the theatre Varenukha had seen plenty, but now he felt his mind becoming paralysed and he could find nothing to say beyond the commonplace and absurd remark :

'It can't be ! '

Rimsky reacted differently. He got up, opened the door and bellowed through it to the usher sitting outside on a stool :

'Don't let anybody in except the telegraph girl,' and locked the door.

He then pulled a sheaf of papers out of his desk drawer and began a careful comparison of the thick, backward-sloping letters in the photogram with the writing in Stepa's memoranda and his signatures, with their typically curly-tailed script. Varenukha, sprawling on the desk, breathed hotly on Rimsky's cheek.

'It's his handwriting,' the treasurer finally said and Varenukha echoed him :

'It's his all right.'

Looking at Rimsky's face the house manager noticed a change in it. A thin man, the treasurer seemed to have grown even thinner and to have aged. Behind their hornrims his eyes had lost their usual aggressiveness. Now they showed only anxiety, even alarm.

Varenukha did everything that people are supposed to do in moments of great stress. He paced up and down the office, twice spread his arms as though he were being crucified, drank a whole glass of brackish water from the carafe and exclaimed :

' 1 don't understand it ! I don't understand it ! I don't under-stand it ! '

Rimsky stared out of the window, thinking hard. The treasurer was in an extremely perplexing situation. He had to find an immediate, on-the-spot, natural solution for a number of very unusual phenomena.

Frowning, the treasurer tried to imagine Stepa in a nightshirt and without his shoes, climbing that morning at about half past eleven into some incredibly super-rapid aeroplane and then the same Stepa, also at half past eleven, standing on Yalta airport in his socks. . . .

Perhaps it wasn't Stepa who had telephoned him from his flat ? No, that was Stepa all right ! As if he didn't know Stepa's voice. Even if it hadn't been Stepa talking to him that morning, he had actually seen the man no earlier than the evening before, when Stepa had rushed in from his own office waving that idiotic contract and had so annoyed Rimsky by his irresponsible behaviour. How could he have flown out of Moscow without saying a word to the theatre ? And if he had flown away yesterday evening he couldn't have reached Yalta before noon today. Or could he ?

' How far is it to Yalta ? ' asked Rimsky.

Varenukha stopped pacing and cried :

' I've already thought of that ! To Sebastopol by rail it's about fifteen hundred kilometres and it's about another eighty kilometres to Yalta. It's less by air, of course.'

Hm . . . Yes . . . No question of his having gone by train. What then ? An Air Force fighter plane ? Who'd let Stepa on board a fighter in his stockinged feet ? And why ? Perhaps he'd

taken his shoes off when he got to Yalta? Same problem—
why? Anyhow, the Air Force wouldn't let him board a fighter
even with his shoes on! No, a fighter was out of the question
too. But the telegram said that he'd appeared at the police
station at half past eleven in the morning and he'd been in
Moscow, talking on the telephone, at . . . Just a moment (his
watch-face appeared before Rimsky's eyes) . . . He remembered
where the hands had been pointing . . . Horrors! It had been
twenty past eleven!

So what was the answer? Supposing that the moment after
his telephone call Stepa had rushed to the airport and got there
in, say, five minutes (which was impossible anyway), then if the
aeroplane had taken off at once it must have covered over a
thousand kilometres in five minutes. Consequently it had been
flying at a speed of more than twelve thousand kilometres per
hour! Impossible, ergo—he wasn't in Yalta!

What other explanation could there be? Hypnosis? There
was no such hypnosis which could hurl a man a thousand kilometres. Could he be imagining that he was in Yalta? *He* might,
but would the Yalta police imagine it? No, no, really, it
was absurd! . . . But they had telegraphed from Yalta, hadn't
they?

The treasurer's face was dreadful to see. By now someone
outside was twisting and rattling the door handle and the usher
could be heard shouting desperately:

'No, you can't! I wouldn't let you in even if you were to
kill me! They're in conference!'

Rimsky pulled himself together as well as he could, picked up
the telephone receiver and said into it:

'I want to put through a priority call to Yalta.'

'Clever!' thought Varenukha.

But the call to Yalta never went through. Rimsky put back
the receiver and said:

'The line's out of order—as if on purpose.'

For some reason the faulty line disturbed him a great deal and
made him reflect. After some thought he picked up the receiver

again with one hand and with the other started writing down
what he was dictating into the telephone :

'Priority telegram. From Variety. Yes. To Yalta police.
Yes. "Today approximately 1130 Likhodeyev telephoned me
Moscow. Stop. Thereafter failed appear theatre and unreach-
able telephone. Stop. Confirm handwriting. Stop. Will take
suggested measures observe Woland Rimsky Treasurer." '

'Very clever ! ' thought Varenukha, but the instant afterwards
he changed his mind : ' No, it's absurd ! He can't be in Yalta ! '

Rimsky was meanwhile otherwise engaged. He carefully laid
all the telegrams into a pile and together with a copy of his own
telegram, put them into an envelope, sealed it up, wrote a few
words on it and handed it to Varenukha, saying :

'Take this and deliver it at once, Ivan Savyelich. Let them
puzzle it out.'

'Now that really is smart ! ' thought Varenukha as he put the
envelope into his briefcase. Then just to be absolutely sure he
dialled the number of Stepa's flat, listened, then winked mysteriously and made a joyful face. Rimsky craned his neck to
listen.

'May I speak to Monsieur Woland, please ? ' asked Varenukha
sweetly.

'He's busy,' answered the receiver in a quavering voice.
'Who wants him ? '

'Varenukha, house manager of the Variety Theatre.'

'Ivan Savyelich ? ' squeaked the earpiece delightedly. 'How
very nice to hear your voice ! How are you ? '

'*Merci*,' replied Varenukha in some consternation. 'Who's
speaking ? '

'This is Koroviev, his assistant and interpreter,' trilled the
receiver. 'At your service, my dear Ivan Savyelich ! Just tell
me what I can do for you. What is it ? '

'I'm sorry . . . is Stepan Bogdanovich Likhodeyev at home ? '

'Alas, no, he isn't,' cried the telephone. 'He's gone out.'

'Where to ? '

'He went out of town for a car-ride.'

' Wha-at ? Car-ride ? When is he coming back ? '

' He said he just wanted a breath of fresh air and then he'd be back.'

' I see . . .' said Varenukha, perplexed. ' *Merci* . . . please tell Monsieur Woland that his act this evening starts after the second interval.'

' Very good. Of course. At once. Immediately. Certainly. I'll tell him,' came the staccato reply from the earpiece.

' Goodbye,' said Varenukha, in amazement.

' Please accept,' said the telephone, ' my warmest and most sincere good wishes for a brilliant success ! It will be a great show—great ! '

' There you are—I told you so ! ' said the house manager excitedly. ' He hasn't gone to Yalta, he's just gone out of town for a drive.'

' Well, if that's the case,' said the treasurer, turning pale with anger, ' he has behaved like an absolute swine ! '

Here the manager leaped into the air and gave such a shout that Rimsky shuddered.

' I remember ! I remember now ! There's a new Turkish restaurant out at Pushkino—it's just opened—and it's called the " Yalta " ! Don't you see ? He went there, got drunk and he's been sending us telegrams from there ! '

' Well, he really has overdone it this time,' replied Rimsky, his cheek twitching and real anger flashing in his eyes. ' This little jaunt is going to cost him dear.' He suddenly stopped and added uncertainly : ' But what about those telegrams from the police ? '

' A lot of rubbish ! More of his practical jokes,' said Varenukha confidently and asked : ' Shall I take this envelope all the same ? '

' You must,' replied Rimsky.

Again the door opened to admit the same woman. ' Oh, not her ! ' sighed Rimsky to himself. Both men got up and walked towards her.

This time the telegram said :

' THANKS CONFIRMATION IDENTITY WIRE ME FIVE

HUNDRED ROUBLES POLICE STATION FLYING MOSCOW
TOMORROW LIKHODEYEV.'

' He's gone mad,' said Varenukha weakly.

Rimsky rattled his key-chain, took some money out of the
safe, counted out five hundred roubles, rang the bell, gave the
money to the usher and sent her off to the post office.

' But Grigory Danilovich,' said Varenukha, unable to believe
his eyes, ' if you ask me you're throwing that money away.'

' It'll come back,' replied Rimsky quietly, ' and then he'll pay
dearly for this little picnic.' And pointing at Varenukha's briefcase he said :

' Go on, Ivan Savyelich, don't waste any time.'

Varenukha picked up his briefcase and trotted off.

He went down to the ground floor, saw a very long queue
outside the box office and heard from the cashier that she was
expecting to have to put up the ' House Full ' notices that
evening because they were being positively overwhelmed since
the special bill had been posted up. Varenukha told her to be
sure not to sell the thirty best seats in the boxes and stalls, then
rushed out of the box office, fought off the people begging for
free tickets and slipped into his own office to pick up his cap.
At that moment the telephone rang.

' Yes ? ' he shouted.

' Ivan Savyelich ? ' enquired the receiver in an odious nasal
voice.

' He's not in the theatre ! ' Varenukha was just about to shout,
but the telephone cut him short :

' Don't play the fool, Ivan Savyelich, and listen. You are not
to take those telegrams anywhere or show them to anybody.'

' Who's that ? ' roared Varenukha. ' Kindly stop playing
these tricks ! You're going to be shown up before long. What's
your telephone number ? '

' Varenukha,' insisted the horrible voice. ' You understand
Russian don't you ? Don't take those telegrams.'

' So you refuse to stop this game do you ? ' shouted the house
manager in a rage. ' Now listen to me—you're going to pay for

this ! ' He went on shouting threats but stopped when he realised that no one was listening to him on the other end.

At that moment his office began to darken. Varenukha ran out, slammed the door behind him and went out into the garden through the side door.

He felt excited and full of energy. After that last insolent telephone call he no longer had any doubt that some gang of hooligans was playing some nasty practical joke and that the joke was connected with Likhodeyev's disappearance. The house manager felt inspired with the urge to unmask the villains and, strange as it may seem, he had a premonition that he was going to enjoy it. It was a longing to be in the limelight, the bearer of sensational news.

Out in the garden the wind blew in his face and threw sand in his eyes as if it were trying to bar his way or warn him. A window-pane on the second floor slammed shut with such force that it nearly broke the glass, the tops of the maples and poplars rustled alarmingly. It grew darker and colder. Varenukha wiped his eyes and noticed that a yellowish-centred thundercloud was scudding low over Moscow. From the distance came a low rumble.

Although Varenukha was in a hurry, an irresistible urge made him turn aside for a second into the open-air men's toilet just to check that the electrician had replaced a missing electric lamp.

Running past the shooting gallery, he passed through a thick clump of lilac which screened the blue-painted lavatory. The electrician seemed to have done his job : the lamp in the men's toilet had been screwed into its socket and the protective wire screen replaced, but the house manager was annoyed to notice that even in the dark before the thunderstorm the pencilled graffiti on the walls were still clearly visible.

' What a . . .' he began, then suddenly heard a purring voice behind him :

' Is that you, Ivan Savyelich ? '

Varenukha shuddered, turned round and saw before him a shortish, fat creature with what seemed like the face of a cat.

'Yes . . .' replied Varenukha coldly.

'Delighted to meet you,' answered the stout, cat-like personage. Suddenly it swung round and gave Varenukha such a box on the ear that his cap flew off and vanished without trace into one of the lavatory pans.

For a moment the blow made the toilet shimmer with a flickering light. A clap of thunder came from the sky. Then there was a second flash and another figure materialised, short but athletically built, with fiery red hair . . . one wall eye, a fang protruding from his mouth . . . He appeared to be left-handed, as he fetched the house manager a shattering clout on his other ear. The sky rumbled again in reply and rain started to drench the wooden roof.

'Look here, com . . .' whispered Varenukha, staggering. It at once occurred to him that the word 'comrades' hardly fitted these bandits who went around assaulting people in public conveniences, so he groaned instead '. . . citizens . . .', realised that they didn't even deserve to be called that and got a third fearful punch. This time he could not see who had hit him, as blood was spurting from his nose and down his shirt.

'What have you got in your briefcase, louse?' shouted the cat-figure. 'Telegrams? Weren't you warned by telephone not to take them anywhere? I'm asking you—weren't you warned?'

'Yes . . . I was . . . warned,' panted Varenukha.

'And you still went? Gimme the briefcase, you skunk!' said the other creature in the same nasal voice that had come through the telephone, and wrenched the briefcase out of Varenukha's trembling hands.

Then they both grabbed the house manager by the arms and frog-marched him out of the garden and along Sadovaya Street. The storm was in full spate, water was roaring and gurgling down the drain-holes in great bubbling waves, it poured off the roofs from the overflowing gutters and out of the drain pipes in foaming torrents. Every living person had vanished from the street and there was no one to help Ivan Savyelich. In one second, leaping over muddy streams and lit by flashes of lightning the bandits had dragged the half-dead Varenukha to No. 302A and fled into the doorway, where two barefoot women stood pressed against the wall, holding their shoes and stockings in their hands. Then they rushed across to staircase 6, carried the nearly insane Varenukha up to the fifth floor and threw him to the ground in the familiar semi-darkness of the hallway of Stepa Likhodeyev's flat.

The two robbers vanished and in their place appeared a completely naked girl—a redhead with eyes that burned with a phosphorescent glitter.

Varenukha felt that this was the most terrible thing that had ever happened to him. With a groan he turned and leaned on the wall. The girl came right up to him and put her hands on his shoulders. Varenukha's hair stood on end. Even through the cold, soaking wet material of his coat he could feel that those palms were even colder, that they were as cold as ice.

'Let me give you a kiss,' said the girl tenderly, her gleaming eyes close to his. Varenukha lost consciousness before he could feel her kiss.

11. The Two Ivans

The wood on the far bank of the river, which an hour before had glowed in the May sunshine, had now grown dim, had blurred and dissolved.

Outside, water was pouring down in solid sheets. Now and again there came a rift in the sky, the heavens split and the patient's room was flooded with a terrifying burst of light.

Ivan was quietly weeping as he sat on his bed and stared out at the boiling, muddied river. At every clap of thunder he cried miserably and covered his face with his hands. Sheets of paper, covered with his writing, blew about on the floor.

The poet's efforts to compose a report on the terrible professor had come to nothing. As soon as he had been given a stub of a pencil and some paper by the fat nurse, whose name was Praskovya Fyodorovna, he had rubbed his hands in a businesslike way and arranged his bedside table for work. The beginning sounded rather well:

' To the Police. From Ivan Nikolayich Bezdomny, Member of MASSOLIT. Statement. Yesterday evening I arrived at Patriarch's Ponds with the late M. A. Berlioz. . . .'

Here the poet stumbled, chiefly because of the words ' the late '. It sounded wrong—how could he have ' arrived ' with ' the late . . .' ? Dead people can't walk. If he wrote like this they really would think he was mad. So Ivan Nikolayich made some corrections, which resulted in : '. . . with M. A. Berlioz, later deceased.' He did not like that either, so he wrote a third version and that was even worse than the previous two : '. . . with Berlioz, who fell under a tram . . .' Here he thought of the composer of the same name and felt obliged to add : ' . . . not the composer.'

Struggling with these two Berliozes, Ivan crossed it all out and decided to begin straight away with a striking phrase which would immediately catch the reader's attention, so he first described how the cat had jumped on the tram and then described the episode of the severed head. The head and the professor's forecast reminded him of Pontius Pilate, so to sound more convincing Ivan decided to give the story of the Procurator in full, from the moment when he had emerged in his white, red-lined cloak into the arcade of Herod's palace.

Ivan worked hard. He crossed out what he had written, put in new words and even tried to draw a sketch of Pontius Pilate, then one showing the cat walking on its hind legs. But his drawings were hopeless and the further he went the more confused his statement grew.

By the time the storm had begun, Ivan felt that he was exhausted and would never be able to write a statement. His wind-blown sheets of paper were in a complete muddle and he began to weep, quietly and bitterly. The kind nurse Praskovya Fyodorovna called on the poet during the storm and was worried to find him crying. She closed the blinds so that the lightning should not frighten the patient, picked up the sheets of paper and went off with them to look for the doctor.

The doctor appeared, gave Ivan an injection in his arm and assured him that he would soon stop crying, that it would pass, everything would be all right and he would forget all about it.

The doctor was right. Soon the wood across the river looked as it always did. The weather cleared until every single tree stood out against a sky which was as blue as before and the river subsided. His injection at once made Ivan feel less depressed. The poet lay quietly down and gazed at the rainbow stretched across the sky.

He lay there until evening and did not even notice how the rainbow dissolved, how the sky faded and saddened, how the wood turned to black.

When he had drunk his hot milk, Ivan lay down again. He was amazed to notice how his mental condition had changed.

The memory of the diabolical cat had grown indistinct, he was no longer frightened by the thought of the decapitated head. Ivan started to muse on the fact that the clinic really wasn't such a bad place, that Stravinsky was very clever and famous and that he was an extremely pleasant man to deal with. The evening air, too, was sweet and fresh after the storm.

The asylum was asleep. The white frosted-glass bulbs in the silent corridors were extinguished and in their place glowed the weak blue night-lights. The nurses' cautious footsteps were heard less and less frequently walking the rubber-tiled floor of the corridor.

Ivan now lay in sweet lassitude; glancing at his bedside lamp, then at the dim ceiling light and at the moon rising in the dark, he talked to himself.

' I wonder why I got so excited about Berlioz falling under that tram ? ' the poet reasoned. ' After all he's dead, and we all die some time. It's not as if I were a relation or a really close friend either. When you come to think of it I didn't even know the man very well. What did I really know about him ? Nothing, except that he was bald and horribly talkative. So, gentlemen,' went on Ivan, addressing an imaginary audience, ' let us consider the following problem : why, I should like to know, did I get in such a rage with that mysterious professor or magician with his empty, black eye ? Why did I chase after him like a fool in those underpants and holding a candle ? Why the ridiculous scene in the restaurant ? '

' Wait a moment, though ! ' said the old Ivan severely to the new Ivan in a voice that was not exactly inside him and not quite by his ear. ' He did know in advance that Berlioz was going to have his head cut off, didn't he ? Isn't that something to get upset about ? '

' What do you mean ? ' objected the new Ivan. ' I quite agree that it's a nasty business—a child could see that. But he's a mysterious, superior being—that's what makes it so interesting. Think of it—a man who knew Pontius Pilate ! Instead of creating that ridiculous scene at Patriarch's wouldn't it have been rather more intelligent to ask him politely what happened next to Pilate and that prisoner Ha-Notsri ? And I had to behave like an idiot ! Of course it's a serious matter to kill the editor of a magazine. But still—the magazine won't close down just because of that, will it ? Man is mortal and as the professor so rightly said mortality can come so suddenly. So God rest his soul and let's get ourselves another editor, perhaps one who's even more of a chatterbox than Berlioz ! '

After dozing for a while the new Ivan said spitefully to the old Ivan :

' And how do I look after this affair ? '

' A fool,' distinctly said a bass voice that belonged to neither of the Ivans and was extremely like the professor's.

Ivan, somehow not offended by the word ' fool ' but even pleasantly surprised by it, smiled and sank into a half-doze. Sleep crept up on him. He had a vision of a palm tree on its elephantine leg and a cat passed by—not a terrible cat but a nice one and Ivan was just about to fall asleep when suddenly the grille slid noiselessly aside. A mysterious figure appeared on the moonlit balcony and pointed a threatening finger at Ivan.

Quite unafraid Ivan sat up in bed and saw a man on the balcony. Pressing his finger to his lips the man whispered : ' Shh ! '

12. Black Magic Revealed

A little man with a crimson pear-shaped nose, in a battered yellow bowler hat, check trousers and patent leather boots pedalled on to the Variety stage on a bicycle. As the band played a foxtrot he rode round in circles a few times, then gave a triumphant yelp at which the bicycle reared up with its front wheel in the air. After a few rounds on the back wheel alone, the man stood on his head, unscrewed the front wheel and threw it into the wings. He then carried on with one wheel, turning the pedals with his hands.

Next a fat blonde girl, wearing a sweater and a very brief skirt strewn with sequins, came in riding a long metal pole with a saddle on the top and a single wheel at the bottom. As they met the man gave a welcoming cry and doffed his bowler hat with his foot.

Finally a little boy of about seven with the face of an old man sneaked in between the two adults on a tiny two-wheeler to which was fixed an enormous motor-car horn.

After a few figures of eight the whole troupe, to an urgent roll of drums from the orchestra, rode at full tilt towards the front of the stage. The spectators in the front rows gasped and ducked, fully expecting all three to crash, cycles and all, into the orchestra pit, but they stopped at the very second that their front wheels threatened to skid into the pit on to the heads of the musicians. With a loud cry of ' Allez-oop ! ' the three cyclists leaped from their machines and bowed, while the blonde blew kisses to the audience and the little boy played a funny tune on his horn.

The auditorium rocked with applause, the blue curtain fell and the cyclists vanished. The lighted green ' Exit ' signs went out and the white globes began to glow brighter and brighter in the web of girders under the dome. The second and last interval had begun.

The only man unaffected by the Giulli family's marvels of cycling technique was Grigory Danilovich Rimsky. He sat alone in his office, biting his thin lips, his face twitching spasmodically. First Likhodeyev had vanished in the most bizarre circumstances and now Varenukha had suddenly disappeared. Rinsky knew where Varenukha had been going to—but the man had simply gone and had never come back. He shrugged his shoulders and muttered to himself:

' But why ? ! '

Nothing would have been simpler for a sensible, practical man like Rimsky to have telephoned the place where Varenukha had gone and to have found out what had happened to him, yet it was ten o'clock that evening before he could bring himself to do so.

At ten Rimsky finally took a grip on himself and picked up the telephone receiver. The telephone was dead. An usher reported that all the other telephones in the building were out of order. This annoying but hardly supernatural occurrence seemed to shock Rimsky, although secretly he was glad, because it absolved him from the need to telephone.

As the little red light above the treasurer's head started flashing to show that the interval was beginning, an usher came in and announced that the foreign magician had arrived. Rimsky's expression changed and he scowled with a mixture of anxiety and irritation. As the only member of the management left in the theatre, it was his duty to go backstage and receive the guest artiste.

As the warning bells rang, inquisitive people were peeping into the star dressing room. Among them were jugglers in bright robes and turbans, a roller-skater in a knitted cardigan, a comedian with a powdered white face and a make-up man. The celebrated guest artiste amazed everyone with his unusually long, superbly cut tail coat and by wearing a black domino. Even more astounding were the black magician's two companions : a tall man in checks with an unsteady pince-nez and a fat black cat which walked into the dressing room on its hind legs and casually sat down on the divan, blinking in the light of the unshaded lamps round the make-up mirror.

With a forced smile which only made him look acidly disagreeable, Rimsky bowed to the silent magician sitting beside the cat on the divan. There were no handshakes, but the man in checks introduced himself smoothly as ' the assistant '. This gave the treasurer an unpleasant shock, as there had not been a word in the contract about an assistant.

Grigory Danilovich enquired stiffly where the professor's equipment might be.

' Why, bless you my dear sir,' replied the magician's assistant, ' we have all the equipment we need with us now—look ! *Eins, zwei, drei!* '

Flourishing his long, knotty fingers in front of Rimsky's eyes he made a pass beside the cat's ear and pulled out of it Rimsky's gold watch and chain, which until that moment had been sitting under the treasurer's buttoned jacket in his waistcoat pocket with the chain threaded through a buttonhole.

Rimsky involuntarily clutched his stomach, the spectators gasped and the make-up man, glancing in from the corridor, clucked with approval.

' Your watch, sir ? There you are,' said the man in checks. Smiling nonchalantly, he proffered the watch to its owner on his dirty palm.

' I wouldn't sit next to *him* in a tram,' whispered the comedian cheerfully to the make-up man.

But the cat put the watch trick in the shade. Suddenly getting up from the divan it walked on its hind legs to the dressing table, pulled the stopper out of a carafe with its forepaw, poured out a glass of water, drank it, replaced the stopper and wiped its whiskers with a make-up cloth.

Nobody even gasped. Their mouths fell open and the make-up man whispered admiringly :

'Bravo . . .'

The last warning bell rang and everybody, excited by the prospect of a good act, tumbled out of the dressing room.

A minute later the house-lights went out, the footlights lit up the fringe of the curtain with a red glow and in the lighted gap between the tabs the audience saw a fat, jolly, clean-shaven man in stained tails and a grubby white dicky. It was Moscow's best known compère, George Bengalsky.

' And now, ladies and gentlemen,' said Bengalsky, smiling his boyish smile, ' you are about to see . . .' Here Bengalsky broke off and started again in a completely different tone of voice : ' I see that our audience has increased in numbers since the interval. Half Moscow seems to be here tonight ! D'you know, I met a friend of mine the other day and I said to him : " Why didn't you come and see our show ? Half the town was there last night." And he said : " I live in the other half ! " ' Bengalsky paused for the laugh, but none came so he went on : ' Well, as I was saying, you are about to see a very famous artiste from abroad, M'sieur Woland, with a session of black magic. Of course we know, don't we . . .' Bengalsky smiled confidentially, ' that there's no such thing really. It's all superstition—or rather Maestro Woland is a past master of the art of conjuring, as you will see from the most interesting part of his act in which he reveals the mysteries of his technique. And now, ladies and gentlemen, since none of us can bear the suspense any longer, I give you . . . Monsieur Woland ! . . .'

Having said his feeble piece, Bengalsky put his hands palm to palm and raised them in a gesture of welcome towards the gap in the curtain, which then rose with a soft rustle.

The entry of the magician with his tall assistant and his cat, who trotted on stage on his hind legs, pleased the audience greatly.

' Armchair, please,' said Woland quietly and instantly an armchair appeared on stage from nowhere. The magician sat down. ' Tell me, my dear Faggot,' Woland enquired of the check-clad buffoon, who apparently had another name besides ' Koroviev,' : ' do you find the people of Moscow much changed ? '

The magician nodded towards the audience, still silent with astonishment at seeing an armchair materialise from nowhere.

' I do, messire,' replied Faggot-Koroviev in a low voice.

' You are right. The Muscovites have changed considerably ... outwardly, I mean ... as, too, has the city itself ... Not just the clothes, but now they have all these ... what d'you call 'em ... tramways, cars ...'

' Buses,' prompted Faggot respectfully.

The audience listened intently to this conversation, assuming it to be the prelude to some magic tricks. The wings were full of actors and stage hands and among their faces could be seen the pale, strained features of Rimsky.

Bengalsky's face, lurking in a corner of the stage, began to show consternation. With an imperceptible raise of one eyebrow he seized the opportunity of a pause in the dialogue to interject :

' Our guest artiste from abroad is obviously delighted with Moscow's technological progress.' This was accompanied by a smile for the stalls and a smile for the gallery.

Woland, Faggot and the cat turned their heads towards the compère.

' Did I say I was delighted ? ' the magician asked Faggot.

' You said nothing of the kind, messire,' replied the latter.

' Then what *is* the man talking about ? '

' He was simply telling lies ! ' announced the chequered clown in a loud voice for the whole theatre to hear and turning to Bengalsky he added : ' D'you hear—you're a liar ! '

There was a burst of laughter from the gallery as Bengalsky spluttered, his eyes popping with indignation.

' But naturally I am not so much interested in the buses and telephones and such like ...'

' Apparatus,' prompted Faggot.

' Precisely, thank you,' drawled the magician in a deep bass, ' as in the much more important question : have the Muscovites changed inwardly ? '

' A vital question indeed, sir.'

In the wings, glances were exchanged, shoulders shrugged ;

Bengalsky was turning purple, Rimsky white. Suddenly, sensing the general air of restlessness, the magician said:

' That's enough talk from us, my dear Faggot—the audience is getting bored. Show us something simple to begin with.'

There was a rustle of relief in the house. Faggot and the cat walked to opposite sides of the footlights. Faggot snapped his fingers, cried : ' Three, four ! ' and seized a pack of cards out of the air, shuffled it and threw it in an unbroken stream to the cat, who caught it and threw it back in the same way. The shiny arc of cards gave a twist, Faggot opened his mouth like a baby bird and swallowed the whole pack card for card. With this the cat bowed and raised a storm of applause.

' Bravo ! Bravo ! ' came the admiring cries from the wings.

Faggot pointed to the stalls and announced :

' That pack of cards, ladies and gentlemen, is now to be found in the seventh row, in comrade Parchevsky's wallet between a three-rouble note and a summons to appear in court for non-payment of alimony to his ex-wife.'

More rustling in the auditorium, people half-rose and finally a man who really was called Parchevsky, purple with embarrassment, removed the pack of cards from his wallet and started waving it in the air, not knowing what to do with it.

' Keep it as a souvenir ! ' shouted Faggot. ' You may need it —didn't you say at dinner yesterday that if it weren't for your poker games life wouldn't be worth living ? '

' That's an old trick ! ' came a shout from the gallery. ' The man in the stalls is a plant.'

' Think so ? ' bawled Faggot, peering up at the gallery. ' In that case you're a plant too, because there's a pack of cards in your pocket ! '

There was a movement in the gallery and a voice cried gleefully :

' He's right ! There is ! Here they are ! . . . Wait . . . there's some money too ! '

The people in the stalls turned their heads. The embarrassed man in the gallery had found a bundle in his pocket, tied up with banker's tape and marked 'One Thousand Roubles'. His neighbours crowded round as he picked at the wrapping with his fingernail to find out whether it was real money or a stage prop.

'My God—it's real money!' came a joyful shout from the gallery.

'I wish you'd play cards with me if you've any more packs like that one,' begged a fat man in the middle of the stalls.

'*Avec plaisir!*' replied Faggot. 'But why should you be the only one? You shall all take part! Everybody look up, please! One!' A pistol appeared in his hand. 'Two!' the pistol was pointed upwards. 'Three!' There was a flash, a bang, and immediately a cascade of white pieces of paper began to float down from the dome above the auditorium.

Turning over and over, some were blown aside and landed in the gallery, some fell towards the orchestra pit or the stage. A few seconds later the shower of money reached the stalls and the audience began catching it.

Hundreds of hands were raised as the audience held the notes up to the light from the stage and found that the watermarks were absolutely genuine. Their smell left no doubt: it was the uniquely delicious smell of newly-printed money. First amusement then wonder seized the entire theatre. From all over the house, amid gasps and delighted laughter, came the words 'money, money!' One man was already crawling in the aisle and fumbling under the seats. Several more were standing up on their seats to catch the drifting, twisting banknotes as they fell.

Gradually a look of perplexity came over the expressions of the police, and the artistes backstage openly pressed forward from the wings. From the dress circle a voice was heard shouting: 'Let go! It's mine—I caught it first!', followed by another voice: 'Stop pushing and grabbing or I'll punch your face in!' There was a muffled crash. A policeman's helmet appeared in the dress circle and a member of the audience was led away. The excitement rose and might have got out of hand if Faggot had not stopped the rain of money by suddenly blowing into the air.

Two young men, grinning purposefully, left their seats and made straight for the bar. A loud buzz filled the theatre : the audience was galvanised with excitement and in an effort to control the situation Bengalsky stirred himself and appeared on stage. With a tremendous effort of self-mastery he went through his habitual motion of washing his hands and in his most powerful voice began :

' We have just seen, ladies and gentlemen, a case of so-called mass hypnosis. A purely scientific experiment, demonstrating better than anything else that there is nothing supernatural about magic. We shall ask Maestro Woland to show us how he did that experiment. You will now see, ladies and gentlemen, how those apparent banknotes will vanish as suddenly as they appeared.'

He began to clap, but he was alone. A confident smile appeared on his face, but the look in his eyes was one of entreaty.

The audience did not care for Bengalsky's speech. Faggot broke the silence :

' And that was a case of so-called fiddlesticks,' he declared in a loud goatish bray. ' The banknotes, ladies and gentlemen, are real.'

' Bravo ! ' abruptly roared a bass from high up in the gallery.

' This man,' Faggot pointed at Bengalsky, ' is starting to bore me. He sticks his nose in everywhere without being asked and ruins the whole act. What shall we do with him ? '

' Cut off his head ! ' said a stern voice.

' What did you say, sir ? ' was Faggot's instant response to this savage proposal. ' Cut off his head ? That's an idea ! Behemoth ! ' he shouted to the cat. ' Do your stuff ! *Eins, zwei, drei!!* '

Then the most incredible thing happened. The cat's fur stood on end and it uttered a harrowing ' miaaow ! ' It crouched, then leaped like a panther straight for Bengalsky's chest and from there to his head. Growling, the cat dug its claws into the compère's glossy hair and with a wild screech it twisted the head clean off the neck in two turns.

Two and a half thousand people screamed as one. Fountains of blood from the severed arteries in the neck spurted up and drenched the man's shirtfront and tails. The headless body waved its legs stupidly and sat on the ground. Hysterical shrieks rang out through the auditorium. The cat handed the head to Faggot who picked it up by the hair and showed it to the audience. The head moaned desperately :

' Fetch a doctor ! '

' Will you go on talking so much rubbish ? ' said Faggot threateningly to the weeping head.

' No, I promise I won't ! ' croaked the head.

' For God's sake stop torturing him ! ' a woman's voice from a box suddenly rang out above the turmoil and the magician turned towards the sound.

' Well, ladies and gentlemen, shall we forgive him ? ' asked Faggot, turning to the audience.

' Yes, forgive him, forgive him ! ' The cries came at first from a few individual voices, mostly women, then merged into a chorus with the men.

' What is your command, messire ? ' Faggot asked the masked professor.

' Well, now,' replied the magician reflectively. ' They're people like any others. They're over-fond of money, but then they always were . . . Humankind loves money, no matter if it's made of leather, paper, bronze or gold. They're thoughtless, of course . . . but then they sometimes feel compassion too . . . . they're ordinary people, in fact they remind me very much of their predecessors, except that the housing shortage has soured them . . .' And he shouted the order : ' Put back his head.'

Taking careful aim the cat popped the head back on its neck, where it sat as neatly as if head and body had never been parted. Most amazing of all—there was not even a scar on the neck. The cat wiped the tailcoat and shirtfront with its paw and every trace of blood vanished. Faggot lifted the seated Bengalsky to his feet, shoved a bundle of money into his coat pocket and led him off stage, saying :

' Go on—off you go, it's more fun without you ! '

Gazing round in a daze and staggering, the compère got no further than the fire-brigade post and collapsed. He cried miserably :

' My head, my head . . . '

Among those who rushed to help him was Rimsky. The compère was weeping, snatching at something in the air and mumbling :

' Give me back my head, my head . . . You can have my flat, you can have all my pictures, only give me back my head . . . ! '

An usher ran for the doctor. They tried to lay Bengalsky on a divan in his dressing-room, but he resisted and became violent. An ambulance was called. When the unfortunate compère had been removed Rimsky ran back to the stage, where new miracles were in progress. It was then, or perhaps a little earlier, that the magician and his faded armchair vanished from the stage. The audience did not notice this at all, as they were absorbed by Faggot's wonderful tricks.

Having seen the compère off the stage, Faggot announced to the audience :

' Now that we have disposed of that old bore, we shall open a shop for the ladies ! '

In a moment half the stage was covered with Persian carpets, some huge mirrors and a row of showcases, in which the audience was astounded to see a collection of Parisian dresses that were the last word in chic. In other showcases were hundreds of ladies' hats, some with feathers and some without, hundreds of pairs of shoes—black shoes, white shoes, yellow shoes, leather shoes, satin shoes, suède shoes, buckled shoes and shoes studded with costume jewellery. Beside the shoes there were flacons of scent, piles of handbags made of buckskin, satin and silk, and next to them piles of gilt lipstick-holders.

A red-haired girl in a black evening dress who had suddenly appeared from nowhere, her beauty only marred by a curious scar on her neck, smiled from the showcases with a proprietorial smile.

With an engaging leer Faggot announced that the firm would exchange, absolutely free of charge, any lady's old dress and shoes for model dresses and shoes from Paris, adding that the offer included handbags and the odds and ends that go in them.

The cat began bowing and scraping, its forepaw gesturing like a commissionaire opening a door.

In a sweet though slightly hoarse voice the girl made an announcement which sounded rather cryptic but which, judging from the faces of the women in the stalls, was very enticing :

' Guerlain, Chanel, Mitsouko, Narcisse Noir, Chanel Number Five, evening dresses, cocktail dresses . . .'

Faggot bent double, the cat bowed and the girl opened the glass-fronted showcases.

' Step up, please ! ' cried Faggot. ' Don't be shy ! '

The audience began to fidget, but no one dared mount the stage. At last a brunette emerged from the tenth row of the stalls and smiling nonchalantly walked up the side stairs on to the stage.

' Bravo ! ' cried Faggot. ' Our first customer ! Behemoth, a chair for the lady ! Shall we start with the shoes, madam ? '

The brunette sat down and Faggot at once spread out a whole heap of shoes on the carpet in front of her. She took off her right shoe, tried on a lilac one, tested it with a walk on the carpet and inspected the heel.

' Won't they pinch ? ' she enquired thoughtfully.

Offended, Faggot cried :

' Oh, come, now ! ' and the cat gave an insulted miaow.

' I'll take them, monsieur,' said the brunette with dignity as she put on the other shoe of the pair. Her old shoes were thrown behind a curtain, followed by the girl herself, the redhead, and Faggot carrying several model dresses on coathangers. The cat busied itself with helping and hung a tape measure round its neck for greater effect.

A minute later the brunette emerged from behind the curtain in a dress that sent a gasp through the entire auditorium. The bold girl, now very much prettier, stopped in front of a mirror, wriggled her bare shoulders, patted her hair and twisted round to try and see her back view.

' The firm begs you to accept this as a souvenir,' said Faggot, handing the girl an open case containing a flacon of scent.

' *Merci*,' replied the girl haughtily and walked down the steps to the stalls. As she went back to her seat people jumped up to touch her scent-bottle.

The ice was broken. Women from all sides poured on to the stage. In the general hubbub of talk, laughter and cries a man's voice was heard, ' I won't let you ! ' followed by a woman's saying : ' Let go of my arm, you narrow-minded little tyrant ! ' Women were disappearing behind the curtain, leaving their old dresses there and emerging in new ones. A row of women was sitting on gilt-legged stools trying on new shoes. Faggot was on his knees, busy with a shoe-horn, while the cat, weighed down by handbags and shoes, staggered from the showcases to the stools and back again, the girl with the scarred neck bustled to and fro, entering so much into the spirit of it all that she was soon chattering away in nothing but French. Strangely enough all the women understood her at once, even those who knew not a word of French.

To everybody's astonishment, a lone man climbed on to the stage. He announced that his wife had a cold and asked to be given something to take home to her. To prove that he was really married he offered to show his passport. This conscientious husband was greeted with a roar of laughter. Faggot declared that he believed him even without his passport and handed the man two pairs of silk stockings. The cat spontaneously added a pot of cold cream.

Latecomers still mounted the steps as a stream of happy women in ball dresses, pyjama suits embroidered with dragons, severe tailor-mades and hats pranced back into the auditorium.

Then Faggot announced that because it was so late, in exactly a minute's time the shop would close until to-morrow evening. This produced an incredible scuffle on stage. Without trying them on, women grabbed any shoes within reach. One woman hurtled behind the screen, threw off her clothes and seized the first thing to hand—a silk dress patterned with enormous bunches of flowers—grabbed a dressing gown and for good measure scooped up two flacons of scent. Exactly a minute later a pistol shot rang out, the mirrors disappeared, the showcases and stools melted away, carpet and curtain vanished into thin air. Last to disappear was the mountain of old dresses and shoes. The stage was bare and empty again.

At this point a new character joined the cast. A pleasant and extremely self-confident baritone was heard from Box No. 2 :

' It's high time, sir, that you showed the audience how you do your tricks, especially the bank-note trick. We should also like to see the compère back on stage. The audience is concerned about him.'

The baritone voice belonged to none other than the evening's guest of honour, Arkady Apollonich Sempleyarov, chairman of the Moscow Theatres' Acoustics Commission.

Arkady Apollonich was sharing his box with two ladies—one elderly, who was expensively and fashionably dressed, the other young and pretty and more simply dressed. The first, as was later established when the official report was compiled, was Arkady Apollonich's wife and the other a distant relative of his, an aspiring young actress from Saratov who lodged in the Sempleyarovs' flat.

' I beg your pardon,' replied Faggot. ' I'm sorry, but there's nothing to reveal. It's all quite plain.'

' Excuse me, but I don't agree. An explanation is essential, otherwise your brilliant act will leave a painful impression. The audience demands an explanation . . .'

' The audience,' interrupted the insolent mountebank, ' has not, to my knowledge, demanded anything of the sort. However, in view of your distinguished position, Arkady Apollonich, I will—since you insist—reveal something of our technique. To do so, will you allow me time for another short number ? '

' Of course,' replied Arkady Apollonich patronisingly. ' But you must show how it's done.'

'Very well, sir, very well. Now—may I ask where you were yesterday evening, Arkady Apollonich?'

At this impertinent question Arkady Apollonich's expression underwent a complete and violent change.

'Yesterday evening Arkady Apollonich was at a meeting of the Acoustics Commission,' said his wife haughtily. 'Surely that has nothing to do with magic?'

'*Oui, madame,*' replied Faggot, 'it has, but you naturally do not know why. As for the meeting, you are quite wrong. When he went to the meeting—which, incidentally, was never scheduled to take place yesterday—Arkady Apollonich dismissed his chauffeur at the Acoustics Commission (a hush came over the whole theatre) and took a bus to Yelokhovskaya Street where he called on an actress called Militsa Andreyevna Pokobatko from the local repertory theatre and spent about four hours in her flat.'

'Oh!' The painful cry rang out from complete silence.

Suddenly Arkady Apollonich's young cousin burst into a low, malicious laugh.

'Of course!' she exclaimed. 'I've suspected him for a long time. Now I see why that tenth-rate ham got the part of Luisa!' And with a sudden wave of her arm she hit Arkady Apollonich on the head with a short, fat, mauve umbrella.

The vile Faggot, who was none other than Koroviev, shouted:

'There, ladies and gentlemen, is your revelation for you, as requested so insistently by Arkady Apollonich!'

'How dare you hit Arkady Apollonich, you little baggage?' said the wife grimly, rising in the box to her full gigantic height.

The young girl was seized with another outburst of satanic laughter.

'I've as much right,' she replied laughing, 'to hit him as you have!' A second dull crack was heard as another umbrella bounced off Arkady Apollonich's head.

'Police! Arrest her!' roared Madame Sempleyarov in a terrifying voice.

Here the cat bounded up to the footlights and announced in a human voice:

' That concludes the evening ! Maestro ! Finale, please ! '

The dazed conductor, scarcely aware of what he was doing, waved his baton and the orchestra struck up, or rather murdered a disorganised excuse for a march, normally sung to obscene but very funny words. However, it was quickly drowned in the ensuing uproar. The police ran to the Sempleyarovs' box, curious spectators climbed on to the ledge to watch, there were explosions of infernal laughter and wild cries, drowned by the golden crash of cymbals from the orchestra.

Suddenly the stage was empty. The horrible Faggot and the sinister cat Behemoth melted into the air and disappeared, just as the magician had vanished earlier in his shabby armchair.

13. Enter the Hero

Ivan swung his legs off the bed and stared. A man was standing on the balcony, peering cautiously into the room. He was aged about thirty-eight, clean-shaven and dark, with a sharp nose, restless eyes and a lock of hair that tumbled over his forehead.

The mysterious visitor listened awhile then, satisfied that Ivan was alone, entered the room. As he came in Ivan noticed that the man was wearing hospital clothes—pyjamas, slippers and a reddish-brown dressing gown thrown over his shoulders.

The visitor winked at Ivan, put a bunch of keys into his pocket and asked in a whisper : ' May I sit down ? ' Receiving an affirmative reply he settled in the armchair.

' How did you get in here ? ' Ivan whispered in obedience to a warning finger. ' The grilles on the windows are locked, aren't they ? '

' The grilles are locked,' agreed the visitor. ' Praskovya Fyodorovna is a dear person but alas, terribly absent-minded. A month ago I removed this bunch of keys from her, which has given me the freedom of the balcony. It stretches along the whole floor, so that I can call on my neighbours whenever I feel like it.'

' If you can get out on to the balcony you can run away. Or is it too high to jump ? ' enquired Ivan with interest.

' No,' answered the visitor firmly, ' I can't escape from here. Not because it's too high but because I've nowhere to go.' After a pause he added : ' So here we are.'

' Here we are,' echoed Ivan, gazing into the man's restless brown eyes.

' Yes . . .' The visitor grew suddenly anxious. ' You're not violent, I hope ? You see, I can't bear noise, disturbance, violence

154

or anything of that sort. I particularly hate the sound of people screaming, whether it's a scream of pain, anger or any other kind of scream. Just reassure me—you're not violent, are you ? '

' Yesterday in a restaurant I clouted a fellow across the snout,' the poet confessed manfully.

' What for ? ' asked the visitor disapprovingly.

' For no reason at all, I must admit,' replied Ivan, embarrassed.

' Disgraceful,' said the visitor reproachfully and added : ' And I don't care for that expression of yours—clouted him across the snout. . . . People have faces, not snouts. So I suppose you mean you punched him in the face. . . . No, you must give up doing that sort of thing.'

After this reprimand the visitor enquired :

' What's your job ? '

' I'm a poet,' admitted Ivan with slight unwillingness.

This annoyed the man.

' Just my bad luck ! ' he exclaimed, but immediately regretted it, apologised and asked : ' What's your name ? '

' Bezdomny.'

' Oh . . .' said the man frowning.

' What, don't you like my poetry ? ' asked Ivan with curiosity.

' No, I don't.'

' Have you read any of it ? '

' I've never read any of your poetry ! ' said the visitor tetchily.

' Then how can you say that ? '

' Why shouldn't I ? ' retorted the visitor. ' I've read plenty of other poetry. I don't suppose by some miracle that yours is any better, but I'm ready to take it on trust. Is your poetry good?'

' Stupendous ! ' said Ivan boldly.

' Don't write any more ! ' said the visitor imploringly.

' I promise not to ! ' said Ivan solemnly.

As they sealed the vow with a handshake, soft footsteps and voices could be heard from the corridor.

' Sshh ! ' whispered the man. He bounded out on to the balcony and closed the grille behind him.

Praskovya Fyodorovna looked in, asked Ivan how he felt and whether he wanted to sleep in the dark or the light. Ivan asked her to leave the light on and Praskovya Fyodorovna departed, wishing him good night. When all was quiet again the visitor returned.

He told Ivan in a whisper that a new patient had been put into No. 119—a fat man with a purple face who kept muttering about dollars in the ventilation shaft and swearing that the powers of darkness had taken over their house on Sadovaya. 'He curses Pushkin for all he's worth and keeps shouting " *Encore, encore!* " ' said the visitor, twitching nervously. When he had grown a little calmer he sat down and said : ' However, let's forget about him,' and resumed his interrupted conversation with Ivan : ' How did you come to be here ? '

' Because of Pontius Pilate,' replied Ivan, staring glumly at the floor.

' What ? ! ' cried the visitor, forgetting his caution, then clapped his hand over his mouth. ' What an extraordinary coincidence ! Do tell me about it, I beg of you ! '

For some reason Ivan felt that he could trust this stranger. Shyly at first, then gaining confidence, he began to describe the previous day's events at Patriarch's Ponds. His visitor treated Ivan as completely sane, showed the greatest interest in the story and as it developed he reached a state of near ecstasy. Now and again he interrupted Ivan, exclaiming :

' Yes, yes ! Please go on ! For heaven's sake don't leave anything out ! '

Ivan left out nothing, as it made the story easier to tell and gradually he approached the moment when Pontius Pilate, in his white cloak lined with blood-red, mounted the platform.

Then the visitor folded his hands as though in prayer and whispered to himself :

' Oh, I guessed it ! I guessed it all ! '

Listening to the terrible description of Berlioz's death, the visitor made an enigmatic comment, his eyes flashing with malice :

' I'm only sorry that it wasn't Latunsky the critic or that hack

Mstislav Lavrovich instead of Berlioz!' And he mouthed silently and ecstatically : ' Go on !'

The visitor was highly amused by the story of how the cat had paid the conductress and he was choking with suppressed laughter as Ivan, stimulated by the success of his story-telling, hopped about on his haunches, imitating the cat stroking his whiskers with a ten-kopeck piece.

' And so,' said Ivan, saddening as he described the scene at Griboyedov, ' here I am.'

The visitor laid a sympathetic hand on the wretched poet's shoulder and said :

' Unhappy poet ! But it's your own fault, my dear fellow. You shouldn't have treated him so carelessly and rudely. Now you're paying for it. You should be thankful that you got off comparatively lightly.'

' But who on earth is he ? ' asked Ivan, clenching his fists in excitement.

The visitor stared at Ivan and answered with a question :

' You won't get violent, will you ? We're all unstable people here . . . There won't be any calls for the doctor, injections or any disturbances of that sort, will there ? '

' No, no ! ' exclaimed Ivan. ' Tell me, who is he ? '

' Very well,' replied the visitor, and said slowly and gravely : ' At Patriarch's Ponds yesterday you met Satan.'

As he had promised, Ivan did not become violent, but he was powerfully shaken.

' It can't be ! He doesn't exist ! '

' Come, come ! Surely you of all people can't say that. You were apparently one of the first to suffer from him. Here you are, shut up in a psychiatric clinic, and you still say he doesn't exist. How strange ! '

Ivan was reduced to speechlessness.

' As soon as you started to describe him,' the visitor went on, ' I guessed who it was that you were talking to yesterday. I must say I'm surprised at Berlioz ! You, of course, are an innocent,' again the visitor apologised for his expression, ' but he, from what I've heard of him, was at least fairly well read. The first remarks that this professor made to you dispelled all my doubts. He's unmistakeable, my friend ! You are . . . do forgive me again, but unless I'm wrong, you are an ignorant person, aren't you ? '

' I am indeed,' agreed the new Ivan.

' Well, you see, even the face you described, the different-coloured eyes, the eyebrows . . . Forgive me, but have you even seen the opera *Faust* ? '

Ivan mumbled an embarrassed excuse.

' There you are, it's not surprising ! But, as I said before, I'm surprised at Berlioz. He's not only well read but extremely cunning. Although in his defence I must say that Woland is quite capable of throwing dust in the eyes of men who are even cleverer than Berlioz.'

' What ? ' shouted Ivan.

' Quiet ! '

With a sweeping gesture Ivan smacked his forehead with his palm and croaked :

' I see it now. There was a letter " W " on his visiting card. Well I'm damned ! ' He sat for a while in perplexity, staring at the moon floating past the grille and then said : ' So he really might have known Pontius Pilate ? He was alive then, I suppose ? And they call me mad ! ' he added, pointing indignantly towards the door.

The visitor's mouth set in a fold of bitterness.

' We must look the facts in the face.' The visitor turned his face towards the moon as it raced through a cloud. ' Both you and I are mad, there's no point in denying it. He gave you a shock and it sent you mad, because you were temperamentally liable to react in that way. Nevertheless what you have described unquestionably happened in fact. But it is so unusual that even Stravinsky, a psychiatrist of genius, naturally didn't believe you. Has he examined you ? (Ivan nodded.) The man you were talking to *was* with Pontius Pilate, he did have breakfast with Kant and now he has paid a call on Moscow.'

'But God knows what he may do here! Shouldn't we try and catch him somehow!' The old Ivan raised his head, uncertain but not yet quite extinguished.

'You've already tried and look where it's got you,' said the visitor ironically. 'I don't advise others to try. But he will cause more trouble, you may be sure of that. How infuriating, though, that you met him and not I. Although I'm a burnt-out man and the embers have died away to ash, I swear that I would have given up Praskovya Fyodorovna's bunch of keys in exchange for that meeting. Those keys are all I have. I am destitute.'

'Why do you want to see him so badly?'

After a long, gloomy silence the visitor said at last:

'You see, it's most extraordinary, but I am in here for exactly the same reason that you are, I mean because of Pontius Pilate.' The visitor glanced uneasily round and said: 'The fact is that a year ago I wrote a novel about Pilate.'

'Are you a writer?' asked the poet with interest.

The visitor frowned, threatened Ivan with his fist and said:

'I am a master.' His expression hardened and he pulled out of his dressing gown pocket a greasy black cap with the letter 'M' embroidered on it in yellow silk. He put the cap on and showed himself to Ivan in profile and full face to prove that he was a master. 'She sewed it for me with her own hands,' he added mysteriously.

'What is your name?'

'I no longer have a name,' replied the curious visitor with grim contempt. 'I have renounced it, as I have renounced life itself. Let us forget it.'

'At least tell me about your novel,' asked Ivan tactfully.

'If you wish. I should say that my life has been a somewhat unusual one,' began the visitor.

A historian by training, two years ago he had, it seemed, been employed in one of the Moscow museums. He was also a translator.

'From which language?' asked Ivan.

'I know five languages beside my own,' replied the visitor.

'English, French, German, Latin and Greek. And I read Italian a little.'

'Phew !' Ivan whistled with envy.

This historian lived alone, had no relatives and knew almost no one in Moscow. One day he won a hundred thousand roubles.

'Imagine my astonishment,' whispered the visitor in his black cap, 'when I fished my lottery ticket out of the laundry basket and saw that it had the same number as the winning draw printed in the paper ! The museum,' he explained, 'had given me the ticket.'

Having won his hundred thousand, Ivan's mysterious guest bought some books, gave up his room on Myasnitskaya Street ...

'Ugh, it was a filthy hole !' he snarled.

... and rented two rooms in the basement of a small house with a garden near the Arbat. He gave up his job in the museum and began writing his novel about Pontius Pilate.

'Ah, that was a golden age !' whispered the narrator, his eyes shining. 'A completely self-contained little flat and a hall with a sink and running water,' he emphasised proudly, 'little windows just above the level of the path leading from the garden gate. Only a few steps away, by the garden fence, was a lilac, a lime tree and a maple. Ah, me ! In winter I rarely saw anyone walking up the garden path or heard the crunch of snow. And there was always a blaze in my little stove ! But suddenly it was spring and through the muddied panes of my windows I saw first the bare branches then the green of the first leaves. And then, last spring, something happened which was far more delightful than winning a hundred thousand roubles. And that, you must agree, is an enormous sum of money !'

'It is,' Ivan agreed, listening intently.

'I had opened the windows and was sitting in the second room, which was quite tiny.' The visitor made measuring gestures. 'Like this—the divan here, another divan along the other wall, a beautiful lamp on a little table between them, a bookcase by the window and over here a little bureau. The main room was huge—fourteen square metres !—books, more books and a stove. It was a marvellous little place. How deliciously the lilac used to smell! I was growing light-headed with fatigue and Pilate was coming to an end . . .'

' White cloak, red lining! How I know the feeling!' exclaimed Ivan.

' Precisely! Pilate was rushing to a conclusion and I already knew what the last words of the novel would be—" the fifth Procurator of Judaea, the knight Pontius Pilate". Naturally I used to go out for walks. A hundred thousand is a huge sum and I had a handsome suit. Or I would go out for lunch to a restaurant. There used to be a wonderful restaurant in the Arbat, I don't know whether it's still there.'

Here his eyes opened wide and as he whispered he gazed at the moon.

' She was carrying some of those repulsive yellow flowers. God knows what they're called, but they are somehow always the first to come out in spring. They stood out very sharply against her black dress. She was carrying yellow flowers! It's an ugly colour. She turned off Tverskaya into a side-street and turned round. You know the Tverskaya, don't you? There must have been a thousand people on it but I swear to you that she saw no one but me. She had a look of suffering and I was struck less by her beauty than by the extraordinary loneliness in her eyes. Obeying that yellow signal I too turned into the side-street and followed her. We walked in silence down that dreary, winding little street without saying a word, she on one side, I on the other. There was not another soul in the street. I was in agony because I felt I had to speak to her and was worried that I might not be able to utter a word, she would disappear and I should never see her again. Then, if you can believe it, she said :

" Do you like my flowers ? "

' I remember exactly how her voice sounded. It was pitched fairly low but with a catch in it and stupid as it may sound I had the impression that it echoed across the street and reverberated from the dirty yellow wall. I quickly crossed to her side and going up to her replied : " No ".

' She looked at me in surprise and suddenly, completely unexpectedly, I realised that I had been in love with this woman all my life. Extraordinary, isn't it ? You'll say I was mad, I expect.'

' I say nothing of the sort,' exclaimed Ivan, adding : ' Please, please go on.'

The visitor continued :

' Yes, she looked at me in surprise and then she said : " Don't you like flowers at all ? "

' There was, I felt, hostility in her voice. I walked on alongside her, trying to walk in step with her and to my amazement I felt completely free of shyness.

' " No, I like flowers, only not these," I said.

' " Which flowers do you like ? "

' " I love roses."

' I immediately regretted having said it, because she smiled guiltily and threw her flowers into the gutter. Slightly em-barrassed, I picked them up and gave them to her but she pushed them away with a smile and I had to carry them.

' We walked on in silence for a while until she pulled the flowers out of my hand and threw them in the roadway, then slipped her black-gloved hand into mine and we went on.'

' Go on,' said Ivan, ' and please don't leave anything out ! '

' Well,' said the visitor, ' you can guess what happened after that.' He wiped away a sudden tear with his right sleeve and went on. ' Love leaped up out at us like a murderer jumping out of a dark alley. It shocked us both—the shock of a stroke of lightning, the shock of a flick-knife. Later she said that this wasn't so, that we had of course been in love for years without knowing each other and never meeting, that she had merely been living with another man and I had been living with . . . that girl, what was her name . . . ? '

' With whom ? ' asked Bezdomny.

' With . . . er, that girl . . . she was called . . .' said the visitor, snapping his fingers in a vain effort to remember.

' Were you married to her ? '

' Yes, of course I was, that's why it's so embarrassing to forget . . . I think it was Varya . . . or was it Manya ? . . . no, Varya, that's it . . . she wore a striped dress, worked at the museum. . . . No good, can't remember. So, she used to say, she had gone out that morning carrying those yellow flowers for me to find her at last and that if it hadn't happened she would have committed suicide because her life was empty.

' Yes, the shock of love struck us both at once. I knew it within the hour when we found ourselves, quite unawares, on the embankment below the Kremlin wall. We talked as though we had only parted the day before, as though we had known each other for years. We agreed to meet the next day at the same place by the Moscow River and we did. The May sun shone on us and soon that woman became my mistress.

' She came to me every day at noon. I began waiting for her from early morning. The strain of waiting gave me hallucinations of seeing things on the table. After ten minutes I would sit at my little window and start to listen for the creak of that ancient garden gate. It was curious : until I met her no one ever came into our little yard. Now it seemed to me that the whole town was crowding in. The gate would creak, my heart would bound and outside the window a pair of muddy boots would appear level with my head. A knife-grinder. Who in our house could possibly need a knife-grinder ? What was there for him to sharpen ? Whose knives ?

' She only came through that gate once a day, but my heart would beat faster from at least ten false alarms every morning. Then when her time came and the hands were pointing to noon, my heart went on thumping until her shoes with their black patent-leather straps and steel buckles drew level, almost soundlessly, with my basement window.

' Sometimes for fun she would stop at the second window and tap the pane with her foot. In a second I would appear at that window but always her shoe and her black silk dress that blocked the light had vanished and I would turn instead to the hall to let her in.

' Nobody knew about our liaison, I can swear to that, although as a rule no one can keep such affairs a complete secret. Her husband didn't know, our friends didn't know. The other tenants in that forgotten old house knew, of course, because they could see that a woman called on me every day, but they never knew her name.'

' Who was she ? ' asked Ivan, deeply fascinated by this love story.

The visitor made a sign which meant that he would never reveal this to anyone and went on with his narrative.

The master and his unknown mistress loved one another so strongly that they became utterly inseparable. Ivan could clearly see for himself the two basement rooms, where it was always twilight from the shade of the lilac bush and the fence : the shabby red furniture, the bureau, the clock on top of it which struck the half-hours and books, books from the painted floor to the smoke-blackened ceiling, and the stove.

Ivan learned that from the very first days of their affair the man and his mistress decided that fate had brought them together on the corner of the Tverskaya and that side-street and that they were made for each other to eternity.

Ivan heard his visitor describe how the lovers spent their day. Her first action on arrival was to put on an apron and light an oil stove on a wooden table in the cramped hall, with its tap and sink that the wretched patient had recalled with such pride. There she cooked lunch and served it on an oval table in the living-room. When the May storms blew and the water slashed noisily past the dim little windows, threatening to flood their home, the lovers stoked up the stove and baked potatoes in it. Steam poured out of the potatoes as they cut them open, the charred skins blackened their fingers. There was laughter in the basement, after the rain the trees in the garden scattered broken branches and white blossom.

When the storms were past and the heat of summer came, the vase was filled with the long-awaited roses that they both loved so much. The man who called himself the master worked

feverishly at his novel and the book cast its spell over the unknown woman.

' At times I actually felt jealous of it,' the moonlight visitor
whispered to Ivan.

Running her sharp, pointed fingernails through her hair, she
ceaselessly read and re-read the manuscript, sewing that same
black cap as she did so. Sometimes she would squat down by the
lower bookshelves or stand by the topmost ones and wipe the
hundreds of dusty spines. Sensing fame, she drove him on and
started to call him ' the master '. She waited impatiently for the
promised final words about the fifth Procurator of Judaea,
reading out in a loud sing-song random sentences that pleased
her and saying that the novel was her life.

It was finished in August and handed to a typist who transcribed
it in five copies. At last came the moment to leave the secret
refuge and enter the outside world.

' When I emerged into the world clutching my novel, my life
came to an end,' whispered the master. He hung his head and
for a long while wagged the black cap with its embroidered
yellow ' M '. He went on with his story but it grew more disjointed and Ivan could only gather that his visitor had suffered
some disaster.

' It was my first sortie into the literary world, but now that it's
all over and I am ruined for everyone to see, it fills me with
horror to think of it ! ' whispered the master solemnly, raising
his hand. ' God, what a shock he gave me ! '

' Who ? ' murmured Ivan, scarcely audibly, afraid to disturb
the master's inspiration.

' The editor, of course, the editor ! Oh yes, he read it. He
looked at me as if I had a swollen face, avoided my eyes and even
giggled with embarrassment. He had smudged and creased the
typescript quite unnecessarily. He asked me questions which I
thought were insane. He said nothing about the substance of
the novel but asked me who I was and where I came from, had
I been writing for long, why had nothing been heard of me
before and finally asked what struck me as the most idiotic

question of all—who had given me the idea of writing a novel on such a curious subject ? Eventually I lost patience with him and asked him straight out whether he was going to print my novel or not. This embarrassed him. He began mumbling something, then announced that he personally was not competent to decide and that the other members of the editorial board would have to study the book, in particular the critics Latunsky and Ariman and the author Mstislav Lavrovich. He asked me to come back a fortnight later. I did so and was received by a girl who had developed a permanent squint from having to tell so many lies.'

' That's Lapshennikova, the editor's secretary,' said Ivan with a smile, knowing the world that his visitor was describing with such rancour.

' Maybe,' he cut in. ' Anyway, she gave me back my novel thoroughly tattered and covered in grease-marks. Trying not to look at me, the girl informed me that the editors had enough material for two years ahead and therefore the question of printing my novel became, as she put it, " redundant ". What else do I remember ? ' murmured the visitor, wiping his forehead. ' Oh yes, the red blobs spattered all over the title page and the eyes of my mistress. Yes, I remember those eyes.'

The story grew more and more confused, full of more and more disjointed remarks that trailed off unfinished. He said something about slanting rain and despair in their basement home, about going somewhere else. He whispered urgently that he would never, never blame her, the woman who had urged him on into the struggle.

After that, as far as Ivan could tell, something strange and sudden happened. One day he opened a newspaper and saw an article by Ariman, entitled ' The Enemy Makes a Sortie,' where the critic warned all and sundry that he, that is to say our hero had tried to drag into print an apologia for Jesus Christ.

' I remember that ! ' cried Ivan. ' But I've forgotten what your name was.'

' I repeat, let's leave my name out of it, it no longer exists,' replied the visitor. ' It's not important. A day or two later another article appeared in a different paper signed by Mstislav Lavrovich, in which the writer suggested striking and striking hard at all this pilatism and religiosity which I was trying to drag (that damned word again !) into print. Stunned by that unheard-of word " pilatism " I opened the third newspaper. In it were two articles, one by Latunsky, the other signed with the initials " N.E." Believe me, Ariman's and Lavrovich's stuff was a mere joke by comparison with Latunsky's article. Suffice it to say that it was entitled " A Militant Old Believer ". I was so absorbed in reading the article about myself that I did not notice her standing in front of me with a wet umbrella and a sodden copy of the same newspaper. Her eyes were flashing fire, her hands cold and trembling. First she rushed to kiss me then she said in a strangled voice, thumping the table, that she was going to murder Latunsky.'

Embarrassed, Ivan gave a groan but said nothing.

' The joyless autumn days came,' the visitor went on, ' the appalling failure of my novel seemed to have withered part of my soul. In fact I no longer had anything to do and I only lived for my meetings with her. Then something began to happen to me. God knows what it was ; I expect Stravinsky has unravelled it long ago. I began to suffer from depression and strange forebodings. The articles, incidentally, did not stop. At first I simply laughed at them, then came the second stage : amazement. In literally every line of those articles one could detect a sense of falsity, of unease, in spite of their confident and threatening tone. I couldn't help feeling—and the conviction grew stronger the more I read—that the people writing those articles were not saying what they had really wanted to say and that *this* was the cause of their fury. And then came the third stage—fear. Don't misunderstand me, I was not afraid of the articles ; I was afraid of something else which had nothing to do with them or with my novel. I started, for instance, to be afraid of the dark. I was reaching the stage of mental derangement. I felt, especially just before going to sleep, that some very cold, supple octopus was fastening its tentacles round my heart. I had to sleep with the light on.

'My beloved had changed too. I told her nothing about the octopus, of course, but she saw that something was wrong with me. She lost weight, grew paler, stopped laughing and kept begging me to have that excerpt from the novel printed. She said I should forget everything and go south to the Black Sea, paying for the journey with what was left of the hundred thousand roubles.

'She was very insistent, so to avoid arguing with her (something told me that I never would go to the Black Sea) I promised to arrange the trip soon. However, she announced that she would buy me the ticket herself. I took out all my money, which was about ten thousand roubles, and gave it to her.

' " Why so much ? " she said in surprise.

'I said something about being afraid of burglars and asked her to keep the money until my departure. She took it, put it in her handbag, began to kiss me and said that she would rather die than leave me alone in this condition, but people were expecting her, she had to go but would come back the next day. She begged me not to be afraid.

'It was twilight, in mid-October. She went. I lay down on my divan and fell asleep without putting on the light. I was awakened by the feeling that the octopus was there. Fumbling in the dark I just managed to switch on the lamp. My watch showed two o'clock in the morning. When I had gone to bed I had been sickening ; when I woke up I was an ill man. I had a sudden feeling that the autumn murk was about to burst the window-panes, flood into the room and I would drown in it as if it were ink. I had lost control of myself. I screamed, I wanted to run somewhere, if only to my landlord upstairs. Wrestling with myself as one struggles with a lunatic, I had just enough strength to crawl to the stove and re-light it. When I heard it begin to crackle and the fire-door started rattling in the draught, I felt slightly better. I rushed into the hall, switched on the light, found a bottle of white wine and began gulping it down from the bottle. This calmed my fright a little, at least enough to stop me from running to my landlord. Instead, I went back to the stove. I opened the fire-door. The heat began to warm my hands and face and I whispered :

' " Something terrible has happened to me . . . Come, come, please come . . . ! "

' But nobody came. The fire roared in the stove, rain whipped against the windows. Then I took the heavy typescript copies of the novel and my handwritten drafts out of the desk drawer and started to burn them. It was terribly hard to do because paper that has been written over in ink doesn't burn easily. Breaking my fingernails I tore up the manuscript books, stuffed them down between the logs and stoked the burning pages with the poker. Occasionally there was so much ash that it put the flames out, but I struggled with it until finally the whole novel, resisting fiercely to the end, was destroyed. Familiar words flickered before me, the yellow crept inexorably up the pages yet I could still read the words through it. They only vanished when the paper turned black and I had given it a savage beating with the poker.

' There was a sound of someone scratching gently at the window. My heart leaped and thrusting the last manuscript book into the fire I rushed up the brick steps from the basement to the door that opened on to the yard. Panting, I reached the door and asked softly :

' " Who's there ? "

' And a voice, her voice, answered :

' " It's me . . ."

' I don't remember how I managed the chain and the key. As soon as she was indoors she fell into my arms, all wet, cheek wet, hair bedraggled, shivering. I could only say :

' " Is it really you ? . . ." then my voice broke off and we ran downstairs into the flat.

' She took off her coat in the hall and we went straight into the living-room. Gasping, she pulled the last bundle of paper out of the stove with her bare hands. The room at once filled with smoke. I stamped out the flames with my foot and she collapsed on the divan and burst into convulsive, uncontrollable tears.

' When she was calm again I said :

' " I suddenly felt I hated the novel and I was afraid. I'm sick. I feel terrible."

' She sat up and said :

' " God how ill you look. Why, why ? But I'm going to save you. What's the matter ? "

' I could see her eyes swollen from smoke and weeping, felt her cool hands smoothing my brow.

' " I shall make you better," she murmured, burying her head in my shoulder. " You're going to write it again. Why, oh why didn't I keep one copy myself ? "

' She ground her teeth with fury and said something indistinct. Then with clamped lips she started to collect and sort the burnt sheets of paper. It was a chapter from somewhere in the middle of the book, I forget which. She carefully piled up the sheets, wrapped them up into a parcel and tied it with string. All her movements showed that she was a determined woman who was in absolute command of herself. She asked for a glass of wine and having drunk it said calmly :

' " This is how one pays for lying," she said, " and I don't want to go on lying any more. I would have stayed with you this evening, but I didn't want to do it like that. I don't want his last memory of me to be that I ran out on him in the middle of the night. He has never done me any harm . . . He was suddenly called out, there's a fire at his factory. But he'll be back soon. I'll tell him tomorrow morning, tell him I love someone else and then come back to you for ever. If you don't want me to do that, tell me."

' " My poor, poor girl," I said to her. " I won't allow you to do it. It will be hell living with me and I don't want you to perish here as I shall perish."

' " Is that the only reason ? " she asked, putting her eyes close to mine.

' " That's the only reason."

' She grew terribly excited, hugged me, embraced my neck and said :

' " Then I shall die with you. I shall be here tomorrow morning."

' The last that I remember seeing of her was the patch of light from my hall and in that patch of light a loose curl of her hair, her beret and her determined eyes, her dark silhouette in the doorway and a parcel wrapped in white paper.

' " I'd see you out, but I don't trust myself to come back alone, I'm afraid."

' " Don't be afraid. Just wait a few hours. I'll be back tomorrow morning."

' Those were the last words that I heard her say.

' Sshh ! ' The patient suddenly interrupted himself and raised his finger. ' It's a restless moonlit night.' He disappeared on to the balcony. Ivan heard the sound of wheels along the corridor, there was a faint groan or cry.

When all was quiet again, the visitor came back and reported that a patient had been put into room No. 120, a man who kept asking for his head back. Both men relapsed into anxious silence for a while, but soon resumed their interrupted talk. The visitor had just opened his mouth but the night, as he had said, was a restless one : voices were heard in the corridor and the visitor began to whisper into Ivan's ear so softly that only the poet could hear what he was saying, with the exception of the first sentence :

' A quarter of an hour after she had left me there came a knock at my window . . .'

The man was obviously very excited by what he was whispering into Ivan's ear. Now and again a spasm would cross his face. Fear and anger sparkled in his eyes. The narrator pointed in the direction of the moon, which had long ago disappeared from the balcony. Only when all the noises outside had stopped did the visitor move away from Ivan and speak louder :

' Yes, so there I stood, out in my little yard, one night in the middle of January, wearing the same overcoat but without any buttons now and I was freezing with cold. Behind me the lilac bush was buried in snowdrifts, below and in front of me were my feebly lit windows with drawn blinds. I knelt down to the first of them and listened—a gramophone was playing in my room. I could hear it but see nothing. After a slight pause I went out of the gate and into the street. A snowstorm was howling along it. A dog which ran between my legs frightened me, and to get away from it I crossed to the other side. Cold and fear, which had become my inseparable companions, had driven me to desperation. I had nowhere to go and the simplest thing would have been to throw myself under a tram then and there where my side street joined the main road. In the distance I could see the approaching tramcars, looking like ice-encrusted lighted boxes, and hear the fearful scrunch of their wheels along the frostbound tracks. But the joke, my dear friend, was that every cell of my body was in the grip of fear. I was as afraid of the tram as I had been of the dog. I'm the most hopeless case in this building, I assure you ! '

' But you could have let her know, couldn't you ? ' said Ivan sympathetically. ' Besides, she had all your money. I suppose she kept it, did she ? '

' Don't worry, of course she kept it. But you obviously don't understand me. Or rather I have lost the powers of description that I once had. I don't feel very sorry for her, as she is of no more use to me. Why should I write to her ? She would be faced,' said the visitor gazing pensively at the night sky, ' by a letter from the madhouse. Can one really write to anyone from an address like this ? . . . I—a mental patient ? How could I make her so unhappy? I . . . I couldn't do it.'

Ivan could only agree. The poet's silence was eloquent of his sympathy and compassion for his visitor, who bowed his head in pain at his memories and said :

' Poor woman . . . I can only hope she has forgotten me . . .'

' But you may recover,' said Ivan timidly.

' I am incurable,' said the visitor calmly. ' Even though Stravinsky says that he will send me back to normal life, I don't believe him. He's a humane man and he only wants to comfort me. I won't deny, though, that I'm a great deal better now than I was. Now, where was I? Oh yes. The frost, the moving tramcars . . . I knew that this clinic had just been opened and I crossed the whole town on foot to come here. It was madness! I would probably have frozen to death but for a lucky chance. A lorry had broken down on the road and I approached the driver. It was four kilometres past the city limits and to my surprise he took pity on me. He was driving here and he took me . . . The toes of my left foot were frost-bitten, but they cured them. I've been here four months now. And do you know, I think this is not at all a bad place. I shouldn't bother to make any great plans for the future if I were you. I, for example, wanted to travel all over the world. Well, it seems that I was not fated to have my wish. I shall only see an insignificant little corner of the globe. I don't think it's necessarily the best bit, but I repeat, it's not so bad. Summer's on the way and the balcony will be covered in ivy, so Praskovya Fyodorovna tells me. These keys have enlarged my radius of action. There'll be a moon at night. Oh, it has set! It's freshening. Midnight is on the way. It's time for me to go.'

' Tell me, what happened afterwards with Yeshua and Pilate?' begged Ivan. ' Please, I want to know.'

' Oh no, I couldn't,' replied the visitor, wincing painfully. ' I can't think about my novel without shuddering. Your friend from Patriarch's Ponds could have done it better than I can. Thanks for the talk. Goodbye.'

Before Ivan had time to notice it, the grille had shut with a gentle click and the visitor was gone.

14. *Saved by Cock-Crow*

His nerves in shreds, Rimsky did not stay for the completion of the police report on the incident but took refuge in his own office. He sat down at the desk and with bloodshot eyes stared at the magic rouble notes spread out in front of him. The treasurer felt his reason slipping. A steady rumbling could be heard from outside as the public streamed out of the theatre on to the street. Suddenly Rimsky's acute hearing distinctly caught the screech of a police whistle, always a sound of ill-omen. When it was repeated and answered by another, more prolonged and authoritative, followed by a clearly audible bellow of laughter and a kind of ululating noise, the treasurer realised at once that something scandalous was happening in the street. However much he might like to disown it, the noise was bound to be closely connected with the terrible act put on that evening by the black magician and his assistants.

The treasurer was right. As he glanced out of the window on to Sadovaya Street he gave a grimace and hissed :

' I knew it ! '

In the bright light of the street lamps he saw below him on the pavement a woman wearing nothing but a pair of violet knickers, a hat and an umbrella. Round the painfully embarrassed woman, trying desperately to crouch down and run away, surged the crowd laughing in the way that had sent shivers down Rimsky's spine. Beside the woman was a man who was ripping off his coat and getting his arm hopelessly tangled in the sleeve.

Shouts and roars of laughter were also coming from the side entrance, and as he turned in that direction Grigory Danilovich saw another woman, this time in pink underwear. She was struggling across the pavement in an attempt to hide in the doorway, but the people coming out barred her way and the wretched victim of her own rashness and vanity, cheated by the sinister Faggot, could do nothing but hope to be swallowed up by the ground. A policeman ran towards the unfortunate woman, splitting the air with his whistle. He was closely followed by some cheerful, cloth-capped young men, the source of the ribald laughter and wolf-whistles.

A thin, moustached horse-cab driver drove up alongside the first undressed woman and smiling all over his whiskered face, reined in his horse with a flourish.

Rimsky punched himself on the head, spat with fury and jumped back from the window. He sat at his desk for a while listening to the noise in the street. The sound of whistles from various directions rose to a climax and then began to fade out. To Rimsky's astonishment the uproar subsided unexpectedly soon.

The time had come to act, to drink the bitter cup of responsibility. The telephones had been repaired during the last act and he now had to ring up, report the incident, ask for help, blame it all on Likhodeyev and exculpate himself.

Twice Rimsky nervously picked up the receiver and twice put it down. Suddenly the deathly silence of the office was broken by the telephone itself ringing. He jumped and went cold. ' My nerves are in a terrible state,' he thought as he lifted the telephone. Immediately he staggered back and turned whiter than paper. A soft, sensual woman's voice whispered into the earpiece :

' Don't ring up, Rimsky, or you'll regret it . . .'

The line went dead. Feeling gooseflesh spreading over his skin, the treasurer replaced the receiver and glanced round to the window behind his back. Through the sparse leaves of a sycamore tree he saw the moon flying through a translucent cloud. He seemed to be mesmerised by the branches of the tree and the longer Rimsky stared at them the more strongly he felt the grip of fear.

Pulling himself together the treasurer finally turned away from the moonlit window and stood up. There was now no longer any question of telephoning and Rimsky could only think of one thing—how to get out of the theatre as quickly as possible.

He listened : the building was silent. He realised that for some time now he had been the only person left on the second floor and a childish, uncontrollable fear overcame him at the thought. He shuddered to think that he would have to walk alone through the empty passages and down the staircase. He feverishly grabbed the magic roubles from his desk, stuffed them into his briefcase and coughed to summon up a little courage. His cough sounded hoarse and weak.

At this moment he noticed what seemed to be a damp, evil-smelling substance oozing under the door and into his office. A tremor ran down the treasurer's spine. Suddenly a clock began to strike midnight and even this made him shudder. But his heart sank completely when he heard the sound of a latch-key being softly turned in the lock. Clutching his briefcase with damp, cold hands Rimsky felt that if that scraping noise in the keyhole were to last much longer his nerves would snap and he would scream.

At last the door gave way and Varenukha slipped noiselessly into the office. Rimsky collapsed into an armchair. Gasping for air, he smiled what was meant to be an ingratiating smile and whispered :

' God, what a fright you gave me. . . .'

Terrifying as this sudden appearance was, it had its hopeful side—it cleared up at least one little mystery in this whole baffling affair.

' Tell me, tell me, quickly ! . . .' croaked Rimsky, clutching at his one straw of certainty in a world gone mad. ' What does this all mean ? "

' I'm sorry,' mumbled Varenukha, closing the door. ' I thought you would have left by now.' Without taking his cap off he crossed to an armchair and sat down beside the desk, facing Rimsky.

There was a trace of something odd in Varenukha's reply, immediately detected by Rimsky, whose sensitivity was now on a par with the world's most delicate seismograph. For one thing, why had Varenukha come to the treasurer's office if he thought he wasn't there? He had his own office, after all. For another, no matter which entrance Varenukha might have used to come into the theatre he must have met one of the night watchmen, who had all been told that Grigory Danilovich was working late in his office. Rimsky, however, did not dwell long on these peculiarities—this was not the moment.

'Why didn't you ring me? And what the hell was all that pantomime about Yalta?'

'It was what I thought,' replied the house manager, making a sucking noise as though troubled by an aching tooth. 'They found him in a bar out at Pushkino.'

'Pushkino? But that's just outside Moscow! What about those telegrams from Yalta?'

'Yalta—hell! He got the Pushkino telegraphist drunk and they started playing the fool, which included sending us those telegrams marked " Yalta ".'

'Aha, aha . . . I see now . . .' crooned Rimsky, his yellowish eyes flashing. In his mind's eye he saw Stepa being solemnly dismissed from his job. Freedom! At last Rimsky would be rid of that idiot Likhodeyev! Perhaps something even worse than the sack was in store for Stepan Bogdanovich . . . 'Tell me all the details!' cried Rimsky, banging his desk with a paperweight.

Varenukha began telling the story. As soon as he had arrived at the place where the treasurer had sent him, he was immediately shown in and listened to with great attention. No one, of course, believed for a moment that Stepa was in Yalta. Everybody at once agreed with Varenukha's suggestion that Likhodeyev was obviously at the ' Yalta ' restaurant in Pushkino.

'Where is he now?' Rimsky interrupted excitedly.

'Where do you think?' replied the house manager with a twisted smile. ' In the police cells, of course, being sobered up! '

' Ah ! Thank God for that ! '

Varenukha went on with his story and the more he said the clearer Rimsky saw the long chain of Likhodeyev's misdeeds, each succeeding link in it worse than the last. What a price he was going to pay for one drunken afternoon at Pushkino ! Dancing with the telegraphist. Chasing terrified women. Picking a fight with the barman at the ' Yalta '. Throwing onions on to the floor. Breaking eight bottles of white wine. Smashing a cab-driver's taximeter for refusing to take him. Threatening to arrest people who tried to stop him. . . .

Stepa was well known in the Moscow theatre world and everybody knew that the man was a menace, but this story was just a shade too much, even for Stepa. . . . Rimsky's sharp eyes bored into Varenukha's face across the desk and the longer the story went on the grimmer those eyes became. The more Varenukha embroidered his account with picturesque and revolting details, the less Rimsky believed him. When Varenukha described how Stepa was so far gone that he tried to resist the men who had been sent to bring him back to Moscow, Rimsky was quite certain that everything the house manager was telling him was a lie—a lie from beginning to end.

Varenukha had never gone to Pushkino, and Stepa had never been there either. There was no drunken telegraphist, no broken glass in the bar and Stepa had not been hauled away with ropes—none of it had ever happened.

As soon as Rimsky felt sure that his colleague was lying to him, a feeling of terror crawled over his body, beginning with his feet and for the second time he had the weird feeling that a kind of malarial damp was oozing across the floor. The house manager was sitting in a curious hunched attitude in the armchair, trying constantly to stay in the shadow of the blue-shaded table lamp and ostensibly shading his eyes from the light with a folded newspaper. Without taking his eyes off Varenukha for a moment, Rimsky's mind was working furiously to unravel this new mystery. Why should the man be lying to him at this late hour in the totally empty and silent building ? Slowly a consciousness of danger, of an unknown but terrible danger took hold of Rimsky. Pretending not to notice Varenukha's fidgeting and tricks with the newspaper, the treasurer concentrated on his face, scarcely listening to what he was saying. There was something else that Rimsky found even more sinister than this slanderous and completely bogus yarn about the goings-on in Pushkino, and that something was a change in the house manager's appearance and manner.

However hard Varenukha tried to pull down the peak of his cap to shade his face and however much he waved the newspaper, Rimsky managed to discern an enormous bruise that covered most of the right side of his face, starting at his nose. What was more, this normally ruddy-cheeked man now had an unhealthy chalky pallor and although the night was hot, he was wearing an old-fashioned striped cravat tied round his neck. If one added to this his newly acquired and repulsive habit of sucking his teeth, a distinct lowering and coarsening of his tone of voice and the furtive, shifty look in his eyes, it was safe to say that Ivan Savyelich Varenukha was unrecognisable.

Something even more insistent was worrying Rimsky, but he could not put his finger on it however much he racked his brain or stared at Varenukha. He was only sure of one thing—that there was something peculiar and unnatural in the man's posture in that familiar chair.

'Well, finally they overpowered him and shoved him into a car,' boomed Varenukha, peeping from under the newspaper and covering his bruise with his hand.

Rimsky suddenly stretched out his arm and with an apparently unthinking gesture of his palm pressed the button of an electric bell, drumming his fingers as he did so. His heart sank. A loud ringing should have been heard instantly throughout the building —but nothing happened, and the bell-push merely sank lifelessly into the desktop. The warning system was out of order.

Rimsky's cunning move did not escape Varenukha, who scowled and said with a clear flicker of hostility in his look:

'Why did you ring?'

' Oh, I just pressed it by mistake, without thinking,' mumbled Rimsky, pulling back his hand and asked in a shaky voice :

' What's that on your face ? '

' The car braked suddenly and I hit myself on the door-handle,' replied Varenukha, averting his eyes.

' He's lying ! ' said Rimsky to himself. Suddenly his eyes gaped with utter horror and he pressed himself against the back of his chair.

On the floor behind Varenukha's chair lay two intersecting shadows, one thicker and blacker than the other. The shadows cast by the back of the chair and its tapering legs were clearly visible, but above the shadow of the chairback there was no shadow of Varenukha's head, just as there was no shadow of his feet to be seen under the chairlegs.

' He throws no shadow ! ' cried Rimsky in a silent shriek of despair. He shuddered helplessly.

Following Rimsky's horrified stare Varenukha glanced furtively round behind the chairback and realised that he had been found out. He got up (Rimsky did the same) and took a pace away from the desk, clutching his briefcase.

' You've guessed, damn you ! You always were clever,' said Varenukha smiling evilly right into Rimsky's face. Then he suddenly leaped for the door and quickly pushed down the latch-button on the lock. The treasurer looked round in desperation, retreated towards the window that gave on to the garden and in that moon-flooded window he saw the face of a naked girl pressed to the glass, her bare arm reaching through the open top pane and trying to open the lower casement.

It seemed to Rimsky that the light of the desk-lamp was going out and that the desk itself was tilting. A wave of icy cold washed over him, but luckily for him he fought it off and did not fall. The remnants of his strength were only enough for him to whisper :

' Help . . .'

Varenukha, guarding the door, was jumping up and down

beside it. He hissed and sucked, signalling to the girl in the window and pointing his crooked fingers towards Rimsky.

The girl increased her efforts, pushed her auburn head through the little upper pane, stretched out her arm as far as she could and began to pluck at the lower catch with her fingernails and shake the frame. Her arm, coloured deathly green, started to stretch as if it were made of rubber. Finally her green cadaverous fingers caught the knob of the window-catch, turned it and the casement opened. Rimsky gave a weak cry, pressed himself to the wall and held his briefcase in front of himself like a shield. His last hour, he knew, had come.

The window swung wide open, but instead of the freshness of the night and the scent of lime-blossom the room was flooded with the stench of the grave. The walking corpse stepped on to the window-sill. Rimsky clearly saw patches of decay on her breast.

At that moment the sudden, joyful sound of a cock crowing rang out in the garden from the low building behind the shooting gallery where they kept the cage birds used on the Variety stage. With his full-throated cry the tame cock was announcing the approach of dawn over Moscow from the east.

Wild fury distorted the girl's face as she swore hoarsely and Varenukha by the door whimpered and collapsed to the floor.

The cock crowed again, the girl gnashed her teeth and her auburn hair stood on end. At the third crow she turned and flew out. Behind her, flying horizontally through the air like an oversized cupid, Varenukha floated slowly across the desk and out of the window.

As white as snow, without a black hair left on his head, the old man who a short while before had been Rimsky ran to the door, freed the latch and rushed down the dark corridor. At the top of the staircase, groaning with terror he fumbled for the switch and lit the lights on the staircase. The shattered, trembling old man fell down on the stairs, imagining that Varenukha was gently bearing down on him from above.

At the bottom Rimsky saw the night-watchman, who had

fallen asleep on a chair in the foyer beside the box office. Rimsky tiptoed past him and slipped out of the main door. Once in the street he felt slightly better. He came to his senses enough to realise, as he clutched his head, that he had left his hat in his office.

Nothing would have induced him to go back for it and he ran panting across the wide street to the cinema on the opposite corner, where a solitary cab stood on the rank. In a minute he had reached it before anyone else could snatch it from him.

' To the Leningrad Station—hurry and I'll make it worth your while,' said the old man, breathing heavily and clutching his heart.

' I'm only going to the garage,' replied the driver turning away with a surly face.

Rimsky unfastened his briefcase, pulled out fifty roubles and thrust them at the driver through the open window.

A few moments later the taxi, shaking like a leaf in a storm, was flying along the ring boulevard. Bouncing up and down in his seat, Rimsky caught occasional glimpses of the driver's delighted expression and his own wild look in the mirror.

Jumping out of the car at the station, Rimsky shouted to the first man he saw, who was wearing a white apron and a numbered metal disc :

' First class single—here's thirty roubles,' he said as he fumbled for the money in his briefcase. ' If there aren't any seats left in the first I'll take second . . . if there aren't any in the second, get me " Hard " class ! '

Glancing round at the illuminated clock the man with the apron snatched the money from Rimsky's hand.

Five minutes later the express pulled out of the glass-roofed station and steamed into the dark. With it vanished Rimsky.

15. The Dream of
Nikanor Ivanovich

It is not hard to guess that the fat man with the purple face who was put into room No. 119 at the clinic was Nikanor Ivanovich Bosoi.

He had not, however, been put into Professor Stravinsky's care at once, but had first spent some time in another place, of which he could remember little except a desk, a cupboard and a sofa.

There some men had questioned Nikanor Ivanovich, but since his eyes were clouded by a flux of blood and extreme mental anguish, the interview was muddled and inconclusive.

' Are you Nikanor Ivanovich Bosoi,' they began, ' chairman of the house committee of No. 302A, Sadovaya Street ? '

Nikanor Ivanovich gave a wild peal of laughter and replied :

' Of course I'm Nikanor ! But why call me chairman ? '

' What do you mean ? ' they asked, frowning.

' Well,' he replied, ' if I'm a chairman I would have seen at once that he was an evil spirit, wouldn't I ? I should have realised, what with his shaky pince-nez, his tattered clothes—how could he have been an interpreter ? '

' Who are you talking about ? '

' Koroviev ! ' cried Nikanor Ivanovich. ' The man who's moved into No. 50. Write it down—Koroviev ! You must find him and arrest him at once. Staircase 6—write it down—that's where you'll find him.'

' Where did you get the foreign currency from ? ' they asked insinuatingly.

' As almighty God's my witness,' said Nikanor Ivanovich, ' I never touched any and I never even suspected that it was foreign money. God will punish me for my sin,' Nikanor Ivanovich went on feelingly, unbuttoning his shirt, buttoning it up again and crossing himself. ' I took the money—I admit that—but it was Soviet money. I even signed a receipt for it. Our secretary Prolezhnov is just as bad—frankly we're all thieves in our house committee. . . . But I never took any foreign money.'

On being told to stop playing the fool and to tell them how the dollars found their way into his ventilation shaft, Nikanor Ivanovich fell on his knees and rocked backwards and forwards with his mouth wide open as though he were trying to swallow the wooden parquet blocks.

' I'll do anything you like,' he groaned, ' that'll make you believe I didn't take the stuff. That Koroviev's nothing less than a devil ! '

Everyone's patience has its limit ; voices were raised behind the desk and Nikanor Ivanovich was told that it was time he stopped talking gibberish.

Suddenly the room was filled with a savage roar from Nikanor Ivanovich as he jumped up from his knees :

' There he is ! There—behind the cupboard ! There—look at him grinning ! And his pince-nez . . . Stop him ! Arrest him ! Surround the building ! '

The blood drained from Nikanor Ivanovich's face. Trembling, he made the sign of the cross in the air, fled for the door, then back again, intoned a prayer and then relapsed into complete delirium.

It was plain that Nikanor Ivanovich was incapable of talking rationally. He was removed and put in a room by himself, where he calmed down slightly and only prayed and sobbed.

Men were sent to the house on Sadovaya Street and inspected flat No. 50, but they found no Koroviev and no one in the building who had seen him or heard of him. The flat belonging to Berlioz and Likhodeyev was empty and the wax seals, quite intact, hung on all the cupboards and drawers in the study. The men left the building, taking with them the bewildered and crushed Prolezhnev, secretary of the house committee.

That evening Nikanor Ivanovich was delivered to Stravinsky's clinic. There he behaved so violently that he had to be given one of Stravinsky's special injections and it was midnight before Nikanor Ivanovich fell asleep in room No. 119, uttering an occasional deep, tormented groan.

But the longer he slept the calmer he grew. He stopped tossing and moaning, his breathing grew light and even, until finally the doctors left him alone.

Nikanor Ivanovich then had a dream, which was undoubtedly influenced by his recent experiences. It began with some men carrying golden trumpets leading him, with great solemnity, to a pair of huge painted doors, where his companions blew a fanfare in Nikanor Ivanovich's honour. Then a bass voice boomed at him from the sky :

' Welcome, Nikanor Ivanovich ! Hand over your foreign currency ! ' Amazed beyond words, Nikanor Ivanovich saw in front of him a black loudspeaker. Soon he found himself in an auditorium lit by crystal candelabra beneath a gilded ceiling and by sconces on the walls. Everything resembled a small but luxurious theatre. There was a stage, closed by a velvet curtain whose dark cerise background was strewn with enlargements of gold ten-rouble pieces ; there was a prompter's box and even an audience.

Nikanor Ivanovich was surprised to notice that the audience was an all-male one and that its members all wore beards. An odd feature of the auditorium was that it had no seats and the entire assembly was sitting on the beautifully polished and extremely slippery floor.

Embarrassed at finding himself in this large and unexpected company, after some hesitation Nikanor Ivanovich followed the general example and sat down Turkish-fashion on the parquet, wedging himself between a stout redbeard and a pale and extremely hirsute citizen. None of the audience paid any attention to the newcomer.

There came the gentle sound of a bell, the house-lights went out, the curtains parted and revealed a lighted stage set with an armchair, a small table on which was a little golden bell, and a heavy black velvet backdrop.

On to the stage came an actor, dinner-jacketed, clean-shaven, his hair parted in the middle above a young, charming face. The audience grew lively and everybody turned to look at the stage. The actor advanced to the footlights and rubbed his hands.

' Are you sitting down ? ' he enquired in a soft baritone and smiled at the audience.

' We are, we are,' chorused the tenors and basses.

' H'mm . . .' said the actor thoughtfully, ' I realise, of course, how bored you must be. Everybody else is out of doors now, enjoying the warm spring sunshine, while you have to squat on the floor in this stuffy auditorium. Is the programme really worth while ? Ah well, chacun à son goût,' said the actor philosophically.

At this he changed the tone of his voice and announced gaily :
' And the next number on our programme is—Nikanor Ivanovich Bosoi, tenants' committee chairman and manager of a diabetic restaurant. This way please, Nikanor Ivanovich ! '

At the sound of the friendly applause which greeted his name, Nikanor Ivanovich's eyes bulged with astonishment and the compère, shading his eyes against the glare of the footlights, located him among the audience and beckoned him to the stage. Without knowing how, Nikanor Ivanovich found himself on stage. His eyes were dazzled from above and below by the glare of coloured lighting which blotted out the audience from his sight.

' Now Nikanor Ivanovich, set us an example,' said the young actor gently and confidingly, ' and hand over your foreign currency.'

Silence. Nikanor Ivanovich took a deep breath and said in a low voice : ' I swear to God, I . . .'

Before he could finish, the whole audience had burst into shouts of disapproval. Nikanor Ivanovich relapsed into uncomfortable silence.

' Am I right,' said the compère, ' in thinking that you were about to swear by God that you had no foreign currency ? ' He gave Nikanov Ivanovich a sympathetic look.

' That's right. I haven't any.'

' I see,' said the actor. ' But . . . if you'll forgive the indelicacy . . . where did those four hundred dollars come from that were found in the lavatory of your flat, of which you and your wife are the sole occupants ? '

' They were magic ones ! ' said a sarcastic voice somewhere in the dark auditorium.

' That's right, they were magic ones,' said Nikanor Ivanovich timidly, addressing no one in particular but adding : ' an evil spirit, that interpreter in a check suit planted them on me.'

Again the audience roared in protest. When calm was restored, the actor said:

' This is better than Lafontaine's fables ! Planted four hundred dollars ! Listen, you're all in the currency racket—I ask you now, as experts : is that possible ? '

' We're not currency racketeers,' cried a number of offended voices from the audience, ' but it's impossible ! '

' I entirely agree,' said the actor firmly, ' and now I'd like to ask you : what sort of things do people plant on other people ? '

' Babies ! ' cried someone at the back.

' Quite right,' agreed the compère. ' Babies, anonymous letters, manifestos, time bombs and God knows what else, but no one would ever plant four hundred dollars on a person because there just isn't anyone idiotic enough to try.' Turning to Nikanor Ivanovich the artist added sadly and reproachfully : ' You've disappointed me, Nikanor Ivanovich. I was relying on you. Well, that number was a flop, I'm afraid.'

The audience began to boo Nikanor Ivanovich.

' He's in the currency black market all right,' came a shout from the crowd, ' and innocent people like us have to suffer because of the likes of him.'

' Don't shout at him,' said the compère gently. ' He'll repent.' Turning his blue eyes, brimming with tears, towards Nikanor

Ivanovich, he said : ' Go back to your place Nikanor Ivanovich.'

After this the actor rang the bell and loudly announced :
' Interval ! '

Shattered by his involuntary debut in the theatre, Nikanor Ivanovich found himself back at his place on the floor. Then he began dreaming that the auditorium was plunged into total darkness and fiery red words leaped out from the walls ' Hand over all foreign cirrency ! '

After a while the curtains opened again and the compère announced:
' Sergei Gerardovich Dunchill on stage, please ! '

Dunchill was a good-looking though very stout man of about fifty.

' Sergei Gerardovich,' the compère addressed him, ' you have been sitting here for six weeks now, firmly refusing to give up your remaining foreign currency, at a time when your country has desperate need of it. You are extremely obstinate. You're an intelligent man, you understand all this perfectly well, yet you refuse to come forward.'

' I'm sorry, but how can I, when I have no more currency ? ' was Dunchill's calm reply.

' Not even any diamonds, perhaps ? ' asked the actor.

' No diamonds either.'

The actor hung his head, reflected for a moment, then clapped his hands. From the wings emerged a fashionably dressed middle-aged woman. The woman looked worried as Dunchill stared at her without the flicker of an eyelid.

' Who is this lady ? ' the compère enquired of Dunchill.

' She is my wife,' replied Dunchill with dignity, looking at the woman with a faint expression of repugnance.

' We regret the inconvenience to you, madame Dunchill,' said the compère, ' but we have invited you here to ask you whether your husband has surrendered all his foreign currency ? '

' He handed it all in when he was told to,' replied madame Dunchill anxiously.

' I see,' said the actor, ' well, if you say so, it must be true.

If he really has handed it all in, we must regretfully deprive our-selves of the pleasure of Sergei Gerardovich's company. You may leave the theatre if you wish, Sergei Gerardovich,' announced the compère with a regal gesture.

Calmly and with dignity Dunchill turned and walked towards the wings.

' Just a minute ! ' The compère stopped him. ' Before you go just let me show you one more number from our programme.' Again he clapped his hands.

The dark backdrop parted and a beautiful young woman in a ball gown stepped on stage. She was holding a golden salver on which lay a thick parcel tied with coloured ribbon, and round her neck she wore a diamond necklace that flashed blue, yellow and red fire.

Dunchill took a step back and his face turned pale. Complete silence gripped the audience.

' Eighteen thousand dollars and a necklace worth forty thousand gold roubles,' the compère solemnly announced, ' be-longing to Sergei Gerardovich and kept for him in Kharkov in the flat of his mistress, Ida Herkulanovna Vors, whom you have the pleasure of seeing before you now and who has kindly con-sented to help in displaying these treasures which, priceless as they are, are useless in private hands. Thank you very much, Ida Herkulanovna.'

The beauty flashed her teeth and fluttered her long eyelashes. ' And as for you,' the actor said to Dunchill, ' we now know that beneath that dignified mask lurks a vicious spider, a liar and a disgrace to our society. For six weeks you have worn us all out with your stupid obstinacy. Go home now and may the hell which your wife is preparing for you be your punish-ment.'

Dunchill staggered and was about to collapse when a sympa-thetic pair of arms supported him. The curtain then fell and hid the occupants of the stage from sight.

Furious applause shook the auditorium until Nikanor Ivanovich thought the lamps were going to jump out of the candelabra. When the curtain rose again there was no one on stage except the actor. To another salvo of applause he bowed and said :

'We have just shown you a typically stubborn case. Only yesterday I was saying how senseless it was to try and conceal a secret hoard of foreign currency. No one who has one can make use of it. Take Dunchill for example. He is well paid and never short of anything. He has a splendid flat, a wife and a beautiful mistress. Yet instead of acting like a law-abiding citizen and handing in his currency and jewellery, all that this incorrigible rogue has achieved is public exposure and a family scandal. So who wants to hand in his currency ? Nobody ? In that case, the next number on our programme will be that famous actor Savva Potapovich Kurolesov in excerpts from " The Covetous Knight " by the poet Pushkin.'

Kurolesov entered, a tall, fleshy, clean-shaven man in tails and white tie. Without a word of introduction he scowled, frowned and began, squinting at the golden bell, to recite in an unnatural voice :

'Hastening to meet his courtesan, the young gallant . . .'

Kurolesov's recital described a tale of evil. He confessed how an unhappy widow had knelt weeping before him in the rain, but the actor's hard heart had remained untouched.

Until this dream, Nikanor Ivanovich knew nothing of the works of Pushkin, although he knew his name well enough and almost every day he used to make remarks like 'Who's going to pay the rent—Pushkin?', or 'I suppose Pushkin stole the light bulb on the staircase', or 'Who's going to buy the fuel-oil for the boilers—Pushkin, I suppose ? ' Now as he listened to one of Pushkin's dramatic poems for the first time Nikanor Ivanovich felt miserable, imagining the woman on her knees in the rain with her orphaned children and he could not help thinking what a beast this fellow Kurolesov must be.

The actor himself, his voice constantly rising, poured out his repentance and finally he completely muddled Nikanor Ivanovich by talking to someone who wasn't on the stage at all, then answered for the invisible man, all the time calling himself first 'king', then 'baron', then 'father', then 'son' until the confusion was total. Nikanor Ivanovich only managed to understand that the actor died a horrible death shouting 'My keys! My keys!', at which he fell croaking to the ground, having first taken care to pull off his white tie.

Having died, Kurolesov got up, brushed the dust from his trousers, bowed, smiled an insincere smile and walked off to faint applause. The compère then said:

'In Savva Potapovich's masterly interpretation we have just heard the story of "The Covetous Knight". That knight saw himself as a Casanova; but as you saw, nothing came of his efforts, no nymphs threw themselves at him, the muses refused him their tribute, he built no palaces and instead he finished miserably after an attack on his hoard of money and jewels. I warn you that something of the kind will happen to you, if not worse, unless you hand over your foreign currency!'

It may have been Pushkin's verse or it may have been the compère's prosaic remarks which had such an effect; at all events a timid voice was heard from the audience:

'I'll hand over my currency.'

'Please come up on stage,' was the compère's welcoming response as he peered into the dark auditorium.

A short blond man, three weeks unshaven, appeared on stage.

'What is your name, please?' enquired the compère.

'Nikolai Kanavkin' was the shy answer.

'Ah! Delighted, citizen Kanavkin. Well?'

'I'll hand it over.'

'How much?'

'A thousand dollars and twenty gold ten-rouble pieces.'

'Bravo! Is that all you have?'

The compère stared straight into Kanavkin's eyes and it seemed to Nikanor Ivanovich that those eyes emitted rays which saw through Kanavkin like X-rays. The audience held its breath.

'I believe you!' cried the actor at last and extinguished his gaze. 'I believe you! Those eyes are not lying! How many times have I said that your fundamental error is to underestimate the significance of the human eye. The tongue may hide the truth but the eyes—never ! If somebody springs a question you may not even flinch ; in a second you are in control of yourself and you know what to say in order to conceal the truth. You can be very convincing and not a wrinkle will flicker in your expression, but alas ! The truth will start forth in a flash from the depths of your soul to your eyes and the game's up ! You're caught ! '

Having made this highly persuasive speech, the actor politely asked Kanavkin :

' Where are they hidden ? '

' At my aunt's, in Prechistenka.'

' Ah ! That will be . . . wait . . . yes, that's Claudia Ilyinishna Porokhovnikova, isn't it ? '

' Yes.'

' Yes, yes, of course. A little bungalow, isn't it ? Opposite a high fence ? Of course, I know it. And where have you put them ? '

' In a box in the cellar.'

The actor clasped his hands.

' Oh, no ! Really ! ' he cried angrily. ' Its so damp there— they'll grow mouldy ! People like that aren't to be *trusted* with money ! What child-like innocence. What will they do next ? '

Kanavkin, realising that he was doubly at fault, hung his curly head.

' Money,' the actor went on, ' should be kept in the State Bank, in dry and specially guarded strongrooms, but never in your aunt's cellar where apart from anything else, the rats may get at it. Really, Kanavkin, you should be ashamed : you—a grown man ! '

Kanavkin did not know which way to look and could only twist the hem of his jacket with his finger.

' All right,' the artist relented slightly, ' since you have owned up we'll be lenient . . .' Suddenly he added unexpectedly : ' By the way . . . we might as well kill two birds with one stone and not waste a car journey . . . I expect your aunt has some of her own hidden away, hasn't she ? '

Not expecting the conversation to take this turn, Kanavkin gave a start and silence settled again on the audience.

' Ah, now, Kanavkin,' said the compère in a tone of kindly reproach, ' I was just going to say what a good boy you were ! And now you have to go and upset it all ! That wasn't very clever, Kanavkin ! Remember what I said just now about your eyes ? Well, I can see from your eyes that your aunt has something hidden. Come on—don't tantalise us ! '

' Yes, she has ! ' shouted Kanavkin boldly.

' Bravo ! ' cried the compère.

' Bravo ! ' roared the audience.

When the noise had died down the compère congratulated Kanavkin, shook him by the hand, offered him a car to take him home and ordered somebody in the wings to go and see the aunt in the same car and invite her to appear in the ladies' section of the programme.

' Oh yes, I nearly forgot to ask you—did your aunt tell you where she has hidden hers ? ' enquired the compère, offering Kanavkin a cigarette and a lighted match. His cigarette lit, the wretched man gave an apologetic sort of grin.

' Of course, I believe you. You don't know,' said the actor with a sigh. ' I suppose the old skinflint wouldn't tell her nephew. Ah well, we shall just have to try and appeal to her better nature. Perhaps we can still touch a chord in her miserly old heart. Goodbye, Kanavkin—and good luck ! '

Kanavkin departed relieved and happy. The actor then enquired whether anyone else wished to surrender his foreign currency, but there was no response.

' Funny, I must say ! ' said the compère with a shrug of his shoulders and the curtain fell.

The lights went out, there was darkness for a while, broken only by the sound of a quavering tenor voice singing :

' Heaps of gold—and mine, all mine . . .'

After a burst of applause, Nikanor Ivanovich's red-bearded neighbour suddenly announced :

' There's bound to be a confession or two in the ladies' programme.' Then with a sigh he added : ' oh, if only they don't get my geese ! I have a flock of geese at Lianozov, you see. They're savage birds, but I'm afraid they'll die if I'm not there. They need a lot of looking after . . . Oh, if only they don't take my geese ! They don't impress *me* by quoting Pushkin . . .' and he sighed again.

The auditorium was suddenly flooded with light and Nikanor Ivanovich began dreaming that a gang of cooks started pouring through all the doors into the auditorium. They wore white chef's hats, carried ladles and they dragged into the theatre a vat full of soup and a tray of sliced black bread. The audience livened up as the cheerful cooks pushed their way down the aisle pouring the soup into bowls and handing out bread.

' Eat up, lads,' shouted the cooks, ' and hand over your currency ! Why waste your time sitting here ? Own up and you can all go home ! '

' What are you doing here, old man ? ' said a fat, red-necked cook to Nikanor Ivanovich as he handed him a bowl of soup with a lone cabbage leaf floating in it.

' I haven't got any ! I haven't, I swear it,' shouted Nikanor Ivanovich in a terrified voice.

' Haven't you ? ' growled the cook in a fierce bass. ' Haven't you ? ' he enquired in a feminine soprano. ' No, I'm sure you haven't,' he muttered gently as he turned into the nurse Praskovya Fyodorovna.

She gently shook Nikanor Ivanovich by the shoulder as he groaned in his sleep. Cooks, theatre, curtain and stage dissolved. Through the tears in his eyes Nikanor Ivanovich stared round at his hospital room and at two men in white overalls. They turned out not to be cooks but doctors, standing beside Praskovya Fyodorovna who instead of a soup-bowl was holding a gauze-covered white enamelled dish containing a hypodermic syringe.

' What are you doing ? ' said Nikanor Ivanovich bitterly as

they gave him an injection. 'I haven't any I tell you! Why doesn't Pushkin hand over his foreign currency? I haven't got any!'

'No, of course you haven't,' said kind Praskovya Fyodorovna, 'and no one is going to take you to court, so you can forget it and relax.'

After his injection Nikanor Ivanovich calmed down and fell into a dreamless sleep.

His unrest, however, had communicated itself to No. 120 where the patient woke up and began looking for his head; No. 118 where the nameless master wrung his hands as he gazed at the moon, remembering that last bitter autumn night, the patch of light under the door in his basement and the girl's hair blown loose.

The anxiety from No. 118 flew along the balcony to Ivan, who woke up and burst into tears.

The doctor soon calmed all his distraught patients and they went back to sleep. Last of all was Ivan, who only dozed off as dawn began to break over the river. As the sedative spread through his body, tranquillity covered him like a slow wave. His body relaxed and his head was filled with the warm breeze of slumber. As he fell asleep the last thing that he heard was the dawn chorus of birds in the wood. But they were soon silent again and he began dreaming that the sun had already set over Mount Golgotha and that the hill was ringed by a double cordon. . . .

16. The Execution

The sun had already set over Mount Golgotha and the hill was ringed by a double cordon.

The cavalry ala that had held up the Procurator that morning had left the city at a trot by the Hebron Gate, its route cleared ahead of it. Infantrymen of the Cappadocian cohort pressed back a crowd of people, mules and camels, and the ala, throwing up pillars of white dust, trotted towards the crossroads where two ways met—one southward to Bethlehem, the other north-westward to Jaffa. The ala took the north-westward route. More of the Cappadocians had been posted along the edge of the road in time to clear the route of all the caravans moving into Jerusalem for Passover. Crowds of pilgrims stood behind the line of troops, leaving the temporary shelter of their tents pitched on the grass. After about a kilometre the ala overtook the second cohort of the Lightning legion and having gone a further kilometre arrived first at the foot of Mount Golgotha. There the commander hastily divided the ala into troops and cordoned off the base of the low hill, leaving only a small gap where a path led from the Jaffa road to the hilltop.

After a while the second cohort arrived, climbed up and formed another cordon round the hill.

Last on the scene was the century under the command of Mark Muribellum. It marched in two single files, one along each edge of the road, and between them, escorted by a secret service detachment, drove the cart carrying the three prisoners. Each wore a white board hung round his neck on which were written the words 'Robber & Rebel' in Aramaic and Greek. Behind the prisoners' cart came others, loaded with freshly sawn posts and cross-pieces, ropes, spades, buckets and axes. They also carried six executioners. Last in the convoy rode Mark the centurion, the captain of the temple guard and the same hooded man with whom Pilate had briefly conferred in a darkened room of the palace.

Although the procession was completely enclosed by troops, it was followed by about two thousand curious sightseers determined to watch this interesting spectacle despite the infernal heat. These spectators from the city were now being joined by crowds of pilgrims, who were allowed to follow the tail of the procession unhindered, as it made its way towards Mount Golgotha to the bark of the heralds' voices as they repeated Pilate's announcement.

The ala allowed them through as far as the second cordon, where the century admitted only those concerned with the execution and then, with a brisk manoeuvre, spread the crowd round the hill between the mounted cordon below and the upper ring formed by the infantry, allowing the spectators to watch the execution through a thin line of soldiery.

More than three hours had gone by since the procession had reached the hill and although the sun over Mount Golgotha had already begun its descent, the heat was still unbearable. The troops in both cordons were suffering from it; stupefied with boredom, they cursed the three robbers and sincerely wished them a quick death.

At the gap in the lower cordon the diminutive commander of the ala, his forehead damp and his white tunic soaked with the sweat of his back, occasionally walked over to the leather bucket in No. 1 Troop's lines, scooped up the water in handfuls, drank and moistened his turban. With this slight relief from the heat he would return and recommence pacing up and down the dusty path leading to the top. His long sword bumped against his laced leather boot. As commander he had to set an example of endurance to his men, but he considerately allowed them to stick their lances into the ground and drape their white cloaks over the tops of the shafts. The Syrians then sheltered from the pitiless sun under these makeshift tents. The buckets emptied quickly and a rota of troopers was kept busy fetching water from a ravine at the foot of the hill, where a muddy stream flowed in the shade of a clump of gaunt mulberry trees. There, making the most of the inadequate shade, the bored grooms lounged beside the horse-lines.

The troops were exhausted and their resentment of the victims was understandable. Fortunately, however, Pilate's fears that disorders might occur in Jerusalem during the execution were unjustified. When the fourth hour of the execution had passed, against all expectation not a man remained between the two cordons. The sun had scorched the crowd and driven it back to Jerusalem. Beyond the ring formed by the two Roman centuries there were only a couple of stray dogs. The heat had exhausted them too and they lay panting with their tongues out, too weary even to chase the green-backed lizards, the only creatures unafraid of the sun, which darted between the broken stones and the spiny, ground-creeping cactus plants.

No one had tried to attack the prisoners, neither in Jerusalem, which was packed with troops, nor on the cordoned hill. The crowd had drifted back into town, bored by this dull execution and eager to join in the preparations for the feast which were already under way in the city.

The Roman infantry forming the second tier was suffering even more acutely than the cavalrymen. Centurion Muribellum's only concession to his men was to allow them to take off their helmets and put on white headbands soaked in water, but he kept them standing, lance in hand. The centurion himself, also wearing a headband though a dry one, walked up and down a short distance from a group of executioners without even removing his heavy silver badges of rank, his sword or his dagger. The sun beat straight down on the centurion without causing him the least distress and such was the glitter from the silver of his lions' muzzles that a glance at them was almost blinding.

Muribellum's disfigured face showed neither exhaustion nor displeasure and the giant centurion seemed strong enough to

198

keep pacing all day, all night and all the next day. For as long as might be necessary he would go on walking with his hands on his heavy bronze-studded belt, he would keep his stern gaze either on the crucified victims or on the line of troops, or just kick at the rubble on the ground with the toe of his rough hide boot, indifferent to whether it was a whitened human bone or a small flint.

The hooded man had placed himself a short way from the gibbets on a three-legged stool and sat in calm immobility, occasionally poking the sand with a stick out of boredom.

It was not quite true that no one was left of the crowd between the cordons. There was one man, but he was partly hidden. He was not near the path, which was the best place from which to see the execution, but on the northern side, where the hill was not smooth and passable but rough and jagged with gulleys and fissures, at a spot where a sickly fig tree struggled to keep alive on that arid soil by rooting itself in a crevice.

Although the fig tree gave no shade, this sole remaining spectator had been sitting beneath it on a stone since the very start of the execution four hours before. He had chosen the worst place to watch the execution, although he had a direct view of the gibbets and could even see the two glittering badges on the centurion's chest. His vantage point seemed adequate, however, for a man who seemed anxious to remain out of sight.

Yet four hours ago this man had behaved quite differently and had made himself all too conspicuous, which was probably the reason why he had now changed his tactics and withdrawn to solitude. When the procession had reached the top of the hill he had been the first of the crowd to appear and he had shown all the signs of a man arriving late. He had run panting up the hill, pushing people aside, and when halted by the cordon he had made a naive attempt, by pretending not to understand their angry shouts, to break through the line of soldiers and reach the place of execution where the prisoners were already being led off the cart. For this he had earned a savage blow on the chest with the blunt end of a lance and had staggered back with a cry, not of pain but of despair. He had stared at the legionary who had hit him with the bleary, indifferent look of a man past feeling physical pain.

Gasping and clutching his chest he had run round to the northern side of the hill, trying to find a gap in the cordon where he might slip through. But it was too late, the chain had been closed. And the man, his face contorted with grief, had had to give up trying to break through to the carts, from which men were unloading the gibbet-posts. Any such attempt would have led to his arrest and as his plans for that day did not include being arrested, he had hidden himself in the crevice where he could watch unmolested.

Now as he sat on his stone, his eyes festering from heat, dust and lack of sleep, the black-bearded man felt miserable. First he would sigh, opening his travel-worn tallith, once blue but now turned dirty grey, and bare his sweating, bruised chest, then he would raise his eyes to the sky in inexpressible agony, following the three vultures who had long been circling the hilltop in expectation of a feast, then gaze hopelessly at the yellow soil where he stared at the half-crushed skull of a dog and the lizards that scurried around it.

The man was in such distress that now and again he would talk to himself.

' Oh, I am a fool,' he mumbled, rocking back and forth in agony of soul and scratching his swarthy chest. ' I'm a fool, as stupid as a woman—and I'm a coward ! I'm a lump of carrion, not a man ! '

He hung his head in silence, then revived by a drink of tepid water from his wooden flask he gripped the knife hidden under his tallith or fingered the piece of parchment lying on a stone in front of him with a stylus and a bladder of ink.

On the parchment were some scribbled notes :

' Minutes pass while I, Matthew the Levite, sit here on Mount Golgotha and still he is not dead ! '

Late :

' The sun is setting and death not yet come.'

Hopelessly, Matthew now wrote with his sharp stylus :

' God ! Why are you angry with him ? Send him death.'

Having written this, he gave a tearless sob and again scratched his chest.

The cause of the Levite's despair was his own and Yeshua's terrible failure. He was also tortured by the fatal mistake which he, Matthew, had committed. Two days before, Yeshua and Matthew had been in Bethphagy near Jerusalem, where they had been staying with a market gardener who had taken pleasure in Yeshua's preaching. All that morning the two men had helped their host at work in his garden, intending to walk on to Jerusalem in the cool of the evening. But for some reason Yeshua had been in a hurry, saying that he had something urgent to do in the city, and had set off alone at noon. That was Matthew the Levite's first mistake. Why, why had he let him go alone ?

That evening Matthew had been unable to go to Jerusalem, as he had suffered a sudden and unexpected attack of sickness. He shivered, his body felt as if it were on fire and he constantly begged for water.

To go anywhere was out of the question. He had collapsed on to a rug in the gardener's courtyard and had lain there until dawn on Friday, when the sickness left Matthew as suddenly as it had struck him. Although still weak, he had felt oppressed by a foreboding of disaster and bidding his host farewell had set out for Jerusalem. There he had learned that his foreboding had not deceived him and that the disaster had occurred. The Levite had been in the crowd that had heard the Procurator pronounce sentence.

When the prisoners were taken away to Mount Golgotha, Matthew the Levite ran alongside the escort amid the crowd of sightseers, trying to give Yeshua an inconspicuous signal that at least he, the Levite, was here with him, that he had not abandoned him on his last journey and that he was praying for Yeshua to be granted a quick death. But Yeshua, staring far ahead to where they were taking him, could not see Matthew.

Then, when the procession had covered half a mile or so of

the way, Matthew, who was being pushed along by the crowd level with the prisoners' cart, was struck by a brilliant and simple idea. In his fervour he cursed himself for not having thought of it before. The soldiers were not marching in close order, but with a gap between each man. With great dexterity and very careful timing it would be possible to bend down and jump between two legionaries, reach the cart and jump on it. Then Yeshua would be saved from an agonising death. A moment would be enough to stab Yeshua in the back with a knife, having shouted to him : ' Yeshua ! I shall save you and depart with you ! I, Matthew, your faithful and only disciple ! '

And if God were to bless him with one more moment of freedom he could stab himself as well and avoid a death on the gallows. Not that Matthew, the erstwhile tax-collector, cared much how he died : he wanted only one thing—that Yeshua, who had never done anyone the least harm in his life, should be spared the torture of crucifixion.

The plan was a very good one, but it had a great flaw—the Levite had no knife and no money.

Furious with himself, Matthew pushed his way out of the crowd and ran back to the city. His head burned with the single thought of how he might at once, by whatever means, find a knife somewhere in town and then catch up with the procession again.

He ran as far as the city gate, slipping through the crowd of pilgrims' caravans pouring into town, and saw on his left the open door of a baker's shop. Breathless from running on the hot road, the Levite pulled himself together, entered the shop very sedately, greeted the baker's wife standing behind the counter, asked her for a loaf from the top shelf which he affected to prefer to all the rest and as she turned round, he silently and quickly snatched off the counter the very thing he had been looking for—a long, razor-sharp breadknife—and fled from the shop.

A few minutes later he was back on the Jaffa road, but the procession was out of sight. He ran. Once or twice he had to drop and lie motionless to regain his breath, to the astonishment of all the passers-by making for Jerusalem on mule-back or on foot. As he lay he could hear the beat of his heart in his chest, in his head and his ears. Rested, he stood up and began running again, although his pace grew slower and slower. When he finally caught sight again of the long, dusty procession, it had already reached the foot of the hill.

' Oh, God ! ' groaned the Levite. He knew he was too late.

With the passing of the fourth hour of the execution Matthew's torments reached their climax and drove him to a frenzy. Rising from his stone, he hurled the stolen knife to the ground, crushed his flask with his foot, thus depriving himself of water, snatched the kefiyeh from his head, tore his flowing hair and cursed himself. As he cursed in streams of gibberish, bellowed and spat, Matthew slandered his father and mother for begetting such a fool.

Since cursing and swearing had no apparent effect at all and changed nothing in that sun-scorched inferno, he clenched his dry fists and raised them heavenwards to the sun as it slowly descended, lengthening the shadows before setting into the Mediterranean. The Levite begged God to perform a miracle and allow Yeshua to die.

When he opened his eyes again nothing on the hill had changed, except that the light no longer flashed from the badges on the centurion's chest. The sun was shining on the victims' backs, as their faces were turned east towards Jerusalem. Then the Levite cried out :

' I curse you, God ! '

In a hoarse voice he shouted that God was unjust and that he would believe in him no more.

' You are deaf ! ' roared Matthew. ' If you were not deaf you would have heard me and killed him in the instant ! '

His eyes tight shut, the Levite waited for the fire to strike him from heaven. Nothing happened. Without opening his eyes, he vented his spite in a torrent of insults to heaven. He shouted that his faith was ruined, that there were other gods and better. No other god would have allowed a man like Yeshua to be scorched to death on a pole.

' No—I was wrong ! ' screamed the Levite, now quite hoarse. ' You are a God of evil ! Or have your eyes been blinded by the smoke of sacrifices from the temple and have your ears grown deaf to everything but the trumpet-calls of the priests ? You are not an almighty God—you are an evil God ! I curse you, God of robbers, their patron and protector ! '

At that moment there was a puff of air in his face and something rustled under his feet. Then came another puff and as he opened his eyes the Levite saw that everything, either as a result of his imprecations or from some other cause, had changed. The sun had been swallowed by a thundercloud looming up, threatening and inexorable, from the west. Its edges were white and ragged, its rumbling black paunch tinged with sulphur. White pillars of dust, raised by the sudden wind, flew along the Jaffa road. The Levite was silent, wondering if the storm which was about to break over Jerusalem might alter the fate of the wretched Yeshua. Watching the tongues of lightning that flickered round the edges of the cloud, he began to pray for one to strike Yeshua's gibbet. Glancing penitently up at the remaining patches of blue sky in which the vultures were winging away to avoid the storm, Matthew knew that he had cursed too soon : God would not listen to him now.

Turning round to look at the foot of the hill, the Levite stared at the cavalry lines and saw that they were on the move. From his height he had a good view of the soldiers' hasty preparations as they pulled their lances out of the ground and threw their cloaks over their shoulders. The grooms were running towards the path, leading strings of troop horses. The regiment was moving out. Shielding his face with his hand and spitting out the sand that blew into his mouth, the Levite tried to think why the cavalry should be preparing to go. He shifted his glance higher up the hill and made out a figure in a purple military chlamys climbing up towards the place of execution. Matthew's heart leaped : he sensed a quick end.

The man climbing Mount Golgotha in the victims' fifth hour of suffering was the Tribune of the Cohort, who had galloped from Jerusalem accompanied by an orderly. At a signal from Muribellum the cordon of soldiers opened and the centurion saluted the Tribune, who took Muribellum aside and whispered something to him. The centurion saluted again and walked over to the executioners, seated on stones under the gibbets. The Tribune meanwhile turned towards the man on the three-legged stool. The seated man rose politely as the Tribune approached him. The officer said something to him in a low voice and both walked over to the gallows, where they were joined by the captain of the temple guard.

Muribellum, with a fastidious grimace at the filthy rags lying on the ground near the crosses—the prisoners' clothes which even the executioners had spurned—called to two of them and gave an order:

' Follow me ! '

A hoarse, incoherent song could just be heard coming from the nearest gibbet. Hestas had been driven out of his mind two hours ago by the flies and the heat and was now softly croaking something about a vineyard. His turbaned head still nodded occasionally, sending up a lazy cloud of flies from his face.

Dismas on the second cross was suffering more than the other two because he was still conscious and shaking his head regularly from side to side.

Yeshua was luckier. He had begun to faint during the first hour, and had then lapsed into unconsciousness, his head drooping in its ragged turban. As a result the mosquitoes and horse-flies had settled on him so thickly that his face was entirely hidden by a black, heaving mask. All over his groin, his stomach and under his armpits sat bloated horseflies, sucking at the yellowing naked body.

At a gesture from the man in the hood one of the executioners picked up a lance and the other carried a bucket and sponge to the gibbet. The first executioner raised the lance and used it to hit Yeshua first on one extended arm and then on the other.

The emaciated body gave a twitch. The executioner then poked Yeshua in the stomach with the handle of the lance. At this Yeshua raised his head, the flies rose with a buzz and the victim's face was revealed, swollen with bites, puff-eyed, unrecognisable.

Forcing open his eyelids, Ha-Notsri looked down. His usually clear eyes were now dim and glazed.

' Ha-Notsri ! ' said the executioner.

Ha-Notsri moved his swollen lips and answered in a hoarse croak :

' What do you want ? Why have you come ? '

' Drink ! ' said the executioner and a water-soaked sponge was raised to Yeshua's lips on the point of a lance. Joy lit up his eyes, he put his mouth to the sponge and greedily sucked its moisture. From the next gibbet came the voice of Dismas :

' It's unjust ! He's as much a crook as me ! '

Dismas strained ineffectually, his arms being lashed to the cross-bar in three places. He arched his stomach, clawed the end of the crossbeam with his nails and tried to turn his eyes, full of envy and hatred, towards Yeshua's cross.

' Silence on the second gibbet ! '

Dismas was silent. Yeshua turned aside from the sponge. He tried to make his voice sound kind and persuasive, but failed and could only croak huskily :

' Give him a drink too.'

It was growing darker. The cloud now filled half the sky as it surged towards Jerusalem ; smaller white clouds fled before the black monster charged with fire and water. There was a flash and a thunderclap directly over the hill. The executioner took the sponge from the lance.

' Hail to the merciful hegemon ! ' he whispered solemnly and gently pierced Yeshua through the heart. Yeshua shuddered and whispered :

' Hegemon . . .'

Blood ran down his stomach, his lower jaw twitched convulsively and his head dropped.

At the second thunderclap the executioner gave the sponge to Dismas with the same words :

' Hail, hegemon . . .' and killed him.

Hestas, his reason gone, cried out in fear as the executioner approached him, but when the sponge touched his lips he gave a roar and sank his teeth into it. A few seconds later his body was hanging as limply as the ropes would allow.

The man in the hood followed the executioner and the centurion ; behind him in turn came the captain of the temple guard. Stopping at the first gibbet the hooded man carefully inspected Yeshua's bloodstained body, touched the pole with his white hand and said to his companions :

' Dead.'

The same was repeated at the other two gallows.

After this the Tribune gestured to the centurion and turned to walk down the hill with the captain of the temple guard and the hooded man.

It was now twilight and lightning was furrowing the black sky. Suddenly there was a brilliant flash and the centurion's shout of ' Fall out, the cordon ! ' was drowned in thunder. The delighted soldiers started running down hill, buckling on their helmets as they went.

A mist had covered Jerusalem.

The downpour struck suddenly and caught the centurion halfway down the hill. The rain fell with such force that turbulent streams began catching them up as they ran. The troops slithered and fell on the muddy soil as they hurried to reach the main road. Moving fast, now scarcely visible in a veil of water, the rain-soaked cavalry was already on its way back to Jerusalem. After a few minutes only one man was left on the hill in the smoking cauldron of wind, water and fire.

Brandishing his stolen knife, for which he now had a use after all, leaping over the slippery rocks, grasping whatever came to hand, at times crawling on his knees, he stumbled towards the gallows in alternate spells of complete darkness and flashes of light.

When he reached the gallows he was already ankle-deep in water and threw off his soaking tallith. Wearing only his shirt Matthew fell at Yeshua's feet. He cut the ropes round his knees, climbed on to the lower crossbar, embraced Yeshua and freed his arms from their bonds. Yeshua's wet, naked body collapsed on to Matthew and dragged him to the ground. The Levite was just about to hoist him on to his shoulders when another thought stopped him. He left the body on the watery ground, its head thrown back and arms outstretched, and ran, slithering, to the other gibbet-posts. He cut their ropes and the two bodies tell to the ground.

A few minutes later only those two water-lashed bodies and three empty gibbets remained on Mount Golgotha. Matthew the Levite and Yeshua were gone.

17. A Day of Anxiety

On Friday morning, the day after the disastrous show, the permanent staff of the Variety Theatre—Vassily Stepanovich Lastochkin the accountant, two bookkeepers, three typists, the two cashiers, the ushers, the commissionaires and the cleaners— were not at work but were instead sitting on the window-ledges looking out on to Sadovaya Street and watching what was happening outside the theatre. There beneath the theatre walls wound a double queue of several thousand people whose tail-end had already reached Kudrinskaya Square. At the head of the queue stood a couple of dozen of the leading lights of the Moscow theatrical world.

The queue was in a state of high excitement, attracting the attention of the passers-by and busily swapping hair-raising stories about the previous evening's incredible performance of black magic. Vassily Stepanovich the accountant, who had not been at yesterday's show, was growing more and more uneasy. The commissionaires were saying unbelievable things, such as how after the show a number of ladies had been seen on the street in a highly improper state. The shy and unassuming Vassily Stepanovich could only blink as he listened to the description of all these sensations and felt utterly unable to decide what to do ; meanwhile something *had* to be done and it was he who had to do it, as he was now the senior remaining member of the Variety's management.

By ten o'clock the ticket queue had swollen to such a size that the police came to hear of it and rapidly sent some detachments of horse and foot to reduce the queue to order. Unfortunately the mere existence of a mile-long queue was enough to cause a minor riot in spite of all the police could do.

Inside the Variety things were as confused as they were outside. The telephone had been ringing since early morning—ringing in Likhodeyev's office, in Rimsky's office, in the accounts department, in the box-office and in Varenukha's office. At first Vassily Stepanovich had attempted to answer, the cashier had tried to cope, the commissionaires had mumbled something into the telephone when it rang, but soon they stopped answering altogether because there was simply no answer to give the people asking where Likhodeyev, Rimsky and Varenukha were. They had been able to put them off the scent for a while by saying that Likhodeyev was in his flat, but this only produced more angry calls later, declaring that they had rung Likhodeyev's flat and been told that he was at the Variety.

One agitated lady rang up and demanded to speak to Rimsky and was advised to ring his wife at home, at which the earpiece, sobbing, replied that she was Rimsky's wife and he was nowhere to be found. Odd stories began to circulate. One of the charwomen was telling everyone that when she had gone to clean the treasurer's office she had found the door ajar, the lights burning, the window on to the garden smashed, a chair overturned on the floor and no one in the room.

At eleven o'clock Madame Rimsky descended on the Variety, weeping and wringing her hands. Vassily Stepanovich was by now utterly bewildered and unable to offer her any advice. Then at half past eleven the police appeared. Their first and very reasonable question was :

' What's happening here ? What is all this ? '

The staff retreated, pushing forward the pale and agitated Vassily Stepanovich. Describing the situation as it really was, he had to admit that the entire management of the Variety, including the general manager, the treasurer and the house manager, had vanished without trace, that last night's compère had been removed to a lunatic asylum and that, in short, yesterday's show had been a catastrophe.

Having done their best to calm her, the police sent the sobbing

Madame Rimsky home, then turned with interest to the char-woman's story about the state of the treasurer's office. The staff were told to go and get on with their jobs and after a short while the detective squad turned up, leading a sharp-eared muscular dog, the colour of cigarette ash and with extremely intelligent eyes. At once a rumour spread among the Variety Theatre staff that the dog was none other than the famous Ace of Diamonds. It was. Its behaviour amazed everybody. No sooner had the animal walked into the treasurer's office than it growled, bared its monstrous yellowish teeth, then crouched on its stomach and crept towards the broken window with a look of mingled terror and hostility. Mastering its fear the dog suddenly leaped on to the window ledge, raised its great muzzle and gave an eerie, savage howl. It refused to leave the window, growled, trembled and crouched as though wanting to jump out of the window.

The dog was led out of the office to the entrance hall, from whence it went out of the main doors into the street and across the road to the taxi-rank. There it lost the scent. After that Ace of Diamonds was taken away.

The detectives settled into Varenukha's office, where one after the other, they called in all the members of the Variety staff who had witnessed the events of the previous evening. At every step the detectives were beset with unforeseen difficulties. The thread kept breaking in their hands.

Had there been any posters advertising the performance? Yes, there had. But since last night new ones had been pasted over them and now there was not a single one to be found anywhere. Where did this magician come from? Nobody knew. Had a contract been signed?

' I suppose so,' replied Vassily Stepanovich miserably.

' And if so it will have gone through the books, won't it? '

' Certainly,' replied Vassily Stepanovich in growing agitation.

' Then where is it? '

' It's not here,' replied the accountant, turning paler and spreading his hands. It was true: there was no trace of a contract in the accounts department files, the treasurer's office, Likhodeyev's office or Varenukha's office.

What was the magician's surname ? Vassily Stepanovich did not know, he had not been at yesterday's show. The commissionaires did not know, the box-office cashier frowned and frowned, thought and thought, and finally said :

' Wo . . . I think it was Woland. . . .'

Perhaps it wasn't Woland ? Perhaps it wasn't. Perhaps it was Foland.

The Aliens' Bureau, it appeared, had never heard of anyone called Woland or Foland or any other black magician. Karpov, an usher, said that as far as he knew the magician was staying at Likhodeyev's flat. Naturally they immediately went to the flat, but there was no sign of a magician living there. Likhodeyev himself was also missing. The maid Grunya was not there and nobody knew where she was. Both the house committee chairman, Nikanor Ivanovich, and the secretary, Prolezhnev, had also vanished.

The investigation so far appeared to amount to a total absurdity : the entire management had vanished, there had been a scandalous show the previous evening—but who had arranged it ? Nobody knew.

Meanwhile it was nearly noon, time for the box office to open. This, of course, was out of the question. A large piece of cardboard was hung on the Variety's doors with the announcement :

TODAY'S

PERFORMANCE

CANCELLED

This caused a stir in the queue, beginning at its head, but the excitement subsided and the queue began to disperse. After an hour there was scarcely a trace of it on Sadovaya Street. The detectives left to pursue their inquiries elsewhere, the staff, except for the watchmen, were dismissed and the doors of the Variety were closed.

Vassily Stepanovich the accountant had two urgent tasks to

perform. Firstly to go to the Commission for Theatrical Spectacles and Light Entertainment with a report on the previous day's events and then to deposit yesterday's takings of 21,711 roubles at the Commission's finance department.

The meticulous and efficient Vassily Stepanovich wrapped the money in newspaper, tied it up with string, put it into his brief-case and following his standing instructions avoided taking a bus or tram but went instead to the nearby taxi-rank.

As soon as the three cab-drivers on the rank saw a fare approaching with a chock-full briefcase under his arm, all three of them instantly drove off empty, scowling back as they went. Amazed, the accountant stood for a while wondering what this odd behaviour could mean. After about three minutes an empty cab drove up the the rank, the driver grimacing with hostility when he saw his fare.

' Are you free ? ' asked Vassily Stepanovich with an anxious cough.

' Show me your money,' snarled the driver.

Even more amazed, the accountant clutched his precious briefcase under one arm, pulled a ten-rouble note out of his wallet and showed it to the driver.

' I'm not taking you,' he said curtly.

' Excuse me, but . . .' The accountant began, but the driver interrupted him :

' Got a three-rouble note ? '

The bewildered accountant took out two three-rouble notes from his wallet and showed them to the driver.

' O.K., get in,' he shouted, slamming down the flag of his meter so hard that he almost broke it. ' Let's go.'

' Are you short of change ? ' enquired the accountant timidly.

' Plenty of change ! ' roared the driver and his eyes, reddened with fury, glared at Vassily Stepanovich from the mirror. ' Third time it's happened to me today. Just the same with the others. Some son of a bitch gives me a tenner and I give him four-fifty change. Out he gets, the bastard ! Five minutes later I look—instead of a tenner there's a label off a soda-water bottle !' Here the driver said several unprintable words. ' Picked up another fare on Zaborskaya. Gives me a tenner—I give him three roubles change. Gets out. I look in my bag and out flies a bee ! Stings me on the finger ! I'll . . .' The driver spat out more unprintable words. ' And there was no tenner. There was a show on at that (unprintable) Variety yesterday evening and some (unprintable) conjurer did a turn with a lot of (unprintable) ten-rouble notes . . .'

The accountant was dumbstruck. He hunched himself up and tried to look as if he was hearing the very word ' Variety ' for the first time in his life as he thought to himself : ' Well I'm damned ! '

Arrived at his destination and paying in proper money, the accountant went into one building and hurried along the corridor to the chief cashier's office, but even before he reached it he realised that he had come at a bad moment. A rumpus was going on in the offices of the Theatrical Commission. A cleaner ran past him with her headscarf awry and bulging eyes.

' He's not there ! He's not there, dear,' she screamed, turning to another man hurrying along the passage. ' His jacket and trousers are there but there's nobody in 'em ! '

She disappeared through a door, from which there at once came the sound of smashing crockery. Vassily Stepanovich then saw the familiar figure of the chief cashier come running out of the secretaries' office and vanish, but the man was in such a state that he failed to recognise Vasilly Stepanovich.

Slightly shaken, the accountant reached the door of the secretaries' office, which was the ante-room to the chairman's office, where he had the greatest shock of all.

Through the far door came a terrible voice, unmistakably belonging to Prokhor Petrovich, the chairman of the Commission. ' I suppose he's telling somebody off,' thought the puzzled accountant. Looking round, he saw something else—there, in a leather armchair, her head resting on the back, sobbing uncontrollably and clutching a wet handkerchief, her legs stretched out to the middle of the floor, lay Prokhor Petrovich's secretary, the beautiful Anna Richardovna. Her chin was smeared with lipstick and streaks of dissolved mascara were running down her peach-skin cheeks.

Seeing him come in, Anna Richardovna jumped up, ran to Vassily Stepanovich, clutched his lapels and began to shake him, howling:

'Thank God! At least there's one of you brave enough! They've all run away, they've all let us down! Come and see him, I don't know what to do!' Still sobbing she dragged him into the chairman's office.

Once inside Vassily Stepanovich dropped his briefcase in horror.

Behind the huge desk with its massive inkwell sat an empty suit. A dry pen was hurrying, unheld, across a sheet of paper. The suit had a shirt and tie, a fountain pen was clipped in its breast-pocket, but above the collar there was no neck and no head and there were no wrists protruding from the cuffs. The suit was hard at work and oblivious of the uproar round about. Hearing someone come in, the suit leaned back in its chair and from somewhere just above the collar came the familiar voice of Prokhor Petrovich:

'What is it? There's a notice on the door saying that I'm not seeing visitors.'

The beautiful secretary moaned and cried, wringing her hands:

'Don't you see? He's not there! Bring him back, oh bring him back!'

Someone peeped round the door, groaned and flew out again. Vassily Stepanovich felt his legs shaking and he sat down on the edge of a chair—not forgetting, though, to hold on to his briefcase. Anna Richardovna pranced round Vassily Stepanovich, pulling at his coat and shrieking:

'I've always, always stopped him whenever he began swearing! Now he's sworn once too often!' The girl ran to the desk and exclaimed in a tender, musical voice, slightly nasal from so much weeping:

'Prosha dear, where are you?'

'Who are you addressing as "Prosha"?' enquired the suit haughtily, drawing further back into the chair.

'He doesn't recognise me! He doesn't recognise me! Don't you see?' sobbed the girl.

'Kindly stop crying in my office!' said the striped suit irritably, stretching out its sleeve for a fresh pile of paper.

'No, I can't look, I can't look!' cried Anna Richardovna and ran back into her office, followed, like a bullet, by the accountant.

'Just imagine—I was sitting here,' began Anna Richardovna trembling with horror and clutching Vassily Stepanovich's sleeve, 'when in came a cat. A great black animal as big as Behemoth. Naturally I shooed it out and it went, but then a fat man came in who also had a face like a cat, said "Do you always say 'shoo' to visitors?" and went straight in to Prokhor Petrovich. So I shouted "What d'you mean by going in there —have you gone crazy?" But the cheeky brute marched straight in to Prokhor Petrovich and sat down in the chair facing him. Well, Prokhor is the nicest man alive, but he's nervous. He lost his temper. He works like a trojan, but he's apt to be nervy and he just flared up. "Why have you come in here without being announced?" he said. And then, if you please, that impudent creature stretched out in his chair and said with a smile: "I've come to have a chat with you on a little matter of business." Prokhor Petrovich snapped at him again: "I'm busy," to which the beast said: "You're not busy at all . . ." How d'you like that? Well, of course, Prokhor Petrovich lost all patience then and shouted: "What is all this? Damn me if I don't have you thrown out of here!" The beast just smiled and said: "Damn you, I think you said? Very well!" And—bang! Before I could even scream, I looked and cat-face had gone and there was this . . . suit . . . sitting . . . Oooooh!' Stretching her mouth into a shapeless cavity Anna Richardovna gave a howl.

Choking back her sobs she took a deep breath but could only gulp nonsensically :

' And it goes on writing and writing and writing ! I must be going off my head ! It talks on the telephone ! The suit ! They've all run away like rabbits ! '

Vassily Stepanovich could only stand there, trembling. Fate rescued him. Into the secretaries' office with a firm, regular tread marched two policemen. Catching sight of them the lovely girl began sobbing even harder and pointed towards the office door.

' Now, now, miss, let's not cry,' said the first man calmly. Vassily Stepanovich, deciding that he was superfluous, skipped away and a minute later was out in the fresh air. His head felt hollow, something inside it was booming like a trumpet and the noise reminded him of the story told by one of the commissionaires about a cat which had taken part in yesterday's show. ' Aha ! Perhaps it's our little pussy up to his tricks again ? '

Having failed to hand in the money at the Commission's head office, the conscientious Vassily Stepanovich decided to go to the branch office, which was in Vagankovsky Street and to calm himself a little he made his way there on foot.

The branch office of the Theatrical Commission was quartered in a peeling old house at the far end of a courtyard, which was famous for the porphyry columns in its hallway. That day, however, the visitors to the house were not paying much attention to the porphyry columns.

Several visitors were standing numbly in the hall and staring at a weeping girl seated behind a desk full of theatrical brochures which it was her job to sell. The girl seemed to have lost interest in her literature and only waved sympathetic enquirers away, whilst from above, below and all sides of the building came the pealing of at least twenty desperate telephones.

Weeping, the girl suddenly gave a start and screamed hysterically :

' There it is again ! ' and began singing in a wobbly soprano :
' *Yo-o, heave-ho! Yo-o heave-ho!* '

A messenger, who had appeared on the staircase, shook his fist at somebody and joined the girl, singing in a rough, tuneless baritone :

' *One more heave, lads, one more heave . . .* '

Distant voices chimed in, the choir began to swell until finally the song was booming out all over the building. In nearby room No. 6, the auditor's department, a powerful hoarse bass voice boomed out an octave below the rest. The chorus was accompanied *crescendo* by a peal of telephone bells.

' *All day lo-ong we must trudge the shore,*' roared the messenger on the staircase.

Tears poured down the girl's face as she tried to clench her teeth, but her mouth opened of its own accord and she sang an octave above the messenger :

' *Work all da-ay and then work more . . .* '

What surprised the dumbfounded visitors was the fact that the singers, spread all through the building, were keeping excellent time, as though the whole choir were standing together and watching an invisible conductor.

Passers-by in Vagankovsky Street stopped outside the court-yard gates, amazed to hear such sounds of harmony coming from the Commission.

As soon as the first verse was over, the singing stopped at once, as though in obedience to a conductor's baton. The messenger swore under his breath and ran off.

The front door opened and in walked a man wearing a light coat on top of a white overall, followed by a policeman.

' Do something, doctor, please ! ' screamed the hysterical girl.

The secretary of the branch office ran out on to the staircase and obviously burning with embarrassment and shame said between hiccups :

' Look doctor, we have a case of some kind of mass hypnosis, so you must . . .' He could not finish his sentence, stuttered and began singing 'Shilka and Nerchinsk . . .'

' Fool ! ' the girl managed to shout, but never managed to

say who she meant and instead found herself forced into a trill and joined in the song about Shilka and Nerchinsk.

'Pull yourselves together! Stop singing!' said the doctor to the secretary.

It was obvious that the secretary would have given anything to stop singing but could not.

When the verse was finished the girl at the desk received a dose of valerian from the doctor, who hurried off to give the secretary and the rest the same treatment.

'Excuse me, miss,' Vassily Stepanovich suddenly asked the girl, 'has a black cat been in here?'

'What cat?' cried the girl angrily. 'There's a donkey in this office—a donkey!' And she went on: 'If you want to hear about it I'll tell you exactly what's happened.'

Apparently the director of the branch office had a mania for organising clubs.

'He does it all without permission from head office!' said the girl indignantly.

In the course of a year the branch director had succeeded in organising a Lermontov Club, a Chess and Draughts Club, a Ping-Pong Club and a Riding Club. In summer he threatened to organise a rowing club and a mountaineering club. And then this morning in came the director at lunch time . . .

'. . . arm in arm with some villain,' said the girl, 'that he'd picked up God knows where, wearing check trousers, with a wobbling pince-nez . . . and an absolutely impossible face!'

There and then, according to the girl, he had introduced him to all the lunchers in the dining-room as a famous specialist in organising choral societies.

The faces of the budding mountaineers darkened, but the director told them to cheer up and the specialist made jokes and assured them on his oath that singing would take up very little time and was a wonderfully useful accomplishment.

Well, of course, the girl went on, the first two to jump up were Fanov and Kosarchuk, both well-known toadies, and announced that they wanted to join. The rest of the staff realised that there was no way out of it, so they all joined the choral society too. It was decided to practise during the lunch break, because all the rest of their spare time was already taken up with Lermontov and draughts. To set an example the director announced that he sang tenor. What happened then was like a bad dream. The check-clad chorus master bellowed : ' *Do, mi, sol, do!* ' He dragged some of the shy members out from behind a cupboard where they had been trying to avoid having to sing, told Kosarchuk that he had perfect pitch, whined, whimpered, begged them to show him some respect as an old choirmaster, struck a tuning fork on his finger and announced that they would begin with ' The Song of the Volga Boatmen '.

They struck up. And they sang very well—the man in the check suit really did know his job. They sang to the end of the first verse. Then the choirmaster excused himself, saying : ' I'll be back in a moment . . .'—and vanished. Everybody expected him back in a minute or two, but ten minutes went by and there was still no sign of him. The staff were delighted—he had run away !

Then suddenly, as if to order, they all began singing the second verse, led by Kosarchuk, who may not have had perfect pitch but who had quite a pleasant high tenor. They finished the verse. Still no conductor. Everybody started to go back to their tables, but they had no time to eat before quite against their will they all started singing again. And they could not stop. There would be three minutes' silence and they would burst out into song again. Silence—then more singing ! Soon people began to realise that something terrible was happening. The director locked himself in his office out of shame.

With this the girl's story broke off—even valerian was no use.

A quarter of an hour later three lorries drove up to the gateway on Vagankovsky Street and the entire branch staff, headed by the director, was put into them. Just as the first lorry drove through the gate and out into the street, the staff, standing in the back of the lorry and holding each other round the shoulders, all opened their mouths and deafened the whole street with a song. The second lorry-load joined in and then the third. On they drove, singing. The passers-by hurrying past on their own business gave the lorries no more than a glance and took no notice, thinking that it was some works party going on an excursion out of town. They were certainly heading out of town, but not for an outing : they were bound for Professor Stravinsky's clinic.

Half an hour later the distracted Vassily Stepanovich reached the accounts department hoping at last to be able to get rid of his large sum of money. Having learned from experience, he first gave a cautious glance into the long hall, where the cashiers sat behind frosted-glass windows with gilt markings. He found no sign of disturbance or upheaval. All was as quiet as it should be in such a respectable establishment.

Vassily Stepanovich stuck his head through the window marked ' Paying In ', said good-day to the clerk and politely asked for a paying-in slip.

' What do you want ? ' asked the clerk behind the window.

The accountant looked amazed.

' I want to pay in, of course. I'm from the Variety.'

' One minute,' replied the clerk and instantly shut his little window.

' Funny ! ' thought Vassily Stepanovich. This was the first time in his life that he had been treated like this. We all know how hard it is to acquire money—the process is strewn with obstacles ; but in his thirty years' experience Vassily Stepanovich had never yet found anyone who had made the least objection to taking money when offered it.

At last the window was pushed open again and the accountant leaned forward again.

' How much have you got ? ' asked the clerk.

' Twenty-one thousand, seven hundred and eleven roubles.'

' Oho ! ' replied the clerk ironically and handed Vassily Stepanovich a green form. Thoroughly familiar with it, he filled it out in a moment and began untying the string on his package.

As he unpacked it a red film came over his eyes and he groaned in agony. In front of him lay heaps of foreign money—Canadian dollars, English pounds, Dutch guilders, Latvian latts, Esthonian crowns . . .

'Here's another of these jokers from the Variety!' said a grim voice behind the accountant. And Vassily Stepanovich was immediately put under arrest.

18. Unwelcome Visitors

Just as Vassily Stepanovich was taking a taxi-ride to meet the suit that wrote by itself, among the passengers from the Kiev express a respectably dressed man carrying a little fibre suitcase emerged from a first-class sleeper on to the Moscow platform. This passenger was none other than the uncle of the late Misha Berlioz, Maximilian Andreyevich Poplavsky, an economist who worked in the Planning Commission and lived in Kiev. The cause of his arrival in Moscow was a telegram that he had received late in the evening two days earlier : HAVE BEEN RUN OVER BY TRAM AT PATRIARCHS FUNERAL THREE O'CLOCK FRIDAY PLEASE COME BERLIOZ

Maximilian Andreyevich was regarded, and rightly so, as one of the most intelligent men in Kiev, but a telegram like this would be liable to put even the brightest of us in a dilemma. If a man telegraphs that he has been run over, obviously he has not been killed. But then why the funeral ? Or is he so desperately ill that he can foresee his own death ? It is possible, but extremely odd to be quite so precise—even if he can predict his death, how does he know that he's going to be buried at three o'clock on Friday ? What an astonishing telegram !

Intelligent people, however, become intelligent by solving complicated problems. It was very simple. There had been a mistake and the wire had arrived in garbled form. Obviously the word ' have ' belonged to some other telegram and had been transmitted in error instead of the word ' Berlioz ', which had been put by mistake at the end of the telegram. Thus corrected, the meaning was quite clear, though, of course, tragic.

When his wife had recovered from her first grief, Maximilian Andreyevich at once prepared to go to Moscow.

Here I should reveal a secret about Maximilian Andreyevich. He genuinely mourned the death of his wife's cousin, cut off in the prime of life, but at the same time, being a practical man, he fully realised that there was no special need for his presence at the funeral. Yet Maximilian Andreyevich was in a great hurry to go to Moscow. What for ? For one thing—the flat. A flat in Moscow was a serious matter. He did not know why, but Maximilian Andreyevich did not like Kiev and the thought of moving to Moscow had lately begun to nag at him with such insistence that it was affecting his sleep.

He took no delight in the spring floods of the Dnieper when, as it drowned the islands on the lower shore, the water spread until it merged with the horizon. He found no pleasure in the staggeringly beautiful view from the foot of the monument to Prince Vladimir. The patches of sunlight that play in spring over the brick pathways leading to the top of St Vladimir's hill meant nothing to him. He wanted none of it. He only wanted to go to Moscow.

Advertisements in the newspapers offering to exchange a flat on University Street in Kiev for a smaller flat in Moscow produced no results. Nobody could be found who wanted to move, except a few whose offers turned out to be fraudulent.

The telegram came as a shock to Maximilian Andreyevich. It was a chance that would be sinful to miss. Practical people know that opportunities of that sort never come twice.

In short he had to make sure, at no matter what cost, that he inherited his nephew's flat in Sadovaya Street. It was going to be complicated, very complicated, but come what might these complications had to be overcome. An experienced man, Maximilian Andreyevich knew that the first and essential step was to arrange a temporary residence permit to stay, for however short a time, in his late nephew's flat.

So on Friday morning Maximilian Andreyevich walked into the office of the Tenants' Association of No. 302A, Sadovaya Street, Moscow. In a mean little room, its wall enlivened by a poster showing in several graphic diagrams how to revive a drowned man, behind a wooden desk there sat a lonely, unshaven middle-aged man with a worried look.

' May I see the chairman, please ? ' enquired the economist politely, taking off his hat and placing his attaché case on a chair by the door. This apparently simple question upset the man behind the desk so much that a complete change came over his expression. Squinting with anxiety he muttered something incoherent about the chairman not being there.

' Is he in his flat ? ' asked Poplavsky. ' I have some very urgent business with him.'

The man gave another indistinct mumble, which meant that he wasn't in his flat either.

' When will he be back ? '

To this the seated man gave no reply except to stare glumly out of the window.

' Aha ! ' said the intelligent Poplavsky to himself and enquired after the secretary. At this the strange man behind the desk actually went purple in the face with strain and again muttered vaguely that the secretary wasn't there either . . . nobody knew when he'd be back again . . . the secretary was ill . . .

' Oho ! ' said Poplavsky to himself. ' Is there anybody here from the Association's management committee ? '

' Me,' said the man in a weak voice.

' Look,' said Poplavsky ingratiatingly, ' I am the sole heir of my nephew Berlioz who as you know died the other day at Patriarch's Ponds and according to law I have to claim my inheritance. All his things are in our flat—No. 50 . . .'

' I don't know anything about it, comrade,' the man interrupted gloomily.

' Excuse me,' said Poplavsky in his most charming voice, ' you are a member of the management committee and you must . . .'

Just then a stranger came into the room. The man behind the desk went pale.

' Are you Pyatnazhko of the management committee ? ' said the stranger.

' Yes, I am,' said the seated man in a tiny voice.

The stranger whispered something to him and the man behind the desk, now completely bewildered, got up and left Poplavsky entirely alone in the empty committee room.

' What a nuisance ! I should have seen the whole committee at once . . .' thought Poplavsky with annoyance as he crossed the courtyard and hurried towards flat No. 50.

He rang the bell, the door was opened and Maximilian Andreyevich walked into the semi-darkness of the hall. He was slightly surprised not to be able to see who had opened the door to him ; there was no one in the hall except an enormous black cat sitting on a chair. Maximilian Andreyevich coughed and tapped his foot, at which the study door opened and Koroviev came into the hall. Maximilian Andreyevich gave him a polite but dignified bow and said :

' My name is Poplavsky. I am the uncle . . .'

But before he could finish Koroviev pulled a dirty handkerchief out of his pocket, blew his nose and burst into tears.

' Of course, of course ! ' said Koroviev, removing the handkerchief from his face. ' I only had to see you to know who you were ! ' He shook with tears and began sobbing : ' Oh, what a tragedy ! How could such a thing happen ? '

' Was he run over by a tram ? ' asked Poplavsky in a whisper.

' Completely ! ' cried Koroviev, tears streaming past his pince-nez. ' Completely ! I saw it happen. Can you believe it ? Bang—his head was off, scrunch—away went his right leg, scrunch—off came his left leg ! What these trams can do.' In his grief, Koroviev leaned his nose against the wall beside the mirror and shook with sobs.

Berlioz's uncle was genuinely moved by the stranger's behaviour. ' There—and they say people have no feelings nowadays ! ' he thought, feeling his own eyes beginning to prick. At the same time, however, an uneasy thought snaked across his mind that perhaps this man had already registered himself in the flat ; such things had been known to happen.

' Excuse me, but were you a friend of Misha's ? ' he enquired, wiping his dry left eye with his sleeve and studying the grief-stricken Koroviev with his right eye. But Koroviev was sobbing so hard that he was inaudible except for ' Scrunch and off it came ! ' His weeping-fit over, Koroviev finally unstuck himself from the wall and said :

' No, I can't bear it ! I shall go and take three hundred drops of valerian in ether . . .' Turning his tear-stained face to Poplavsky he added : ' Ah, these trams ! '

' I beg your pardon, but did you send me a telegram ? ' asked Maximilian Andreyevich, racking his brains to think who this extraordinary weeping creature might be.

' He sent it,' replied Koroviev, pointing to the cat.

Poplavsky, his eyes bulging, assumed that he had misheard.

' No, I can't face it any longer,' went on Koroviev, sniffing. ' When I think of that wheel going over his leg . . . each wheel weighs 360 pounds . . . scrunch ! . . . I must go and lie down, sleep is the only cure.' And he vanished from the hall.

The cat jumped down from the chair, stood up on its hind legs, put its forelegs akimbo, opened its mouth and said :

' I sent the telegram. So what ? '

Maximilian Andreyevich's head began to spin, his arms and legs gave way so that he dropped his case and sat down in a chair facing the cat.

' Don't you understand Russian ? ' said the cat severely. ' What do you want to know ? '

Poplavsky was speechless.

' Passport ! ' barked the cat and stretched out a fat paw.

Completely dumbfounded and blind to everything except the twin sparks in the cat's eyes, Poplavsky pulled his passport out of his pocket like a dagger. The cat picked up a pair of spectacles in thick black rims from the table under the mirror, put them on its snout, which made it look even more imposing, and took the passport from Poplavsky's shaking hand.

' I wonder—have I fainted or what ? ' thought Poplavsky. From the distance came the sound of Koroviev's blubbering, the hall was filled with the smell of ether, valerian and some other nauseating abomination.

'Which department issued this passport?' asked the cat. There was no answer.

'Department four hundred and twenty,' said the cat to itself, drawing its paw across the passport which it was holding upside-down. 'Well, of course! I know that department, they issue passports to anybody who comes along. I wouldn't have given one to someone like you. Not on any account. One look at your face and I'd have refused!' The cat had worked itself up into such a temper that it threw the passport to the ground. 'You may not attend the funeral,' went on the cat in an official voice. 'Kindly go home at once.' And it shouted towards the door: 'Azazello!'

At this a small, red-haired man limped into the hall. He had one yellow fang, a wall eye and was wearing a black sweater with a knife stuck into a leather belt. Feeling himself suffocating, Poplavsky stood up and staggered back, clutching his heart.

'See him out, Azazello!' ordered the cat and went out.

'Poplavsky,' said the fanged horror in a nasal whine, 'I hope you understand?'

Poplavsky nodded.

'Go back to Kiev at once,' Azazello went on, 'stay at home as quiet as a mouse and forget that you ever thought of getting a flat in Moscow. Got it?'

The little man only came up to Poplavsky's shoulder, but he reduced him to mortal terror with his fang, his knife and his wall-eyed squint and he had an air of cool, calculating energy.

First he picked up the passport and handed it to Maximilian Andreyevich, who took it with a limp hand. Then Azazello took the suitcase in his left hand, flung open the front door with his right and taking Berlioz's uncle by the arm led him out on to the landing. Poplavsky leaned against the wall. Without a key Azazello opened the little suitcase, took out of it an enormous roast chicken minus one leg wrapped in greaseproof paper and put it on the floor. Then he pulled out two sets of clean underwear, a razor-strop, a book and a leather case and kicked them all downstairs except the chicken. The empty suitcase followed it. It could be heard crashing downstairs and to judge by the sound, the lid broke off as it went.

Then the carrot-haired ruffian picked up the chicken by its leg and hit Poplavsky a terrible blow across the neck with it, so violently that the carcase flew apart leaving Azazello with the leg in his hand. 'Everything was in a mess in the Oblonskys' house' as Leo Tolstoy so truly put it, a remark which applied exactly to the present situation. Everything was in a mess for Poplavsky. A long spark of light flashed in front of him, then he had a vision of a funeral procession on a May afternoon and Poplavsky fell downstairs.

When he reached the landing he knocked a pane out of the window with his foot and sat down on the step. A legless chicken rolled past him, disintegrating as it went. On the upper landing Azazello devoured the chicken-leg in a flash, stuffed the bone into his pocket, turned back into the flat and slammed the door behind him.

From below there came the sound of a man's cautious steps coming upstairs. Poplavsky ran down another flight and sat down on a little wooden bench on the landing to draw breath.

A tiny little old man with a painfully sad face, wearing an old-fashioned tussore suit and a straw boater with a green ribbon, came up the stairs and stopped beside Poplavsky.

'Would you mind telling me, sir,' enquired the man in tussore sadly, 'where No. 50 might be?'

'Upstairs,' gasped Poplavsky.

'Thank you very much, sir,' said the little man as gloomily as before and plodded upward, whilst Poplavsky stood up and walked on downstairs.

You may ask whether Maximilian Andreyevich hurried to the police to complain about the ruffians who had handled him with such violence in broad daylight. He most certainly did not. How could he walk into a police station and say that a cat had been reading his passport and that a man in a sweater armed with a knife . . . ? No, Maximilian Andreyevich was altogether too intelligent for that.

He had by now reached the ground floor and noticed just beside the main door another little door, with a broken glass pane, leading into a storage cupboard. Poplavsky put his passport into his pocket and hunted round for the scattered contents of his suitcase. There was no trace of them. He was amazed to notice how little this worried him. Another and rather intriguing idea now occupied him—to stay and see what happened when the little old man went into the sinister flat. Since he had asked the way to No. 50, he must be going there for the first time and was heading straight for the clutches of the gang that had moved into the flat. Something told Poplavsky that the little man was going to come out of that flat again in quick time. Naturally he had given up any idea of going to his nephew's funeral and there was plenty of time before the train left for Kiev. The economist glanced round and slipped into the cupboard.

Just then came the sound of a door closing upstairs. ' He's gone in . . .' thought Poplavsky anxiously. It was damp and cold in the cupboard and it smelled of mice and boots. Maximilian Andreyevich sat down on a log of wood and decided to wait. He was in a good position to watch the staircase and the doorway leading on to the courtyard.

However he had to wait longer than he had expected. The staircase remained empty. At last the door on the fifth floor was heard shutting. Poplavsky froze. Yes, those were his footsteps. ' He's coming down . . .' A door opened one floor lower. The footsteps stopped. A woman's voice. A sad man's voice—yes, that was him . . . saying something like ' Stop it, for heaven's sake . . .' Poplavsky stuck his ear out through the broken pane and caught the sound of a woman's laughter. Quick, bold steps coming downstairs and a woman flashed past. She was carrying a green oilcloth bag and hurried out into the courtyard. Then came the little man's footsteps again. ' That's odd ! He's going back into the flat again ! Surely he's not one of the gang ? Yes, he's going back. They've opened the door upstairs again. Well, let's wait a little longer and see . . .'

This time there was not long to wait. The sound of the door. Footsteps. The footsteps stopped. A despairing cry. A cat miaowing. A patter of quick footsteps coming down, down, down !

Poplavsky waited. Crossing himself and muttering the sad little man rushed past, hatless, an insane look on his face, his bald head covered in scratches, his trousers soaking wet. He began struggling with the door handle, so terrified that he failed to see whether it opened inwards or outwards, finally mastered it and flew out into the sunlit courtyard.

The experiment over and without a further thought for his dead nephew or for his flat, trembling to think of the danger he had been through and muttering, ' I see it all, I see it all ! ' Maximilian Andreyevich ran outside. A few minutes later a trolley-bus was carrying the economist towards the Kiev station.

While the economist had been lurking in the downstairs cupboard, the little old man had been through a distressing experience. He was a barman at the Variety Theatre and his name was Andrei Fokich Sokov. During the police investigation at the theatre, Andrei Fokich had kept apart from it all and the only thing noticeable about him was that he grew even sadder-looking than usual. He also found out from Karpov, the usher, where the magician was staying.

So, leaving the economist on the landing, the barman climbed up to the fifth floor and rang the bell at No. 50.

The door was opened immediately, but the barman shuddered and staggered back without going in. The door had been opened by a girl, completely naked except for an indecent little lace apron, a white cap and a pair of little gold slippers. She had a perfect figure and the only flaw in her looks was a livid scar on her neck.

'Well, come on in, since you rang,' said the girl, giving the barman an enticing look.

Andrei Fokich groaned, blinked and stepped into the hall, taking off his hat. At that moment the telephone rang. The shameless maid put one foot on a chair, lifted the receiver and said into it:

'Hullo!'

The barman did not know where to look and shifted from foot to foot, thinking: 'These foreigners and their maids! Really, it's disgusting!' To save himself from being disgusted he stared the other way.

The large, dim hallway was full of strange objects and pieces of clothing. A black cloak lined with fiery red was thrown over the back of a chair, while a long sword with a shiny gold hilt lay on the console under the mirror. Three swords with silver hilts stood in one corner as naturally as if they had been umbrellas or walking sticks, and berets adorned with eagles' plumes hung on the antlers of a stag's head.

'Yes,' said the girl into the telephone. 'I beg your pardon? Baron Maigel? Very good, sir. Yes. The professor is in today. Yes, he'll be delighted to see you. Yes, it's formal . . . Tails or dinner jacket. When? At midnight.' The conversation over, she put back the receiver and turned to the barman.

'What do you want?'

'I have to see the magician.'

'What, the professor himself?'

'Yes,' replied the barman miserably.

'I'll see,' said the maid, hesitating, then she opened the door into Berlioz's study and announced: 'Sir, there's a little man here. He says he has to see messire in person.'

'Show him in,' said Koroviev's cracked voice from the study.

'Go in, please,' said the girl as naturally as if she had been normally dressed, then opened the door and left the hall.

As he walked in the barman was so amazed at the furnishing of the room that he forgot why he had come. Through the stained-glass windows (a fantasy of the jeweller's widow) poured a strange ecclesiastical light. Although the day was hot there was a log fire in the vast old-fashioned fireplace, yet it gave no heat and instead the visitor felt a wave of damp and cold as though he had walked into a tomb. In front of the fireplace sat a great black tomcat on a tiger-skin rug blinking pleasurably at the fire. There was a table, the sight of which made the God-fearing barman shudder—it was covered with an altar-cloth and on top of it was an army of bottles—bulbous, covered in mould and dust. Among the bottles glittered a plate, obviously of solid gold. By the fireplace a little red-haired man with a knife in his belt was roasting a piece of meat on the end of a long steel blade. The fat dripped into the flames and the smoke curled up the chimney. There was a smell of roasting meat, another powerful scent and the odour of incense, which made the barman wonder, as he had read of Berlioz's death and knew that this had been his flat, whether they were performing some kind of requiem for the dead man, but as soon as it came to him he abandoned the idea as clearly ridiculous.

Suddenly the stupefied barman heard a deep bass voice :

' Well sir, and what can I do for you ? '

Andrei Fokich turned round and saw the man he was looking for.

The black magician was lolling on a vast, low, cushion-strewn divan. As far as the barman could see the professor was wearing nothing but black underwear and black slippers with pointed toes.

' I am,' said the little man bitterly, ' the head barman at the Variety Theatre.'

The professor stretched out a hand glittering with precious stones as though to stop the barman's mouth and interrupted heatedly :

' No, no, no ! Not another word ! Never, on any account ! I shall never eat or drink a single mouthful at that buffet of yours ! I went past your counter the other day, my dear sir, and I shall never forget the sight of that smoked sturgeon and that cheese !

My dear fellow, cheese isn't supposed to be green, you know—someone must have given you the wrong idea. It's meant to be white. And the tea! It's more like washing-up water. With my own eyes I saw a slut of a girl pouring grey water into your enormous samovar while you went on serving tea from it. No, my dear fellow, that's not the way to do it!'

'I'm sorry,' said Andrei Fokich, appalled by this sudden attack, 'but I came about something else, I don't want to talk about the smoked sturgeon . . .'

'But I insist on talking about it—it was stale!'

'The sturgeon they sent was second-grade-fresh,' said the barman.

'Really, what nonsense!'

'Why nonsense?'

'"Second-grade-fresh"—that's what I call nonsense! There's only one degree of freshness—the first, and it's the last. If your sturgeon is "second-grade-fresh" that means it's stale.'

'I'm sorry . . .' began the barman, at a loss to parry this insistent critic.

'No, it's unforgivable,' said the professor.

'I didn't come to see you about that,' said the barman again, now utterly confused.

'Didn't you?' said the magician, astonished. 'What did you come for then? As far as I remember I've never known anybody connected with your profession, except for a *vivandière*, but that was long before your time. However, I'm delighted to make your acquaintance. Azazello! A stool for the head barman!'

The man who was roasting meat turned round, terrifying the barman at the sight of his wall eye, and neatly offered him one of the dark oaken stools. There were no other seats in the room.

The barman said: 'Thank you very much,' and sat down on the stool. One of its back legs immediately broke with a crash and the barman, with a groan, fell painfully backward onto the floor. As he fell he kicked the leg of another stool and upset a full glass of red wine all over his trousers.

The professor exclaimed :

' Oh ! Clumsy ! '

Azazello helped the barman to get up and gave him another stool. In a miserable voice the barman declined his host's offer to take off his trousers and dry them in front of the fire. Feeling unbearably awkward in his wet trousers and underpants, he took a cautious seat on the other stool.

' I love a low seat,' began the professor. ' One's not so likely to fall. Ah, yes, we were talking about sturgeon. First and last, my dear fellow, it must be fresh, fresh, fresh ! That should be the motto of every man in your trade. Oh yes, would you like to taste . . .'

In the red glow of the fire a sword glittered in front of the barman, and Azazello laid a sizzling piece of meat on a gold plate, sprinkled it with lemon juice and handed the barman a golden two-pronged fork.

' Thank you, but I . . .'

' No, do taste it ! '

Out of politeness the barman put a little piece into his mouth and found that he was chewing something really fresh and unusually delicious. As he ate the succulent meat, however, he almost fell off his stool again. A huge dark bird flew in from the next room and softly brushed the top of the barman's bald head with its wing. As it perched on the mantelpiece beside a clock, he saw that the bird was an owl. ' Oh my God ! ' thought Andrei Fokich, nervous as all barmen are, ' what a place ! '

' Glass of wine ? White or red ? What sort of wine do you like at this time of day ? '

' Thanks but . . . I don't drink . . .'

' You poor fellow ! What about a game of dice then ? Or do you prefer some other game ? Dominoes ? Cards ? '

' I don't play,' replied the barman, feeling weak and thoroughly muddled.

'How dreadful for you,' said the host. 'I always think, present company excepted of course, that there's something unpleasant lurking in people who avoid drinking, gambling, table-talk and pretty women. People like that are either sick or secretly hate their fellow-men. Of course there may be exceptions. I have had some outright scoundrels sitting at my table before now ! Now tell me what I can do for you.'

'Yesterday you did some tricks . . .'

'I did ? Tricks ? ' exclaimed the magician indignantly. 'I beg your pardon ! What a rude suggestion ! '

'I'm sorry,' said the barman in consternation. 'I mean . . . black magic . . . at the theatre.'

'Oh, that ! Yes, of course. I'll tell you a secret, my dear fellow. I'm not really a magician at all. I simply wanted to see some Muscovites en masse and the easiest way to do so was in a theatre. So my staff '—he nodded towards the cat—'arranged this little act and I just sat on stage and watched the audience. Now, if that doesn't shock you too much, tell me what brings you here in connection with my performance ? '

'During your act you made bank-notes float down from the ceiling. . . .' The barman lowered his voice and looked round in embarrassment. 'Well, all the audience picked them up and a young man came to my bar and handed me a ten-rouble note, so I gave him eight roubles fifty change . . . Then another one came . . .'

'Another young man ? '

'No, he was older. Then there was a third and a fourth . . . I gave them all change. And today when I came to check the till there was nothing in it but a lot of strips of paper. The bar was a hundred and nine roubles short.'

'Oh dear, dear, dear ! ' exclaimed the professor. 'Don't tell me people thought those notes were real ? I can't believe they did it on purpose.'

The barman merely stared miserably round him and said nothing.

'They weren't swindlers, were they ? ' the magician asked in a worried voice. 'Surely there aren't any swindlers here in Moscow?'

The barman replied with such a bitter smile that there could be no doubt about it : there were plenty of swindlers in Moscow.

'That's mean!' said Woland indignantly. 'You're a poor man . . . you are a poor man, aren't you?'

Andrei Fokich hunched his head into his shoulders to show that he was a poor man.

'How much have you managed to save?'

Although the question was put in a sympathetic voice, it was tactless. The barman squirmed.

'Two hundred and forty nine thousand roubles in five different savings banks,' said a quavering voice from the next room, 'and under the floor at home he's got two hundred gold ten-rouble pieces.'

Andrei Fokich seemed to sink into his stool.

'Well, of course, that's no great sum of money,' said Woland patronisingly. 'All the same, you don't need it. When are you going to die?'

Now it was the barman's turn to be indignant.

'Nobody knows and it's nobody's business,' he replied.

'Yes, nobody knows,' said the same horrible voice from the next room. 'But by Newton's binomial theorem I predict that he will die in nine months' time in February of next year of cancer of the liver, in Ward No. 4 of the First Moscow City Hospital.'

The barman's face turned yellow.

'Nine months . . .' Woland calculated thoughtfully. 'Two hundred and forty-nine thousand . . . that works out at twenty-seven thousand a month in round figures . . . not much, but enough for a man of modest habits . . . then there are the gold coins . . .'

'The coins will not be cashed,' said the same voice, turning Andrei Fokich's heart to ice. 'When he dies the house will be demolished and the coins will be impounded by the State Bank.'

'If I were you I shouldn't bother to go into hospital,' went on the professor. 'What's the use of dying in a ward surrounded by a lot of groaning and croaking incurables? Wouldn't it be much better to throw a party with that twenty-seven thousand and take poison and depart for the other world to the sound of violins, surrounded by lovely drunken girls and happy friends?'

The barman sat motionless. He had aged. Black rings encircled his eyes, his cheeks were sunken, his lower jaw sagged.

'But we're daydreaming,' exclaimed the host. 'To business! Show me those strips of paper.'

Fumbling, Andrei Fokich took a package out of his pocket, untied it and sat petrified—the sheet of newspaper was full of ten-rouble notes.

'My dear chap, you really are sick,' said Woland, shrugging his shoulders.

Grinning stupidly, the barman got up from his stool.

'B-b-but . . .' he stammered, hiccupping, 'if they vanish again . . . what then?'

'H'm,' said the professor thoughtfully. 'In that case come back and see us. Delighted to have met you. . . .'

At this Koroviev leaped out of the study, clasped the barman's hand and shook it violently as he begged Andrei Fokich to give his kindest regards to everybody at the theatre. Bewildered, Andrei Fokich stumbled out into the hall.

'Hella, see him out!' shouted Koroviev.

The same naked girl appeared in the hall. The barman staggered out, just able to squeak 'Goodbye', and left the flat as though he were drunk. Having gone a little way down, he stopped, sat down on a step, took out the package and checked—the money was still there.

Just then a woman with a green bag came out of one of the flats on that landing. Seeing a man sitting on the step and staring dumbly at a packet of bank-notes, she smiled and said wistfully:

'What a dump this is . . . drunks on the staircase at this hour of the morning . . . and they've smashed a window on the staircase again !'

After a closer look at Andrei Fokich she added :

' Mind the rats don't get all that money of yours. . . . Wouldn't you like to share some of it with me ? '

' Leave me alone, for Christ's sake ! ' said the barman and promptly hid the money.

The woman laughed.

' Oh, go to hell, you old miser ! I was only joking. . . .' And she went on downstairs.

Andrei Fokich slowly got up, raised his hand to straighten his hat and discovered that it was not on his head. He desperately wanted not to go back, but he missed his hat. After some hesitation he made up his mind, went back and rang the bell.

' What do you want now ? ' asked Hella.

' I forgot my hat,' whispered the barman, tapping his bald head. Hella turned round and the little man shut his eyes in horror. When he opened them, Hella was offering him his hat and a sword with a black hilt.

' It's not mine. . . .' whispered the barman, pushing away the sword and quickly putting on his hat.

' Surely you didn't come without a sword ? ' asked Hella in surprise.

Andrei Fokich muttered something and hurried off downstairs. His head felt uncomfortable and somehow too hot. He took off his hat and gave a squeak of horror—he was holding a velvet beret with a bedraggled cock's feather. The barman crossed himself. At that moment the beret gave a miaou and changed into a black kitten. It jumped on to Andrei Fokich's head and dug its claws into his bald patch. Letting out a shriek of despair, the wretched man hurled himself downstairs as the kitten jumped off his head and flashed back to No. 50.

Bursting out into the courtyard, the barman trotted out of the gate and left the diabolical No. 302A for ever.

It was not, however, the end of his adventures. Once in the

street he stared wildly round as if looking for something. A minute later he was in a chemist's shop on the far side of the road. No sooner had he said:

'Tell me, please . . .' when the woman behind the counter shrieked:

'Look! Your head! It's cut to pieces!'

Within five minutes Andrei's head was bandaged and he had discovered that the two best specialists in diseases of the liver were Professor Bernadsky and Professor Kuzmin. Enquiring which was the nearest, he was overjoyed to learn that Kuzmin lived literally round the corner in a little white house and two minutes later he was there.

It was an old-fashioned but very comfortable little house. Afterwards the barman remembered first meeting a little old woman who wanted to take his hat, but since he had no hat the old woman hobbled off, chewing her toothless gums. In her place appeared a middle-aged woman, who immediately announced that new patients could only be registered on the 19th of the month and not before. Instinct told Andrei Fokich what to do. Giving an expiring glance at the three people in the waiting-room he whispered:

'I'm dying. . . .'

The woman glanced uncertainly at his bandaged head, hesitated, then said:

'Very well. . . .' and led the barman through the hall.

At that moment a door opened to reveal a bright gold pince-nez. The woman in the white overall said:

'Citizens, this patient has priority.'

Andrei Fokich had not time to look round before he found himself in Professor Kuzmin's consulting room. It was a long, well-proportioned room with nothing frightening, solemn or medical about it.

'What is your trouble?' enquired Professor Kuzmin in a pleasant voice, glancing slightly anxiously at the bandaged head.

240

' I have just learned from a reliable source,' answered the barman, staring wildly at a framed group photograph, ' that I am going to die next February from cancer of the liver. You must do something to stop it.'

Professor Kuzmin sat down and leaned against the tall leather back of his Gothic chair.

' I'm sorry I don't understand you . . . You mean . . . you saw a doctor? Why is your head bandaged? '

' Him? He's no doctor . . .' replied the barman and suddenly his teeth began to chatter. ' Don't bother about my head, that's got nothing to do with it . . . I haven't come about my head . . . I've got cancer of the liver—you must do something about it! '

' But who told you? '

' You must believe him! ' Andrei Fokich begged fervently. ' He knows! '

' I simply don't understand,' said the professor, shrugging his shoulders and pushing his chair back from the desk. ' How can he know when you're going to die? Especially as he's not a doctor.'

' In Ward No. 4,' was all the barman could say.

The professor stared at his patient, at his head, at his damp trousers, and thought: ' This is the last straw—some madman . . .' He asked:

' Do you drink? '

' Never touch it,' answered the barman.

In a minute he was undressed and lying on a chilly striped couch with the professor kneading his stomach. This cheered the barman considerably. The professor declared categorically that at the present moment at least there were no signs of cancer, but since . . . since he was worried about it and some charlatan had given him a fright, he had better have some tests done.

The professor scribbled on some sheets of paper, explaining where Andrei Fokich was to go and what he should take with him. He also gave him a note to a colleague, Professor Burye, the neuropathologist, saying that his nerves, at any rate, were in a shocking condition.

' How much should I pay you, professor ? ' asked the barman in a trembling voice, pulling out a fat notecase.

' As much as you like,' replied the professor drily.

Andrei Fokich pulled out thirty roubles and put them on the table, then furtively, as though his hands were cat's paws, put a round, chinking, newspaper-wrapped pile on top of the ten-rouble notes.

' What's that ? ' asked Kuzmin, twirling one end of his moustache.

' Don't be squeamish, professor,' whispered the barman. ' You can have anything you want if you'll stop my cancer.'

' Take your gold,' said the professor, feeling proud of himself as he said it. ' You'd be putting it to better use if you spent it on having your nerves treated. Produce a specimen of urine for analysis tomorrow, don't drink too much tea and don't eat any salt in your food.'

' Can't I even put salt in my soup ? ' asked the barman.

' Don't put salt in anything,' said Kuzmin firmly.

' Oh dear . . .' exclaimed the barman gloomily, as he gazed imploringly at the professor, picked up his parcel of gold coins and shuffled backwards to the door.

The professor did not have many patients that evening and as twilight began to set in, the last one was gone. Taking off his white overall, the professor glanced at the place on the desk where Andrei Fokich had left the three ten-rouble notes and saw that there were no longer any bank-notes there, but three old champagne bottle labels instead.

' Well, I'm damned ! ' muttered Kuzmin, trailing the hem of his overall across the floor and fingering the pieces of paper. ' Apparently he's not only a schizophrenic but a crook as well. But what can he have wanted out of me ? Surely not a chit for a urine test ? Ah ! Perhaps he stole my overcoat ! ' The professor dashed into the hall, dragging his overall by one sleeve. ' Xenia

Nikitishna!' he screamed in the hall. 'Will you look and see if my overcoat's in the cupboard?'

It was. But when the professor returned to his desk having finally taken off his overall, he stopped as though rooted to the parquet, staring at the desk. Where the labels had been there now sat a black kitten with a pathetically unhappy little face, miaowing over a saucer of milk.

'What is going on here? This is...' And Kuzmin felt a chill run up his spine.

Hearing the professor's plaintive cry, Xenia Nikitishna came running in and immediately calmed him by saying that the kitten had obviously been abandoned there by one of the patients, a thing they were sometimes prone to do.

'I expect they're poor,' explained Xenia Nikitishna, 'whereas we...'

They tried to guess who might have left the animal there. Suspicion fell on an old woman with a gastric ulcer.

'Yes, it must be her,' said Xenia Nikitishna. 'She'll have thought to herself: I'm going to die anyway, but it's hard on the poor little kitty.'

'Just a moment!' cried Kuzmin. 'What about the milk? Did she bring the milk? And the saucer too?'

'She must have had a saucer and a bottle of milk in her bag and poured it out here,' explained Xenia Nikitishna.

'At any rate remove the kitten and the saucer, please,' said Kuzmin and accompanied Xenia Nikitishna to the door.

As he hung up his overall the professor heard laughter from the courtyard. He looked round and hurried over to the window. A woman, wearing nothing but a shirt, was running across the courtyard to the house opposite. The professor knew her—she was called Marya Alexandrovna. A boy was laughing at her.

'Really, what behaviour,' said Kuzmin contemptuously.

Just then the sound of a gramophone playing a foxtrot came from his daughter's room and at the same moment the professor heard the chirp of a sparrow behind his back. He turned round and saw a large sparrow hopping about on his desk.

' H'm . . . steady now ! ' thought the professor. ' It must have flown in when I walked over to the window. I'm quite all right ! ' said the professor to himself severely, feeling that he was all wrong, thanks to this intruding sparrow. As he looked at it closer, the professor at once realised that it was no ordinary sparrow. The revolting bird was leaning over on its left leg, making faces, waving its other leg in syncopation—in short it was dancing a foxtrot in time to the gramophone, cavorting like a drunk round a lamppost and staring cheekily at the professor.

Kuzmin's hand was on the telephone and he was just about to ring up his old college friend Burye and ask him what it meant to start seeing sparrows at sixty, especially if they made your head spin at the same time.

Meanwhile the sparrow had perched on his presentation inkstand, fouled it, then flew up, hung in the air and dived with shattering force at a photograph showing the whole class of '94 on graduation day, smashing the glass to smithereens. The bird then wheeled smartly and flew out of the window.

The professor changed his mind and instead of ringing up Burye dialled the number of the Leech Bureau and asked them to send a leech to his house at once. Replacing the receiver on the rest, the professor turned back to his desk and let out a wail. On the far side of the desk sat a woman in nurse's uniform with a bag marked ' Leeches '. The sight of her mouth made the professor groan again—it was a wide, crooked, man's mouth with a fang sticking out of it. The nurse's eyes seemed completely dead.

' I'll take the money,' said the nurse, ' it's no good to you now.' She grasped the labels with a bird-like claw and began to melt into the air.

Two hours passed. Professor Kuzmin was sitting up in bed with leeches dangling from his temples, his ears and his neck. At his feet on the buttoned quilt sat the grey-haired Professor

Burye, gazing sympathetically at Kuzmin and comforting him by assuring him that it was all nonsense. Outside it was night.

We do not know what other marvels happened in Moscow that night and we shall not, of course, try to find out—especially as the time is approaching to move into the second half of this true story. Follow me, reader!

BOOK TWO

19. Margarita

Follow me, reader! Who told you that there is no such thing as real, true, eternal love? Cut out his lying tongue!

Follow me, reader, and only me and I will show you that love!

The master was wrong when he told Ivan with such bitterness, in the hospital that hour before midnight, that she had forgotten him. It was impossible. Of course she had not forgotten him.

First let us reveal the secret that the master refused to tell Ivan. His beloved mistress was called Margarita Nikolayevna. Everything the master said about her to the wretched poet was the strict truth. She was beautiful and clever. It is also true that many women would have given anything to change places with Margarita Nikolayevna. Thirty years old and childless, Margarita was married to a brilliant scientist, whose work was of national importance. Her husband was young, handsome, kind, honest and he adored his wife. Margarita Nikolayevna and her husband lived alone in the whole of the top floor of a delightful house in a garden in one of the side streets near the Arbat. It was a charming place. You can see for yourself whenever you feel like having a look. Just ask me and I'll tell you the address and how to get there; the house is standing to this day.

Margarita Nikolayevna was never short of money. She could buy whatever she liked. Her husband had plenty of interesting friends. Margarita never had to cook. Margarita knew nothing of the horrors of living in a shared flat. In short . . . was she happy? Not for a moment. Since the age of nineteen when she had married and moved into her house she had never been happy. Ye gods! What more did the woman need? Why did her eyes always glow with a strange fire? What else did she want, that witch with a very slight squint in one eye, who always decked herself with mimosa every spring? I don't know. Obviously she was right when she said she needed him, the master, instead of a Gothic house, instead of a private garden, instead of money. She was right—she loved him.

Even I, the truthful narrator, yet a mere onlooker, feel a pain when I think what Margarita went through when she came back to the master's basement the next day (fortunately she had not been able to talk to her husband, who failed to come home at the time arranged) and found that the master was not there. She did everything she could to discover where he might be, but in vain. Then she returned home and took up her old life.

But when the dirty snow disappeared from the roads and pavements, as soon as the raw, live wind of spring blew in through the upper casement, Margarita Nikolayevna felt even more wretched than in winter. She often wept in secret, long and bitterly. She had no idea whether her lover was dead or alive. The longer the hopeless days marched on, the oftener, especially at twilight, she began to suspect that her man was dead. She must either forget him or die herself. Her present existence was intolerable. She had to forget him at all costs. But unfortunately he was not a man one could forget.

' Yes, I made exactly the same mistake,' said Margarita, sitting by the stove and watching the fire, lit in memory of the fire that used to burn while he was writing about Pontius Pilate. ' Why did I leave him that night? Why? I must have been mad. I came back the next day just as I had promised, but it was too late. Yes, I came too late like poor Matthew the Levite!'

All this, of course, was nonsense, because what would have been changed if she had stayed with the master that night? Would she have saved him? The idea's absurd . . . but she was a woman and she was desperate.

On the same day that witnessed the ridiculous scandal caused by the black magician's appearance in Moscow, that Friday when Berlioz's uncle was sent packing back to Kiev, when the accountant was arrested and a host of other weird and improbable events took place, Margarita woke up around midday in her bedroom, that looked out of an attic window of their top-floor flat.

Waking, Margarita did not burst into tears, as she frequently did, because she had woken up with a presentiment that today, at last, something was going to happen. She kept the feeling warm and encouraged it, afraid that it might leave her.

' I believe it ! ' whispered Margarita solemnly. ' I believe something is going to happen, must happen, because what have I done to be made to suffer all my life ? I admit I've lied and been unfaithful and lived a secret life, but even that doesn't deserve such a cruel punishment . . . something will happen, because a situation like this can't drag on for ever. Besides, my dream was prophetic, that I'll swear. . . .'

With a sense of unease Margarita Nikolayevna dressed and brushed her short curly hair in front of her triple dressing-table mirror.

The dream that Margarita had dreamed that night had been most unusual. Throughout her agony of the past winter she had never dreamed of the master. At night he left her and it was only during the day that her memory tormented her. And now she had dreamed of him.

Margarita had dreamed of a place, mournful, desolate under a dull sky of early spring. The sky was leaden, with tufts of low, scudding grey cloud and filled with a numberless flock of rooks. There was a little hump-backed bridge over a muddy, swollen stream ; joyless, beggarly, half-naked trees. A lone aspen, and in the distance, past a vegetable garden stood a log cabin that looked like a kind of outhouse. The surroundings looked so life-less and miserable that one might easily have been tempted to hang oneself on that aspen by the little bridge. Not a breath of wind, not a cloud, not a living soul. In short—hell. Suddenly the door of this hut was flung open and he appeared in it, at a fair distance but clearly visible. He was dressed in some vague, slightly tattered garment, hair in untidy tufts, unshaven. His eyes looked anxious and sick. He waved and called. Panting in the lifeless air, Margarita started running towards him over the uneven, tussocky ground. At that moment she woke up.

' That dream can only mean one of two things,' Margarita Nikolayevna reasoned with herself, ' if he is dead and beckoned me that means that he came for me and I shall die soon. If so, I'm glad ; that means that my agony will soon be over. Or if he's alive, the dream can only mean that he is reminding me of himself. He wants to tell me that we shall meet again . . . yes, we shall meet again—soon.'

Still in a state of excitement, Margarita dressed, telling herself that everything was working out very well, that one should know how to seize such moments and make use of them. Her husband had gone away on business for three whole days. She was left to herself for three days and no one was going to stop her thinking or dreaming of whatever she wished. All five rooms on the top floor of the house, a flat so big that tens of thousands of people in Moscow would have envied her, was entirely at her disposal.

Yet free as she was for three days in such luxurious quarters, Margarita chose the oddest part of it in which to spend her time. After a cup of tea she went into their dark, windowless attic where they kept the trunks, the lumber and two large chests of drawers full of old junk. Squatting down she opened the bottom drawer of the first chest and from beneath a pile of odds and ends of material she drew out the one thing which she valued most of all. It was an old album bound in brown leather, which contained a photograph of the master, a savings bank book with a deposit of ten thousand roubles in his name, a few dried rose petals pressed between some pieces of cigarette paper and several sheets of typescript with singed edges.

Returning to her bedroom with this treasure, Margarita Nikolayevna propped up the photograph against her dressing-table mirror and sat for about an hour, the burnt typescript on her knees, turning the pages and re-reading what the fire had not destroyed : ' . . . The mist that came from the Mediterranean sea blotted out the city that Pilate so detested. The suspension bridges connecting the temple with the grim fortress of Antonia vanished, the murk descended from the sky and drowned the winged gods above the hippodrome, the crenellated Hasmonaean palace, the bazaars, the caravanserai, the alleyways, the pools . . . Jerusalem, the great city, vanished as though it had never been. . . .'

Margarita wanted to read on, but there was nothing more except the charred, uneven edge.

Wiping away her tears, Margarita Nikolayevna put down the script, leaned her elbows on the dressing-table and sat for a long time in front of her reflection in the mirror staring at the photograph. After a while she stopped crying. Margarita carefully folded away her hoard, a few minutes later it was buried again under the scraps of silk and the lock shut with a click in the dark room.

Margarita put on her overcoat in the hall to go out for a walk. Her pretty maid Natasha enquired what she was to do tomorrow and being told that she could do what she liked, she started talking to her mistress to pass the time and mentioned something vague about a magician who had done such fantastic tricks in the theatre yesterday that everybody had gasped, that he had handed out two bottles of French perfume and two pairs of stockings to everybody for nothing and then, when the show was over and the audience was coming out—bang!—they were all naked! Margarita Nikolayevna collapsed on to the hall chair and burst out laughing.

'Natasha, really! Aren't you ashamed of yourself?' said Margarita. 'You're a sensible, educated girl . . . and you repeat every bit of rubbishy gossip that you pick up in queues!'

Natasha blushed and objected hotly, saying that she never listened to queue gossip and that she had actually seen a woman that morning come into a delicatessen on the Arbat wearing some new shoes and while she was standing at the cash desk to pay, her shoes had vanished and she was left standing in her stockinged feet. She looked horrified, because she had a hole in the heel of one stocking! The shoes were the magic ones that she had got at the show.

' And she walked out barefoot ? '

' Yes, she did! ' cried Natasha, turning even pinker because no one would believe her. ' And yesterday evening, Margarita Nikolayevna, the police arrested a hundred people. Some of the women who'd been at the show were running along the Tverskaya in nothing but a pair of panties.'

' That sounds to me like one of your friend Darya's stories,' said Margarita Nikolayevna. ' I've always thought she was a frightful liar.'

This hilarious conversation ended with a pleasant surprise for Natasha. Margarita Nikolayevna went into her bedroom and came out with a pair of stockings and a bottle of eau-de-cologne. Saying to Natasha that she wanted to do a magic trick too, Margarita gave her the stockings and the scent; she told her that she could have them on one condition—that she promised not to run along the Tverskaya in nothing but stockings and not to listen to Darya's gossip. With a kiss mistress and maid parted.

Leaning back on her comfortable upholstered seat in the trolley-bus, Margarita Nikolayevna rolled along the Arbat, thinking of her own affairs and half-listening to what two men on the seat in front were whispering. Glancing round occasionally for fear of being overheard, they seemed to be talking complete nonsense. One, a plump, hearty man with sharp pig-like eyes, who was sitting by the window, was quietly telling his smaller neighbour how they had been forced to cover the open coffin with a black cloth . . .

' Incredible! ' whispered the little one in amazement. ' It's unheard-of! So what did Zheldybin do ? '

Above the steady hum of the trolley-bus came the reply from the window seat :

' Police . . . scandal . . . absolute mystery ! '

Somehow Margarita Nikolayevna managed to construct a fairly coherent story from these snatches of talk. The men were whispering that someone had stolen the head of a corpse (they did not mention the dead man's name) from a coffin that morning. This, apparently, was the cause of Zheldybin's anxiety and the two men whispering in the trolley-bus also appeared to have some connection with the victim of this ghoulish burglary.

'Shall we have time to buy some flowers?' enquired the smaller man anxiously. 'You said the cremation was at two o'clock, didn't you?'

In the end Margarita Nikolayevna grew bored with their mysterious whispering about the stolen head and she was glad when it was time for her to get out.

A few minutes later she was sitting under the Kremlin wall on one of the benches in the Alexander Gardens facing the Manège. Margarita squinted in the bright sunlight, recalling her dream and she remembered that exactly a year ago to the hour she had sat on this same bench beside him. Just as it had then, her black handbag lay on the bench at her side. Although the master was not there this time, Margarita Nikolayevna carried on a mental conversation with him : ' If you've been sent into exile why haven't you at least written to tell me? Don't you love me any more? No, somehow I don't believe that. In that case you have died in exile . . .' If you have, please release me, let me go free to lead my life like other people!' Margarita answered for him : 'You're free . . . I'm not keeping you by force.' Then she replied : 'What sort of an answer is that? I won't be free until I stop thinking of you . . .'

People were walking past. One man gave a sideways glance at this well-dressed woman. Attracted by seeing a pretty girl alone, he coughed and sat down on Margarita Nikolayevna's half of the bench. Plucking up his courage he said :

'What lovely weather it is today . . .'

Margarita turned and gave him such a grim look that he got up and went away.

'That's what I mean,' said Margarita silently to her lover. 'Why did I chase that man away? I'm bored, there was nothing wrong with that Casanova, except perhaps for his highly unoriginal remark . . . Why do I sit here alone like an owl ? Why am I cut off from life ? '

She had worked herself into a state of complete depression, when suddenly the same wave of urgent expectancy that she had felt that morning overcame her again. ' Yes, something's going to happen ! ' The wave struck her again and she then realised that it was a wave of sound. Above the noise of traffic there clearly came the sound of approaching drum-beats and the braying of some off-key trumpets.

First to pass the park railings was a mounted policeman, followed by three more on foot. Next came the band on a lorry, then a slow-moving open hearse carrying a coffin banked with wreaths and a guard of honour of four people—three men and a woman. Even from a distance Margarita could see that the members of the guard of honour looked curiously distraught. This was particularly noticeable in the woman, who was standing at the left-hand rear corner of the hearse. Her fat cheeks seemed to be more than normally puffed out by some secret joke and her protuberant little eyes shone with a curiously ambiguous sparkle. It was as if the woman was liable at any moment to wink at the corpse and say ' Did you ever see such a thing ? Stealing a dead man's head . . . ! ' The three hundred-odd mourners, who were slowly following the cortège on foot, looked equally mystified.

Margarita watched the cortège go by, listening to the mournful beat of the kettle-drum as its monotonous ' boom, boom, boom' slowly faded away and she thought : ' What a strange funeral . . . and how sad that drum sounds ! I'd sell my soul to the devil to know whether he's alive or not . . . I wonder who that odd-looking crowd is going to bury ? '

' Mikhail Alexandrovich Berlioz,' said a slightly nasal man's voice beside her, ' the late chairman of MASSOLIT.'

Margarita Nikolayevna turned in astonishment and saw a man on her bench who must have sat down noiselessly while she had been watching the funeral procession. Presumably she had absentmindedly spoken her last question aloud. Meanwhile the procession had stopped, apparently held up by the traffic lights.

' Yes,' the stranger went on, ' it's an odd sort of funeral. They're carrying the man off to the cemetery in the usual way but all they can think about is—what's happened to his head ? '

' Whose head ? ' asked Margarita, glancing at her unexpected neighbour. He was short, with fiery red hair and one protruding fang, wearing a starched shirt, a good striped suit, patent-leather shoes and a bowler hat. His tie was bright. One strange feature was his breast pocket : instead of the usual handkerchief or fountain pen, it contained a gnawed chicken bone.

' This morning,' explained the red-haired man, ' the head was pulled off the dead man's body during the lying-in-state at Griboyedov.'

' How ever could that have happened ? ' asked Margarita, suddenly remembering the two whispering men in the trolley-bus.

' Devil knows how,' said the man vaguely. ' I suspect Behemoth might be able to tell you. It must have been a neat job, but why bother to steal a head ? After all, who on earth would want it ? '

Preoccupied though she was, Margarita Nikolayevna could not help being intrigued by this stranger's extraordinary conversation.

' Just a minute ! ' she suddenly exclaimed. ' Who is Berlioz ? Is he the one in the newspapers today who . . .'

' Yes, yes.'

' So those were writers in the guard of honour round the coffin ? ' enquired Margarita, suddenly baring her teeth.

' Yes, of course . . .'

' Do you know them by sight ? '

' Every one,' the man replied.

' Tell me,' said Margarita, her voice dropping, ' is one of them a critic by the name of Latunsky ? '

' How could he fail to be there ? ' answered the man with red hair. ' That's him, on the far side of the fourth rank.'

' The one with fair hair ? ' asked Margarita, frowning.

' Ash-blond. Look, he's staring up at the sky.'

' Looking rather like a Catholic priest ? '

' That's him ! '

Margarita asked no more questions but stared hard at Latunsky.

'You, I see,' said the stranger with a smile, 'hate that man Latunsky. 'Yes, and someone else too,' said Margarita between clenched teeth, 'but I'd rather not talk about it.'

Meanwhile the procession had moved on again, the mourners being followed by a number of mostly empty cars.

'Then we won't discuss it, Margarita Nikolayevna!'

Astounded, Margarita said:

'Do you know me?'

Instead of replying the man took off his bowler hat and held it in his outstretched hand.

'A face like a crook,' thought Margarita, as she stared at him.

'But I don't know you,' she said frigidly.

'Why should you? However, I have been sent on a little matter that concerns you.'

Margarita paled and edged away. 'Why didn't you say so at once,' she said, 'instead of making up that fairy tale about a stolen head? Have you come to arrest me?'

'Nothing of the sort!' exclaimed the man with red hair. 'Why does one only have to speak to a person for them to imagine they're going to be arrested? I simply have a little matter to discuss with you.'

'I don't understand—what matter?'

The stranger glanced round and said mysteriously:

'I have been sent to give you an invitation for this evening.'

'What are you talking about? What invitation?'

'You are invited by a very distinguished foreign gentleman,' said the red-haired man portentously, with a frown.

Margarita blazed with anger.

'I see that pimps work in the streets now!' she said as she got up to go.

'Is that all the thanks I get?' exclaimed the man, offended. And he growled at Margarita's retreating back:

'Stupid bitch!'

'Swine!' she flung back at him over her shoulder.

Immediately she heard the stranger's voice behind her:

' The mist that came from the Mediterranean sea blotted out the city that Pilate so detested. The suspension bridges connecting the temple with the grim fortress of Antonia vanished, the murk descended from the sky and drowned the winged gods above the hippodrome, the crenellated Hasmonaean palace, the bazaars, the caravanserai, the alleyways, the pools. . . . Jerusalem, the great city, vanished as though it had never been. . . . So much for your charred manuscript and your dried rose petals ! Yet you sit here alone on a bench and beg him to let you go, to allow you to be free and to forget him ! '

White in the face, Margarita turned back to the bench. The man sat frowning at her.

' I don't understand it,' said Margarita Nikolayevna in a hushed voice. ' You might have found out about the manuscript . . . you might have broken in, stolen it, looked at it . . . I suppose you bribed Natasha. But how could you know what I was thinking ? ' She wrinkled her brow painfully and added ' Tell me, who are you ? What organisation do you belong to ? '

' Oh, lord, not that . . .' muttered the stranger in exasperation. In a louder voice he said : 'I'm sorry. As I said, I have not come to arrest you and I don't belong to any " organisation." Please sit down.'

Margarita obediently did as she was told, but once seated could not help asking again :

' Who are you ? '

' Well if you must know my name is Azazello, although it won't mean anything to you.'

' And won't you tell me how you knew about the manuscript and how you read my thoughts ? '

' I will not,' said Azazello curtly.

' Do you know anything about *him* ? ' whispered Margarita imploringly.

' Well, let's say I do.'

' Tell me, I beg of you, just one thing—is he alive ? Don't torture me ! '

' Yes, he's alive all right,' said Azazello reluctantly.

'Oh, God!'

'No scenes, please,' said Azazello with a frown.

'I'm sorry, I'm sorry,' said Margarita humbly. 'I'm sorry I lost my temper with you. But you must admit that if someone comes up to a woman in the street and invites her . . . I have no prejudices, I assure you.' Margarita laughed mirthlessly. 'But I never meet foreigners and I have never wanted to . . . besides that, my husband . . . my tragedy is that I live with a man I don't love . . . but I can't bring myself to ruin his life . . . he has never shown me anything but kindness . . .'

Azazello listened to this incoherent confession and said severely:

'Please be quiet for a moment.'

Margarita obediently stopped talking.

'My invitation to this foreigner is quite harmless. And not a soul will know about it. That I swear.'

'And what does he want me for?' asked Margarita insinuatingly.

'You will discover that later.'

'I see now . . . I am to go to bed with him,' said Margarita thoughtfully.

To this Azazello snorted and replied:

'Any woman in the world, I can assure you, would give anything to do so'—his face twisted with a laugh—'but I must disappoint you. He doesn't want you for that.'

'Who is this foreigner?' exclaimed Margarita in perplexity, so loudly that several passers-by turned to look at her. 'And why should I want to go and see him?'

Azazello leaned towards her and whispered meaningly:

'For the best possible reason . . . you can use the opportunity . . .'

'What?' cried Margarita, her eyes growing round. 'If I've understood you correctly, you're hinting that I may hear some news of him there?'

Azazello nodded silently.

'I'll go!' Margarita burst out and seized Azazello by the arm. 'I'll go wherever you like!'

With a sigh of relief Azazello leaned against the back of the bench, covering up the name 'Manya' carved deep into its wood, and said ironically: 'Difficult people, these woman!' He stuck his hands into his pockets and stretched his feet out far in front of him. 'Why did he have to send me on this job? Behemoth should have done it, he's got such charm . . .'

With a bitter smile Margarita said:

'Stop mystifying me and talking in riddles. I'm happy and you're making use of it . . . I may be about to let myself in for some dubious adventure, but I swear it's only because you have enticed me by talking about him! All this mystery is making my head spin . . .'

'Please don't make a drama out of it,' replied Azazello with a grimace. 'Think of what it's like being in my position. Punch a man on the nose, kick an old man downstairs, shoot somebody or any old thing like that, that's my job. But argue with women in love—no thank you! Look, I've been at it with you for half an hour now . . . Are you going or not?'

'I'll go,' replied Margarita Nikolayevna simply.

'In that case allow me to present you with this,' said Azazello, taking a little round gold box out of his pocket and saying as he handed it to Margarita: 'Hide it, or people will see it. It will do you good, Margarita Nikolayevna; unhappiness has aged you a lot in the last six months—' Margarita bridled but said nothing,. and Azazello went on: 'This evening, at exactly half past eight, you will kindly strip naked and rub this ointment all over your face and your body. After that you can do what you like, but don't go far from the telephone. At nine I shall ring you up and tell you what you have to do. You won't have to worry about anything, you'll be taken to where you're going and nothing will be done to upset you. Understood?'

Margarita said nothing for a moment, then replied:

'I understand. This thing is solid gold, I can tell by its weight. I quite see that I am being seduced into something shady which I shall bitterly regret . . .'

'What's that?' Azazello almost hissed. 'You're not having second thoughts are you?'

'No, no, wait!'

'Give me back the cream!'

Margarita gripped the box tighter and went on:

'No, please wait . . . I know what I'm letting myself in for. I'm ready to go anywhere and do anything for his sake, only because I have no more hope left. But if you are planning to ruin or destroy me, you will regret it. Because if I die for his sake I shall have died out of love.'

'Give it back!' shouted Azazello in fury. 'Give it back and to hell with the whole business. They can send Behemoth!'

'Oh, no!' cried Margarita to the astonishment of the passers-by. 'I agree to everything, I'll go through the whole pantomime of smearing on the ointment, I'll go to the ends of the earth! I won't give it back!'

'Bah!' Azazello suddenly roared and staring at the park railings, pointed at something with his finger.

Margarita turned in the direction that he was pointing, but saw nothing in particular. Then she turned to Azazello for some explanation of his absurd cry of 'Bah!', but there was no one to explain : Margarita Nikolayevna's mysterious companion had vanished.

Margarita felt in her handbag and made sure that the gold box was still where she had put it. Then without stopping to reflect she hurried away from the Alexander Gardens.

20. *Azazello's Cream*

Through the branches of the maple tree a full moon hung in the clear evening sky. The limes and acacias traced a complex pattern of shadows on the grass. A triple casement window in the attic, open but with the blind drawn, shone with a glare of electric light. Every lamp was burning in Margarita Nikolayevna's bedroom and lighting up the chaotically untidy room.

On the bedspread lay blouses, stockings and underwear, more crumpled underwear was piled on the floor beside a packet of cigarettes that had been squashed in the excitement. A pair of slippers was on the bedside table alongside a cold, unfinished cup of coffee and an ashtray with a smouldering cigarette end. A black silk dress hung across the chairback. The room smelled of perfume and from somewhere there came the reek of a hot iron.

Margarita Nikolayevna was sitting in front of a full-length mirror in nothing but black velvet slippers, a bath-wrap thrown over her naked body. Her gold wrist-watch lay in front of her alongside the little box given her by Azazello, and Margarita was staring at the watch-face.

At times she felt that the watch had broken and the hands were not moving. They were moving, but so slowly that they seemed to have stuck. At last the minute hand pointed to twenty nine minutes past eight. Margarita's heart was thumping so violently that at first she could hardly pick up the box. With an effort she opened it and saw that it contained a greasy yellowish cream. It seemed to smell of swamp mud. With the tip of her finger Margarita put a little blob of the cream on her palm, which produced an even stronger smell of marsh and forest, and then she began to massage the cream into her forehead and cheeks.

The ointment rubbed in easily and produced an immediate tingling effect. After several rubs Margarita looked into the mirror and dropped the box right on to the watch-glass, which shivered into a web of fine cracks. Margarita shut her eyes, then looked again and burst into hoots of laughter.

Her eyebrows that she had so carefully plucked into a fine line had thickened into two regular arcs above her eyes, which had taken on a deeper green colour. The fine vertical furrow between her eyebrows which had first appeared in October when the master disappeared, had vanished without trace. Gone too were the yellowish shadows at her temples and two barely detectable sets of crowsfeet round the corners of her eyes. The skin of her cheeks was evenly suffused with pink, her brow had become white and smooth and the frizzy, artificial wave in her hair had straightened out.

A dark, naturally curly-haired woman of twenty, teeth bared and laughing uncontrollably, was looking out of the mirror at the thirty-year-old Margarita.

Laughing, Margarita jumped out of her bath-wrap with one leap, scooped out two large handfuls of the slightly fatty cream and began rubbing it vigorously all over her body. She immediately glowed and turned a healthy pink. In a moment her headache stopped, after having pained her all day since the encounter in the Alexander Gardens. The muscles of her arms and legs grew firmer and she even lost weight.'

She jumped and stayed suspended in the air just above the carpet, then slowly and gently dropped back to the ground.

' Hurray for the cream ! ' cried Margarita, throwing herself into an armchair.

The anointing had not only changed her appearance. Joy surged through every part of her body, she felt as though bubbles were shooting along every limb. Margarita felt free, free of everything, realising with absolute clarity that what was happening was the fulfilment of her presentiment of that morning, that she was going to leave her house and her past life for ever. But one thought from her past life hammered persistently in her mind and she knew that she had one last duty to perform before she took off into the unknown, into the air. Naked as she was she ran out of the bedroom, flying through the air, and into her husband's study, where she turned on the light and flew to his desk. She tore a sheet off his note-pad and in one sweep, erasing nothing and changing nothing, she quickly and firmly pencilled this message :

Forgive me and forget me as quickly as you can. I am leaving you for ever. Don't look for me, it will be useless. Misery and unhappiness have turned me into a witch. It is time for me to go. Farewell. Margarita.

With a sense of absolute relief Margarita flew back into the bedroom. Just then Natasha came in, loaded with clothes and shoes. At once the whole pile, dresses on coathangers, lace blouses, blue silk shoes on shoe trees, belts, all fell on to the floor and Natasha clasped her hands.

' Pretty, aren't I ? ' cried Margarita Nikolayevna in a loud, slightly husky voice.

' What's happened ? ' whispered Natasha, staggering back. ' What have you done, Margarita Nikolayevna ? '

' It's the cream ! The cream ! ' replied Margarita, pointing to the gleaming gold box and twirling round in front of the mirror. Forgetting the heap of crumpled clothes on the floor, Natasha ran to the dressing table and stared, eyes hot with longing, at the remains of the ointment. Her lips whispered a few words in silence. She turned to Margarita and said with something like awe :

' Oh, your skin—look at your skin, Margarita Nikolayevna, it's shining ! ' Then she suddenly remembered herself, picked up the dress she had dropped and started to smooth it out.

' Leave it, Natasha ! Drop it ! ' Margarita shouted at her. ' To hell with it ! Throw it all away ! No—wait—you can have it all. As a present from me. You can have everything there is in the room ! '

Dumbfounded, Natasha gazed at Margarita for a while then clasped her round the neck, kissing her and shouting :

' You're like satin ! Shiny satin ! And look at your eyebrows ! '

' Take all these rags, take all my scent and put it all in your bottom drawer, you can keep it,' shouted Margarita. ' but don't take the jewellery or they'll say you stole it.'

Natasha rummaged in the heap for whatever she could pick up—stockings, shoes, dresses and underwear—and ran out of the bedroom.

At that moment from an open window on the other side of the street came the loud strains of a waltz and the spluttering of a car engine as it drew up at the gate.

' Azazello will ring soon ! ' cried Margarita, listening to the sound of the waltz. ' He's going to ring ! And this foreigner is harmless, I realise now that he can never harm me ! '

The car's engine roared as it accelerated away. The gate slammed and footsteps could be heard on the flagged path.

' It's Nikolai Ivanovich, I recognise his tread,' thought Margarita. ' I must do something funny as a way of saying goodbye to him ! '

Margarita flung the shutters open and sat sideways on the windowsill, clasping her knees with her hands. The moonlight caressed her right side. Margarita raised her head towards the moon and put on a reflective and poetic face. Two more footsteps were heard and then they suddenly stopped. With another admiring glance at the moon and a sigh for fun, Margarita turned to look down at the garden, where she saw her neighbour of the floor below, Nikolai Ivanovich. He was clearly visible in the moonlight, sitting on a bench on which he had obviously just sat down with a bump. His pince-nez was lop-sided and he was clutching his briefcase in his arms.

' Hullo, Nikolai Ivanovich ! ' said Margarita Nikolayevna in a sad voice. ' Good evening ! Have you just come from the office ? '

Nikolai Ivanovich said nothing.

' And here am I,' Margarita went on, leaning further out into the garden, ' sitting all alone as you can see, bored, looking at the moon and listening to a waltz . . .'

Margarita Nikolayevna ran her left hand along her temple, arranging a lock of hair, then said crossly :

' It's very impolite of you, Nikolai Ivanovich ! I am a woman, after all ! It's rude not to answer when someone speaks to you.'

Nikolai Ivanovich, visible in the bright moonlight down to the last button on his grey waistcoat and the last hair on his little pointed beard, suddenly gave an idiotic grin and got up from his bench. Obviously half-crazed with embarrassment, instead of taking off his hat he waved his briefcase and flexed his knees as though just about to break into a Russian dance.

' Oh how you bore me, Nikolai Ivanovich ! ' Margarita went on. ' You all bore me inexpressibly and I can't tell you how happy I am to be leaving you ! You can all go to hell ! '

Just then the telephone rang in Margarita's bedroom. She slipped off the windowsill and forgetting Nikolai Ivanovich completely she snatched up the receiver.

' Azazello speaking,' said a voice.

' Dear, dear Azazello,' cried Margarita.

' It's time for you to fly away,' said Azazello and she could hear from his tone that he was pleased by Margarita's sincere outburst of affection. ' As you fly over the gate shout " I'm invisible "—then fly about over the town a bit to get used to it and then turn south, away from Moscow straight along the river. They're waiting for you ! '

Margarita hung up and at once something wooden in the next room started bumping about and tapping on the door. Margarita flung it open and a broom, bristles upward, danced into the bedroom. Its handle beat a tattoo on the floor, tipped itself up horizontally and pointed towards the window. Margarita whimpered with joy and jumped astride the broomstick. Only then did she remember that in the excitement she had forgotten to get dressed. She galloped over to the bed and picked up the first thing to hand, which was a blue slip. Waving it like a banner she flew out of the window. The waltz rose to a crescendo.

Margarita dived down from the window and saw Nikolai Ivanovich sitting on the bench. He seemed to be frozen to it, listening stunned to the shouts and bangs that had been coming from the top-floor bedroom.

' Goodbye, Nikolai Ivanovich ! ' cried Margarita, dancing about in front of him.

The wretched man groaned, fidgeted and dropped his briefcase.

' Farewell for ever, Nikolai Ivanovich ! I'm flying away ! ' shouted Margarita, drowning the music of the waltz. Realising that her slip was useless she gave a malicious laugh and threw it over Nikolai Ivanovich's head. Blinded, Nikolai Ivanovich fell off the bench on to the flagged path with a crash.

Margarita turned round for a last look at the house where she had spent so many years of unhappiness and saw the astonished face of Natasha in the lighted window.

' Goodbye, Natasha ! ' Margarita shouted, waving her broom. ' I'm invisible ! Invisible ! ' she shouted at the top of her voice as she flew off, the maple branches whipping her face, over the gate and out into the street. Behind her flew the strains of the waltz, rising to a mad crescendo.

21. *The Flight*

Invisible and free ! Reaching the end of her street, Margarita turned sharp right and flew on down a long, crooked street with its plane trees and its patched roadway, its oil-shop with a warped door where they sold kerosene by the jugful and the bottled juice of parasites. Here Margarita discovered that although she was invisible, free as air and thoroughly enjoying herself, she still had to take care. Stopping herself by a miracle she just avoided a lethal collison with an old, crooked lamp-post. As she swerved away from it, Margarita gripped her broomstick harder and flew on more slowly, glancing at the passing signboards and electric cables.

The next street led straight to the Arbat. By now she had thoroughly mastered the business of steering her broom, having found that it answered to the slightest touch of her hands or legs and that when flying around the town she had to be very careful to avoid collisions. It was now quite obvious that the people in the street could not see her. Nobody turned their head, nobody shouted ' Look, look ! ', nobody stepped aside, nobody screamed, fell in a faint or burst into laughter.

Margarita flew silently and very slowly at about second-storey height. Slow as her progress was, however, she made slightly too wide a sweep as she flew into the blindingly-lit Arbat and hit her shoulder against an illuminated glass traffic sign. This annoyed her. She stopped the obedient broomstick, flew back, aimed for the sign and with a sudden flick of the end of her broom, smashed it to fragments. The pieces crashed to the ground, passers-by jumped aside, a whistle blew and Margarita burst into laughter at her little act of wanton destruction.

' I shall have to be even more careful on the Arbat,' she

thought to herself. ' There are so many obstructions, it's like a maze.' She began weaving between the cables. Beneath her flowed the roofs of trolley-buses, buses and cars, and rivers of hats surged along the pavements. Little streams diverged from these rivers and trickled into the lighted caves of all-night stores.

' What a maze,' thought Margarita crossly. ' There's no room to manoeuvre here ! '

She crossed the Arbat, climbed to fourth-floor height, past the brilliant neon tubes of a corner theatre and turned into a narrow side-street flanked with tall houses. All their windows were open and radio music poured out from all sides. Out of curiosity Margarita glanced into one of them. She saw a kitchen. Two Primuses were roaring away on a marble ledge, attended by two women standing with spoons in their hands and swearing at each other.

' You should put the light out when you come out of the lavatory, I've told you before, Pelagea Petrovna,' said the woman with a saucepan of some steaming decoction, ' otherwise we'll have you chucked out of here.'

' You can't talk,' replied the other.

' You're both as bad as each other,' said Margarita clearly, leaning over the windowsill into the kitchen.

The two quarrelling women stopped at the sound of her voice and stood petrified, clutching their dirty spoons. Margarita carefully stretched out her arm between them and turned off both primuses. The women gasped. But Margarita was already bored with this prank and had flown out again into the street.

Her attention was caught by a massive and obviously newly-built eight-storey block of flats at the far end of the street. Margarita flew towards it and as she landed she saw that the building was faced with black marble, that its doors were wide, that a porter in gold-laced peaked cap and buttons stood in the hall. Over the doorway was a gold inscription reading ' Dramlit House '.

Margarita frowned at the inscription, wondering what the word 'Dramlit' could mean. Tucking her broomstick under her arm, Margarita pushed open the front door, to the amazement of the porter, walked in and saw a huge black notice-board that listed the names and flat numbers of all the residents. The inscription over the name-board, reading 'Drama and Literature House,' made Margarita give a suppressed yelp of predatory anticipation. Rising a little in the air, she began eagerly to read the names: Khustov, Dvubratsky, Quant, Beskudnikov, Latunsky . . .

'Latunsky!' yelped Margarita. 'Latunsky! He's the man . . . who ruined the master!'

The porter jumped up in astonishment and stared at the name-board, wondering why it had suddenly given a shriek.

Margarita was already flying upstairs, excitedly repeating :

'Latunsky, eighty-four . . . Latunsky, eighty-four . . . Here we are, left—eighty-two, right—eighty-three, another floor up, left—eighty-four ! Here it is and there's his name—" O. Latunsky ".'

Margarita jumped off her broomstick and the cold stone floor of the landing felt pleasantly cool to her hot bare feet. She rang once, twice. No answer. Margarita pressed the button harder and heard the bell ringing far inside Latunsky's flat. Latunsky should have been grateful to his dying day that the chairman of MASSOLIT had fallen under a tramcar and that the memorial gathering was being held that very evening. Latunsky must have been born under a lucky star, because the coincidence saved him from an encounter with Margarita, newly turned witch that Friday.

No one came to open the door. At full speed Margarita flew down, counting the floors as she went, reached the bottom, flew out into the street and looked up. She counted the floors and tried to guess which of the windows belonged to Latunsky's flat. Without a doubt they were the five unlighted windows on the eighth floor at the corner of the building. Feeling sure that she was right, Margarita flew up and a few seconds later found her way through an open window into a dark room lit only by a silver patch of moonlight. Margarita walked across and fumbled tor the switch. Soon all the lights in the flat were burning. Parking her broom in a corner and making sure that nobody was at home, Margarita opened the front door and looked at the nameplate. This was it.

People say that Latunsky still turns pale when he remembers that evening and that he always pronounces Berlioz's name with gratitude. If he had been at home God knows what violence might have been done that night.

Margarita went into the kitchen and came out with a massive hammer.

Naked and invisible, unable to restrain herself, her hands shook with impatience. Margarita took careful aim and hit the keys of the grand piano, sending a crashing discord echoing through the flat. The innocent piano, a Bäcker baby grand, howled and sobbed. With the sound of a revolver shot, the polished sounding-board split under a hammer-blow. Breathing hard, Margarita smashed and battered the strings until she collapsed into an armchair to rest.

An ominous sound of water came from the kitchen and the bathroom. 'It must be overflowing by now . . .' thought Margarita and added aloud:

'But there's no time to sit and gloat.'

A flood was already pouring from the kitchen into the passage. Wading barefoot, Margarita carried buckets of water into the critic's study, and emptied them into the drawers of his desk. Then having smashed the glass-fronted bookcase with a few hammer-blows, she ran into the bedroom. There she shattered the mirror in the wardrobe door, pulled out all Latunsky's suits and flung them into the bathtub. She found a large bottle of ink in the study and poured its contents all over the huge, luxurious double bed.

Although all this destruction was giving her the deepest pleasure, she somehow felt that its total effect was inadequate and too easily repaired.

She grew wilder and more indiscriminate. In the room with the piano, she smashed the flower vases and the pots holding rubber plants. With savage delight she rushed into the bedroom with a cook's knife, slashed all the sheets and broke the glass in the photograph frames. Far from feeling tired, she wielded her weapon with such ferocity that the sweat poured in streams down her naked body.

Meanwhile in No. 82, immediately beneath Latunsky's flat, Quant's maid was drinking a cup of tea in the kitchen and wondering vaguely why there was so much noise and running about upstairs. Looking up at the ceiling she suddenly saw it change colour from white to a deathly grey-blue. The patch spread visibly and it began to spout drops of water. The maid sat there for a few minutes, bewildered at this phenomenon, until a regular shower began raining down from the ceiling and pattering on the floor. She jumped up and put a bowl under the stream, but it was useless as the shower was spreading and was already pouring over the gas stove and the dresser. With a shriek Quant's maid ran out of the flat on to the staircase and started ringing Latunsky's front-door bell.

' Ah, somebody's ringing . . . time to go,' said Margarita. She mounted the broom, listening to a woman's voice shouting through the keyhole.

' Open up, open up ! Open the door, Dusya ! Your water's overflowing ! We're being flooded ! '

Margarita flew up a few feet and took a swing at the chandelier. Two lamps broke and glass fragments flew everywhere. The shouts at the keyhole had stopped and there was a tramp of boots on the staircase. Margarita floated out of the window, where she turned and hit the glass a gentle blow with her hammer. It shattered and cascaded in smithereens down the marble façade on to the street below. Margarita flew on to the next window. Far below people were running about on the pavement, and one of the cars standing outside the entrance started up and drove away.

Having dealt with all Latunsky's windows, Margarita floated

on towards the next flat. The blows became more frequent, the street resounded with bangs and tinkles. The porter ran out of the front door, looked up, hesitated for a moment in amazement, popped a whistle into his mouth and blew like a maniac. The noise inspired Margarita to even more violent action on the eighth-floor windows and then to drop down a storey and to start work on the seventh.

Bored by his idle job of hanging around the entrance hall, the porter put all his pent-up energy into blowing his whistle, playing a woodwind obbligato in time to Margarita's enthusiastic percussion. In the intervals as she moved from window to window, he drew breath and then blew an ear-splitting blast from distended cheeks at each stroke of Margarita's hammer. Their combined efforts produced the most impressive results. Panic broke out in Dramlit House. The remaining unbroken window-panes were flung open, heads were popped out and instantly withdrawn, whilst open windows were hastily shut. At the lighted windows of the building opposite appeared figures, straining forward to try and see why for no reason all the windows of Dramlit House were spontaneously exploding.

All along the street people began running towards Dramlit House and inside it others were pelting senselessly up and down the staircase. The Quants' maid shouted to them that they were being flooded out and she was soon joined by the Khustovs' maid from No. 80 which lay underneath the Quants'. Water was pouring through the Khustovs' ceiling into the bathroom and the kitchen. Finally an enormous chunk of plaster crashed down from Quants' kitchen ceiling, smashing all the dirty crockery on the draining-board and letting loose a deluge as though someone upstairs were pouring out buckets of dirty rubbish and lumps of sodden plaster. Meanwhile a chorus of shouts came from the staircase.

Flying past the last window but one on the fourth floor, Margarita glanced into it and saw a panic-stricken man putting on a gas mask. Terrified at the sound of Margarita's hammer tapping on the window, he vanished from the room.

Suddenly the uproar stopped. Floating down to the third floor Margarita looked into the far window, which was shaded by a flimsy blind. The room was lit by a little night-light. In a cot with basketwork sides sat a little boy of about four, listening nervously. There were no grownups in the room and they had obviously all run out of the flat.

'Windows breaking,' said the little boy and cried : 'Mummy !'

Nobody answered and he said :

'Mummy, I'm frightened.'

Margarita pushed aside the blind and flew in at the window.

'I'm frightened,' said the little boy again, shivering.

'Don't be frightened, darling,' said Margarita, trying to soften her now raucous, harsh voice. 'It's only some boys breaking windows.'

'With a catapult ?' asked the boy, as he stopped shivering.

'Yes, with a catapult,' agreed Margarita. 'Go to sleep now.'

'That's Fedya,' said the boy. 'He's got a catapult.'

'Of course, it must be Fedya.'

The boy glanced slyly to one side and asked :

'Where are you, aunty ?'

'I'm nowhere,' replied Margarita. 'You're dreaming about me.'

'I thought so,' said the little boy.

'Now you lie down,' said Margarita, 'put your hand under your cheek and I'll send you to sleep.'

'All right,' agreed the boy and lay down at once with his cheek on his palm.

'I'll tell you a story,' Margarita began, laying her hot hand on the child's cropped head. 'Once upon a time there was a lady . . . she had no children and she was never happy. At first she just used to cry, then one day she felt very naughty . . .' Margarita stopped and took away her hand. The little boy was asleep.

Margarita gently put the hammer on the windowsill and flew out of the window. Below, disorder reigned. People were shouting and running up and down the glass-strewn pavement, policemen among them. Suddenly a bell started clanging and round the corner from the Arbat drove a red fire-engine with an extending ladder.

Margarita had already lost interest. Steering her way past any cables, she clutched the broom harder and in a moment was flying high above Dramlit House. The street veered sideways and vanished. Beneath her now was only an expanse of roofs, criss-crossed with brilliantly lit roads. Suddenly it all slipped sideways, the strings of light grew blurred and vanished.

Margarita gave another jerk, at which the sea of roofs disappeared, replaced below her by a sea of shimmering electric lights. Suddenly the sea of light swung round to the vertical and appeared over Margarita's head whilst the moon shone under her legs. Realising that she had looped the loop, Margarita righted herself, turned round and saw that the sea had vanished ; behind her there was now only a pink glow on the horizon. In a second that too had disappeared and Margarita saw that she was alone with the moon, sailing along above her and to the left. Margarita's hair streamed out behind her in wisps as the moonlight swished past her body. From the two lines of widely-spaced lights meeting at a point in the distance and from the speed with which they were vanishing behind her Margarita guessed that she was flying at prodigious speed and was surprised to discover that it did not take her breath away.

After a few seconds' travel, far below in the earthbound blackness an electric sunrise flared up and rolled beneath Margarita's feet, then twisted round and vanished. Another few seconds, another burst of light.

' Towns ! Towns ! ' shouted Margarita.

Two or three times she saw beneath her what looked like dull glinting bands of steel ribbon that were rivers.

Glancing upward and to the left she stared at the moon as it flew past her, rushing backwards to Moscow, yet strangely appearing to stand still. In the moon she could clearly see a mysterious dark shape—not exactly a dragon, not quite a little hump-backed horse, its sharp muzzle pointed towards the city she was leaving.

The thought then came to Margarita that there was really no reason for her to drive her broom at such a speed. She was missing a unique chance to see the world from a new viewpoint and savour the thrill of flight. Something told her that wherever her destination might be, her hosts would wait for her.

There was no hurry, no reason to make herself dizzy with speed or to fly at such a height, so she tilted the head of her broom downwards and floated, at a greatly reduced speed, almost down to ground level. This headlong dive, as though on an aerial toboggan, gave her the utmost pleasure. The earth rose up to her and the moonlit landscape, until then an indistinguishable blur, was revealed in exquisite detail. Margarita flew just above the veil of mist over meadow and pond; through the wisps of vapour she could hear the croaking of frogs, from the distance came the heart-stopping moan of a train. Soon Margarita caught sight of it. It was moving slowly, like a caterpillar blowing sparks from the top of its head. She overtook it, crossed another lake in which a reflected moon swam beneath her legs, then flew still lower, nearly brushing the tops of the giant pines with her feet.

Suddenly Margarita caught the sound of heavy, snorting breath behind her and it seemed to be slowly catching her up. Gradually another noise like a flying bullet and a woman's raucous laughter could be heard. Margarita looked round and saw that she was being followed by a dark object of curious shape. As it drew nearer it began to look like someone flying astride, until as it slowed down to draw alongside her Margarita saw clearly that it was Natasha.

Completely naked too, her hair streaming behind her, she was flying along mounted on a fat pig, clutching a briefcase in its front legs and furiously pounding the air with its hind trotters. A pince-nez, which occasionally flashed in the moonlight, had fallen off its nose and was dangling on a ribbon, whilst the pig's hat kept falling forward over its eyes. After a careful look

Margarita recognised the pig as Nikolai Ivanovich and her laughter rang out, mingled with Natasha's, over the forest below.

' Natasha ! ' shrieked Margarita. ' Did you rub the cream on yourself ? '

' Darling ! ' answered Natasha, waking the sleeping pine forests with her screech. ' I smeared it on his bald head ! '

' My princess ! ' grunted the pig miserably.

' Darling Margarita Nikolayevna ! ' shouted Natasha as she galloped alongside. ' I confess—I took the rest of the cream. Why shouldn't I fly away and live, too ? Forgive me, but I could never come back to you now—not for anything. This is the life for me ! ... He made me a proposition.'—Natasha poked her finger into the back of the pig's neck—' The old lecher. I didn't think he had it in him, did you ? What did you call me ? ' she yelled, leaning down towards the pig's ear.

' Goddess ! ' howled the animal. ' Slow down, Natasha, please ! There are important papers in my briefcase and I may lose them ! '

' To hell with your papers,' shouted Natasha, laughing. ' Oh, please don't shout like that, somebody may hear us ! ' roared the pig imploringly.

As she flew alongside Margarita, Natasha laughingly told her what had happened in the house after Margarita Nikolayevna had flown away over the gate.

Natasha confessed that without touching any more of the things she had been given she had torn her clothes off, rushed to the cream and started to anoint herself. The same transformation took place. Laughing aloud with delight, she was standing in front of the mirror admiring her magical beauty when the door opened and in walked Nikolai Ivanovich. He was highly excited and was holding Margarita Nikolayevna's slip, his briefcase and his hat. At first he was riveted to the spot with horror, then announced, as red as a lobster, that he thought he should bring the garment back. . . .

' The things he said, the beast ! ' screamed Natasha, roaring

with laughter. 'The things he suggested! The money he
offered me! Said his wife would never find out. It's true, isn't
it?' Natasha shouted to the pig, which could do nothing but
wriggle its snout in embarrassment.

As they had romped about in the bedroom, Natasha smeared
some of the cream on Nikolai Ivanovich and then it was her
turn to freeze with astonishment. The face of her respectable
neighbour shrank and grew a snout, whilst his arms and legs
sprouted trotters. Looking at himself in the mirror Nikolai
Ivanovich gave a wild, despairing squeal but it was too late. A
few seconds later, with Natasha astride him, he was flying
through the air away from Moscow, sobbing with chagrin.

'I demand to be turned back to my usual shape!' the pig
suddenly grunted, half angry, half begging. 'I refuse to take
part in an illegal assembly! Margarita Nikolayevna, kindly take
your maid off my back.'

'Oh, so I'm a maid now, am I! What d'you mean—maid!'
cried Natasha, tweaking the pig's ear. 'I was a goddess just
now! What did you call me?'

'Venus!' replied the pig miserably, brushing a hazel-bush
with its feet as they flew low over a chattering, fast-flowing
stream.

'Venus! Venus!' screamed Natasha triumphantly, putting
one arm akimbo and waving the other towards the moon.

'Margarita! Queen Margarita! Ask them to let me stay a
witch! You have the power to ask for whatever you like and
they'll do it for you.'

Margarita replied:

'Very well, I promise.'

'Thanks!' screamed Natasha, raising her voice still higher to
shout: 'Hey, go on—faster, faster! Faster than that!'

She dug her heels into the pig's thin flanks, sending it flying
forward. In a moment Natasha could only be seen as a dark
spot far ahead and as she vanished altogether the swish of her
passage through the air died away.

Margarita flew on slowly through the unknown, deserted

countryside, over hills strewn with occasional rocks and sparsely grown with giant fir trees. She was no longer flying over their tops, but between their trunks, silvered on one side by the moonlight. Her faint shadow flitted ahead of her, as the moon was now at her back.

Sensing that she was approaching water, Margarita guessed that her goal was near. The fir trees parted and Margarita gently floated through the air towards a chalky hillside. Below it lay a river. A mist was swirling round the bushes growing on the cliff-face, whilst the opposite bank was low and flat. There under a lone clump of trees was the flicker of a camp fire, surrounded by moving figures, and Margarita seemed to hear the insistent beat of music. Beyond, as far as the eye could see, there was not a sign of life.

Margarita bounded down the hillside to the water, which looked tempting after her chase through the air. Throwing aside the broom, she took a run and dived head-first into the water. Her body, as light as air, plunged in and threw up a column of spray almost to the moon. The water was as warm as a bath and as she glided upwards from the bottom Margarita revelled in the freedom of swimming alone in a river at night. There was no one near Margarita in the water, but further away near some bushes by the shore, she could hear splashing and snorting. Someone else was having a bathe.

Margarita swam ashore and ran up the bank. Her body tingled. She felt no fatigue after her long flight and gave a little dance of pure joy on the damp grass. Suddenly she stopped and listened. The snorting was moving closer and from a clump of reeds there emerged a fat man, naked except for a dented top hat perched on the back of his head. He had been plodding his way through sticky mud, which made him seem to be wearing black boots. To judge from his breath and his hiccups he had had a great deal to drink, which was confirmed by a smell of brandy rising from the water around him.

Catching sight of Margarita the fat man stared at her, then cried with a roar of joy :

' Surely it can't be ! It is—Claudine, the merry widow ! What brings you here ? ' He waddled forward to greet her. Margarita retreated and replied in a dignified voice :

' Go to hell ! What d'you mean—Claudine ? Who d'you think you're talking to ? ' After a moment's reflection she rounded off her retort with a long, satisfying and unprintable obscenity. Its effect on the fat man was instantly sobering.

' Oh dear,' he exclaimed, flinching. ' Forgive me—I didn't see you, your majesty, Queen Margot. It's the fault of the brandy.' The fat man dropped on to one knee, took off his top hat, bowed and in a mixture of Russian and French jabbered some nonsense about having just come from a wedding in Paris, about brandy and about how deeply he apologised for his terrible mistake.

' You might have put your trousers on, you great fool,' said Margarita, relenting though still pretending to be angry.

The fat man grinned with delight as he realised that Margarita had forgiven him and he announced cheerfully that he just happened to be without his trousers at this particular moment because he had absent-mindedly left them on the bank of the river Yenisei where he had been bathing just before flying here, but would go back for them at once. With an effusive volley of farewells he began bowing and walking backwards, until he slipped and fell headlong into the water. Even as he fell, however, his side-whiskered face kept its smile of cheerful devotion. Then Margarita gave a piercing whistle, mounted the obedient broomstick and flew across to the far bank, which lay in the full moonlight beyond the shadow cast by the chalk cliff.

As soon as she touched the wet grass the music from the clump of willows grew louder and the stream of sparks blazed upwards with furious gaiety. Under the willow branches, hung with thick catkins, sat two rows of fat-cheeked frogs, puffed up as if they were made of rubber and playing a march on wooden pipes. Glow-worms hung on the willow twigs in front of the musicians to light their sheets of music whilst a flickering glow from the camp fire played over the frogs' faces.

The march was being played in Margarita's honour as part of a solemn ceremony of welcome. Translucent water-sprites stopped their dance to wave fronds at her as their cries of welcome floated across the broad water-meadow. Naked witches jumped down from the willows and curtsied to her. A goat-legged creature ran up, kissed her hand and, as he spread out a silken sheet on the grass, enquired if she had enjoyed her bathe and whether she would like to lie down and rest.

As Margarita lay down the goat-legged man brought her a goblet of champagne, which at once warmed her heart. Asking where Natasha was, she was told that Natasha had already bathed. She was already flying back to Moscow on her pig to warn them that Margarita would soon be coming and to help in preparing her attire.

Margarita's short stay in the willow-grove was marked by a curious event : a whistle split the air and a dark body, obviously missing its intended target, sailed through the air and landed in the water. A few moments later Margarita was faced by the same fat man with side whiskers who had so clumsily introduced himself earlier. He had obviously managed to fly back to the Yenisei because although soaking wet from head to foot, he now wore full evening dress. He had been at the brandy again, which had caused him to land in the water, but as before his smile was indestructible and in his bedraggled state he was permitted to kiss Margarita's hand.

All prepared to depart. The water-sprites ended their dance and vanished. The goat-man politely asked how she had arrived at the river and on hearing that she had ridden there on a broom he cried :

' Oh, how uncomfortable ! ' In a moment he had twisted two branches into the shape of a telephone and ordered someone to send a car at once, which was done in a minute.

A brown open car flew down to the island. Instead of a driver the chauffeur's seat was occupied by a black, long-beaked crow in a check cap and gauntlets. The island emptied as the witches flew away in the moonlight, the fire burned out and the glowing embers turned to grey ash.

The goat-man opened the door for Margarita, who sprawled on the car's wide back seat. The car gave a roar, took off and climbed almost to the moon. The island fell away, the river disappeared and Margarita was on her way to Moscow.

22. By Candlelight

The steady hum of the car as it flew high above the earth lulled Margarita to sleep and the moonlight felt pleasantly warm. Closing her eyes she let the wind play on her face and thought wistfully of that strange riverbank which she would probably never see again. After so much magic and sorcery that evening she had already guessed who her host was to be, but she felt quite unafraid. The hope that she might regain her happiness made her fearless. In any case she was not given much time to loll in the car and dream about happiness. The crow was a good driver and the car a fast one. When Margarita opened her eyes she no longer saw dark forests beneath her but the shimmering jewels of the lights of Moscow. The bird-chauffeur unscrewed the right-hand front wheel as they flew along, then landed the car at a deserted cemetery in the Dorogomilov district.

Opening the door to allow Margarita and her broom to alight on a gravestone the crow gave the car a push and sent it rolling towards the ravine beyond the far edge of the cemetery. It crashed over the side and was shattered to pieces. The crow saluted politely, mounted the wheel and flew away on it.

At that moment a black cloak appeared from behind a headstone. A wall eye glistened in the moonlight and Margarita recognised Azazello. He gestured to Margarita to mount her broomstick, leaped astride his own long rapier, and they both took off and landed soon afterwards, unnoticed by a soul, near No. 302A, Sadovaya Street.

As the two companions passed under the gateway into the courtyard, Margarita noticed a man in cap and high boots, apparently waiting for somebody. Light as their footsteps were, the lonely man heard them and shifted uneasily, unable to see who it was.

At the entrance to staircase 6 they encountered a second man, astonishingly similar in appearance to the first, and the same performance was repeated. Footsteps ... the man turned round uneasily and frowned. When the door opened and closed he hurled himself in pursuit of the invisible intruders and peered up the staircase but failed, of course, to see anything. A third man, an exact copy of the other two, was lurking on the third-floor landing. He was smoking a strong cigarette and Margarita coughed as she walked past him. The smoker leaped up from his bench as though stung, stared anxiously around, walked over to the banisters and glanced down. Meanwhile Margarita and her companion had reached flat No. 50.

They did not ring, but Azazello silently opened the door with his key. Margarita's first surprise on walking in was the darkness. It was as dark as a cellar, so that she involuntarily clutched Azazello's cloak from fear of an accident, but soon from high up and far away a lighted lamp flickered and came closer. As they went Azazello took away Margarita's broom and it vanished soundlessly into the darkness.

They then began to mount a broad staircase, so vast that to Margarita it seemed endless. She was surprised that the hallway of an ordinary Moscow flat could hold such an enormous, invisible but undeniably real and apparently unending staircase. They reached a landing and stopped. The light drew close and Margarita saw the face of the tall man in black holding the lamp. Anybody unlucky enough to have crossed his path in those last few days would have recognised him at once. It was Koroviev, alias Faggot.

His appearance, it is true, had greatly changed. The guttering flame was no longer reflected in a shaky pince-nez long due for the dustbin, but in an equally unsteady monocle. The moustaches on his insolent face were curled and waxed. He appeared black for the simple reason that he was wearing tails and black trousers. Only his shirt front was white.

Magician, choirmaster, wizard, or the devil knows what, Koroviev bowed and with a broad sweep of his lamp invited Margarita to follow him. Azazello vanished.

' How strange everything is this evening ! ' thought Margarita. ' I was ready for anything except this. Are they trying to save current, or what ? The oddest thing of all is the size of this place . . . how on earth can it fit into a Moscow flat ? It's simply impossible ! '

Despite the feebleness of the light from Koroviev's lamp, Margarita realised that she was in a vast, colonnaded hall, dark and apparently endless. Stopping beside a small couch, Koroviev put his lamp on a pedestal, gestured to Margarita to sit down and then placed himself beside her in an artistic pose, one elbow leaned elegantly on the pedestal.

' Allow me to introduce myself,' said Koroviev in a grating voice. ' My name is Koroviev. Are you surprised that there's no light ? Economy, I suppose you were thinking ? Never ! May the first murderer to fall at your feet this evening cut my throat if that's the reason. It is simply because messire doesn't care for electric light and we keep it turned off until the last possible moment. Then, believe me, there will be no lack of it. It might even be better if there were not quite so much.'

Margarita liked Koroviev and she found his flow of light-hearted nonsense reassuring.

' No,' replied Margarita, ' what really puzzles me is where you have found the space for all this.' With a wave of her hand Margarita emphasised the vastness of the hall they were in.

Koroviev smiled sweetly, wrinkling his nose.

' Easy ! ' he replied. ' For anyone who knows how to handle the fifth dimension it's no problem to expand any place to whatever size you please. No, dear lady, I will say more—to the devil knows what size. However, I have known people,' Koroviev burbled on, ' who though quite ignorant have done wonders in enlarging their accommodation. One man in this town, so I was told, was given a three-roomed flat on the Zemlyanoi Rampart and in a flash, without using the fifth dimension or anything like that, he had turned it into four rooms by dividing one of the rooms in half with a partition. Then he exchanged it for two separate flats in different parts of Moscow, one with three rooms and the other with two. That, you will agree, adds up to five rooms. He exchanged the three-roomed one for two separate two-roomers and thus became the owner, as you will have noticed, of six rooms altogether, though admittedly scattered all over Moscow. He was just about to pull off his last and most brilliant coup by putting an advertisement in the newspaper offering six rooms in various districts of Moscow in exchange for one five-roomed flat on the Zemlyanoi Rampart, when his activities were suddenly and inexplicably curtailed. He may have a room somewhere now, but not, I can assure you, in Moscow. There's a sharp operator for you—and you talk of the fifth dimension ! '

Although it was Koroviev and not Margarita who had been talking about the fifth dimension, she could not help laughing at the way he told his story of the ingenious property tycoon. Koroviev went on :

' But to come to the point, Margarita Nikolayevna. You are a very intelligent woman and have naturally guessed who our host is.'

Margarita's heart beat faster and she nodded.

' Very well, then,' said Koroviev. ' I will tell you more. We dislike all mystery and ambiguity. Every year messire gives a ball. It is known as the springtime ball of the full moon, or the ball of the hundred kings. Ah, the people who come ! . . .' Here Koroviev clutched his cheek as if he had a toothache. ' However, you will shortly be able to see for yourself. Messire is a bachelor as you will realise, but there has to be a hostess.' Koroviev spread his hands : ' You must agree that without a hostess . . .'

Margarita listened to Koroviev, trying not to miss a word. Her heart felt cold with expectancy, the thought of happiness made her dizzy. ' Firstly, it has become a tradition,' Koroviev went on, ' that the hostess of the ball must be called Margarita and secondly, she must be a native of the place where the ball is held. We, as you know, are always on the move and happen to be in Moscow at present. We have found a hundred and twenty-one Margaritas in Moscow and would you believe it . . .'— Koroviev slapped his thigh in exasperation—'. . . not one of them was suitable ! Then at last, by a lucky chance . . .'

Koroviev grinned expressively, bowing from the waist, and again Margarita's heart contracted.

' Now to the point ! ' exclaimed Koroviev. ' To be brief—you won't decline this responsibility, will you ? '

' I will not,' replied Margarita firmly.

' Of course,' said Koroviev, raising his lamp, and added: ' Please follow me.'

They passed a row of columns and finally emerged into another hall which for some reason smelled strongly of lemons. A rustling noise was heard and something landed on Margarita's head. She gave a start.

' Don't be afraid,' Koroviev reassured her, taking her arm. ' Just some stunt that Behemoth has dreamed up to amuse the guests tonight, that's all. Incidentally, if I may be so bold, Margarita Nikolayevna, my advice to you is to be afraid of nothing you may see. There's no cause for fear. The ball will be extravagantly luxurious, I warn you. We shall see people who in their time wielded enormous power. But when one recalls how microscopic their influence really was in comparison with the powers of the one in whose retinue I have the honour to serve they become quite laughable, even pathetic . . . You too, of course, are of royal blood.'

' How can I be of royal blood ? ' whispered Margarita, terrified, pressing herself against Koroviev.

' Ah, your majesty,' Koroviev teased her, ' the question of blood is the most complicated problem in the world! If you were to ask certain of your great-great-great-grandmothers, especially those who had a reputation for shyness, they might tell you some remarkable secrets, my dear Margarita Nikolayevna !

To draw a parallel—the most amazing combinations can result if you shuffle the pack enough. There are some matters in which even class barriers and frontiers are powerless. I rather think that a certain king of France of the sixteenth century would be most astonished if somebody told him that after all these years I should have the pleasure of walking arm in arm round a ballroom in Moscow with his great-great-great-great-great-grandaughter. Ah—here we are ! '

Koroviev blew out his lamp, it vanished from his hand and Margarita noticed a patch of light on the floor in front of a black doorway. Koroviev knocked gently. Margarita grew so excited that her teeth started chattering and a shiver ran up her spine.

The door opened into a small room. Margarita saw a wide oak bed covered in dirty, rumpled bedclothes and pillows. In front of the bed was a table with carved oaken legs bearing a candelabra whose sockets were made in the shape of birds' claws. Seven fat wax candles burned in their grasp. On the table there was also a large chessboard set with elaborately carved pieces. A low bench stood on the small, worn carpet. There was one more table laden with golden beakers and another candelabra with arms fashioned like snakes. The room smelled of damp and tar. Shadows thrown by the candlelight criss-crossed on the floor.

Among the people in the room Margarita at once recognised Azazello, now also wearing tails and standing near the bed-head. Now that Azazello was smartly dressed he no longer looked like the ruffian who had appeared to Margarita in the Alexander Gardens and he gave her a most gallant bow.

The naked witch, Hella, who had so upset the respectable barman from the Variety Theatre and who luckily for Rimsky had been driven away at cock-crow, was sitting on the floor by the bed and stirring some concoction in a saucepan which gave off a sulphurous vapour. Besides these, there was an enormous black cat sitting on a stool in front of the chessboard and holding a knight in its right paw.

Hella stood up and bowed to Margarita. The cat jumped down

from its stool and did likewise, but making a flourish it dropped the knight and had to crawl under the bed after it.

Faint with terror, Margarita blinked at this candlelit pantomime. Her glance was drawn to the bed, on which sat the man whom the wretched Ivan had recently assured at Patriarch's Ponds that he did not exist.

Two eyes bored into Margarita's face. In the depths of the right eye was a golden spark that could pierce any soul to its core; the left eye was as empty and black as a small black diamond, as the mouth of a bottomless well of dark and shadow. Woland's face was tilted to one side, the right-hand corner of his mouth pulled downward and deep furrows marked his forehead parallel to his eyebrows. The skin of his face seemed burned by timeless sunshine.

Woland was lying sprawled on the bed, dressed only in a long, dirty black nightshirt, patched on the left shoulder. One bare leg was tucked up beneath him, the other stretched out on the bench. Hella was massaging his knees with a steaming ointment.

On Woland's bare, hairless chest Margarita noticed a scarab on a gold chain, intricately carved out of black stone and marked on its back with an arcane script. Near Woland was a strange globe, lit from one side, which seemed almost alive.

The silence lasted for several seconds. ' He is studying me,' thought Margarita and by an effort of will tried to stop her legs from trembling.

At last Woland spoke. He smiled, causing his one sparkling eye to flash.

' Greetings, my queen. Please excuse my homely garb.'

Woland's voice was so low-pitched that on certain syllables it faded off into a mere growl.

Woland picked up a long sword from the bed, bent over, poked it under the bed and said :

' Come out now. The game's over. Our guest has arrived.'

' Please . . .' Koroviev whispered anxiously into Margarita's ear like a prompter.

' Please . . .' began Margarita.

'Messire . . .' breathed Koroviev.

'Please, messire,' Margarita went on quietly but firmly : 'I beg you not to interrupt your game. I am sure the chess journals would pay a fortune to be allowed to print it.'

Azazello gave a slight croak of approval and Woland, staring intently at Margarita, murmured to himself :

'Yes, Koroviev was right. The result can be amazing when you shuffle the pack. Blood will tell.'

He stretched out his arm and beckoned Margarita.

She walked up to him, feeling no ground under her bare feet. Woland placed his hand—as heavy as stone and as hot as fire—on Margarita's shoulder, pulled her towards him and sat her down on the bed by his side.

'Since you are so charming and kind,' he said, 'which was no more than I expected, we shan't stand on ceremony.' He leaned over the edge of the bed again and shouted : 'How much longer is this performance under the bed going to last ? Come on out !'

'I can't find the knight,' replied the cat in a muffled falsetto from beneath the bed. 'It's galloped off somewhere and there's a frog here instead.'

'Where do you think you are—on a fairground ?' asked Woland, pretending to be angry. 'There's no frog under the bed ! Save those cheap tricks for the Variety ! If you don't come out at once we'll begin to think you've gone over to the enemy, you deserter !'

'Never, messire !' howled the cat, crawling out with the knight in its paw.

'Allow me to introduce to you . . .' Woland began, then interrupted himself. 'No, really, he looks too ridiculous ! Just look what he's done to himself while he was under the bed !'

The cat, covered in dust and standing on its hind legs, bowed to Margarita. Round its neck it was now wearing a made-up white bow tie on an elastic band, with a pair of ladies' mother-of-pearl binoculars hanging on a cord. It had also gilded its whiskers.

'What have you done ? ' exclaimed Woland. ' Why have you gilded your whiskers ? And what on earth do you want with a white tie when you haven't even got any trousers ? '

' Trousers don't suit cats, messire,' replied the cat with great dignity. ' Why don't you tell me to wear boots ? Cats always wear boots in fairy tales. But have you ever seen a cat going to a ball without a tie ? I don't want to make myself look ridiculous. One likes to look as smart as one can. And that also applies to my opera-glasses, messire ! '

' But your whiskers ? . . .'

' I don't see why,' the cat objected coldly, ' Azazello and Koroviev are allowed to cover themselves in powder and why powder is better than gilt. I just powdered my whiskers, that's all. It would be a different matter if I'd shaved myself ! A clean-shaven cat is something monstrous, that I agree. But I see . . .' —here the cat's voice trembled with pique—' . . . that this is a conspiracy to be rude about my appearance. Clearly I am faced with a problem—shall I go to the ball or not ? What do you say, messire ? '

Outraged, the cat had so inflated itself that it looked about to explode at any second.

' Ah, the rogue, the sly rogue,' said Woland shaking his head. ' Whenever he's losing a game he starts a spiel like a quack-doctor at a fair. Sit down and stop all this hot air.'

' Very well,' replied the cat, sitting down, ' but I must object. My remarks are by no means all hot air, as you so vulgarly put it, but a series of highly apposite syllogisms which would be appreciated by such connoisseurs as Sextus Empiricus, Martian Capella, even, who knows, Aristotle himself.

' Check,' said Woland.

' Check it is,' rejoined the cat, surveying the chessboard through his lorgnette.

' So,' Woland turned to Margarita, ' let me introduce my retinue. That creature who has been playing the fool is the cat Behemoth. Azazello and Koroviev you have already met ; this is my maid, Hella. She's prompt, clever, and there's no service she cannot perform for you.'

The beautiful Hella turned her green eyes on Margarita and smiled, continuing to scoop out the ointment in the palm of her hand and to rub it on Woland's knee.

' Well, there they are,' concluded Woland, wincing as Hella massaged his knee rather too hard. ' A charming and select little band.' He stopped and began turning his globe, so cleverly made that the blue sea shimmered in waves and the polar cap was of real ice and snow. On the chessboard, meanwhile, confusion reigned. Distraught, the white king was stamping about on his square and waving his arms in desperation. Three white pawns, armed with halberds, were staring in bewilderment at a bishop who was waving his crozier and pointing forwards to where Woland's black knights sat mounted on two hot-blooded horses, one pawing the ground of a white square, the other on a black square.

Margarita was fascinated by the game and amazed to see that the chessmen were alive.

Dropping its lorgnette, the cat gently nudged his king in the back, at which the wretched king covered his face in despair.

' You're in trouble, my dear Behemoth,' said Koroviev in a voice of quiet malice.

' The position is serious but far from hopeless,' retorted Behemoth. ' What is more, I am confident of ultimate victory. All it needs is a careful analysis of the situation.'

His method of analysis took the peculiar form of pulling faces and winking at his king.

' That won't do you any good,' said Koroview.

' Oh ! ' cried Behemoth, ' all the parrots have flown away, as I said they would.'

From far away came the sound of innumerable wings. Koroviev and Azazello rushed out of the room.

' You're nothing but a pest with all your arrangements for the ball,' grumbled Woland, preoccupied with his globe.

As soon as Koroviev and Azazella had gone, Behemoth's

winking increased until at last the white king guessed what was required of him. He suddenly pulled off his cloak, dropped it on his square and walked off the board. The bishop picked up the royal cloak, threw it round his shoulders and took the king's place.

Koroviev and Azazello returned.

' False alarm, as usual,' growled Azazello.

' Well, I thought I heard something,' said the cat.

' Come on, how much longer do you need ? ' asked Woland. ' Check.'

' I must have mis-heard you, *mon maître*,' replied the cat. ' My king is not in check and cannot be.'

' I repeat—check.'

' Messire,' rejoined the cat in a voice of mock anxiety, ' you must be suffering from over-strain. I am not in check ! '

' The king is on square K2,' said Woland, without looking at the board.

' Messire, you amaze me,' wailed the cat, putting on an amazed face, ' there is no king on that square.'

' What ? ' asked Woland, with a puzzled look at the board. The bishop, standing in the king's square, turned his head away and covered his face with his hand.

' Aha, you rogue,' said Woland reflectively.

' Messire ! I appeal to the laws of logic ! ' said the cat, clasping its paws to its chest, ' if a player says check and there is no king on the board, then the king is not in check ! '

' Do you resign or not ? ' shouted Woland in a terrible voice.

' Give me time to consider, please,' said the cat meekly. It put its elbows on the table, covered its ears with its paws and began to think. Finally, having considered, it said. ' I resign.'

' He needs murdering, the obstinate beast,' whispered Azazello.

' Yes, I resign,' said the cat, ' but only because I find it impossible to play when I'm distracted by jealous, hostile spectators ! ' He stood up and the chessmen ran back into their box.

' It's time for you to go, Hella,' said Woland and Hella left the room. 'My leg has started hurting again and now there is this ball . . .' he went on.

'Allow me,' Margarita suggested gently.

Woland gave her a searching stare and moved his knee towards her.

The ointment, hot as lava, burned her hands but without flinching Margarita massaged it into Woland's knee, trying not to cause him pain.

'My friends maintain that it's rheumatism,' said Woland, continuing to stare at Margarita, 'but I strongly suspect that the pain is a souvenir of an encounter with a most beautiful witch that I had in 1571, on the Brocken in the Harz Mountains.'

'Surely not!' said Margarita.

'Oh, give it another three hundred years or so and it will go. I've been prescribed all kinds of medicaments, but I prefer to stick to traditional old wives' remedies. I inherited some extraordinary herbal cures from my terrible old grandmother. Tell me, by the way—do you suffer from any complaint? Perhaps you have some sorrow which is weighing on your heart?'

'No messire, I have no such complaint,' replied Margarita astutely. 'In any case, since I have been with you I have never felt better.'

'As I said—blood will tell . . .' said Woland cheerfully to no one in particular, adding: 'I see my globe interests you.'

'I have never seen anything so ingenious.'

'Yes, it is nice. I confess I never like listening to the news on the radio. It's always read out by some silly girl who can't pronounce foreign names properly. Besides, at least one in three of the announcers is tongue-tied, as if they chose them specially. My globe is much more convenient, especially as I need exact information. Do you see that little speck of land, for instance, washed by the sea on one side? Look, it's just bursting into flames. War has broken out there. If you look closer you'll see it in detail.'

Margarita leaned towards the globe and saw that the little square of land was growing bigger, emerging in natural colours and turning into a kind of relief map. Then she saw a river and a village beside it. A house the size of a pea grew until it was as large as a matchbox. Suddenly and noiselessly its roof flew upwards in a puff of black smoke, the walls collapsed leaving nothing of the two-storey matchbox except a few smoking heaps of rubble. Looking even closer Margarita discerned a tiny female figure lying on the ground and beside her in a pool of blood a baby with outstretched arms.

' It's all over now,' said Woland, smiling. ' He was too young to have sinned. Abadonna has done his work impeccably.'

' I wouldn't like to be on the side that is against Abadonna,' said Margarita. ' Whose side is he on ? '

' The more I talk to you,' said Woland kindly, ' the more convinced I am that you are very intelligent. Let me reassure you. He is utterly impartial and is equally sympathetic to the people fighting on either side. Consequently the outcome is always the same for both sides. Abadonna ! ' Woland called softly and from the wall appeared the figure of a man wearing dark glasses. These glasses made such a powerful impression on Margarita that she gave a low cry, turned away and hit her head against Woland's leg. ' Stop it ! ' cried Woland. ' How nervous people are nowadays ! ' He slapped Margarita on the back so hard that her whole body seemed to ring. ' He's only wearing spectacles, that's all. There never has been and never will be a case when Abadonna comes to anyone too soon. In any case, I'm here—you're my guest. I just wanted to show him to you.'

Abadonna stood motionless.

' Could he take off his glasses for a moment ? ' asked Margarita, pressing against Woland and shuddering, though now with curiosity.

' No, that is impossible,' replied Woland in a grave tone. At a wave of his hand, Abadonna vanished. ' What did you want to say, Azazello ? '

' Messire,' answered Azazello, ' two strangers have arrived— a beautiful girl who is whining and begging to be allowed to stay with her mistress, and with her there is, if you'll forgive me, her pig.'

' What odd behaviour for a girl ! ' said Woland.

' It's Natasha—my Natasha ! ' exclaimed Margarita.

' Very well, she may stay here with her mistress. Send the pig to the cooks.'

' Are you going to kill it ? ' cried Margarita in fright. ' Please, messire, that's Nikolai Ivanovich, my neighbour. There was a mistake—she rubbed the cream on him . . .'

' Who said anything about killing him ? ' said Woland. ' I merely want him to sit at the cooks' table, that's all. I can't allow a pig into the ballroom, can I ? '

' No, of course not,' said Azazello, then announced : ' Midnight approaches, Mêssire.'

' Ah, good.' Woland turned to Margarita. ' Now let me thank you in advance for your services tonight. Don't lose your head and don't be afraid of anything. Drink nothing except water, otherwise it will sap your energy and you will find yourself flagging. Time to go ! '

As Margarita got up from the carpet Koroviev appeared in the doorway.

23. Satan's Rout

Midnight was approaching, time to hurry. Peering into the dim surroundings, Margarita discerned some candles and an empty pool carved out of onyx. As Margarita stood in the pool Hella, assisted by Natasha, poured a thick, hot red liquid all over her. Margarita tasted salt on her lips and realised that she was being washed in blood. The bath of blood was followed by another liquid—dense, translucent and pink, and Margarita's head swam with attar of roses. Next she was laid on a crystal couch and rubbed with large green leaves until she glowed.

The cat came in and began to help. It squatted on its haunches at Margarita's feet and began polishing her instep like a shoe-black.

Margarita never remembered who it was who stitched her shoes out of pale rose petals or how those shoes fastened themselves of their own accord. A force lifted her up and placed her in front of a mirror : in her hair glittered a diamond crown. Koroviev appeared and hung on Margarita's breast a picture of a black poodle in a heavy oval frame with a massive chain. Queen Margarita found this ornament extremely burdensome, as the chain hurt her neck and the picture pulled her over forwards. However, the respect with which Koroviev and Behemoth now treated her was some recompense for the discomfort.

' There's nothing for it,' murmured Koroviev at the door of the room with the pool. ' You must wear it round your neck— you must . . . Let me give you a last word of advice, your majesty. The guests at the ball will be mixed--oh, very mixed—but you must show no favouritism, queen Margot! If you don't like anybody . . . I realise that you won't show it in your face, of course not—but you must not even let it cross your mind! If you do, the guest is bound to notice it instantly. You must be sweet and kind to them all, your majesty. For that, the hostess of the ball will be rewarded a hundredfold. And another thing—don't neglect anybody or fail to notice them. Just a smile if you haven't time to toss them a word, even just a little turn of your head! Anything you like except inattention—they can't bear that. . . .'

Escorted by Koroviev and Behemoth, Margarita stepped out of the bathing hall and into total darkness.

' Me, me,' whispered the cat, ' let me give the signal ! '

' All right, give it,' replied Koroviev from the dark.

' Let the ball commence ! ' shrieked the cat in a piercing voice. Margarita screamed and shut her eyes for several seconds. The ball burst upon her in an explosion of light, sound and smell. Arm in arm with Koroviev, Margarita found herself in a tropical forest. Scarlet-breasted parrots with green tails perched on lianas and hopping from branch to branch uttered deafening screeches of ' Ecstasy ! Ecstasy ! ' The forest soon came to an end and its hot, steamy air gave way to the cool of a ballroom with columns made of a yellowish, iridescent stone. Like the forest the ballroom was completely empty except for some naked Negroes in silver turbans holding candelabra. Their faces paled with excitement when Margarita floated into the ballroom with her suite, to which Azazello had now attached himself. Here Koroviev released Margarita's arm and whispered :

' Walk straight towards the tulips ! '

A low wall of white tulips rose up in front of Margarita. Beyond it she saw countless lights in globes, and rows of men in tails and starched white shirts. Margarita saw then where the sound of ball music had been coming from. A roar of brass deafened her and the soaring violins that broke through it poured over her body like blood. The orchestra, all hundred and fifty of them, were playing a polonaise.

Seeing Margarita the tail-coated conductor turned pale, smiled and suddenly raised the whole orchestra to its feet with a wave of his arm. Without a moment's break in the music the orchestra stood and engulfed Margarita in sound. The conductor turned away from the players and gave a low bow. Smiling, Margarita waved to him.

' No, no, that won't do,' whispered Koroviev. ' He won't sleep all night. Shout to him " Bravo, king of the waltz ! " '

Margarita shouted as she was told, amazed that her voice, full as a bell, rang out over the noise of the orchestra. The conductor gave a start of pleasure, placed his left hand on his heart and with his right went on waving his white baton at the orchestra.

' Not enough,' whispered Koroviev. ' Look over there at the first violins and nod to them so that every one of them thinks you recognise him personally. They are all world famous. Look, there . . . on the first desk—that's Joachim ! That's right ! Very good . . . Now—on we go.'

' Who is the conductor ? ' asked Margarita as she floated away.

' Johann Strauss ! ' cried the cat. ' May I be hung from a liana in the tropical forest if any ball has ever had an orchestra like this ! I arranged it ! And not one of them was ill or refused to come ! '

There were no columns in the next hall, but instead it was flanked by walls of red, pink, and milky-white roses on one side and on the other by banks of Japanese double camellias. Fountains played between the walls of flowers and champagne bubbled in three ornamental basins, the first of which was a translucent violet in colour, the second ruby, the third crystal. Negroes in scarlet turbans were busy with silver scoops filling shallow goblets with champagne from the basins. In a gap in the wall of roses was a man bouncing up and down on a stage in a red swallow-tail coat, conducting an unbearably loud jazz band. As soon as he saw Margarita he bent down in front of her until his hands touched the floor, then straightened up and said in a piercing yell :

' Alleluia ! '

He slapped himself once on one knee, then twice on the other, snatched a cymbal from the hands of a nearby musician and struck it against a pillar.

As she floated away Margarita caught a glimpse of the virtuoso bandleader, struggling against the polonaise that she could still hear behind her, hitting the bandsmen on the head with his cymbal while they crouched in comic terror.

At last they regained the platform where Koroviev had first met Margarita with the lamp. Now her eyes were blinded with the light streaming from innumerable bunches of crystal grapes. Margarita stopped and a little amethyst pillar appeared under her left hand.

' You can rest your hand on it if you find it becomes too tiring,' whispered Koroviev.

A black-skinned boy put a cushion embroidered with a golden poodle under Margarita's feet. Obeying the pressure of an invisible hand she bent her knee and placed her right foot on the cushion.

Margarita glanced around. Koroviev and Azazello were standing in formal attitudes. Besides Azazello were three young men, who vaguely reminded Margarita of Abadonna. A cold wind blew in her back. Looking round Margarita saw that wine was foaming out of the marble wall into a basin made of ice. She felt something warm and velvety by her left leg. It was Behemoth.

Margarita was standing at the head of a vast carpeted staircase stretching downwards in front of her. At the bottom, so far away that she seemed to be looking at it through the wrong end of a telescope, she could see a vast hall with an absolutely immense fireplace, into whose cold, black maw one could easily have driven a five-ton lorry. The hall and the staircase, bathed in painfully bright light, were empty. Then Margarita heard the sound of distant trumpets. For some minutes they stood motionless.

' Where are the guests ? ' Margarita asked Koroviev.

' They will be here at any moment, your majesty. There will be no lack of them. I confess I'd rather be sawing logs than receiving them here on this platform.'

' Sawing logs ? ' said the garrulous cat. ' I'd rather be a tramconductor and there's no job worse than that.'

'Everything must be prepared in advance, your majesty,' explained Koroviev, his eye glittering behind the broken lens of his monocle. 'There can be nothing more embarrassing than for the first guest to wait around uncomfortably, not knowing what to do, while his lawful consort curses him in a whisper for arriving too early. We cannot allow that at our ball, queen Margot.'

'I should think not', said the cat.

'Ten seconds to midnight,' said Koroviev, 'it will begin in a moment.'

Those ten seconds seemed unusually long to Margarita. They had obviously passed but absolutely nothing seemed to be happening. Then there was a crash from below in the enormous fireplace and out of it sprang a gallows with a half-decayed corpse bouncing on its arm. The corpse jerked itself loose from the rope, fell to the ground and stood up as a dark, handsome man in tailcoat and lacquered pumps. A small, rotting coffin then slithered out of the fireplace, its lid flew off and another corpse jumped out. The handsome man stepped gallantly towards it and offered his bent arm. The second corpse turned into a nimble little woman in black slippers and black feathers on her head and then man and woman together hurried up the staircase.

'The first guests !' exclaimed Koroviev. 'Monsieur Jacques and his wife. Allow me to introduce to you, your majesty, a most interesting man. A confirmed forger, a traitor to his country but no mean alchemist. He was famous,' Koroviev whispered into Margarita's ear, 'for having poisoned the king's mistress. Not everybody can boast of that, can they ? See how good-looking he is ! '

Turning pale and open-mouthed with shock, Margarita looked down and saw gallows and coffin disappear through a side door in the hall.

'We are delighted ! ' the cat roared to Monsieur Jacques as he mounted the steps.

Just then a headless, armless skeleton appeared in the fireplace below, fell down and turned into yet another man in a tailcoat.

Monsieur Jacques' wife had by now reached the head of the staircase where she knelt down, pale with excitement, and kissed Margarita's foot.

'Your majesty . . .' murmured Madame Jacques.

'Her majesty is charmed!' shouted Koroviev.

'Your majesty . . .' said Monsieur Jacques in a low voice.

'We are charmed!' intoned the cat. The young men beside Azazello, smiling lifeless but welcoming smiles, were showing Monsieur and Madame Jacques to one side, where they were offered goblets of champagne by the Negro attendants. The single man in tails came up the staircase at a run.

'Count Robert,' Koroviev whispered to Margarita. 'An equally interesting character. Rather amusing, your majesty— the case is reversed : he was the queen's lover and poisoned his own wife.'

'We are delighted, Count,' cried Behemoth.

One after another three coffins bounced out of the fireplace, splitting and breaking open as they fell, then someone in a black cloak who was immediately stabbed in the back by the next person to come down the chimney. There was a muffled shriek. When an almost totally decomposed corpse emerged from the fireplace, Margarita frowned and a hand, which seemed to be Natasha's, offered her a flacon of sal volatile.

The staircase began to fill up. Now on almost every step there were men in tailcoats accompanied by naked women who only differed in the colour of their shoes and the feathers on their heads.

Margarita noticed a woman with the downcast gaze of a nun hobbling towards her, thin, shy, hampered by a strange wooden boot on her left leg and a broad green kerchief round her neck.

'Who's that woman in green?' Margarita enquired.

'A most charming and respectable lady,' whispered Koroviev. 'Let me introduce you—Signora Toffana. She was extremely popular among the young and attractive ladies of Naples and Palermo, especially among those who were tired of their husbands. Women do get bored with their husbands, your majesty . . .'

'Yes,' replied Margarita dully, smiling to two men in evening dress who were bowing to kiss her knee and her foot.

'Well,' Koroviev managed to whisper to Margarita as he simultaneously cried : 'Duke ! A glass of champagne ? We are charmed ! . . . Well, Signora Toffana sympathised with those poor women and sold them some liquid in a bladder. The woman poured the liquid into her husband's soup, who ate it, thanked her for it and felt splendid. However, after a few hours he would begin to feel a terrible thirst, then lay down on his bed and a day later another beautiful Neapolitan lady was as free as air.'

'What's that on her leg ?' asked Margarita, without ceasing to offer her hand to the guests who had overtaken Signora Toffana on the way up. 'And why is she wearing green round her neck ? Has she a withered neck ?'

'Charmed, Prince !' shouted Koroviev as he whispered to Margarita : 'She has a beautiful neck, but something unpleasant happened to her in prison. The thing on her leg, your majesty, is a Spanish boot and she wears a scarf because when her jailers found out that about five hundred ill-matched husbands had been dispatched from Naples and Palermo for ever, they strangled Signora Toffana in a rage.'

'How happy I am, your majesty, that I have the great honour . . .' whispered Signora Toffana in a nun-like voice, trying to fall on one knee but hindered by the Spanish boot. Koroviev and Behemoth helped Signora Toffana to rise.

'I am delighted,' Margarita answered her as she gave her hand to the next arrival.

People were now mounting the staircase in a flood. Margarita ceased to notice the arrivals in the hall. Mechanically she raised and lowered her hand, bared her teeth in a smile for each new guest. The landing behind her was buzzing with voices, and music like the waves of the sea floated out from the ball-rooms.

'Now this woman is a terrible bore.' Koroviev no longer bothered to whisper but shouted it aloud, certain that no one could hear his voice over the hubbub. 'She loves coming to a ball because it gives her a chance to complain about her hand-kerchief.'

Among the approaching crowd Margarita's glance picked out the woman at whom Koroviev was pointing. She was young, about twenty, with a remarkably beautiful figure but a look of nagging reproach.

' What handkerchief ? ' asked Margarita.

' A maid has been assigned to her,' Koroviev explained, ' who for thirty years has been putting a handkerchief on her bedside table. It is there every morning when she wakes up. She burns it in the stove or throws it in the river but every morning it appears again beside her.'

' What handkerchief ? ' whispered Margarita, continuing to lower and raise her hand to the guests.

' A handkerchief with a blue border. One day when she was a waitress in a café the owner enticed her into the storeroom and nine months later she gave birth to a boy, carried him into the woods, stuffed a handkerchief into his mouth and then buried him. At the trial she said she couldn't afford to feed the child.'

' And where is the café-owner ? ' asked Margarita.

' But your majesty,' the cat suddenly growled, ' what has the café-owner got to do with it ? It wasn't he who stifled the baby in the forest, was it ? '

Without ceasing to smile and to shake hands with her right hand, she dug the sharp nails of her left hand into Behemoth's ear and whispered to the cat :

' If you butt into the conversation once more, you little horror . . .'

Behemoth gave a distinctly unfestive squeak and croaked : ' Your majesty . . . you'll make my ear swell . . . why spoil the ball with a swollen ear ? I was speaking from the legal point of view . . . I'll be quiet, I promise, pretend I'm not a cat, pretend I'm a fish if you like but please let go of my ear ! '

Margarita released his ear.

The woman's grim, importunate eyes looked into Margarita's :

' I am so happy, your majesty, to be invited to the great ball of the full moon.'

' And I am delighted to see you,' Margarita answered her, ' quite delighted. Do you like champagne ? '

' Hurry up, your majesty ! ' hissed Koroviev quietly but desperately. ' You're causing a traffic-jam on the staircase.'

' Yes, I like champagne,' said the woman imploringly, and began to repeat mechanically : ' Frieda, Frieda, Frieda ! My name is Frieda, your majesty ! '

' Today you may get drunk, Frieda, and forget about everything,' said Margarita.

Frieda stretched out both her arms to Margarita, but Koroviev and Behemoth deftly took an arm each and whisked her off into the crowd.

By now people were advancing from below like a phalanx bent on assaulting the landing where Margarita stood. The naked women mounting the staircase between the tail-coated and white-tied men floated up in a spectrum of coloured bodies that ranged from white through olive, copper and coffee to quite black. In hair that was red, black, chestnut or flaxen, sparks flashed from precious stones. Diamond-studded orders glittered on the jackets and shirt-fronts of the men. Incessantly Margarita felt the touch of lips to her knee, incessantly she offered her hand to be kissed, her face stretched into a rigid mask of welcome.

' Charmed,' Koroviev would monotonously intone, ' We are charmed . . . her majesty is charmed . . .'

' Her majesty is charmed,' came a nasal echo from Azazello, standing behind her.

' I am charmed ! ' squeaked the cat.

' Madame la marquise,' murmured Koroviev, ' poisoned her father, her two brothers and two sisters for the sake of an inheritance . . . Her majesty is delighted, Mme. Minkin ! . . . Ah, how pretty she is ! A trifle nervous, though. Why *did* she have to burn her maid with a pair of curling-tongs ? Of course, in the way she used them it was bound to be fatal . . . Her majesty is charmed ! . . . Look, your majesty—the Emperor Rudolf—

magician and alchemist . . . Another alchemist—he was hanged
. . . Ah, there she is ! What a magnificent brothel she used to
keep in Strasbourg ! . . . We are delighted, madame ! . . . That
woman over there was a Moscow dressmaker who had the
brilliantly funny idea of boring two peep-holes in the wall of her
fitting-room . . .'

'And didn't her lady clients know ? enquired Margarita.

'Of course, they all knew, your majesty,' replied Koroviev.

'Charmed ! . . . That young man over there was a dreamer
and an eccentric from childhood. A girl fell in love with him and
he sold her to a brothel-keeper . . .

On and on poured the stream from below. Its source—the
huge fireplace—showed no sign of drying up. An hour passed,
then another. Margarita felt her chain weighing more and more.
Something odd was happening to her hand : she found she could
not lift it without wincing. Koroviev's remarks ceased to
interest her. She could no longer distinguish between slant-eyed
Mongol faces, white faces and black faces. They all merged into a
blur and the air between them seemed to be quivering. A
sudden sharp pain like a needle stabbed at Margarita's right
hand, and clenching her teeth she leaned her elbow on the little
pedestal. A sound like the rustling of wings came from the
rooms behind her as the horde of guests danced, and Margarita
could feel the massive floors of marble, crystal and mosaic
pulsating rhythmically.

Margarita showed as little interest in the emperor Caius
Caligula and Messalina as she did in the rest of the procession
of kings, dukes, knights, suicides, poisoners, gallows-birds,
procuresses, jailers, card-sharpers, hangmen, informers, traitors,
madmen, detectives and seducers. Her head swam with their
names, their faces merged into a great blur and only one face
remained fixed in her memory—Malyuta Skuratov with his fiery
beard. Margarita's legs were buckling and she was afraid that
she might burst into tears at any moment. The worst pain came
from her right knee, which all the guests had kissed. It was
swollen, the skin on it had turned blue in spite of Natasha's

constant attention to it with a sponge soaked in fragrant ointment. By the end of the third hour Margarita glanced wearily
down and saw with a start of joy that the flood of guests was
thinning out.

' Every ball is the same, your majesty,' whispered Koroviev,
' at about this time the arrivals begin to decrease. I promise you
that this torture will not last more than a few minutes longer.
Here comes a party of witches from the Brocken, they're always
the last to arrive. Yes, there they are. And a couple of drunken
vampires . . . is that all ? Oh, no, there's one more . . . no, two
more.'

The last two guests mounted the staircase.

' Now this is someone new,' said Koroviev, peering through
his monocle. ' Oh, yes, now I remember. Azazello called on him
once and advised him, over a glass of brandy, how to get rid of
a man who was threatening to denounce him. So he made his
friend, who was under an obligation to him, spray the other
man's office walls with poison.'

' What's his name ? ' asked Margarita.

' I'm afraid I don't know,' said Koroviev, ' You'd better ask
Azazello.

' And who's that with him ? '

' That's his friend who did the job. Delighted to welcome you ! '
cried Koroviev to the last two guests.

The staircase was empty, and although the reception committee
waited a little longer to make sure, no one else appeared from the
fireplace.

A second later, half-fainting, Margarita found herself beside
the pool again where, bursting into tears from the pain in her
arm and leg, she collapsed to the floor. Hella and Natasha
comforted her, doused her in blood and massaged her body until
she revived again.

' Once more, queen Margot,' whispered Koroviev. ' You
must make the round of the ballrooms just once more to show
our guests that they are not being neglected.'

Again Margarita floated away from the pool. In place of

Johan Strauss' orchestra the stage behind the wall of tulips had been taken over by a jazz band of frenetic apes. An enormous gorilla with shaggy sideburns and holding a trumpet was leaping clumsily up and down as he conducted. Orang-utan trumpeters sat in the front row, each with a chimpanzee accordionist on his shoulders. Two baboons with manes like lions' were playing the piano, their efforts completely drowned by the roaring, squeaking and banging of the saxophones, violins and drums played by troops of gibbons, mandrils and marmosets. Innumerable couples circled round the glass floor with amazing dexterity, a mass of bodies moving lightly and gracefully as one. Live butterflies fluttered over the dancing horde, flowers drifted down from the ceiling. The electric light had been turned out, the capitals of the pillars were now lit by myriads of glow-worms, and will-o'-the-wisps danced through the air.

Then Margarita found herself by the side of another pool, this time of vast dimensions and ringed by a colonnade. A gigantic black Neptune was pouring a broad pink stream from his great mouth. Intoxicating fumes of champagne rose from the pool. Joy reigned untrammelled. Women, laughing, handed their bags to their escorts or to the Negroes who ran along the sides holding towels, and dived shrieking into the pool. Spray rose in showers. The crystal bottom of the pool glowed with a faint light which shone through the sparkling wine to light up the silvery bodies of the swimmers, who climbed out of the pool again completely drunk. Laughter rang out beneath the pillars until it drowned even the jazz band.

In all this debauch Margarita distinctly saw one totally drunken woman's face with eyes that were wild with intoxication yet still imploring—Frieda.

Margarita's head began to spin with the fumes of the wine and she was just about to move on when the cat staged one of his tricks in the swimming pool. Behemoth made a few magic passes in front of Neptune's mouth; immediately all the champagne drained out of the pool, and Neptune began spewing forth a stream of brown liquid. Shrieking with delight the women screamed : ' Brandy ! ' In a few seconds the pool was full. Spinning round three times like a top the cat leaped into the air and dived into the turbulent sea of brandy. It crawled out, spluttering, its tie soaked, the gilding gone from its whiskers, and minus its lorgnette. Only one woman dared follow Behemoth's example —the dressmaker—procuress and her escort, a handsome young mulatto. They both dived into the brandy, but before she had time to see any more Margarita was led away by Koroviev.

They seemed to take wing and in their flight Margarita first saw great stone tanks full of oysters, then a row of hellish furnaces blazing away beneath the glass floor and attended by a frantic crew of diabolical chefs. In the confusion she remembered a glimpse of dark caverns lit by candles where girls were serving meat that sizzled on glowing coals and revellers drank Margarita's health from vast mugs of beer. Then came polar bears playing accordions and dancing a Russian dance on a stage, a salamander doing conjuring tricks unharmed by the flames around it . . . And for a second time Margarita felt her strength beginning to flag.

' The last round,' whispered Koroviev anxiously, ' and then we're free.'

Escorted by Koroviev, Margarita returned to the ballroom, but now the dance had stopped and the guests were crowded between the pillars, leaving an open space in the middle of the room. Margarita could not remember who helped her up to a platform which appeared in the empty space. When she had mounted it, to her amazement she heard a bell strike midnight, although by her reckoning midnight was long past. At the last chime of the invisible clock silence fell on the crowd of guests.

Then Margarita saw Woland. He approached surrounded by Abadonna, Azazello and several young men in black resembling Abadonna. She now noticed another platform beside her own, prepared for Woland. But he did not make use of it. Margarita was particularly surprised to notice that Woland appeared at the ball in exactly the same state in which he had been in the bedroom. The same dirty, patched nightshirt hung from his shoulders and his feet were in darned bedroom slippers. Woland was armed with his sword but he leaned on the naked weapon as though it were a walking stick.

Limping, Woland stopped beside his platform. At once Azazello appeared in front of him bearing a dish. On that dish Margarita saw the severed head of a man with most of its front teeth missing. There was still absolute silence, only broken by the distant sound, puzzling in the circumstances, of a door-bell ringing.

' Mikhail Alexandrovich,' said Woland quietly to the head, at which its eyelids opened. With a shudder Margarita saw that the eyes in that dead face were alive, fully conscious and tortured with pain.

' It all came true, didn't it ? ' said Woland, staring at the eyes of the head. ' Your head was cut off by a woman, the meeting didn't take place and I am living in your flat. That is a fact. And a fact is the most obdurate thing in the world. But what interests us now is the future, not the facts of the past. You have always been a fervent proponent of the theory that when a man's head is cut off his life stops, he turns to dust and he ceases to exist. I am glad to be able to tell you in front of all my guests—despite the fact that their presence here is proof to the contrary—that your theory is intelligent and sound. Now—one theory deserves another. Among them there is one which maintains that a man will receive his deserts in accordance with his beliefs. So be it ! You shall depart into the void and from the goblet into which your skull is about to be transformed I shall have the pleasure of drinking to life eternal ! '

Woland raised his sword. Immediately the skin of the head darkened and shrank, then fell away in shreds, the eyes disappeared and in a second Margarita saw on the dish a yellowed skull, with emerald eyes and pearl teeth, mounted on a golden stand. The top of the skull opened with a hinge.

' In a second, messire,' said Koroviev, noticing Woland's enquiring glance, ' he will stand before you. I can hear the creak of his shoes and the tinkle as he puts down the last glass of champagne of his lifetime. Here he is.'

A new guest, quite alone, entered the ballroom. Outwardly he was no different from the thousands of other male guests, except in one thing—he was literally staggering with fright. Blotches glowed on his cheeks and his eyes were swivelling with alarm. The guest was stunned. Everything that he saw shocked him, above all the way Woland was dressed.

Yet he was greeted with marked courtesy.

' Ah, my dear Baron Maigel,' Woland said with a welcoming smile to his guest, whose eyes were starting out of his head. ' I am happy to introduce to you,' Woland turned towards his guests, ' Baron Maigel, who works for the Entertainments Commission as a guide to the sights of the capital for foreign visitors.'

Then Margarita went numb. She recognised this man Maigel. She had noticed him several times in Moscow theatres and restaurants. ' Has he died too ? ' Margarita wondered. But the matter was soon explained.

' The dear Baron,' Woland continued with a broad smile, ' was charming enough to ring me up as soon as I arrived in Moscow and to offer me his expert services as a guide to the sights of the city. Naturally I was happy to invite him to come and see me.'

Here Margarita noticed that Azazello handed the dish with the skull to Koroviev.

' By the way, Baron,' said Woland, suddenly lowering his voice confidentially, ' rumours have been going round that you have an unquenchable curiosity. This characteristic, people say, together with your no less developed conversational gifts, has begun to attract general attention. What is more, evil tongues have let slip the words " eavesdropper" and " spy." What is more, there is a suggestion that this may bring you to an unhappy end in less than a month from now. So in order to save you from the agonising suspense of waiting, we have decided to come to your help, making use of the fact that you invited yourself to see me with the aim of spying and eavesdropping as much as you could.'

The Baron turned paler than the pallid Abadonna and then something terrible happened. Abadonna stepped in front of the Baron and for a second took off his spectacles. At that moment there was a flash and a crack from Azazello's hand and the Baron staggered, crimson blood spurting from his chest and drenching his starched shirtfront and waistcoat. Koroviev placed the skull under the pulsating stream of blood and when the goblet was full handed it to Woland. The Baron's lifeless body had meanwhile crumpled to the floor.

'Your health, ladies and gentlemen,' said Woland and raised the goblet to his lips.

An instant metamorphosis took place. The nightshirt and darned slippers vanished. Woland was wearing a black gown with a sword at his hip. He strode over to Margarita, offered her the goblet and said in a commanding voice:

'Drink!'

Margarita felt dizzy, but the cup was already at her lips and a voice was whispering in her ears:

'Don't be afraid, your majesty . . . don't be afraid, your majesty, the blood has long since drained away into the earth and grapes have grown on the spot.'

Her eyes shut, Margarita took a sip and the sweet juice ran through her veins, her ears rang. She was deafened by cocks crowing, a distant band played a march. The crowd of guests faded—the tailcoated men and the women withered to dust and before her eyes the bodies began to rot, the stench of the tomb filled the air. The columns dissolved, the lights went out, the fountains dried up and vanished with the camellias and the tulips. All that remained was what had been there before: poor Berlioz's drawing-room, with a shaft of light falling through its half-open door. Margarita opened it wide and went in.

24. *The Master is Released*

Everything in Woland's bedroom was as it had been before the ball. Woland was sitting in his nightshirt on the bed, only this time Hella was not rubbing his knee, and a meal was laid on the table in place of the chessboard. Koroviev and Azazello had removed their tailcoats and were sitting at table, alongside them the cat, who still refused to be parted from his bow-tie even though it was by now reduced to a grubby shred. Tottering, Margarita walked up to the table and leaned on it. Woland beckoned her, as before, to sit beside him on the bed.

' Well, was it very exhausting ? ' enquired Woland.

' Oh no, messire,' replied Margarita in a scarcely audible voice.

' Noblesse oblige,' remarked the cat, pouring out a glassful of clear liquid for Margarita.

' Is that vodka ? ' Margarita asked weakly.

The cat jumped up from its chair in indignation.

' Excuse me, your majesty,' he squeaked, ' do you think I would give vodka to a lady ? That is pure spirit ! '

Margarita smiled and tried to push away the glass.

' Drink it up,' said Woland and Margarita at once picked up the glass.

' Sit down, Hella,' ordered Woland, and explained to Margarita : ' The night of the full moon is a night of celebration, and I dine in the company of my close friends and my servants. Well, how do you feel ? How did you find that exhausting ball ? '

' Shattering ! ' quavered Koroviev. ' They were all charmed, they all fell in love with her, they were all crushed ! Such tact, such savoir-faire, such fascination, such charm ! '

Woland silently raised his glass and clinked it with Margarita's. She drank obediently, expecting the spirit to knock her out.

It had no ill effect, however. The reviving warmth flowed through her body, she felt a mild shock in the back of her neck, her strength returned as if she had just woken from a long refreshing sleep and she felt ravenously hungry. Remembering that she had not eaten since the morning of the day before, her hunger increased and she began wolfing down caviar.

Behemoth cut himself a slice of pineapple, salted and peppered it, ate it and chased it down with a second glass of spirit with a flourish that earned a round of applause.

After Margarita's second glassful the light in the candelabra burned brighter and the coals in the fireplace glowed hotter, yet she did not feel the least drunk. As her white teeth bit into the meat Margarita savoured the delicious juice that poured from it and watched Behemoth smearing an oyster with mustard.

'If I were you I should put a grape on top of it, too,' said Hella, digging the cat in the ribs.

'Kindly don't teach your grandmother to suck eggs,' Behemoth replied. 'I know how to behave at table, so mind your own business.'

'Oh, how nice it is to dine like this, at home,' tinkled Koroviev's voice, 'just among friends . . .'

'No, Faggot,' said the cat. 'I like the ball—it's so grand and exciting.'

'It's not in the least exciting and not very grand either, and those idiotic bears and the tigers in the bar—they nearly gave me migraine with their roaring,' said Woland.

'Of course, messire,' said the cat. 'If you think it wasn't very grand, I immediately find myself agreeing with you.'

'And so I should think,' replied Woland.

'I was joking,' said the cat meekly 'and as for those tigers, I'll have them roasted.'

'You can't eat tiger-meat' said Hella.

'Think so? Well, let me tell you a story,' retorted the cat. Screwing up its eyes with pleasure it told a story of how it had once spent nineteen days wandering in the desert and its only food had been the meat of a tiger it had killed. They all listened with fascination and when Behemoth came to the end of his story they all chorussed in unison :

' Liar ! '

' The most interesting thing about that farrago,' said Woland, ' was that it was a lie from first to last.'

' Oh, you think so, do you ? ' exclaimed the cat and everybody thought that it was about to protest again, but it only said quietly : ' History will be my judge.'

' Tell me,' revived by the vodka Margot turned to Azazello : ' did you shoot that ex-baron ? '

' Of course,' replied Azazello, ' why not ? He needed shooting.'

' I had such a shock ! ' exclaimed Margarita, ' it happened so unexpectedly ! '

' There was nothing unexpected about it,' Azazello objected, and Koroviev whined :

' Of course she was shocked. Why, even I was shaking in my shoes ! Bang ! Crash ! Down went the baron ! '

' I nearly had hysterics,' added the cat, licking a caviar-smeared spoon.

' But there's something I can't understand,' said Margarita, her eyes sparkling with curiosity. ' Couldn't the music and general noise of the ball be heard outside ? '

' Of course not, your majesty,' said Koroviev. ' We saw to that. These things must be done discreetly.'

' Yes, I see . . . but what about that man on the staircase when Azazello and I came up . . . and the other one at the foot of the staircase ? I had the impression that they were keeping watch on your flat.'

' You're right, you're right,' cried Koroviev, ' you're right, my dear Margarita Nikolayevna ! You have confirmed my suspicions. Yes, he was watching our flat. For a while I thought he was some absent-minded professor or a lover mooning about on the staircase. But no ! I had an uncomfortable feeling he might be watching the flat. And there was another one at the bottom of the stairs too ? And the one at the main entrance— did he look the same ? '

' Suppose they come and arrest you ? ' asked Margarita.

' Oh, they'll come all right, fairest one, they'll come ! ' answered Koroviev. ' I feel it in my bones. Not now, of course, but they'll come when they're ready. But I don't think they'll have much luck.'

' Oh, what a shock I had when the Baron fell ! ' said Margarita, obviously still feeling the effects of seeing her first murder. ' I suppose you're a good shot ? '

' Fair,' answered Azazello.

' At how many paces ? '

' As many as you like,' replied Azazello. ' It's one thing to hit Latunsky's windows with a hammer, but it's quite another to hit him in the heart.'

' In the heart ! ' exclaimed Margarita, clutching her own heart. ' In the heart ! ' she repeated grimly.

' What's this about Latunsky ? ' enquired Woland, frowning at Margarita.

Azazello, Koroviev and Behemoth looked down in embarrassment and Margarita replied, blushing :

' He's a critic. I wrecked his flat this evening.'

' Did you now ! Why ? '

' Because, messire,' Margarita explained, ' he destroyed a certain master.'

' But why did you put yourself to such trouble ? ' asked Woland.

' Let me do it, messire ! ' cried the cat joyfully, jumping to its feet.

' You sit down,' growled Azazello, rising. ' I'll go at once.'

' No ! ' cried Margarita. ' No, I beg you, messire, you mustn't ! '

' As you wish, as you wish,' replied Woland. Azazello sat down again.

' Where were we, precious queen Margot ? ' said Koroviev. ' Ah yes, his heart . . . He can hit a man's heart all right,' Koroviev pointed a long finger at Azazello. ' Anywhere you like. Just name the auricle—or the ventricle.'

For a moment Margarita did not grasp the implication of this, then she exclaimed in amazement :

' But they're inside the body—you can't see them ! '

' My dear,' burbled Koroviev, ' that's the whole point—you can't see them ! That's the joke ! Any fool can hit something you can see ! '

Koroviev took the seven of spades out of a box, showed it to Margarita and asked her to point at one of the pips. Margarita chose the one in the upper right-hand corner. Hella hid the card under a pillow and shouted :

' Ready ! '

Azazello, who was sitting with his back to the pillow, took a black automatic out of his trouser pocket, aimed the muzzle over his shoulder and, without turning round towards the bed, fired, giving Margarita an enjoyable shock. The seven of spades was removed from under the pillow. The upper right-hand pip was shot through.

' I wouldn't like to meet you when you've got a revolver,' said Margarita with a coquettish look at Azazello. She had a passion for people who did things well.

' My precious queen,' squeaked Koroviev, ' I don't recommend anybody to meet him even without his revolver ! I give you my word of honour as an ex-choirmaster that anybody who did would regret it.'

During the trial of marksmanship the cat had sat scowling. Suddenly it announced :

' I bet I can shoot better than that.'

Azazello snorted, but Behemoth was insistent and demanded not one but two revolvers. Azazello drew another pistol from his left hip pocket and with a sarcastic grin handed them both to the cat. Two pips on the card were selected. The cat took a long time to prepare, then turned its back on the cushion. Margarita sat down with her fingers in her ears and stared at the owl dozing on the mantelpiece. Behemoth fired from both revolvers, at which there came a yelp from Hella, the owl fell dead from the mantelpiece and the clock stopped from a bullet in its vitals. Hella, one finger bleeding, sank her nails into the cat's fur. Behemoth in retaliation clawed at her hair and the pair of them rolled on the floor in a struggling heap. A glass fell off the table and broke.

' Somebody pull this she-devil off me ! ' wailed the cat, lashing out at Hella who had thrown the animal on its back and was sitting astride it. The combatants were separated and Koroviev healed Hella's wounded finger by blowing on it.

' I can't shoot properly when people are whispering about me behind my back ! ' shouted Behemoth, trying to stick back into place a large handful of fur that had been torn off his back.

' I bet you,' said Woland with a smile at Margarita, ' that he did that on purpose. He can shoot perfectly well.'

Hella and the cat made friends again and sealed their reconciliation with a kiss. Someone removed the card from under the cushion and examined it. Not a single pip, except the one shot through by Azazello had been touched.

' I don't believe it,' said the cat, staring through the hole in the card at the light of the candelabra.

Supper went gaily on. The candles began to gutter, a warm dry heat suffused the room from the fireplace. Having eaten her fill, a feeling of well-being came over Margarita. She watched as Azazello blew smoke-rings at the fireplace and the cat spiked them on the end of his sword. She felt no desire to go, although by her timing it was late—probably, she thought, about six o'clock in the morning. During a pause Margarita turned to Woland and said timidly :

' Excuse me, but it's time for me to go . . . it's getting late . . .'

' Where are you going in such a hurry ? ' enquired Woland politely but a little coldly. The others said nothing, pretending to be watching the game with the smoke-rings.

' Yes, it's time,' said Margarita uneasily and turned round as if looking for a cloak or something else to wear. Her nakedness was beginning to embarrass her. She got up from the table. In silence Woland picked up his greasy dressing-gown from the bed and Koroviev threw it over Margarita's shoulders.

' Thank you, messire,' whispered Margarita with a questioning glance at Woland. In reply he gave her a polite but apathetic smile. Black depression at once swelled up in Margarita's heart. She felt herself cheated. No one appeared to be going to offer her any reward for her services at the ball and nobody made a move to prevent her going. Yet she realised quite well that she had nowhere to go. A passing thought that she might have to go back home brought on an inner convulsion of despair. Dared she ask about the master, as Azazello had so temptingly suggested in the Alexander Gardens ? ' No, never ! ' she said to herself.

' Goodbye, messire,' she said aloud, thinking : ' If only I can get out of here, I'll make straight for the river and drown myself ! '

' Sit down,' Woland suddenly commanded her.

A change came over Margarita's face and she sat down.

' Perhaps you'd like to say something in farewell ? '

' Nothing, messire,' replied Margarita proudly, ' however, if you still need me I am ready to do anything you wish. I am not at all tired and I enjoyed the ball. If it had lasted longer I would have been glad to continue offering my knee to be kissed by thousands more gallows-birds and murderers.'

Margarita felt she was looking at Woland through a veil ; her eyes had filled with tears. ' Well said ! ' boomed Woland in a terrifying voice. ' That was the right answer ! '

' The right answer ! ' echoed Woland's retinue in unison.

' We have put you to the test,' said Woland. ' You should never ask anyone for anything. Never—and especially from those who are more powerful than yourself. They will make the offer and they will give of their own accord. Sit down, proud woman ! ' Woland pulled the heavy dressing-gown from Margarita's back and she again found herself sitting beside him on the bed. ' So, Margot,' Woland went on, his voice softening. ' What do you want for having been my hostess tonight ? What reward do you want for having spent the night naked ? What price do you set on your bruised knee ? What damages did you suffer at the hands of my guests, whom just now you called gallows-birds? Tell me! You can speak without constraint now, because it was I who made the offer.'

Margarita's heart began to knock, she sighed deeply and tried to think of something.

' Come now, be brave! ' said Woland encouragingly. ' Use your imagination! The mere fact of having watched the murder of that worn-out old rogue of a baron is worth a reward, especially for a woman. Well? '

Margarita caught her breath. She was about to utter her secret wish when she suddenly turned pale, opened her mouth and stared. ' Frieda! . . . Frieda, Frieda! ' a sobbing, imploring voice cried in her ear. ' My name is Frieda! ' and Margarita said, stuttering :

' Can I ask . . . for one thing? '

' Demand, don't ask, *madonna mia*,' replied Woland with an understanding smile. ' You may demand one thing.'

With careful emphasis Woland repeated Margarita's own words : ' one thing '.

Margarita sighed again and said :

' I want them to stop giving Frieda back the handkerchief she used to stifle her baby.'

The cat looked up at the ceiling and sighed noisily, but said nothing, obviously remembering the damage done to his ear.

' In view of the fact,' said Woland, smiling, ' that the possibility of your having taken a bribe from that idiot Frieda is, of course, excluded—it would in any case have been unfitting to your queenly rank—I don't know what to do. So there only remains one thing—to find yourself some rags and use them to block up all the cracks in my bedroom.'

' What do you mean, messire? ' said Margarita, puzzled.

' I quite agree, messire,' interrupted the cat. ' Rags—that's it! ' And the cat banged its paw on the table in exasperation.

' I was speaking of compassion,' explained Woland, the gaze of his fiery eye fixed on Margarita. ' Sometimes it creeps in through the narrowest cracks. That is why I suggested using rags to block them up . . .'

' That's what I meant, too ! ' exclaimed the cat, for safety's sake edging away from Margarita and covering its pointed ears with paws smeared in pink cream.

' Get out,' Woland said to the cat.

' I haven't had my coffee,' replied Behemoth. ' How can you expect me to go yet ? Surely you don't divide your guests into two grades on a festive night like this, do you—first-grade and second-grade-fresh, in the words of that miserable cheeseparing barman ? '

' Shut up,' said Woland, then turning to Margarita enquired : ' To judge from everything about you, you seem to be a good person. Am I right ? '

' No,' replied Margarita forcefully. ' I know that I can only be frank with you and I tell you frankly—I am headstrong. I only asked you about Frieda because I was rash enough to give her a firm hope. She's waiting, messire, she believes in my power. And if she's cheated I shall be in a terrible position. I shall have no peace for the rest of my life. I can't help it—it just happened.'

' That's quite understandable,' said Woland.

' So will you do it ? ' Margarita asked quietly.

' Out of the question,' replied Woland. ' The fact is, my dear queen, that there has been a slight misunderstanding. Each department must stick to its own business. I admit that our scope is fairly wide, in fact it is much wider than a number of very sharp-eyed people imagine . . .'

' Yes, much wider,' said the cat, unable to restrain itself and obviously proud of its interjections.

' Shut up, damn you ! ' said Woland, and he turned and went on to Margarita. ' But what sense is there, I ask you, in doing something which is the business of another department, as I call it ? So you see I can't do it ; you must do it yourself.'

' But can I do it ? '

Azazello squinted at Margarita, gave an imperceptible flick of his red mop and sneered.

' That's just the trouble—to do it,' murmured Woland. He

had been turning the globe, staring at some detail on it, apparently absorbed in something else while Margarita had been talking.

' Well, as to Frieda . . .' Koroviev prompted her.

' Frieda ! ' cried Margarita in a piercing voice.

The door burst open and a naked, dishevelled but completely sober woman with ecstatic eyes ran into the room and stretched out her arms towards Margarita, who said majestically :

' You are forgiven. You will never be given the handkerchief again.'

Frieda gave a shriek and fell spreadeagled, face downward on the floor in front of Margarita. Woland waved his hand and Frieda vanished.

' Thank you. Goodbye,' said Margarita and rose to go.

' Now, Behemoth,' said Woland, ' as tonight is a holiday we shan't take advantage of her for being so impractical, shall we ? ' He turned to Margarita. ' All right, that didn't count, because I did nothing. What do you want for yourself ? '

There was silence, broken by Koroviev whispering to Margarita :

' *Madonna bellissima*, this time I advise you to be more sensible. Or your luck may run out.'

' I want you to give me back instantly, this minute, my lover —the master,' said Margarita, her face contorted.

A gust of wind burst into the room, flattening the candle flames. The heavy curtain billowed out, the window was flung open and high above appeared a full moon—not a setting moon, but the midnight moon. A dark green cloth stretched from the window-sill to the floor and down it walked Ivan's night visitor, the man who called himself the master. He was wearing his hospital clothes—dressing-gown, slippers and the black cap from which he was never parted. His unshaven face twitched in a grimace, he squinted with fear at the candle flames and a flood of moonlight boiled around him.

Margarita recognised him at once, groaned, clasped her hands and ran towards him. She kissed him on the forehead, the lips, pressed her face to his prickly cheek and her long-suppressed tears streamed down her face. She could only say, repeating it like a senseless refrain :

'It's you . . . it's you . . . it's you . . .'

The master pushed her away and said huskily :

'Don't cry, Margot, don't torment me, I'm very ill,' and he grasped the windowsill as though preparing to jump out and run away again. Staring round at the figures seated in the room he cried : 'I'm frightened, Margot ! I'm getting hallucinations again . . .'

Stifled with sobbing, Margarita whispered, stammering :

'No, no . . . don't be afraid . . . I'm here . . . I'm here . . .'

Deftly and unobtrusively Koroviev slipped a chair behind the master. He collapsed into it and Margarita fell on her knees at his side, where she grew calmer. In her excitement she had not noticed that she was no longer naked and that she was now wearing a black silk gown. The master's head nodded forward and he stared gloomily at the floor.

'Yes,' said Woland after a pause, 'they have almost broken him.'

He gave an order to Koroviev :

'Now, sir, give this man something to drink.'

In a trembling voice Margarita begged the master :

'Drink it, drink it ! Are you afraid ? No, no, believe me, they want to help you ! '

The sick man took the glass and drank it, but his hand trembled, he dropped the glass and it shattered on the floor.

'*Mazel tov!*' Koroviev whispered to Margarita. 'Look, he's coming to himself already.'

It was true. The patient's stare was less wild and distraught.

'Is it really you, Margot ? asked the midnight visitor.

'Yes, it really is,' replied Margarita.

'More ! ' ordered Woland.

When the master had drained the second glass his eyes were fully alive and conscious.

' That's better,' said Woland with a slight frown. ' Now we can talk. Who are you ? '

' I am no one,' replied the master with a lopsided smile.

' Where have you just come from ? '

' From the madhouse. I am a mental patient,' replied the visitor.

Margarita could not bear to hear this and burst into tears again. Then she wiped her eyes and cried :

' It's terrible—terrible ! He is a master, messire, I warn you ! Cure him—he's worth it ! '

' You realise who I am, don't you ? ' Woland asked. ' Do you know where you are ? '

'I know,' answered the master. 'My next-door neighbour in the madhouse is that boy, Ivan Bezdomny. He told me about you.'

' Did he now ! ' replied Woland. ' I had the pleasure of meeting that young man at Patriarch's Ponds. He nearly drove *me* mad, trying to prove that I didn't exist. But you believe in me, I hope ? '

' I must,' said the visitor, ' although I would much prefer it if I could regard you as a figment of my own hallucination. Forgive me,' added the master, recollecting himself.

' By all means regard me as such if that makes you any happier,' replied Woland politely.

' No, no ! ' said Margarita with anxiety, shaking the master by the shoulder. ' Think again ! It really is him ! '

' But I really am like a hallucination. Look at my profile in the moonlight,' said Behemoth. The cat moved into a shaft of moonlight and was going to say something else, but was told to shut up and only said :

' All right, all right, I'll be quiet. I'll be a silent hallucination.'

' Tell me, why does Margarita call you the master? ' enquired Woland.

The man laughed and said :

' An understandable weakness of hers. She has too high an opinion of a novel that I've written.'

' Which novel ? '

' A novel about Pontius Pilate.'

Again the candle flames flickered and jumped and the crockery rattled on the table as Woland gave a laugh like a clap of thunder. Yet no one was frightened or shocked by the laughter ; Behemoth even applauded.

' About what ? About whom ? ' said Woland, ceasing to laugh. ' But that's extraordinary ! In this day and age ? Couldn't you have chosen another subject ? Let me have a look.' Woland stretched out his hand palm uppermost.

' Unfortunately I cannot show it to you,' replied the master, ' because I burned it in my stove.'

' I'm sorry but I don't believe you,' said Woland. ' You can't have done. Manuscripts don't burn.' He turned to Behemoth and said : ' Come on, Behemoth, give me the novel.'

The cat jumped down from its chair and where he had been sitting was a pile of manuscripts. With a bow the cat handed the top copy to Woland. Margarita shuddered and cried out, moved to tears :

' There's the manuscript ! There it is ! '

She flung herself at Woland's feet and cried ecstatically: ' You are all-powerful ! '

Woland took it, turned it over, put it aside and turned, unsmiling, to stare at the master. Without apparent cause the master had suddenly relapsed into uneasy gloom ; he got up from his chair, wrung his hands and turning towards the distant moon he started to tremble, muttering :

' Even by moonlight there's no peace for me at night . . . Why do they torment me ? Oh, ye gods . . .'

Margarita clutched his hospital dressing-gown, embraced him and moaned tearfully :

' Oh God, why didn't that medicine do you any good ? '

' Don't be upset,' whispered Koroviev, edging up to the master, ' another little glassful and I'll have one myself to keep you company . . .'

A glass winked in the moonlight. It began to work. The master sat down again and his expression grew calmer.

' Well, that makes everything quite clear,' said Woland, tapping the manuscript with his long finger.

' Quite clear,' agreed the cat, forgetting its promise to be a silent hallucination. ' I see the gist of this great opus quite plainly now. What do you say, Azazello ? '

' I say,' drawled Azazello, ' that you ought to be drowned.'

' Be merciful, Azazello', the cat replied, ' and don't put such thoughts into my master's head. I'd come and haunt you every night and beckon you to follow me. How would you like that, Azazello ? '

' Now Margarita,' said Woland, ' say whatever you wish to say.'

Margarita's eyes shone and she said imploringly to Woland :

' May I whisper to him ? '

Woland nodded and Margarita leaned over the master's ear and whispered something into it. Aloud, he replied :

' No, it's too late. I want nothing more out of life except to see you. But take my advice and leave me, otherwise you will be destroyed with me.'

' No, I won't leave you,' replied Margarita, and to Woland she said : ' Please send us back to his basement in that street near the Arbat, light the lamp again and make everything as it was before.'

The master laughed, and clasping Margarita's dishevelled head he said :

' Don't listen to this poor woman, messire ! Somebody else is living in that basement now and no one can turn back the clock.' He laid his cheek on his mistress's head, embraced Margarita and murmured :

' My poor darling . . .'

' No one can turn the clock back, did you say ? ' said Woland ' That's true. But we can always try. Azazello ! '

Immediately a bewildered man in his underclothes crashed through the ceiling to the floor, with a suitcase in his hand and wearing a cap. Shaking with fear, the man bowed.

' Is your name Mogarych ? ' Azazello asked him.

' Aloysius Mogarych,' said the new arrival, trembling.

' Are you the man who lodged a complaint against this man '
—pointing to the master—' after you had read an article about
him by Latunsky, and denounced him for harbouring illegal
literature ? ' asked Azazello.

The man turned blue and burst into tears of penitence.

' You did it because you wanted to get his flat, didn't you ? '
said Azazello in a confiding, nasal whine.

The cat gave a hiss of fury and Margarita, with a howl of:
' I'll teach you to thwart a witch ! ' dug her nails into Aloysius
Mogarych's face.

There was a brisk scuffle.

' Stop it ! ' cried the master in an agonised voice. ' Shame on
you, Margot ! '

' I protest ! There's nothing shameful in it ! ' squeaked the cat.
Koroviev pulled Margarita away.

' I put in a bathroom . . .' cried Mogarych, his face streaming
blood. His teeth were chattering and he was babbling with fright.
' I gave it a coat of whitewash . . .'

' What a good thing that you put in a bathroom,' said Azazello
approvingly. ' He'll be able to have baths now.' And he shouted
at Mogarych : ' Get out ! '

The man turned head over heels and sailed out of the open
window of Woland's bedroom.

His eyes starting from his head, the master whispered :

' This beats Ivan's story ! ' He stared round in amazement
then said to the cat : ' Excuse me, but are you . . .' he hesitated,
not sure how one talked to a cat : ' Are you the same cat who
boarded the tramcar ? '

' I am,' said the cat, flattered, and added : ' It's nice to hear
someone speak so politely to a cat. People usually address cats
as " pussy ", which I regard as an infernal liberty.'

' It seems to me that you're not entirely a cat . . .' replied the
master hesitantly. ' The hospital people are bound to catch me
again, you know,' he added to Woland resignedly.

' Why should they ? ' said Koroviev reassuringly. Some

papers and books appeared in his hand : ' Is this your case-history ? '

' Yes . . . '

Koroviev threw the case-history into the fire. ' Remove the document—and you remove the man,' said Koroviev with satisfaction.

' And is this your landlord's rent-book ? '

' Yes . . . '

' What is the tenant's name ? Aloysius Mogarych ? ' Koroviev blew on the page. ' Hey presto ! He's gone and, please note, he was never there. If the landlord is surprised, tell him he was dreaming about Aloysius. Mogarych ? What Mogarych ? Never heard of him ! ' At this the rent-book evaporated from Koroviev's hands. ' Now it's back on the landlord's desk.'

' You were right,' said the master, amazed at Koroviev's efficiency, ' when you said that once you remove the document, you remove the man as well. I no longer exist now—I have no papers.'

' Oh no, I beg your pardon,' exclaimed Koroviev. ' That is just another hallucination. Here are your papers ! ' He handed the master some documents, then said with a wink to Margarita : ' And here is your property, Margarita Nikolayevna.' Koroviev handed Margarita a manuscript-book with burnt edges, a dried rose, a photograph and, with special care, a savings-bank book : ' The ten thousand that you deposited, Margarita Nikolayevna. We have no use for other people's money.'

' May my paws drop off before I touch other people's money,' exclaimed the cat, bouncing up and down on a suitcase to flatten the copies of the ill-fated novel that were inside it.

' And a little document of yours,' Koroviev went on, handing Margarita a piece of paper. Then turning to Woland he announced respectfully : ' That is everything, messire.'

' No, it's not everything,' answered Woland, turning away from the globe. ' What would you like me to do with your retinue, Madonna ? I have no need of them myself.'

Natasha, stark naked, flew in at the open window and cried to

Margarita : ' I hope you'll be very happy, Margarita Nikolayevna ! ' She nodded towards the master and went on : ' You
see, I knew about it all the time.'

' Servants know everything,' remarked the cat, wagging its
paw sagely. ' It's a mistake to think they're blind.'

' What do you want, Natasha ? ' asked Margarita. ' Go back
home.'

' Dear Margarita Nikolayevna,' said Natasha imploringly and
fell on her knees, ' ask him,' she nodded towards Woland, ' to
let me stay a witch. I don't want to go back to that house ! Last
night at the ball Monsieur Jacques made me an offer.' Natasha
unclenched her fist and showed some gold coins.

Margarita looked enquiringly at Woland, who nodded. Natasha
embraced Margarita, kissed her noisily and with a triumphant
cry flew out of the window.

Natasha was followed by Nikolai Ivanovich. He had regained
human form, but was extremely glum and rather cross.

' Now here's someone I shall be especially glad to release,'
said Woland, looking at Nikolai Ivanovich with repulsion. ' I
shall be delighted to see the last of him.'

' Whatever you do, please give me a certificate,' said Nikolai
Ivanovich, anxiously but with great insistence, ' to prove where
I was last night.'

' What for ? ' asked the cat sternly.

' To show to my wife and to the police,' said Nikolai Ivanovich firmly.

' We don't usually give certificates,' replied the cat frowning,
' but as it's for you we'll make an exception.'

Before Nikolai Ivanovich knew what was happening, the naked
Hella was sitting behind a typewriter and the cat dictating to her.

' This is to certify that the Bearer, Nikolai Ivanovich, spent
the night in question at Satan's Ball, having been enticed there
in a vehicular capacity . . . Hella, put in brackets after that
" (pig) ". Signed—Behemoth.'

' What about the date ? ' squeaked Nikolai Ivanovich.

' We don't mention the date, the document becomes invalid if it's dated,' replied the cat, waving the piece of paper. Then the animal produced a rubber stamp, breathed on it in the approved fashion, stamped 'Paid' on the paper and handed the document to Nikolai Ivanovich. He vanished without trace, to be unexpectedly replaced by another man.

'Now who's this?' asked Woland contemptuously, shielding his eyes from the candlelight.

Varenukha hung his head, sighed and said in a low voice:

'Send me back, I'm no good as a vampire. Hella and I nearly frightened Rimsky to death, but I'll never make a vampire—I'm just not bloodthirsty. Please let me go.'

'What is he babbling about?' asked Woland, frowning. 'Who is this Rimsky? What is all this nonsense?'

'Nothing to worry about, messire,' said Azazello and he turned to Varenukha: 'Don't play the fool or tell lies on the telephone any more. Understand? You're not going to, are you?'

Overcome with relief, Varenukha beamed and stammered:

'Thank Go ... I mean ... your maj ... as soon as I've had my supper ...' He pressed his hand to his heart and gazed imploringly at Azazello.

'All right. Off you go home!' said Azazello and Varenukha melted away.

'Now all of you leave me alone with these two,' ordered Woland, pointing to the master and Margarita.

Woland's command was obeyed instantly. After a silence he said to the master:

'So you're going back to your basement near the Arbat. How will you be able to write now? Where are your dreams, your inspiration?'

'I have no more dreams and my inspiration is dead,' replied the master, 'nobody interests me any longer except her'—he laid his hand again on Margarita's head—'I'm finished. My only wish is to return to that basement.'

'And what about your novel? What about Pilate?'

' I hate that novel,' replied the master. ' I have been through too much because of it.'

' Please,' begged Margarita piteously, ' don't talk like that. Why are you torturing me ? You know I've put my whole life into your work,' and she added, turning to Woland : ' Don't listen to him, messire, he has suffered too much.'

' But won't you need to re-write some of it ? ' asked Woland. ' Or if you've exhausted your Procurator, why not write about somebody else—that Aloysius, for instance . . .'

The master smiled.

' Lapshennikova would never print it and in any case that doesn't interest me.'

' How will you earn your living, then ? Won't you mind being poor ? '

' Not a bit,' said the master, drawing Margarita to him. Embracing her round the shoulders he added : ' She'll leave me when she comes to her senses.'

' I doubt it,' said Woland, teeth clenched. He went on : ' So the creator of Pontius Pilate proposes to go and starve in a basement ? '

Margarita unlinked her arms from the master's and said passionately :

' I've done all I can. I whispered to him the most tempting thing of all. And he refused.'

' I know what you whispered to him,' said Woland, ' but that is not what tempts him most. Believe me,' he turned with a smile to the master, ' your novel has some more surprises in store for you.'

' What a grim prospect,' answered the master.

' No, it is not grim at all,' said Woland. ' Nothing terrible will come of it, I assure you. Well now, Margarita Nikolayevna, everything is arranged. Have you any further claims on me ? '

' How can I, messire ? '

' Then take this as a souvenir,' said Woland and took a small golden, diamond-studded horseshoe from under a cushion.

' No—I couldn't take it. Haven't you done enough for me ? '

' Are you arguing with me ? ' asked Woland, smiling.

As Margarita had no pocket in her gown she wrapped the horseshoe in a napkin and knotted it. Then something seemed to worry her. She looked out of the window at the moon and said : ' One thing I don't understand—it still seems to be midnight. Shouldn't it be morning ? '

' It's pleasant to stop the clock on a festive night such as this,' replied Woland. ' And now—good luck ! '

Margarita stretched both hands to Woland in entreaty, but found she could come no nearer to him.

' Goodbye ! Goodbye ! '

' *Au revoir*,' said Woland.

Margarita in her black cloak and the master in his hospital dressing-gown walked out into the corridor of Berlioz's flat, where the light was burning and Woland's retinue was waiting for them. As they passed along the corridor Hella, helped by the cat, carried the suitcase with the novel and Margarita Nikolayevna's few belongings.

At the door of the flat Koroviev bowed and vanished, while the others escorted them down the staircase. It was empty. As they passed the third floor landing a faint bump was heard, but no one paid it any attention. At the front door of staircase 6 Azazello blew into the air and as they entered the dark courtyard they saw a man in boots and peaked cap sound asleep on the doorstep and a large, black car standing by the entrance with dimmed lights. Barely visible in the driver's seat was the outline of a crow.

Margarita was just about to sit down when she gave a stifled cry of despair :

' Oh God, I've lost the horseshoe.'

' Get into the car,' said Azazello, ' and wait for me. I'll be back in a moment as soon as I've looked into this.' He walked back through the doorway.

What had happened was this : shortly before Margarita, the master and their escort had left No. 50, a shrivelled woman carrying a bag and a tin can had emerged from No. 48, the flat immediately below. It was Anna—the same Anna who the previous Wednesday had spilt the sunflower-seed oil near the turnstile with such disastrous consequences for Berlioz.

Nobody knew and no one probably ever will know what this woman was doing in Moscow or what she lived on. She was to be seen every day either with her tin can or her bag or both, sometimes at the oil-shop, sometimes at the market, sometimes outside the block of flats or on the staircase, but mostly in the kitchen of flat No. 48, where she lived. She was notorious for being a harbinger of disaster wherever she went and she was nicknamed ' Anna the Plague '.

Anna the Plague usually got up very early in the morning, but this morning something roused her long before dawn, soon after midnight. Her key turned in the door, her nose poked through and was followed by Anna herself, who slammed the door behind her. She was just about to set off on some errand when the door banged on the upstairs landing, a man came bounding downstairs, crashed into Anna and knocked her sideways so hard that she hit the back of her head against the wall.

' Where the hell do you think you're going like that—in your underpants ? ' whined Anna, rubbing the back of her head.

The man, who was wearing underclothes and a cap and carrying a suitcase, answered in a sleepy voice with his eyes closed :

' Bath . . . whitewash . . . cost me a fortune . . .' and bursting into tears he bellowed : ' I've been kicked out ! '

Then he dashed off—not downstairs but upstairs again to where the windowpane had been broken by Poplavsky's foot, and through it he glided feet first out into the courtyard. Forgetting about her aching head, Anna gasped and rushed up to the broken window. She lay flat on the landing floor and stuck her head out in the courtyard, expecting to see the mortal remains of the man with the suitcase lit up by the courtyard lamp. But there was absolutely nothing to be seen on the courtyard pavement.

As far as Anna could tell, this weird sleepwalker had flown

out of the house like a bird, leaving not a trace. She crossed
herself and thought: 'It's that No. 50! No wonder people say
it's haunted . . .'

The thought had hardly crossed her mind before the door
upstairs slammed again and someone else came running down.
Anna pressed herself to the wall and saw a respectable looking
gentleman with a little beard and, so it seemed to her, a slightly
piggish face, who slipped past her and like the first man left the
building through the window, also without hitting the ground
below. Anna had long since forgotten her original reason for
coming out, and stayed on the staircase, crossing herself, moaning
and talking to herself. After a short while a third man, with no
beard but with a round clean-shaven face and wearing a shirt,
emerged and shot through the window in turn.

To give Anna her due she was of an enquiring turn of mind
and she decided to wait and see if there were to be any further
marvels. The upstairs door opened again and a whole crowd
started coming downstairs, this time not running but walking
like ordinary people. Anna ran down from the window back
to her own front door, quickly opened it, hid behind it and kept
her eye, wild with curiosity, fixed to the crack which she left
open.

An odd sick-looking man, pale with a stubbly beard, in a black
cap and dressing-gown, was walking unsteadily downstairs, carefully helped by a lady wearing what looked to Anna in the gloom
like a black cassock. The lady was wearing some transparent
slippers, obviously foreign, but so torn and shredded that she
was almost barefoot. It was indecent—bedroom slippers and
quite obviously naked except for a black gown billowing out as
she walked! 'That No. 50!' Anna's mind was already savouring
the story she was going to tell the neighbours tomorrow.

After this lady came a naked girl carrying a suitcase and helped
by an enormous black cat. Rubbing her eyes, Anna could barely
help bursting into a shriek of pure amazement. Last in the procession was a short, limping foreigner with a wall eye, no jacket,
a white evening-dress waistcoat and a bow tie. Just as the whole

party had filed downstairs past Anna's door, something fell on to the landing with a gentle thump.

When the sound of footsteps had died away, Anna wriggled out of her doorway like a snake, put down her tin can, dropped on to her stomach and started groping about on the landing floor. Suddenly she found herself holding something heavy wrapped in a table-napkin. Her eyes started from her head as she untied the napkin and lifted the jewel close to eyes that burned with a wolfish greed. A storm of thoughts whirled round her mind:

' See no sights and tell no tales ! Shall I take it to my nephew ? Or split it up into pieces ? I could ease the stones out and sell them off one at a time. . . .'

Anna hid her find in the front of her blouse, picked up her tin can and was just about to abandon her errand and slip back indoors when she was suddenly confronted by the coatless man with the white shirtfront, who whispered to her in a soft voice:

' Give me that horseshoe wrapped in a serviette ! '

' What serviette ? What horseshoe ? ' said Anna, prevaricating with great skill. ' Never seen a serviette. What's the matter with you—drunk ? '

Without another word but with fingers as hard and as cold as the handrail of a bus, the man in the white shirtfront gripped Anna's throat so tightly that he prevented all air from entering her lungs. The tin can fell from her hand. Having stopped Anna from breathing for a while, the jacketless stranger removed his fingers from her neck. Gasping for breath, Anna smiled.

' Oh, you mean the little horseshoe ? ' she said. ' Of course ! Is it yours ? I looked and there it was wrapped in a serviette, I picked it up on purpose in case anybody else might find it and vanish with it ! '

With the horseshoe in his possession again, the stranger began bowing and scraping to Anna, shook her by the hand and thanked her warmly in a thick foreign accent:

' I am most deeply grateful to you, madame. This horseshoe is dear to me as a memory. Please allow me to give you two hundred roubles for saving it.' At which he pulled the money from his waistcoat pocket and gave it to Anna, who could only exclaim with a bewildered grin :

'Oh, thank you so much ! *Merci!*'

In one leap the generous stranger had jumped down a whole flight of stairs, but before vanishing altogether he shouted up at her, this time without a trace of an accent :

'Next time you find someone else's things, you old witch, hand it in to the police instead of stuffing it down your front !'

Utterly confused by events and by the singing in her ears, Anna could do nothing for a long time but stand on the staircase and croak : '*Merci! Merci!*' until long after the stranger had vanished.

Having returned Woland's present to Margarita, Azazello said goodbye to her, enquiring if she was comfortably seated ; Hella gave her a smacking kiss and the cat pressed itself affectionately to her hand. With a wave to the master as he lowered himself awkwardly into his seat and a wave to the crow, the party vanished into thin air, without bothering to return indoors and walk up the staircase. The crow switched on the headlights and drove out of the courtyard past the man asleep at the entrance. Finally the lights of the big black car were lost as they merged into the rows of streetlamps on silent, empty Sadovaya Street.

An hour later Margarita was sitting, softly weeping from shock and happiness, in the basement of the little house in one of the sidestreets off the Arbat. In the master's study all was as it had been before that terrible autumn night of the year before. On the table, covered with a velvet cloth, stood a vase of lily-of-the-valley and a shaded lamp. The charred manuscript-book lay in front of her, beside it a pile of undamaged copies. The house was silent. Next door on a divan, covered by his hospital dressing-gown, the master lay in a deep sleep, his regular breathing inaudible from the next room.

Drying her tears, Margarita picked up one of the unharmed folios and found the place that she had been reading before she had met Azazello beneath the Kremlin wall. She had no wish to sleep. She smoothed the manuscript tenderly as one strokes a favourite cat and turning it over in her hands she inspected it from every angle, stopping now on the title page, now at the end. A fearful thought passed through her mind that it was nothing more than a piece of wizardry, that the folio might vanish from sight, that she would wake up and find that she was in her bedroom at home and it was time to get up and stoke the boiler. But this was only a last terrible fantasy, the echo of long-borne suffering. Nothing vanished, the all-powerful Woland really was all-powerful and Margarita was able to leaf through the manuscript to her heart's content, till dawn if she wanted to, stare at it, kiss it and re-read the words :

' The mist that came from the Mediterranean sea blotted out the city that Pilate so detested . . .'

25. How the Procurator Tried to Save Judas of Karioth

The mist that came from the Mediterranean sea blotted out the city that Pilate so detested. The suspension bridges connecting the temple with the grim fortress of Antonia vanished, the murk descended from the sky and drowned the winged gods above the hippodrome, the crenellated Hasmonaean palace, the bazaars, the caravanserai, the alleyways, the pools . . . Jerusalem, the great city, vanished as though it had never been. The mist devoured everything, frightening every living creature in Jerusalem and its surroundings. The city was engulfed by a strange cloud which had crept over it from the sea towards the end of that day, the fourteenth of the month of Nisan.

It had emptied its belly over Mount Golgotha, where the executioners had hurriedly despatched their victims, it had flowed over the temple of Jerusalem, pouring down in smoky cascades from the mound of the temple and invading the Lower City. It had rolled through open windows and driven people indoors from the winding streets. At first it held back its rain and only spat lightning, the flame cleaving through the smoking black vapour, lighting up the great pile of the temple and its glittering, scaly roof. But the flash passed in a moment and the temple was plunged again into an abyss of darkness. Several times it loomed through the murk to vanish again and each time its disappearance was accompanied by a noise like the crack of doom.

Other shimmering flashes lit up the palace of Herod the Great facing the temple on the western hill; as they did so the golden statues, eyeless and fearful, seemed to leap up into the black sky and stretch their arms towards it. Then the fire from heaven would be quenched again and a great thunderclap would banish the gilded idols into the mist.

The rainstorm burst suddenly and the storm turned into a hurricane. On the very spot near a marble bench in the garden, where that morning the Procurator had spoken to the High Priest, a thunderbolt snapped the trunk of a cypress as though it had been a twig. With the water vapour and the hail, the balcony under the arcade was swept with torn rose-heads, magnolia leaves, small branches and sand as the hurricane scourged the garden.

At the moment when the storm broke only the Procurator was left beneath the arcade.

He was no longer sitting in a chair but lying on a couch beside a small low table laid with food and jugs of wine. Another, empty, couch stood on the far side of the table. An untidy, blood-red puddle lay spread out at the Procurator's feet amid the sherds of a broken jug. The servant who had laid the Procurator's table had been so terrified by his look and so nervous at his apparent displeasure that the Procurator had lost his temper with him and smashed the jug on the mosaic floor, saying :

' Why don't you look me in the eyes when you serve me ? Have you stolen something ? '

The African's black face turned grey, mortal terror came into his eyes and he trembled so much that he almost broke another jug, but the Procurator waved him away and the slave ran off, leaving the pool of spilt wine.

As the hurricane struck, the African hid himself in a niche beside a statue of a white, naked woman with bowed head, afraid to show himself too soon yet frightened of missing the call should the Procurator summon him.

Lying on his couch in the half-darkness of the storm the Procurator poured out his own wine, drank it in long gulps, stretching out his arm for an occasional piece of bread which he crumbled and ate in little pieces. Now and again he would swallow an oyster, chew a slice of lemon and drink again.

Without the roar of water, without the claps of thunder which seemed to be about to smash the palace roof, without the crash of hail that hammered on the steps leading up to the balcony, a listener might have heard the Procurator muttering as he talked to himself. And if the momentary flashes of lightning had shone with a steady light an observer might have noticed that the Procurator's face, the eyes inflamed with insomnia and wine, showed impatience ; that the Procurator's glance was not only taken up by the two yellow roses drowning in the red puddle, but that he was constantly turning his face towards the garden, towards the water-lashed sand and mud ; that he was expecting someone, waiting impatiently.

A little time passed and the veil of water in front of the Procurator began to thin out. The storm, though still furious, was abating. No more branches creaked and fell. The lightning and thunder grew more infrequent. The cloud hovering over Jerusalem was no longer violet edged with white but a normal grey, the rearguard of the storm that was now moving onwards towards the Dead Sea.

Soon the sound of the rain could be distinguished from the noise of water running down the gutters and on to the staircase down which the Procurator had walked to the square to pronounce sentence. At last even the tinkle of the fountain, drowned until now, could be heard. It grew lighter. Windows of blue began to appear in the grey veil as it fled eastward.

Then from far away, above the weak patter of rain, the Procurator heard faint trumpet-calls and the tattoo of several score of horses' hooves. The sound caused the Procurator to stir and his expression to liven. The ala was returning from Mount Golgotha. To judge from the sound, they were just crossing the hippodrome square.

At last the Procurator heard the long-awaited footsteps and the slap of shoe-leather on the staircase leading to the upper terrace of the garden in front of the balcony. The Procurator craned his neck and his eyes shone expectantly.

Between the two marble lions there appeared first the cowled

341

head, then the figure of a man closely wrapped in his soaking wet cloak. It was the same man with whom the Procurator, before pronouncing sentence, had held a whispered conference in a darkened room of the palace, and who had watched the execution as he played with a stick seated on a three-legged stool.

Walking straight through the puddles, the cowled man crossed the terrace, crossed the mosaic floor of the balcony, and raising his hand said in a pleasant, high-pitched voice :

' Hail, Procurator ! ' The visitor spoke in Latin.

' Gods ! ' exclaimed Pilate. ' There's not a dry stitch on you ! What a storm ! Please go to my room at once and change.'

The man pushed back his cowl, revealing a completely wet head with the hair plastered down over his forehead. With a polite smile on his clean-shaven face he declined the offer of a change of clothing, assuring the Procurator that a little rain would do him no harm.

' I won't hear of it,' replied Pilate. He clapped his hands, summoning his cowering servant, and ordered him to help the visitor to change and then to bring him some hot food.

The Procurator's visitor needed only a short while to dry his hair, change his clothes, his footgear, and tidy himself up, and he soon reappeared on the balcony in dry sandals, in a purple army cloak and with his hair combed.

At that moment the sun returned to Jerusalem and before setting in the Mediterranean it sent its parting rays over the Procurator's hated city and gilded the balcony steps. The fountain was now playing again at full strength, pigeons had landed on the terrace, cooing and hopping between the broken twigs and pecking at the sand. The red puddle was mopped up, the fragments removed, a steaming plateful of meat was set on the table.

' I await the Procurator's orders,' said the visitor as he approached the table.

' Forget about my orders until you have sat down and drunk your wine,' answered Pilate kindly, pointing to the other couch.

The man reclined, the servant poured some thick red wine

into his cup. Another servant, bending cautiously over Pilate's shoulder, filled the Procurator's cup, after which he dismissed them both with a gesture.

While the visitor ate and drank Pilate sipped his wine and watched his guest through narrowed eyes. The man was middle-aged with very pleasant, neat, round features and a fleshy nose. The colour of his hair was vague, though its colour lightened as it dried out. His nationality was hard to guess. His main feature was a look of good nature, which was belied by his eyes —or rather not so much by his eyes as by a peculiar way of looking at the person facing him. Usually the man kept his small eyes shielded under eyelids that were curiously enlarged, even swollen. At these moments the chinks in his eyelids showed nothing but mild cunning, the look of a man with a sense of humour. But there were times when the man who was now the Procurator's guest opened his eyelids wide and gave a person a sudden, unwavering stare as though to search out an inconspicuous spot on his nose. It only lasted a moment, after which the lids dropped, the eyes narrowed again and they shone with goodwill and sly intelligence.

The visitor accepted a second cup of wine, swallowed a few oysters with obvious relish, tasted the boiled vegetables and ate a piece of meat. When he had eaten his fill he praised the wine :

' An excellent vintage, Procurator—is it Falernian ? '

' Cecuba—thirty years old,' replied the Procurator amiably.

The visitor placed his hand on his heart and declined the offer of more to eat, saying that he had had enough. Pilate refilled his own cup and his guest did the same. The two men each poured a libation into the dish of meat and the Procurator, raising his cup, said in a loud voice :

' To thee, O Caesar, father of thy people, best and most beloved of men.'

Both drank their wine to its dregs and the Africans cleared the dishes from the table, leaving fruit and jugs of wine. The Procurator dismissed the servants, and was left alone with his visitor under the arcade.

' So,' began Pilate quietly, ' what have you to tell me of the mood of the city ? ' Involuntarily he turned his glance downwards to where, past the terraces of the garden, the colonnades and flat roofs glowed in the golden rays of the setting sun.

' I believe, Procurator,' said his visitor, ' that the mood of Jerusalem can now be regarded as satisfactory.'

' So I can rely on there being no further disorders ? '

' One can only rely,' Arthanius replied with a reassuring glance at the Procurator, ' on one thing in this world—on the power of great Caesar.'

' May the gods send him long life ! ' Pilate said fervently, ' And universal peace ! ' He was silent for a moment then went on : ' What do you think—can we withdraw the troops now ? '

' I think the cohort from the Lightning can be sent away,' replied the visitor, and added : ' It would be a good idea if it were to parade through the city before leaving.'

' A very good idea,' said the Procurator approvingly. ' I shall order it away the day after tomorrow. I shall also go myself and—I swear to you by the feast of the twelve gods, I swear by the Lares—I would have given a lot to have been able to do so today ! '

' Does the Procurator not like Jerusalem ? ' enquired the visitor amicably.

' Merciful heavens ! ' exclaimed the Procurator, smiling. ' It's the most unsettling place on earth. It isn't only the climate— I'm ill every time I have to come here—that's only half the trouble. But these festivals ! Magicians, sorcerers, wizards, the hordes of pilgrims. Fanatics—all of them. And what price this messiah of theirs, which they're expecting this year ? Every moment there's likely to be some act of gratuitous bloodshed. I spend all my time shuffling the troops about or reading denunciations and complaints, half of which are directed at you. You must admit it's boring. Oh, if only I weren't in the imperial service ! '

' Yes, the festivals here are trying times,' agreed the visitor.

' I wish with all my heart that this one was over,' said Pilate forcibly. ' Then I can go back to Caesarea. Do you know, this lunatic building of Herod's '—the Procurator waved at the arcade, embracing the whole palace in a gesture—' is positively driving me out of my mind. I can't bear sleeping in it. It is the most extraordinary piece of architecture in the world . . . However, to business. First of all—is that cursed Bar-Abba giving you any trouble ? '

At this the visitor directed his peculiar stare at the Procurator, but Pilate was gazing wearily into the distance, frowning with distaste and contemplating the quarter of the city which lay at his feet, fading into the dusk. The visitor's glance also faded and his eyelids lowered again.

' I think that Bar is now as harmless as a lamb,' said the visitor, his round face wrinkling. ' He is hardly in a position to make trouble now.'

' Too busy ? ' asked Pilate, smiling.

' The Procurator, as usual, has put the point with great finesse.'

' But at all events,' remarked the Procurator anxiously and raised a long, thin finger adorned with a black stone, ' we must . . .'

' The Procurator may rest assured that as long as I am in Judaea Bar will not move a step without my being on his heels.'

' That is comforting. I am always comforted when you are here.'

' The Procurator is too kind.'

' Now tell me about the execution,' said Pilate.

' What interests the Procurator in particular ? '

' Chiefly, whether there were any attempts at insurrection from the mob ? '

' None,' answered the visitor.

' Good. Did you personally confirm that they were dead ? '

' Of that the Procurator may be sure.'

' And tell me . . . were they given a drink before being gibbeted ? '

' Yes. But he '—the visitor closed his eyes—' refused to drink.'

'Who did ? ' asked Pilate.

' I beg your pardon, hegemon ! ' exclaimed the visitor. ' Didn't I say ? Ha-Notsri ! '

' Madman ! ' said Pilate, grimacing. A vein twitched under his left eye. ' To die of sunstroke ! Why refuse what the law provides for ? How did he refuse ? '

' He said,' replied the guest, shutting his eyes again, ' that he was grateful and blamed no one for taking his life.'

' Whom did he thank ? ' asked Pilate in a low voice.

' He did not say, hegemon . . .'

' He didn't try to preach to the soldiers, did he ? '

' No, hegemon, he was not very loquacious on this occasion. His only words were that he regarded cowardice as one of the worst human sins.'

' What made him say that ? ' The Procurator's voice suddenly trembled.

' I have no idea. His behaviour was in any case strange, as it always has been.'

' In what way strange ? '

' He kept staring at individuals among the people standing around him, and always with that curiously vague smile on his face.'

' Nothing more ? ' asked the husky voice.

' Nothing more.'

The jug clattered against his cup as the Procurator poured himself some more wine. Having drained it he said :

' My conclusion is as follows : although we have not been able—at least not at present—to find any followers or disciples of his, we nevertheless cannot be certain that he had none.'

The visitor nodded, listening intently.

' Therefore to avoid any untoward consequences,' the Procurator went on, ' please remove the three victims' bodies from the face of the earth, rapidly and without attracting attention. Bury them secretly and silently so that nothing more is heard of them.'

' Very good, hegemon,' said the visitor. He stood up and

said : ' As this matter is important and will present certain difficulties, may I have your permission to go at once ? '

' No, sit down again,' said Pilate, restraining his visitor with a gesture. ' I have a couple more questions to ask you. Firstly—your remarkable diligence in carrying out your task as chief of the secret service to the Procurator makes it my pleasant duty to mention it in a report to Rome.'

The visitor blushed as he rose, bowed to the Procurator and said :

' I am only doing my duty as a member of the imperial service.'

' But,' said the hegemon, ' if you are offered promotion and transfer to another post, I should like to ask you to refuse it and stay here. I do not wish to be parted from you on any account. I shall see to it that you are rewarded in other ways.'

' I am happy to serve under you, hegemon.'

' I am very glad to hear it. Now for the second question. It concerns that man . . . what's his name ? . . . Judas of Karioth.'

At this the visitor again gave the Procurator his open-eyed glance, then, as was fitting, hooded his eyes again.

' They say,' the Procurator went on, lowering his voice, ' that he is supposed to have been paid for the way he took that idiot home and made him so welcome.'

' *Will* be paid,' corrected the visitor gently.

' How much ? '

' No one can tell, hegemon.'

' Not even you ? ' said the hegemon, praising the man by his surprise.

' Alas, not even I,' replied the visitor calmly. ' But I do know that he will be paid this evening. He has been summoned to Caiaphas' palace today.'

' Ah, he must be greedy, that old man from Karioth ! ' said the Procurator with a smile. ' I suppose he is an old man, isn't he ? '

' The Procurator is never mistaken, but on this occasion he

has been misinformed,' replied the man kindly. ' This man from Karioth is a young man.'

' Really ? Can you describe him ? Is he a fanatic ? '

' Oh no, Procurator.'

' I see. What else do you know about him ? '

' He is very good-looking.'

' What else ? Has he perhaps a special passion ? '

' It is hard to know so much with certainty in this huge city, Procurator.'

' Come now, Arthanius ! You underestimate yourself.'

' He has one passion, Procurator.' The visitor made a tiny pause. ' He has a passion for money.'

' What is his occupation ? '

Arthanius looked up, reflected and answered :

' He works for one of his relatives who has a money-changer's booth.'

' I see, I see.' The Procurator was silent, looked round to make sure that there was no one on the balcony and then said in a low voice : ' The fact is—I have received information that he is to be murdered tonight.'

At this the visitor not only turned his glance on the Procurator but held it for a while and then replied :

' You have flattered me, Procurator, but I fear I have not earned your commendation. I have no such information.'

' You deserve the highest possible praise,' replied the Procurator, ' but there is no doubting this information.'

' May I ask its source ? '

' You must allow me not to divulge that for the present, particularly as it is casual, vague and unreliable. But it is my duty to allow for every eventuality. I place great reliance on my instinct in these matters, because it has never failed me yet. The information is that one of Ha-Notsri's secret followers, revolted by this money-changer's monstrous treachery, has plotted with his confederates to kill the man tonight and to return his blood-money to the High Priest with a note reading : " Take back your accursed money ! " '

The chief of the secret service gave the hegemon no more of his startling glances and listened, frowning, as Pilate continued :

' Do you think the High Priest will be pleased at such a gift on Passover night ? '

' Not only will he not be pleased,' replied the visitor with a smile, ' but I think, Procurator, that it will create a major scandal.'

' I think so too. That is why I am asking you to look after the affair and take all possible steps to protect Judas of Karioth.'

' The hegemon's orders will be carried out,' said Arthanius, ' but I can assure the hegemon that these villains have set themselves a very difficult task. After all, only think '—the visitor glanced round as he spoke—' they have to trace the man, kill him, then find out how much money he received and return it to Caiaphas by stealth. All that in one night ? Today ? '

' Nevertheless he will be murdered tonight,' Pilate repeated firmly. ' I have a presentiment, I tell you ! And it has never yet played me false.' A spasm crossed the Procurator's face and he rubbed his hands.

' Very well,' said the visitor obediently. He rose, straightened up and suddenly said coldly :

' You say he will be murdered, hegemon ? '

' Yes,' answered Pilate, ' and our only hope is your extreme efficiency.'

The visitor adjusted the heavy belt under his cloak and said :
' Hail and farewell, Procurator ! '

' Ah, yes,' cried Pilate, ' I almost forgot. I owe you some money.'

The visitor looked surprised.

' I am sure you do not, Procurator.'

' Don't you remember ? When I arrived in Jerusalem there was a crowd of beggars, I wanted to throw them some money, I had none and borrowed from you.'

' But Procurator, that was a trifle ! '

' One should remember trifles.' Pilate turned, lifted a cloak lying on a chair behind him, picked up a leather purse from beneath it and handed it to Arthanius. The man bowed, took the purse and put it under his cloak.

'I expect,' said Pilate, 'a report on the burial and on the matter of Judas of Karioth tonight, do you hear, Arthanius, tonight. The guards will be given orders to wake me as soon as you appear. I shall be waiting for you.'

'Very well,' said the chief of the secret service and walked out on to the balcony. For a while Pilate could hear the sound of wet sand under his feet, then the clatter of his sandals on the marble paving between the two stone lions. Then legs, torso and finally cowl disappeared. Only then did the Procurator notice that the sun had set and twilight had come.

26. The Burial

It may have been the twilight which seemed to cause such a sharp change in the Procurator's appearance. He appeared to have aged visibly and he looked hunched and worried. Once he glanced round and shuddered, staring at the empty chair with his cloak thrown over its back. The night of the feast was approaching, the evening shadows were playing tricks and the exhausted Procurator may have thought he had seen someone sitting in the chair. In a moment of superstitious fear the Procurator shook the cloak, then walked away and began pacing the balcony, occasionally rubbing his hands, drinking from the goblet on the table, or halting to stare unseeingly at the mosaic floor as though trying to decipher some writing in it.

For the second time that day a brooding depression overcame him. Wiping his brow, where he felt only a faintly nagging memory of the hellish pain from that morning, the Procurator racked his brain in an attempt to define the cause of his mental agony. He soon realised what it was, but unable to face it, he tried to deceive himself. It was clear to him that this morning he had irretrievably lost something and now he was striving to compensate for that loss with a trivial substitute, which took the form of belated action. His self-deception consisted in trying to persuade himself that his actions this evening were no less significant than the sentence which he had passed earlier in the day. But in this attempt the Procurator had little success.

At one of his turns he stopped abruptly and whistled. In reply there came a low bark from the twilight shadows and a gigantic grey-coated dog with pointed ears bounded in from the garden, wearing a gold-studded collar.

' Banga, Banga,' cried the Procurator weakly.

The dog stood up on its hind legs, put its forepaws on its master's shoulders, almost knocking him over, and licked his cheek. The Procurator sat down in a chair. Banga, tongue hanging out and panting fast, lay down at Pilate's feet with an expression of delight that the thunderstorm was over, the only thing in the world that frightened this otherwise fearless animal ; delighted, too, because it was back again with the man it loved, respected and regarded as the most powerful being on earth, the ruler of all men, thanks to whom the dog too felt itself a specially privileged and superior creature. But lying at his feet and gazing into the twilit garden without even looking at Pilate the dog knew at once that its master was troubled. It moved, got up, went round to Pilate's side and laid its forepaws and head on the Procurator's knees, smearing the hem of his cloak with wet sand. Banga's action seemed to mean that he wanted to comfort his master and was prepared to face misfortune with him. This he tried to express in his eyes and in the forward set of his ears. These two, dog and man who loved each other, sat in vigil together on the balcony that night of the feast.

Meanwhile Arthanius was busy. Leaving the upper terrace of the garden, he walked down the steps to the next terrace and turned right towards the barracks inside the palace grounds. These quarters housed the two centuries who had accompanied the Procurator to Jerusalem for the feast-days, together with the Procurator's secret bodyguard commanded by Arthanius. He spent a little while in the barracks, no longer than ten minutes, but immediately afterwards three carts drove out of the barrack yard loaded with entrenching tools and a vat of water, and escorted by a section of fifteen mounted men wearing grey cloaks. Carts and escort left the palace grounds by a side-gate, set off westward, passed through a gateway in the city wall and first took the Bethlehem road northward ; they reached the crossroads by the Hebron gate and there turned on to the Jaffa road, along the route taken by the execution party that morning. By now it was dark and the moon had risen on the horizon.

Soon after the carts and their escort section had set off, Arthanius also left the palace on horseback, having changed into a shabby black chiton, and rode into the city. After a while he could have been seen riding towards the fortress of Antonia, situated immediately north of the great temple. The visitor spent an equally short time in the fortress, after which his route took him to the winding, crooked streets of the Lower City. He had now changed his mount to a mule.

Thoroughly at home in the city, the man easily found the street he was looking for. It was known as the street of the Greeks, as it contained a number of Greek shops, including one that sold carpets. There the man stopped his mule, dismounted and tethered it to a ring outside the gate. The shop was shut. The guest passed through a wicket gate in the wall beside the shop door and entered a small rectangular courtyard, fitted out as a stables. Turning the corner of the yard the visitor reached the ivy-grown verandah of the owner's house and looked round him. House and stables were dark, the lamps not yet lit. He called softly :

' Niza ! '

At the sound of his voice a door creaked and a young woman, her head uncovered, appeared on the verandah in the evening dusk. She leaned over the railings, looking anxiously to see who had arrived. Recognising the visitor, she gave him a welcoming smile, nodded and waved.

' Are you alone ? ' asked Arthanius softly in Greek.

' Yes, I am,' whispered the woman on the verandah. ' My husband went to Caesarea this morning '—here the woman glanced at the door and added in a whisper—' but the servant is here.' Then she beckoned him to come in.

Arthanius glanced round, mounted the stone steps and went indoors with the woman. Here he spent no more than five minutes, after which he left the house, pulled his cowl lower over his eyes and went out into the street. By now candles were being lit in all the houses, there was a large feast-day crowd in the streets, and Arthanius on his mule was lost in the stream of riders and people on foot. Where he went from there is unknown.

When Arthanius had left her, the woman called Niza began to change in a great hurry, though despite the difficulty of finding the things she needed in her dark room she lit no candle and did not call her servant. Only when she was ready, with a black shawl over her head, did she say :

' If anybody asks for me tell them that I've gone to see Enanta.'

Out of the dark her old serving-woman grumbled in reply :

' Enanta ? That woman ! You know your husband's forbidden you to see her. She's nothing but a procuress, that Enanta of yours. I'll tell your husband . . .'

' Now, now, now, be quiet,' retorted Niza and slipped out of doors like a shadow, her sandals clattering across the paved courtyard. Still grumbling, the servant shut the verandah door and Niza left her house.

At the same time a young man left a tumbledown little house with its blind side to the street and whose only windows gave on to the courtyard, and passed through the wicket into an unpaved alley that descended in steps to one of the city's pools. He wore a white kefiyeh falling to his shoulders, a new dark-blue fringed tallith for the feast-day, and creaking new sandals. Dressed up for the occasion, the handsome, hook-nosed young man set off boldly, overtaking passers-by as he hurried home to the solemn Passover-night table, watching the candles as they were lit in house after house. The young man took the road leading past the bazaar towards the palace of Caiaphas the High Priest at the foot of the temple hill.

After a while he entered the gates of Caiaphas' palace and left it a short time later.

Leaving the palace, already bright with candles and torches and festive bustle, the young man returned, with an even bolder and more cheerful step, to the Lower City. At the corner where the street joined the bazaar square, he was passed in the seething crowd by a woman walking with the hip-swinging gait of a prostitute and wearing a black shawl low over her eyes. As she overtook him the woman raised her shawl slightly and flashed a glance in the young man's direction, but instead of slowing down she walked faster as though trying to run away from him.

The young man not only noticed the woman but recognised her. He gave a start, halted, stared perplexedly at her back and at once set off to catch her up. Almost knocking over a man carrying a jug, the young man drew level with the woman and panting with agitation called out to her :

' Niza ! '

The woman turned, frowned with a look of chilling irritation and coldly replied in Greek :

' Oh, it's you, Judas. I didn't recognise you. Still, it's lucky. We have a saying that if you don't recognise a person he's going to be rich. . . .'

So excited that his heart began to leap like a wild bird in a cage, Judas asked in a jerky whisper, afraid that the passers-by might hear :

' Where are you going, Niza ? '

' Why do you want to know ? ' answered Niza, slackening her pace and staring haughtily at Judas.

In a childish, pleading voice Judas whispered distractedly :

' But Niza . . . we agreed . . . I was to come to see you, you said you'd be at home all evening . . .'

' Oh no,' replied Niza, pouting capriciously, which to Judas made her face, the most beautiful he had ever seen in the world, even prettier, ' I'm bored. It's a feast-day for you, but what do you expect me to do ? Sit and listen to you sighing on the verandah ? And always frightened of the servant telling my husband ? No, I've decided to go out of town and listen to the nightingales.'

' Out of town ? ' asked Judas, bewildered. ' What—alone ? '

' Yes, of course,' replied Niza.

' Let me go with you,' whispered Judas with a sigh. His mind was confused, he had forgotten about everything and he gazed pleadingly into Niza's blue eyes that now seemed black in the darkness.

Niza said nothing but walked faster.

' Why don't you say something, Niza ? ' asked Judas miserably, hastening to keep pace with her.

' Won't I be bored with you ? ' Niza asked suddenly and stopped. Judas now felt utterly hopeless.

' All right,' said Niza, relenting at last. ' Come on ! '

' Where to ? '

' Wait . . . let's go into this courtyard and arrange it, otherwise I'm afraid of someone seeing me and then telling my husband that I was out on the streets with my lover.'

Niza and Judas vanished from the bazaar and began whispering under the gateway of a courtyard.

' Go to the olive-grove,' whispered Niza, pulling her shawl down over her eyes and turning away from a man who came into the courtyard carrying a bucket, ' in Gethsemane, over Kedron, do you know where I mean ? '

' Yes, yes . . .'

' I'll go first,' Niza went on, ' but don't follow close behind me, go separately. I'll go ahead. . . . When you've crossed the stream . . . do you know where the grotto is ? '

' Yes, I know, I know . . .'

' Go on through the olive grove on the hill and then turn right towards the grotto. I'll be there. But whatever you do, don't follow me at once, be patient, wait a while here.' With these words Niza slipped out of the gateway as though she had never spoken to Judas.

Judas stood alone for some time, trying to collect his whirling thoughts. Among other things he tried to think how he would explain his absence from the Passover table to his parents. He stood and tried to work out some lie, but in his excitement his mind refused to function properly, and still lacking an excuse he slowly walked out of the gateway.

Now he took another direction and instead of making for the Lower City he turned back towards the palace of Caiaphas. The celebrations had already begun. From windows on all sides came the murmur of the Passover ceremony. Latecomers hastening home urged on their donkeys, whipping them and shouting at them. On foot Judas hurried on, not noticing the menacing turrets of the fortress of Antonia, deaf to the call of trumpets from the fortress, oblivious of the Roman mounted patrol with their torches that threw an alarming glare across his path.

As he turned past the fortress Judas saw that two gigantic seven-branched candlesticks had been lit at a dizzy height above the temple. But he only saw them in a blur. They seemed like dozens of lamps that burned over Jerusalem in rivalry with the single lamp climbing high above the city—the moon.

Judas had no thought for anything now but his urgent haste to leave the city as quickly as possible by the Gethsemane gate. Occasionally he thought he could see, among the backs and faces of the people in front of him, a figure dancing along and drawing him after it. But it was an illusion. Judas realised that Niza must be well ahead of him. He passed a row of money-changers' shops and at last reached the Gethsemane gate. Here, burning with impatience, he was forced to wait. A camel caravan was coming into the city, followed by a mounted Syrian patrol, which Judas mentally cursed. . . .

But the delay was short and the impatient Judas was soon outside the city wall. To his left was a small cemetery, beside it the striped tents of a band of pilgrims. Crossing the dusty, moonlit road Judas hurried on towards the stream Kedron and crossed it, the water bubbling softly under his feet as he leaped from stone to stone. Finally he reached the Gethsemane bank and saw with joy that the road ahead was deserted. Not far away could be seen the half-ruined gateway of the olive grove.

After the stifling city Judas was struck by the intoxicating freshness of the spring night. Across a garden fence the scent of myrtles and acacia was blown from the fields of Gethsemane.

The gateway was unguarded and a few minutes later Judas was far into the olive grove and running beneath the mysterious shadows of the great, branching olive trees. The way led uphill. Judas climbed, panting, occasionally emerging from darkness into chequered carpets of moonlight which reminded him of the carpets in the shop kept by Niza's jealous husband.

Soon an oil-press came in sight in a clearing to Judas' left, with its heavy stone crushing-wheel and a pile of barrels. There was no one in the olive grove—work had stopped at sunset and choirs of nightingales were singing above Judas' head.

He was near his goal. He knew that in a moment from the darkness to his right he would hear the quiet whisper of running water from the grotto. There was the sound now and the air was cooler near the grotto. He checked his pace and called:

' Niza ! '

But instead of Niza slipping out from behind a thick olive trunk, the stocky figure of a man jumped out on to the path. Something glittered momentarily in his hand. With a faint cry Judas started running back, but a second man blocked his way.

The first man asked Judas :

' How much did you get ? Talk, if you want to save your life.'

Hope welled up in Judas' heart and he cried desperately :

' Thirty tetradrachms ! Thirty tetradrachms ! I have it all on me. There's the money ! Take it, but don't kill me ! '

The man snatched the purse from Judas' hand. At the same moment a knife was rammed into Judas' back under his shoulder-blade. He pitched forward, throwing up his hands, fingers clutching. The man in front caught Judas on his knife and thrust it up to the hilt into Judas' heart.

' Ni . . . za . . .' said Judas, in a low, reproachful growl quite unlike his own, youthful, high-pitched voice and made not another sound. His body hit the ground so hard that the air whistled as it was knocked out of his lungs.

Then a third figure stepped out on to the path, wearing a hooded cloak.

' Don't waste any time,' he ordered. The cowled man gave the murderers a note and they wrapped purse and note into a piece of leather which they bound criss-cross with twine. The hooded man put the bundle down his shirt-front, then the two assassins ran off the path and were swallowed by the darkness between the olive trees.

The third man squatted down beside the body and looked

into his face. It seemed as white as chalk, with an expression not unlike spiritual beauty.

A few seconds later there was not a living soul on the path. The lifeless body lay with arms outstretched. Its left foot was in a patch of moonlight that showed up every strap and lace of the man's sandal. The whole of Gethsemane rang with the song of nightingales.

The man with the hood left the path and plunged deep through the olive grove, heading southward. He climbed over the wall at the southernmost corner of the olive grove where the upper course of masonry jutted out. Soon he reached the bank of Kedron, where he waded in and waited in midstream until he saw the distant outlines of two horses and a man beside them, also standing in the stream. Water flowed past, washing their hooves. The groom mounted one of the horses, the cowled man the other and both set off walking down the bed of the stream, pebbles crunching beneath the horses' hooves. The riders left the water, climbed up the bank and followed the line of the city walls at a walk. Then the groom galloped ahead and disappeared from sight while the man in the cowl stopped his horse, dismounted on the empty road, took off his cloak, turned it inside out, and producing a flat-topped, uncrested helmet from the folds, put it on. The rider was now in military uniform with a short sword at his hip. He flicked the reins and the fiery cavalry charger broke into a trot. He had not far to go before he rode up to the southern gate of Jerusalem.

Torch-flames danced and flickered restlessly under the arch of the gate where the sentries from the second cohort of the Lightning legion sat on stone benches playing dice. As the mounted officer approached the soldiers jumped up, the officer waved to them and rode into the city.

The town was lit up for the festival. Candle flames played at every window and from each one came the sound of sing-song incantations. Glancing occasionally into the windows that opened on to the street the rider saw people at their tables set with kid's meat and cups of wine between the dishes of bitter herbs. Whistling softly the rider made his way at a leisurely trot through the deserted streets of the Lower City, heading towards the fortress of Antonia and looking up now and then at vast seven-branched candlesticks flaring over the temple or at the moon above them.

The palace of Herod the Great had no part in the ceremonies of Passover night. Lights were burning in the outbuildings on the south side where the officers of the Roman cohort and the Legate of the Legion were quartered, and there were signs of movement and life. The frontal wings, with their one involuntary occupant—the Procurator—with their arcades and gilded statues, seemed blinded by the brilliance of the moonlight. Inside the palace was darkness and silence.

The Procurator, as he had told Arthanius, preferred not to go inside. He had ordered a bed to be prepared on the balcony where he had dined and where he had conducted the interrogation that morning. The Procurator lay down on the couch, but he could not sleep. The naked moon hung far up in the clear sky and for several hours the Procurator lay staring at it.

Sleep at last took pity on the hegemon towards midnight. Yawning spasmodically, the Procurator unfastened his cloak and threw it off, took off the strap that belted his tunic with its steel sheath-knife, put it on the chair beside the bed, took off his sandals and stretched out. Banga at once jumped up beside him on the bed and lay down, head to head. Putting his arm round the dog's neck the Procurator at last closed his eyes. Only then did the dog go to sleep.

The couch stood in half darkness, shaded from the moon by a pillar, though a long ribbon of moonlight stretched from the staircase to the bed. As the Procurator drifted away from reality he set off along that path of light, straight up towards the moon. In his sleep he even laughed from happiness at the unique beauty of that transparent blue pathway. He was walking with Banga and the vagrant philosopher beside him. They were arguing about a weighty and complex problem over which neither could gain the upper hand. They disagreed entirely, which made their argument the more absorbing and interminable. The execution, of course, had been a pure misunderstanding : after all this same man, with his ridiculous philosophy that all men were good, was walking beside him—consequently he was alive. Indeed the very thought of executing such a man was absurd. There had been no execution ! It had never taken place ! This thought comforted him as he strode along the moonlight pathway.

They had as much time to spare as they wanted, the storm would not break until evening. Cowardice was undoubtedly one of the most terrible sins. Thus spake Yeshua Ha-Notsri. No, philosopher, I disagree—it is the most terrible sin of all !

Had *he* not shown cowardice, the man who was now Procurator of Judaea but who had once been a Tribune of the legion on that day in the Valley of the Virgins when the wild Germans had so nearly clubbed Muribellum the Giant to death ? Have pity on me, philosopher ! Do you, a man of your intelligence, imagine that the Procurator of Judaea would ruin his career for the sake of a man who had committed a crime against Caesar ?

' Yes, yes . . .' Pilate groaned and sobbed in his sleep.

Of course he would risk ruining his career. This morning he had not been ready to, but now at night, having thoroughly weighed the matter, he was prepared to ruin himself if need be. He would do anything to save this crazy, innocent dreamer, this miraculous healer, from execution.

' You and I will always be together,' said the ragged tramp-philosopher who had so mysteriously become the travelling companion of the Knight of the Golden Lance. ' Where one of us goes, the other shall go too. Whenever people think of me they will think of you—me, an orphan child of unknown parents and you the son of an astrologer-king and a miller's daughter, the beautiful Pila ! '

' Remember to pray for me, the astrologer's son,' begged Pilate in his dream. And reassured by a nod from the pauper from Ein-Sarid who was his companion, the cruel Procurator of Judaea wept with joy and laughed in his sleep.

The hegemon's awakening was all the more fearful after the euphoria of his dream. Banga started to growl at the moon, and the blue pathway, slippery as butter, collapsed in front of the Procurator. He opened his eyes and the first thing he remembered was that the execution had taken place. Then the Procurator groped mechanically for Banga's collar, then turned his aching eyes in search of the moon and noticed that it had moved slightly to one side and was silver in colour. Competing with its light was another more unpleasant and disturbing light that flickered in front of him. Holding a flaming, crackling torch, Muribellum scowled with fear and dislike at the dangerous beast, poised to spring.

' Lie down, Banga,' said the Procurator in a suffering voice, coughing. Shielding his eyes from the torch-flame, he went on :

' Even by moonlight there's no peace for me at night. . . . Oh, ye gods ! You too have a harsh duty, Mark. You have to cripple men. . . .'

Startled, Mark stared at the Procurator, who recollected himself. To excuse his pointless remark, spoken while still half-dreaming, the Procurator said :

' Don't be offended, centurion. My duty is even worse, I assure you. What do you want ? '

' The chief of the secret service has come to see you,' said Mark calmly.

' Send him in, send him in,' said the Procurator, clearing his throat and fumbling for his sandals with bare feet. The flame danced along the arcade, the centurion's caligae rang out on the mosaic as he went out into the garden.

' Even by moonlight there's no peace for me,' said the Procurator to himself, grinding his teeth.

The centurion was replaced by the man in the cowl.

' Lie down, Banga,' said the Procurator quietly, pressing down on the dog's head.

Before speaking Arthanius gave his habitual glance round and moved into a shadow. Having ensured that apart from Banga there were no strangers on the balcony, he said :

' You may charge me with negligence, Procurator. You were right. I could not save Judas of Karioth from being murdered. I deserve to be court-martialled and discharged.'

Arthanius felt that of the two pairs of eyes watching him; one was a dog's, the other a wolf's. From under his tunic he took out a bloodstained purse that was sealed with two seals.

' The murderers threw this purseful of money into the house of the High Priest. There is blood on it—Judas of Karioth's blood.'

' How much money is there in it ? ' asked Pilate, nodding towards the purse.

' Thirty tetradrachms.'

The Procurator smiled and said :

' Not much.'

Arthanius did not reply.

' Where is the body ? '

' I do not know,' replied the cowled man with dignity. ' This morning we will start the investigation.'

The Procurator shuddered and gave up trying to lace his sandal, which refused to tie.

' But are you certain he was killed ? '

To this the Procurator received the cool reply :

' I have been working in Judaea for fifteen years, Procurator. I began my service under Valerius Gratus. I don't have to see a body to be able to say that a man is dead and I am stating that the man called Judas of Karioth was murdered several hours ago.'

' Forgive me, Arthanius,' replied Pilate. ' I made that remark because I haven't quite woken up yet. I sleep badly,' the Procurator smiled, ' I was dreaming of a moonbeam. It was funny, because I seemed to be walking along it. . . . Now, I want your suggestions for dealing with this affair. Where are you going to look for him ? Sit down.'

Arthanius bowed, moved a chair closer to the bed and sat down, his sword clinking.

' I shall look for him not far from the oil-press in the Gethsemane olive-grove.'

' I see. Why there ? '

' I believe, hegemon, that Judas was killed neither in Jerusalem itself nor far from the city, but somewhere in its vicinity.'

' You are an expert at your job. I don't know about Rome itself, but in the colonies there's not a man to touch you. Why do you think that ? '

' I cannot believe for one moment,' said Arthanius in a low voice, ' that Judas would have allowed himself to be caught by any ruffians within the city limits. The street is no place for a clandestine murder. Therefore he must have been enticed into some cellar or courtyard. But the secret service has already made a thorough search of the Lower City and if he were there they would have found him by now. They have not found him and I am therefore convinced that he is not in the city. If he had been killed a long way from Jerusalem, then the packet of money could not have been thrown into the High Priest's palace so soon. He was murdered near the city after they had lured him out.'

' How did they manage to do that ? '

' That, Procurator, is the most difficult problem of all and I am not even sure that I shall ever be able to solve it.'

' Most puzzling, I agree. A believing Jew leaves the city to go heaven knows where on the eve of Passover and is killed. Who could have enticed him and how ? Might it have been done by a woman ? ' enquired the Procurator, making a sudden inspired guess.

Arthanius replied gravely :

' Impossible, Procurator. Out of the question. Consider it logically : who wanted Judas done away with ? A band of vagrant cranks, a group of visionaries which, above all, contains no women. To marry and start a family needs money, Procurator. But to kill a man with a woman as decoy or accomplice needs a very great deal of money indeed and these men are tramps—homeless and destitute. There was no woman involved in this affair, Procurator. What is more, to theorise on those lines may even throw us off the scent and hinder the investigation.'

'I see, Arthanius, that you are quite right,' said Pilate. 'I was merely putting forward a hypothesis.'

'It is, alas, a faulty one, Procurator.'

'Well then—what is your theory?' exclaimed the Procurator, staring at Arthanius with avid curiosity.

'I still think that the bait was money.'

'Remarkable! Who, might I ask, would be likely to entice him out of the city limits in the middle of the night to offer him money?'

'No one, of course, Procurator. No, I can only make one guess and if it is wrong, then I confess I am at a loss.' Arthanius leaned closer to Pilate and whispered: 'Judas intended to hide his money in a safe place known only to himself.'

'A very shrewd explanation. That must be the answer. I see it now: he was not lured out of town—he went of his own accord. Yes, yes, that must be it.'

'Precisely. Judas trusted nobody. He wanted to hide his money.'

'You said Gethsemane . . . Why there? That, I confess, I don't understand.'

'That, Procurator, is the simplest deduction of all. No one is going to hide money in the road or out in the open. Therefore Judas did not take the road to Hebron or to Bethany. He will have gone to somewhere hidden, somewhere where there are trees. It's obvious—there is no place round about Jerusalem that answers to that description except Gethsemane. He cannot have gone far.'

'You have completely convinced me. What is your next move?'

'I shall immediately start searching for the murderers who followed Judas out of the city and meanwhile, as I have already proposed to you, I shall submit myself to be court-martialled.'

'What for?'

'My men lost track of Judas this evening in the bazaar after he had left Caiaphas' palace. How it occurred, I don't know. It has never happened to me before. He was put under observation immediately after our talk, but somewhere in the bazaar area he gave us the slip and disappeared without trace.'

' I see. You will be glad to hear that I do not consider it necessary for you to be court-martialled. You did all you could and no one in the world,'—the Procurator smiled—' could possibly have done more. Reprimand the men who lost Judas. But let me warn you that I do not wish your reprimand to be a severe one. After all, we did our best to protect the scoundrel. Oh yes—I forgot to ask '—the Procurator wiped his forehead—' how did they manage to return the money to Caiaphas ? '

' That was not particularly difficult, Procurator. The avengers went behind Caiaphas' palace, where that back street overlooks the rear courtyard. Then they threw the packet over the fence.'

' With a note ? '

' Yes, just as you said they would, Procurator. Oh, by the way . . .' Arthanius broke the seals on the packet and showed its contents to Pilate.

' Arthanius ! Take care what you're doing. Those are temple seals.'

' The Procurator need have no fear on that score,' replied Arthanius as he wrapped up the bag of money.

' Do you mean to say that you have copies of all their seals ? ' asked Pilate, laughing.

' Naturally, Procurator,' was Arthanius' curt, unsmiling reply.

' I can just imagine how Caiaphas must have felt ! '

' Yes, Procurator, it caused a great stir. They sent for me at once.'

Even in the dark Pilate's eyes could be seen glittering.

' Interesting . . .'

' If you'll forgive my contradicting, Procurator, it was most uninteresting. A boring and time-wasting case. When I enquired whether anybody in Caiaphas' palace had paid out this money I was told categorically that no one had.'

' Really ? Well, if they say so, I suppose they didn't. That will make it all the harder to find the murderers.'

' Quite so, Procurator.'

' Arthanius, it has just occurred to me—might he not have killed himself ? '

' Oh no, Procurator,' replied Arthanius, leaning back in his chair and staring in astonishment, ' that, if you will forgive me, is most unlikely ! '

' Ah, in this city anything is likely. I am prepared to bet that before long the city will be full of rumours about his suicide.'

Here Arthanius gave Pilate his peculiar stare, thought a moment, and answered :

' That may be, Procurator.'

Pilate was obviously obsessed with the problem of the murder of Judas of Karioth, although it had been fully explained.

He said reflectively :

' I should have liked to have seen how they killed him.'

' He was killed with great artistry, Procurator,' replied Arthanius, giving Pilate an ironic look.

' How do you know ? '

' If you will kindly inspect the bag, Procurator,' Arthanius replied, ' I can guarantee from its condition that Judas' blood flowed freely. I have seen some murdered men in my time.'

' So he will not rise again ? '

' No, Procurator. He will rise again,' answered Arthanius, smiling philosophically, ' when the trumpet-call of their messiah sounds for him. But not before.'

' All right, Arthanius, that case is dealt with. Now what about the burial ? '

' The executed prisoners have been buried, Procurator.'

' Arthanius, it would be a crime to court-martial you. You deserve the highest praise. What happened ? '

While Arthanius had been engaged on the Judas case, a secret service squad under the command of Arthanius' deputy had reached the hill shortly before dark. At the hilltop one body was missing. Pilate shuddered and said hoarsely :

' Ah, now why didn't I foresee that ? '

' There is no cause for worry, Procurator,' said Arthanius and went on : ' The bodies of Dismas and Hestas, their eyes picked out by carrion crows, were loaded on to a cart. The men at once set off to look for the third body. It was soon found. A man called . . .'

' Matthew the Levite,' said Pilate. It was not a question but an affirmation.

' Yes, Procurator . . . Matthew the Levite was hidden in a cave on the northern slope of Mount Golgotha, waiting for darkness. With him was Ha-Notsri's naked body. When the guard entered the cave with a torch, the Levite fell into a fit. He shouted that he had committed no crime and that according to the law every man had a right to bury the body of an executed criminal if he wished to. Matthew the Levite refused to leave the body. He was excited, almost delirious, begging, threatening, cursing . . .'

' Did they have to arrest him ? ' asked Pilate glumly.

' No, Procurator,' replied Arthanius reassuringly. ' They managed to humour the lunatic by telling him that the body would be buried. The Levite calmed down but announced that he still refused to leave the body and wanted to assist in the burial. He said he refused to go even if they threatened to kill him and even offered them a bread knife to kill him with.'

' Did they send him away ? ' enquired Pilate in a stifled voice.

' No, Procurator. My deputy allowed him to take part in the burial.'

' Which of your assistants was in charge of this detail ? '

' Tolmai,' replied Arthanius, adding anxiously : ' Did I do wrong ? '

' Go on,' replied Pilate. ' You did right. I am beginning to think, Arthanius, that I am dealing with a man who never makes a mistake—I mean you.'

' Matthew the Levite was taken away by cart, together with the bodies, and about two hours later they reached a deserted cave to the north of Jerusalem. After an hour working in shifts the squad had dug a deep pit in which they buried the bodies of the three victims.'

' Naked ? '

' No, Procurator, the squad had taken chitons with them for the purpose. Rings were put on the bodies' fingers : Yeshua's ring had one incised stroke, Dismas' two and Hestas' three. The pit was filled and covered with stones. Tolmai knows the recognition mark.'

' Ah, if only I could have known ! ' said Pilate, frowning. ' I wanted to see that man Matthew the Levite.'

' He is here, Procurator.'

Pilate stared at Arthanius for a moment with wide-open eyes, then said :

' Thank you for everything you have done on this case. Tomorrow please send Tolmai to see me and before he comes tell him that I am pleased with him. And you, Arthanius,'— the Procurator took out a ring from the pocket of his belt and handed it to the chief of secret service—' please accept this as a token of my gratitude.'

With a bow Arthanius said :

' You do me a great honour, Procurator.'

' Please give my commendation to the squad that carried out the burial and a reprimand to the men who failed to protect Judas. And send Matthew the Levite to me at once. I need certain details from him on the case of Yeshua.'

' Very good, Procurator,' replied Arthanius and bowed himself out. The Procurator clapped his hands and shouted :

' Bring me candles in the arcade ! '

Arthanius had not even reached the garden when servants began to appear bearing lights. Three candlesticks were placed on the table in front of the Procurator and instantly the moonlit night retreated to the garden as though Arthanius had taken it with him. In his place a small, thin stranger mounted to the balcony accompanied by the giant centurion. At a nod from the Procurator Muribellum turned and marched out.

Pilate studied the new arrival with an eager, slightly fearful look, in the way people look at someone of whom they have heard a great deal, who has been in their thoughts and whom they finally meet.

The man who now appeared was about forty, dark, ragged, covered in dried mud, with a suspicious, wolfish stare. In a word he was extremely unsightly and looked most of all like one of the city beggars who were to be found in crowds on the terraces of the temple or in the bazaars of the noisy and dirty Lower City.

The silence was long and made awkward by the man's strange behaviour. His face worked, he staggered and he would have fallen if he had not put out a dirty hand to grasp the edge of the table.

' What's the matter with you ? ' Pilate asked him.

' Nothing,' replied Matthew the Levite, making a movement as though he were swallowing something. His thin, bare, grey neck bulged and subsided again.

' What is it—answer me,' Pilate repeated.

' I am tired,' answered the Levite and stared dully at the floor.

' Sit down,' said Pilate, pointing to a chair.

Matthew gazed mistrustfully at the Procurator, took a step towards the chair, gave a frightened look at its gilded armrests and sat down on the floor beside it.

' Why didn't you sit in the chair ? ' asked Pilate.

' I'm dirty, I would make it dirty too,' said the Levite staring at the floor.

' You will be given something to eat shortly.'

' I don't want to eat.'

' Why tell lies ? ' Pilate asked quietly. ' You haven't eaten all day and probably longer. All right, don't eat. I called you here to show me your knife.'

' The soldiers took it away from me when they brought me here,' replied the Levite and added dismally : ' You must give it back to me, because I have to return it to its owner. I stole it.'

' Why ? '

' To cut the ropes.'

' Mark ! ' shouted the Procurator and the centurion stepped into the arcade. ' Give me his knife.'

The centurion pulled a dirty breadknife out of one of the two leather sheaths on his belt, handed it to the Procurator and withdrew.

'Where did you steal the knife?'

'In a baker's shop just inside the Hebron gate, on the left.'

Pilate inspected the wide blade and tested the edge with his finger. Then he said:

'Don't worry about the knife, it will be returned to the shop. Now I want something else—show me the parchment you carry with you on which you have written what Yeshua has said.'

The Levite looked at Pilate with hatred and smiled a smile of such ill-will that his face was completely distorted.

'Are you going to take it away from me? The last thing I possess?'

'I didn't say " give it ",' answered Pilate. 'I said " show it to me".'

The Levite fumbled in his shirt-front and pulled out a roll of parchment. Pilate took it, unrolled it, spread it out in the light of two candles and with a frown began to study the barely decipherable script. The uneven strokes were hard to understand and Pilate frowned and bent over the parchment, tracing the lines with his finger. He nevertheless managed to discern that the writings were a disjointed sequence of sayings, dates, household notes and snatches of poetry. Pilate managed to read: ' there is no death . . . yesterday we ate sweet cakes . . .'

Grimacing with strain, Pilate squinted and read: ' . . . we shall see a pure river of the water of life . . . mankind will look at the sun through transparent crystal . . .'

Pilate shuddered. In the last few lines of the parchment he deciphered the words: '. . . greatest sin . . . cowardice . . .'

Pilate rolled up the parchment and with a brusque movement handed it back to the Levite.

'There, take it,' he said, and after a short silence he added: 'I see you are a man of learning and there is no need for you, living alone, to walk around in such wretched clothes and without a home. I have a large library at Caesarea, I am very rich and I would like you to come and work for me. You would catalogue and look after the papyruses, you would be fed and clothed.'

The Levite stood up and replied :

' No, I don't want to.'

' Why not ? ' asked the Procurator, his expression darkening. ' You don't like me . . . are you afraid of me ? '

The same evil smile twisted Matthew's face and he said :

' No, because you would be afraid of me. You would not find it very easy to look me in the face after having killed him.'

' Silence,' Pilate cut him off. ' Take this money.'

The Levite shook his head and the Procurator went on :

' You, I know, consider yourself a disciple of Yeshua, but I tell you that you have acquired nothing of what he taught you. For if you had, you would have certainly accepted something from me. Remember—before he died he said that he blamed no one—' Pilate raised his finger significantly and his face twitched —' and I know that he would have accepted something. You are hard. He was not a hard man. Where will you go ? '

Matthew suddenly walked over to Pilate's table, leaned on it with both hands and staring at the Procurator with burning eyes he whispered to him :

' Know, hegemon, that there is one man in Jerusalem whom I shall kill. I want to tell you this so that you are warned— there will be more blood.'

' I know that there will be more blood,' answered Pilate. ' What you have said does not surprise me. You want to murder me, I suppose ? '

' I shall not be able to murder you,' replied the Levite, baring his teeth in a smile. ' I am not so stupid as to count on that. But I shall kill Judas of Karioth if it takes the rest of my life.'

At this the Procurator's eyes gleamed with pleasure. Beckoning Matthew the Levite closer he said :

' You will not succeed, but it will not be necessary. Judas was murdered tonight.'

The Levite jumped back from the table, stared wildly round and cried :

' Who did it ? '

Pilate answered him :

' I did it.

' You must not be jealous,' said Pilate, baring his teeth mirth-lessly and rubbing his hands, ' but I'm afraid he had other admirers beside yourself.'

' Who did it ? ' repeated the Levite in a whisper.

Matthew opened his mouth and stared at the Procurator, who said quietly :

' It is not much, but I did it.' And he added : ' Now will you accept something ? '

The Levite thought for a moment, relented and finally said :

' Order them to give me a clean piece of parchment.'

An hour had passed since the Levite had left the palace. The dawn silence was only disturbed by the quiet tread of the sentries in the garden. The moon was fading and on the other edge of heaven there appeared the whitish speck of the morning star. The candles had long been put out. The Procurator lay on his couch. He was sleeping with his hand under his cheek and breathing noiselessly. Beside him slept Banga.

Thus Pontius Pilate, fifth Procurator of Judaea, met the dawn of the fifteenth of Nisan.

27. The Last of Flat No. 50

Day was breaking as Margarita read the last words of the chapter '. . . Thus Pontius Pilate, fifth Procurator of Judaea, met the dawn of the fifteenth of Nisan.'

From the yard she could hear the lively, cheerful early morning chatter of sparrows in the branches of the willow and the lime tree.

Margarita got up from her chair, stretched and only then realised how physically exhausted she felt and how much she wanted to sleep. Mentally, though, Margarita was in perfect form. Her mind was clear and she was completely unmoved by the fact that she had spent a night in the supernatural. It caused her no distress to think that she had been at Satan's ball, that by some miracle the master had been restored to her, that the novel had risen from the ashes, that everything was back in its place in the basement flat after the expulsion of the wretched Aloysius Mogarych. In a word, her encounter with Woland had done her no psychological harm. Everything was as it should be.

She went into the next room, made sure that the master was sound asleep, put out the unnecessary light on the bedside table and stretched out on the other little divan, covering herself with an old, torn blanket. A minute later she was in a dreamless sleep. Silence reigned in the basement rooms and in the whole house, silence filled the little street.

But on that early Saturday morning there was no sleep for a whole floor of a certain Moscow office which was busy investigating the Woland case ; in nine offices the lamps had been burning all night. Their windows, looking out on to a large asphalted square which was being cleaned by slow, whirring vehicles with revolving brushes, competed with the rising sun in brightness.

Although the outlines of the case had been quite clear since the day before, when they had closed the Variety as a result of the disappearance of its management and the scandalous performance of black magic, everything was complicated by the incessant flow of new evidence.

The department in charge of this strange case now had the task of drawing together all the strands of the varied and confusing events, occurring all over Moscow, which included an apparent mixture of sheer devilry, hypnotic conjuring tricks and barefaced crime.

The first person summoned to the glaring electric light of that unsleeping floor was Arkady Apollonich Sempleyarov, the chairman of the Acoustics Commission.

On Friday evening after dinner, the telephone rang in his flat on Kamenny Most and a man's voice asked to speak to Arkady Apollonich. His wife, who had answered the call, announced grimly that Arkady Apollonich was unwell, had gone to lie down and could not come to the telephone. Nevertheless Arkady Apollonich was obliged to come when the voice said who was calling.

' Of course . . . at once . . . right away,' stammered Arkady's usually arrogant spouse and she flew like an arrow to rouse Arkady Apollonich from the couch where he had lain down to recover from the horrific scenes caused by the theatre incident and the stormy expulsion from their flat of his young cousin from Saratov. In a quarter of a minute, in underclothes and one slipper, Arkady Apollonich was babbling into the telephone :

' Yes, it's me. Yes, I will . . .'

His wife, all thought of Arkady Apollonich's infidelity instantly forgotten, put her terrified face round the door, waving a slipper in the air and whispering :

' Put your other slipper on . . . you'll catch cold . . .' At this Arkady Apollonich, waving his wife away with a bare leg and rolling his eyes at her, muttered into the receiver :

' Yes, yes, yes, of course . . . I understand . . . I'll come at once . . .'

Arkady Apollonich spent the rest of the evening with the investigators.

The ensuing conversation was painful and unpleasant in the extreme ; he was not only made to give a completely frank account of that odious show and the fight in the box, but was obliged to tell everything about Militsa Andreyevna Pokobatko from Yelokhovskaya Street, as well as all about his cousin from Saratov and much more besides, the telling of which caused Arkady Apollonich inexpressible pain.

Naturally the evidence given by Arkady Apollonich—an intelligent and cultured man who had been an eyewitness of the show and who as an articulate and informed observer was not only able to give an excellent description of the mysterious masked magician and his two rascally assistants but who actually remembered that the magician's name was Woland—helped considerably to advance the enquiry. When Arkady Apollonich's evidence was compared with the evidence of the others, among them several of the ladies who had suffered such embarrassment after the show (including the woman in violet knickers who had so shocked Rimsky) and Karpov the usher who had been sent to Flat No. 50 at 302A, Sadovaya Street—it became immediately obvious where the culprit was to be found.

They went to No. 50 more than once and not only searched it with extreme thoroughness but tapped on the walls, examined the chimney-flues and looked for secret doors. None of this, however, produced any results and nothing was found during the visits to the flat. Yet someone was living in the flat, despite the fact that every official body in Moscow concerned with visiting foreigners stated firmly and categorically that there was not and could not be a magician called Woland in Moscow.

He had definitely not registered on entry, he had shown no one his passport or any other documents, contracts or agreements and no one had so much as heard of him. Kitaitsev, the director of the programmes department of the Theatrical Commission, swore by all the saints that the missing Stepa Likhodeyev had never sent him a programme schedule for anyone called Woland for confirmation and had never telephoned Kitaitsev a word about Woland's arrival. Therefore he, Kitaitsev, failed completely to understand how Stepa could have allowed a show of this sort to be put on at the Variety. When he was told that Arkady Apollonich had seen the performance with his own eyes, Kitaitsev could only spread his hands and raise his eyes to heaven. From those eyes alone it was obvious that Kitaitsev was as pure as crystal.

Prokhor Petrovich, the chairman of the Entertainments Commission . . .

He, incidentally, had re-entered his suit as soon as the police reached his office, to the ecstatic joy of Anna Richardovna and to the great annoyance of the police, who had been alerted for nothing. As soon as he was back at his post and wearing his striped grey suit, Prokhor Petrovich fully approved all the minutes that his suit had drafted during his short absence.

So Prokhor Petrovich obviously knew nothing about Woland either.

The sum total of their enquiries amounted to a conclusion which was little short of farcical : thousands of spectators, plus the Variety Theatre staff plus, finally, Arkady Apollonich, that highly intelligent man, had seen this magician and his thrice-cursed assistants, yet in the meantime all four had completely vanished. What could it mean ? Had Woland been swallowed up by the earth or had he, as some claimed, never come to Moscow at all ? If one accepted the first alternative, then he had apparently spirited away the entire Variety management with him ; if you believed the second alternative, it meant that the theatre management itself, having first indulged in a minor orgy of destruction had decamped from Moscow leaving no trace.

The officer in charge of the case was, to give him his due, a man who knew his job. Rimsky, for instance, was tracked down with astounding speed. Merely by linking the Ace of Diamonds' behaviour at the taxi-rank near the cinema with certain timings, such as the time of the end of the show and the time at which Rimsky could have vanished, they were able to send an immediate telegram to Leningrad. An hour later (on Friday evening) the reply came back that Rimsky had been found in room 412 at the Astoria Hotel, on the fourth floor next to the room containing the repertory manager of one of the Moscow theatres then on tour in Leningrad, in that famous room with the blue-grey furniture and the luxurious bathroom.

Rimsky, found hiding in the wardrobe of his room at the Astoria, was immediately arrested and interrogated in Leningrad, after which a telegram reached Moscow stating that treasurer Rimsky was an irresponsible witness who had proved unwilling or incapable of replying coherently to questions and had done nothing but beg to be put into an armourplated strong-room under armed guard. An order was telegraphed to Leningrad for Rimsky to be escorted back to Moscow, and he returned under guard by the Friday evening train.

By Friday evening, too, they were on the track of Likhodeyev. Telegrams asking for information on Likhodeyev had been sent to every town and a reply came from Yalta that Likhodeyev was there but about to leave for Moscow by aeroplane.

The only person whose trail they failed to pick up was Varen-ukha. This man, known to the entire theatrical world of Moscow, seemed to have vanished without trace.

Meanwhile investigations were in hand on related incidents in other parts of Moscow. An explanation was needed, for instance, of the baffling case of the office staff who had sung the ' Volga Boatmen ' song (Stravinsky, incidentally, cured them all within two hours by subcutaneous injections) and of other cases of people (and their victims) who had proffered various pieces of rubbish under the illusion that they were banknotes. The nastiest, the most scandalous and the most insoluble of all these episodes was, of course, the theft, in broad daylight, of Berlioz's head from the open coffin at Griboyedov.

The job of the team of twelve men assigned to the case was rather like that of someone with a knitting-needle trying to pick up stitches dropped all over Moscow.

One of the detectives called on Professor Stravinsky's clinic and began by asking for a list of all patients admitted during the past three days. By this means they discovered Nikanor Ivanovich Bosoi and the unfortunate compère whose head had been wrenched off, although they were not greatly interested in these two. It was obvious now that they had both merely been victimised by the gang headed by this weird magician. In Ivan Nikolayich Bezdomny, however, the detective showed the very greatest interest.

Early on Friday evening the door of Ivan's room opened to admit a polite, fresh-faced young man. He looked quite unlike a detective, yet he was one of the best in the Moscow force. He saw lying in bed a pale, pinched-looking young man with lack-lustre, wandering eyes. The detective, a man of considerable charm and tact, said that he had come to see Ivan for a talk about the incident at Patriarch's Ponds two days previously.

The poet would have been triumphant if the detective had called earlier, on Thursday for instance when Ivan had been trying so loudly and passionately to induce someone to listen to his story about Patriarch's Ponds. Now people were at last coming to hear his version of the affair—just when his urge to help capture Professor Woland had completely evaporated.

For Ivan, alas, had altogether changed since the night of Berlioz's death. He was quite prepared to answer the detective's questions politely, but his voice and his expression betrayed his utter disinterest. The poet no longer cared about Berlioz's fate.

While Ivan had been dozing before the detective's arrival, a succession of images had passed before his mind's eye. He saw a strange, unreal, vanished city with great arcaded marble piles ; with roofs that flashed in the sunlight ; with the grim, black and pitiless tower of Antonia ; with a palace on the western hill plunged almost to roof-level in a garden of tropical greenery, and above the garden bronze statues that glowed in the setting sun ; with Roman legionaries clad in armour marching beneath the city walls.

In his half-waking dream Ivan saw a man sitting motionless in a chair, a clean-shaven man with taut, yellowing skin who wore a white cloak lined with red, who sat and stared with loathing at this alien, luxuriant garden. Ivan saw, too, a treeless ochre-coloured hill with three empty cross-barred gibbets.

The events at Patriarch's Ponds no longer interested Ivan Bezdomny the poet.

' Tell me, Ivan Nikolayich, how far were you from the turnstile when Berlioz fell under the tram ? '

A barely detectable smile of irony crossed Ivan's lips as he replied :

' I was far away.'

' And was the man in checks standing beside the turnstile ? '

' No, he was on a bench nearby.'

' You distinctly remember, do you, that he did not approach the turnstile at the moment when Berlioz fell ? '

' I do remember. He didn't move. He was on the bench and he stayed there.'

These were the detective's last questions. He got up, shook hands with Ivan, wished him a speedy recovery and said that he soon hoped to read some new poetry of his.

' No,' said Ivan quietly. ' I shall not write any more poetry.'

The detective smiled politely and assured the poet that although he might be in a slight state of depression at the moment, it would soon pass.

' No,' said Ivan, staring not at the detective but at the distant twilit horizon, ' it will never pass. The poetry I wrote was bad poetry. I see that now.'

The detective left Ivan, having gathered some extremely important evidence. Following the thread of events backwards from end to beginning, they could now pinpoint the source of the whole episode. The detective had no doubt that the events in question had all begun with the murder at Patriarch's Ponds. Neither Ivan, of course, nor the man in the check suit had pushed the unfortunate chairman of MASSOLIT under the tramcar; no one had physically caused him to fall under the wheels, but the detective was convinced that Berlioz had thrown himself (or had fallen) beneath the tram while under hypnosis.

Although there was plenty of evidence and it was obvious whom they should arrest and where, it proved impossible to lay hands on them. There was no doubt that someone was in flat No. 50. Occasionally the telephone was answered by a quavering or a nasal voice, occasionally someone in the flat opened a window and the sound of a gramophone could be heard floating out. Yet whenever they went there the place was completely empty. They searched it at various hours of the day, each time going over it with a fine-tooth comb. The flat had been under suspicion for some time and a watch had been placed on both the main stairs and the back stairs; men were even posted on the roof among the chimney pots. The flat was playing tricks and there was nothing that anyone could do about it.

The case dragged on in this way until midnight on Friday, when Baron Maigel, wearing evening dress and patent-leather pumps, entered flat No. 50 as a guest. He was heard being let in. Exactly ten minutes later the authorities entered the flat without a sound. It was not only empty of tenants, but worse, there was not even a trace of Baron Maigel.

There things rested until dawn on Saturday, when some new and valuable information came to light as a six-seater passenger aeroplane landed at Moscow airport having flown from the Crimea. Among its passengers was one extremely odd young man. He had heavy stubble on his face, had not washed for three days, his eyes were red with exhaustion and fright, he had no luggage and was somewhat eccentrically dressed. He wore a sheepskin hat, a felt cloak over a nightshirt and brand-new blue leather bedroom slippers. As he stepped off the gangway from the aircraft cabin, a group of expectant men approached him. A short while later the one and only manager of the Variety Theatre, Stepan Bogdanovich Likhodeyev, was facing the detectives. He added some new information. They were now able to establish that Woland had tricked his way into the Variety after hypnotising Stepa Likhodeyev and had then spirited Stepa God knows how many kilometres away from Moscow. This gave the authorities more evidence, but far from making their job any easier it made it if anything rather harder, because it was obviously not going to be so simple to arrest a person capable of the kind of sleight-of-hand to which Stepan Bogdanovich had fallen victim. Likhodeyev, at his own request, was locked up in a strong-room.

The next witness was Varenukha, arrested at home where he had returned after an unexplained absence lasting nearly forty-eight hours. In spite of his promise to Azazello, the house manager began by lying. He should not, however, be judged too harshly for this—Azazello had, after all, only forbidden him to lie on the telephone and in this instance Varenukha was talking without the help of a telephone. With a shifty look Ivan Savyelich announced that on Thursday he had shut himself up in his office and had got drunk, after which he had gone somewhere—he couldn't remember where; then somewhere else and drunk some 100-proof vodka; had collapsed under a hedge—again he couldn't remember where. He was then told that his stupid and irrational behaviour was prejudicial to the course of justice and that he would be held responsible for it. At this Varenukha broke down, sobbing, and whispered in a trembling voice, glancing round fearfully, that he was only telling lies out of fear of Woland's gang, who had already roughed him up once and that he begged, prayed, longed to be locked up in an armoured cell.

' There soon won't be room for them all in that strong-room ! '
growled one of the investigators.

' These villains have certainly put the fear of God into them,'
said the detective who had questioned Ivan.

They calmed Varenukha as well as they could, assuring him
that he would be given protection without having to resort to a
strong-room. He then admitted that he had never drunk any
100-proof vodka but had been beaten up by two characters, one
with a wall eye and the other a stout man . . .

' Looking like a cat ? '

' Yes, yes,' whispered Varenukha, almost swooning with fear
and glancing round every moment, adding further details of
how he had spent nearly two days in flat No. 50 as a vampire's
decoy and had nearly caused Rimsky's death . . .

Just then Rimsky himself was brought in from the Leningrad
train, but this grey-haired, terror-stricken, psychologically disturbed old man, scarcely recognisable as the treasurer of the
Variety Theatre, stubbornly refused to speak the truth. Rimsky
claimed that he had never seen Hella at his office window that
night, nor had he seen Varenukha; he had simply felt ill and
had taken the train to Leningrad in a fit of amnesia. Needless to
say the ailing treasurer concluded his evidence by begging to be
locked up in a strong-room.

Anna was arrested while trying to pay a store cashier with a
ten-dollar bill. Her story about people flying out of the landing
window and the horseshoe, which she claimed to have picked
up in order to hand it over to the police, was listened to
attentively.

' Was the horseshoe really gold and studded with diamonds ? '
they asked Anna.

' Think I don't know diamonds when I see them ? ' replied
Anna.

' And did he really give you ten-rouble notes ? '

' Think I don't know a tenner when I see one ? '

' When did they turn into dollars ? '

' I don't know what dollars are and I never saw any ! ' whined

Anna. ' I know my rights ! I was given the money as a reward and went to buy some material with it.' Then she started raving about the whole thing being the fault of the house management committee which had allowed evil forces to move in on the fifth floor and made life impossible for everybody else.

Here a detective waved a pen at Anna to shut up because she was boring them, and signed her release on a green form with which, to the general satisfaction, she left the building.

There followed a succession of others, among them Nikolai Ivanovich, who had been arrested thanks to the stupidity of his jealous wife in telling the police that her husband was missing. The detectives were not particularly surprised when Nikolai Ivanovich produced the joke certificate testifying that he had spent his time at Satan's ball. Nikolai Ivanovich departed slightly from the truth, however, when he described how he had carried Margarita Nikolayevna's naked maid through the air to bathe in the river at some unknown spot and how Margarita Nikolayevna herself had appeared naked at the window. He thought it unnecessary to recall, for instance, that he had appeared in the bedroom carrying Margarita's abandoned slip or that he had called Natasha ' Venus.' According to him, Natasha had flown out of the window, mounted him and made him fly away from Moscow . . .

' I was forced to obey under duress,' said Nikolai Ivanovich, finishing his tale with a request not to tell a word of it to his wife, which was granted.

Nikolai Ivanovich's evidence established the fact that both Margarita Nikolayevna and her maid Natasha had vanished without trace. Steps were taken to find them.

So the investigation progressed without a moment's break until Saturday morning. Meanwhile the city was seething with the most incredible rumours, in which a tiny grain of truth was embellished with a luxuriant growth of fantasy. People were saying that after the show at the Variety all two thousand spectators had rushed out into the street as naked as the day they were born ; that the police had uncovered a magic printing-press for counterfeiting money on Sadovaya Street; that a gang had kidnapped the five leading impresarios in Moscow but that the police had found them all again, and much more that was unrepeatable.

As it grew near lunchtime a telephone bell rang in the investigators' office. It was a report from Sadovaya Street that the haunted flat was showing signs of life again. Someone inside had apparently opened the windows, sounds of piano music and singing had been heard coming from it, and a black cat had been observed sunning itself on a windowsill.

At about four o'clock on that warm afternoon a large squad of men in plain clothes climbed out of three cars that had stopped a little way short of No. 302A, Sadovaya Street. Here the large squad divided into two smaller ones, one of which entered the courtyard through the main gateway and headed straight for staircase 6, while the other opened a small door, normally locked, leading to the back staircase and both began converging on flat No. 50 by different stairways.

While this was going on Koroviev and Azazello, in their normal clothes instead of festive tailcoats, were sitting in the dining-room finishing their lunch. Woland, as was his habit, was in the bedroom and no one knew where the cat was, but to judge from the clatter of saucepans coming from the kitchen Behemoth was presumably there, playing the fool as usual.

' What are those footsteps on the staircase ? ' asked Koroviev, twirling his spoon in a cup of black coffee.

' They're coming to arrest us,' replied Azazello and drained a glass of brandy.

' Well, well . . .' was Koroviev's answer.

The men coming up the front staircase had by then reached the third-floor landing, where a couple of plumbers were fiddling with the radiator. The party exchanged meaning looks with the plumbers.

' They're all at home,' whispered one of the plumbers, tapping the pipe with his hammer.

At this the leader of the squad drew a black Mauser from under his overcoat and the man beside him produced a skeleton key. All the men were suitably armed. Two of them had thin, easily unfurled silk nets in their pockets, another had a lasso and the sixth man was equipped with gauze masks and an ampoule of chloroform.

In a second the front door of No. 50 swung open and the party was in the hall, whilst the knocking on the door from the kitchen to the back staircase showed that the second squad had also arrived on time.

This time at least partial success seemed to be in their grasp. Men at once fanned out to all the rooms and found no one, but on the dining-room table were the remains of an obviously recently finished meal and in the drawing-room, alongside a crystal jug, a huge black cat was perched on the mantelpiece, holding a Primus in its front paws.

There was a long pause as the men gazed at the cat.

' H'm, yes . . . that's him . . .' whispered one of them.

' I'm doing no harm—I'm not playing games, I'm mending the Primus,' said the cat with a hostile scowl, ' and I'd better warn you that a cat is an ancient and inviolable animal.'

' Brilliant performance,' whispered a man and another said loudly and firmly :

' All right, you inviolable ventriloquist's dummy, come here ! '

The net whistled across the room but the man missed his target and only caught the crystal jug, which broke with a loud crash.

' Missed ! ' howled the cat. ' Hurrah ! ' Putting aside the Primus the cat whipped a Browning automatic from behind its back. In a flash it took aim at the nearest man, but the detective beat the cat to the draw and fired first. The cat flopped head first from the mantelpiece, dropping the Browning and upsetting the Primus.

' It's all over,' said the cat in a weak voice, stretched out in a pool of blood. ' Leave me for a moment, let me say goodbye. Oh my friend Azazello,' groaned the cat, streaming blood,

' where are you ? ' The animal turned its expiring gaze towards the door into the dining-room. ' You didn't come to my help when I was outnumbered . . . you left poor Behemoth, betraying him for a glass of brandy—though it was very good brandy ! Well, my death will be on your conscience but I'll bequeath you my Browning . . .'

' The net, the net,' whispered the men urgently round the cat. But the net somehow got tangled up in the man's pocket and would not come out.

' The only thing that can save a mortally wounded cat,' said Behemoth, ' is a drink of paraffin.' Taking advantage of the confusion it put its mouth to the round filler-hole of the Primus and drank some paraffin. At once the blood stopped pouring from above its left forepaw. The cat jumped up bold and full of life, tucked the Primus under its foreleg, leaped back with it on to the mantelpiece and from there, tearing the wallpaper, crawled along the wall and in two seconds it was high above the invaders, sitting on a metal pelmet.

In a moment hands were grabbing the curtains and pulling them down together with the pelmet, bringing the sunlight flooding into the darkened room. But neither the cat nor the Primus fell. Without dropping the Primus the cat managed to leap through the air and jump on to the chandelier hanging in the middle of the room.

' Step-ladder ! ' came the cry from below.

' I challenge you to a duel ! ' screamed the cat, sailing over their heads on the swinging chandelier. The Browning appeared in its paw again and it lodged the Primus between the arms of the chandelier. The cat took aim and, as it swung like a pendulum over the detectives' heads, opened fire on them. The sound of gunfire rocked the flat. Fragments of crystal strewed the floor, the mirror over the fireplace was starred with bullet holes, plaster dust flew everywhere, ejected cartridge cases pattered to the floor, window panes shattered and paraffin began to spurt from the punctured tank of the Primus. There was now no question of taking the cat alive and the men were aiming hard at its head, stomach, breast and back. The sound of gunfire started panic in the courtyard below.

But this fusillade did not last long and soon died down. It had not, in fact, caused either the men or the cat any harm. There were no dead and no wounded. No one, including the cat, had been hit. As a final test one man fired five rounds into the beastly animal's stomach and the cat retaliated with a whole volley that had the same result—not a scratch. As it swung on the chandelier, whose motion was gradually shortening all the time, it blew into the muzzle of the Browning and spat on its paw.

The faces of the silent men below showed total bewilderment. This was the only case, or one of the only cases, in which gunfire had proved to be completely ineffectual. Of course the cat's Browning might have been a toy, but this was certainly not true of the detectives' Mausers. The cat's first wound, which had undoubtedly occurred, had been nothing but a trick and a villainous piece of deception, as was its paraffin-drinking act.

One more attempt was made to seize the cat. The lasso was thrown, it looped itself round one of the candles and the whole chandelier crashed to the floor. Its fall shook the whole building, but it did not help matters. The men were showered with splinters while the cat flew through the air and landed high up under the ceiling on the gilded frame of the mirror over the mantelpiece. It made no attempt to bolt but from its relatively safe perch announced :

' I completely fail to understand the reason for this rough treatment . . .'

Here the cat's speech was interrupted by a low rumbling voice that seemed to come from nowhere :

' What's happening in this flat ? It's disturbing my work . . .'

Another voice, ugly and nasal, cried :

' It's Behemoth, of course, damn him ! '

A third, quavering voice said :

' Messire ! Saturday. The sun is setting. We must go.'

' Excuse me, I've no more time to spare talking,' said the cat from the mirror. 'We must go.' It threw away its Browning, smashing two window panes, then poured the paraffin on to the floor where it burst spontaneously into a great flame as high as the ceiling.

It burned fast and hard, with even more violence than is usual with paraffin. At once the wallpaper started to smoke, the torn curtain caught alight and the frames of the broken windowpanes began to smoulder. The cat crouched, gave a miaow, jumped from the mirror to the windowsill and disappeared, clutching the Primus. Shots were heard from outside. A man sitting on an iron fire-escape on the level of No. 50's windows fired at the cat as it sprang from windowsill to windowsill heading for the drainpipe on the corner of the building. The cat scrambled up the drainpipe to the roof. There it came under equally ineffective fire from the men covering the chimney-pots and the cat faded into the westering sunlight that flooded the city.

Inside the flat the parquet was already crackling under the men's feet and in the fireplace, where the cat had shammed dead, there gradually materialised the corpse of Baron Maigel, his little beard jutting upwards, his eyes glassy. The body was impossible to move.

Hopping across the burning blocks of parquet, beating out their smouldering clothes, the men in the drawing-room retreated to the study and the hall. The men who had been in the dining-room and the bedroom ran out into the passage. The drawing-room was already full of smoke and fire. Someone managed to dial the fire brigade and barked into the receiver :

'Sadovaya, 302A !'

They could stay no longer. Flame was lashing into the hallway and it was becoming difficult to breathe.

As soon as the first wisps of smoke appeared through the shattered windows of the haunted flat, desperate cries were heard from the courtyard :

'Fire ! Fire ! Help ! We're on fire !'

In several flats people were shouting into the telephone :

'Sadovaya ! Sadovaya, 302A !'

The Master and Margarita

Just as the heart-stopping sound of bells was heard from the long red fire-engines racing towards Sadovaya Street from all over the city, the crowd in the courtyard saw three dark figures, apparently men, and one naked woman, float out of the smoking windows on the fifth floor.

28. *The Final Adventure of Koroviev and Behemoth*

No one, of course, can say for certain whether those figures were real or merely imagined by the frightened inhabitants of that ill-fated block on Sadovaya Street. If they were real, no one knows exactly where they were going; but we do know that about a quarter of an hour after the outbreak of fire on Sadovaya Street, a tall man in a check suit and a large black cat appeared outside the glass doors of the Torgsin Store in Smolensk Market.

Slipping dexterously between the passers-by, the man opened the outer door of the store only to be met by a small, bony and extremely hostile porter who barred his way and said disagreeably :

' No cats allowed ! '

' I beg your pardon,' quavered the tall man, cupping his knotty hand to his ear as though hard of hearing, ' no cats, did you say ? What cats ? '

The porter's eyes bulged, and with reason : there was no cat by the man's side, but instead a large fat man in a tattered cap, with vaguely feline looks and holding a Primus, was pushing his way into the shop.

For some reason the misanthropic porter did not care for the look of this couple.

' You can only buy with foreign currency here,' he croaked, glaring at them from beneath ragged, moth-eaten eyebrows.

' My dear fellow,' warbled the tall man, one eye glinting through his broken pince-nez, ' how do you know that I haven't got any ? Are you judging by my suit ? Never do that, my good man. You may make a terrible mistake. Read the story of the famous caliph Haroun-al-Rashid and you'll see what I mean. But for the present, leaving history aside for a moment, I warn you I shall complain to the manager and I shall tell him such tales about you that you'll wish you had never opened your mouth.'

' This Primus of mine may be full of foreign currency for all you know,' said the stout cat-like figure. An angry crowd was forming behind them. With a look of hatred and suspicion at the dubious pair, the porter stepped aside and our friends Koroviev and Behemoth found themselves in the store. First they looked around and then Koroviev announced in a penetrating voice, audible everywhere :

' What a splendid store ! A very, very good store indeed ! '

The customers turned round from the counters to stare at Koroviev in amazement, although there was every reason to praise the store. Hundreds of different bolts of richly coloured poplins stood in holders on the floor, whilst behind them the shelves were piled with calico, chiffon and worsted. Racks full of shoes stretched into the distance where several women were sitting on low chairs, a worn old shoe on their right foot, a gleaming new one on their left. From somewhere out of sight came the sound of song and gramophone music.

Spurning all these delights Koroviev and Behemoth went straight to the delicatessen and confectionery departments. These were spaciously laid out and full of women in headscarves and berets. A short, completely square, blue-jowled little man wearing horn-rims, a pristine hat with unstained ribbon, dressed in a fawn overcoat and tan kid gloves, was standing at a counter and booming away in an authoritative voice at an assistant in a clean white overall and blue cap. With a long sharp knife, very like the knife Matthew the Levite stole, he was easing the snake-like skin away from the fat, juicy flesh of a pink salmon.

' This department is excellent, too,' Koroviev solemnly pronounced ' and that foreigner looks a nice man.' He pointed approvingly at the fawn coat.

' No, Faggot, no' answered Behemoth thoughtfully. ' You're

wrong. I think there is something missing in that gentleman's face.'

The fawn back quivered, but it was probably coincidence, because he was after all a foreigner and could not have understood what Koroviev and his companion had been saying in Russian.

'Is goot?' enquired the fawn customer in a stern voice.

'First class!' replied the assistant, showing off his blade-work with a flourish that lifted a whole side of skin from the salmon.

'Is goot—I like, is bad—I not like,' added the foreigner.

'But of course!' rejoined the salesman.

At this point our friends left the foreigner to his salmon and moved over to the cakes and pastries.

'Hot today,' said Koroviev to a pretty, red-cheeked young salesgirl, to which he got no reply.

'How much are the tangerines?' Koroviev then asked her.

'Thirty kopeks the kilo,' replied the salesgirl.

'They look delicious,' said Koroviev with a sigh, 'Oh, dear' . . . He thought for a while longer, then turned to his friend. 'Try one, Behemoth.'

The stout cat-person tucked his Primus under his arm, took the uppermost tangerine off the pyramid, ate it whole, skin and all, and took another.

The salesgirl was appalled.

'Hey—are you crazy?' she screamed, the colour vanishing from her cheeks. 'Where are your travellers' cheques or foreign currency?' She threw down her pastry-tongs.

'My dear, sweet girl,' cooed Koroviev, leaning right across the counter and winking at the assistant, 'I can't help it but we're just out of currency today. I promise you I'll pay you it all cash down next time, definitely not later than Monday! We live near-by on Sadovaya, where the house caught fire . . .'

Having demolished a third tangerine, Behemoth thrust his paw into an ingenious structure built of chocolate bars, pulled out the bottom one, which brought the whole thing down with a crash, and swallowed the chocolate complete with its gold wrapper.

The assistant at the fish counter stood petrified, knife in hand, the fawn-coated foreigner turned round towards the looters, revealing that Behemoth was wrong : far from his face lacking something it was if anything over-endowed—huge pendulous cheeks and bright, shifty eyes.

The salesgirl, now pale yellow, wailed miserably.

' Palosich ! Palosich ! '

The sound brought customers running from the drapery department. Meanwhile Behemoth had wandered away from the temptations of the confectionery counter and thrust his paw into a barrel labelled ' Selected Kerch Salted Herrings,' pulled out a couple of herrings, gulped them both down and spat out the tails.

' Palosich ! ' came another despairing shriek from the confectionery counter and the man at the fish counter, his goatee wagging in fury, barked :

' Hey, you—what d'you think you're doing ! '

Pavel Yosifovich (reduced to ' Palosich' in the excitement) was already hurrying to the scene of action. He was an imposing man in a clean white overall like a surgeon, with a pencil sticking out of his breast pocket. He was clearly a man of great experience. Catching sight of a herring's tail protruding from Behemoth's mouth he summed up the situation in a moment and refusing to join in a shouting match with the two villains, waved his arm and gave the order :

' Whistle ! '

The porter shot out into Smolensk Market and relieved his feelings with a furious whistle-blast. As customers began edging up to the rogues and surrounding them, Koroviev went into action.

' Citizens ! ' he cried in a vibrant ringing voice, ' What's going on here ? Eh ? I appeal to you ! This poor man '—Koroviev put a tremor into his voice and pointed at Behemoth, who had immediately assumed a pathetic expression—' this poor man has been mending a Primus all day. He's hungry . . . where could he get any foreign currency ? '

Pavel Yosifovich, usually calm and reserved, shouted grimly : ' Shut up, you ! ' and gave another impatient wave of his arm.

Just then the automatic bell on the door gave a cheerful tinkle.

Koroviev, quite undisturbed by the manager's remark, went on:

' I ask you—where ? He's racked with hunger and thirst, he's hot. So the poor fellow tried a tangerine. It's only worth three kopecks at the most, but they have to start whistling like nightingales in springtime, bothering the police and stopping them from doing their proper job. But it's all right for *him* isn't it ?! '

Koroviev pointed at the fat man in the fawn coat, who exhibited violent alarm. ' Who is he ? Mm ? Where's he from ? Why is he here ? Were we dying of boredom without him ? Did we invite him ? Of course not ! ' roared the ex-choirmaster, his mouth twisted into a sarcastic leer. ' Look at him—in his smart fawn coat, bloated with good Russian salmon, pockets bulging with currency, and what about our poor comrade here ? What about him, I ask you ? ' wailed Koroviev, completely overcome by his own oratory.

This ridiculous, tactless and doubtless politically dangerous speech made Pavel Yosifovich shake with rage, but strangely enough it was clear from the looks of the customers that many of them approved of it. And when Behemoth, wiping his eyes with a ragged cuff, cried tragically : ' Thank you, friend, for speaking up for a poor man,' a miracle happened. A quiet, dignified, little old man, shabbily but neatly dressed, who had been buying three macaroons at the pastry counter, was suddenly transformed. His eyes flashed fire, he turned purple, threw his bagfull of macaroons on to the floor and shouted in a thin, childish voice : ' He's right ! ' Then he picked up a tray, threw away the remains of the chocolate-bar Eiffel Tower that Behemoth had ruined, waved it about, pulled off the foreigner's hat with his left hand, swung the tray with his right and brought it down with a crash on the fawn man's balding head. There was a noise

of the kind you hear when sheet steel is thrown down from a
lorry. Turning pale, the fat man staggered and fell backwards into
the barrel of salted herrings, sending up a fountain of brine and
fish-scales. This produced a second miracle. As the fawn man
fell into the barrel of fish he screamed in perfect Russian without
a trace of an accent :

' Help ! Murder ! They're trying to kill me ! ' The shock
had obviously given him sudden command of a hitherto unknown language.

The porter had by now stopped whistling and through the
crowd of excited customers could be seen the approach of two
police helmets. But the cunning Behemoth poured paraffin from
the Primus on to the counter and it burst spontaneously into
flame. It flared up and ran along the counter, devouring the
beautiful paper ribbons decorating the baskets of fruit. The
salesgirls leaped over the counter and ran away screaming as the
flames caught the blinds on the windows and more paraffin
caught alight on the floor.

With a shriek of horror the customers shuffled out of the
confectionery, sweeping aside the helpless Pavel Yosifovich,
while the fish salesmen galloped away towards the staff door,
clutching their razor-sharp knives.

Heaving himself out of the barrel the fawn man, covered in
salt-herring juice, staggered past the salmon counter and followed
the crowd. There was a tinkling and crashing of glass at the
doorway as the public fought to get out, whilst the two villains,
Koroviev and the gluttonous Behemoth, disappeared, no one
knew where. Later, witnesses described having seen them float
up to the ceiling and then burst like a couple of balloons. This
story sounds too dubious for belief and we shall probably never
know what really happened.

We do know however that exactly a minute later Behemoth
and Koroviev were seen on the boulevard pavement just outside Griboyedov House. Koroviev stopped by the railings and
said :

' Look, there's the writers' club. You know, Behemoth,

that house has a great reputation. Look at it, my friend. How lovely to think of so much talent ripening under that roof.'

'Like pineapples in a hothouse,' said Behemoth, climbing up on to the concrete plinth of the railings for a better look at the yellow, colonnaded house.

'Quite so,' agreed his inseparable companion Koroviev, 'and what a delicious thrill one gets, doesn't one, to think that at this moment in that house there may be the future author of a *Don Quixote*, or a *Faust* or who knows—*Dead Souls* ? '

'It could easily happen,' said Behemoth.

'Yes,' Koroviev went on, wagging a warning finger, 'but— but, I say, and I repeat—*but* ! . . . provided that those hot-house growths are not attacked by some micro-organism, pro-vided they're not nipped in the bud, provided they don't rot ! And it can happen with pineapples, you know ! Ah, yes, it can happen ! '

'Frightening thought,' said Behemoth.

'Yes,' Koroviev went on, 'think what astonishing growths may sprout from the seedbeds of that house and its thousands of devotees of Melpomene, Polyhymnia and Thalia. Just imagine the furore if one of them were to present the reading public with a *Government Inspector* or at least a *Eugene Onegin* ! '

'By the way,' enquired the cat poking its round head through a gap in the railings. 'what are they doing on the verandah ? '

'Eating,' explained Koroviev. 'I should add that this place has a very decent, cheap restaurant. And now that I think of it, like any tourist starting on a long journey I wouldn't mind a snack and large mug of iced beer.'

'Nor would I,' said Behemoth and the two rogues set off under the lime trees and up the asphalt path towards the unsuspecting restaurant.

A pale, bored woman in white ankle-socks and a white tasselled beret was sitting on a bentwood chair at the corner entrance to the verandah, where there was an opening in the creeper-grown trellis. In front of her on a plain kitchen table lay a large book like a ledger, in which for no known reason the woman wrote the names of the people entering the restaurant. She stopped Koroviev and Behemoth.

'Your membership cards?' she said, staring in surprise at Koroviev's pince-nez, at Behemoth's Primus and grazed elbow.

'A thousand apologies, madam, but what membership cards?' asked Koroviev in astonishment.

'Are you writers?' asked the woman in return.

'Indubitably,' replied Koroviev with dignity.

'Where are your membership cards?' the woman repeated.

'Dear lady . . .' Koroviev began tenderly.

'I'm not a dear lady,' interrupted the woman.

'Oh, what a shame,' said Koroviev in a disappointed voice and went on : 'Well, if you don't want to be a dear lady, which would have been delightful, you have every right not to be. But look here—if you wanted to make sure that Dostoyevsky was a writer, would you really ask him for his membership card? Why, you only have to take any five pages of one of his novels and you won't need a membership card to convince you that the man's a writer. I don't suppose he ever had a membership card, anyway! What do you think?' said Koroviev, turning to Behemoth.

'I'll bet he never had one,' replied the cat, putting the Primus on the table and wiping the sweat from its brow with its paw.

'You're not Dostoyevsky,' said the woman to Koroviev.

'How do you know?'

'Dostoyevsky's dead,' said the woman, though not very confidently.

'I protest!' exclaimed Behemoth warmly. 'Dostoyevsky is immortal!'

'Your membership cards, please,' said the woman.

'This is really all rather funny!' said Koroviev, refusing to give up. 'A writer isn't a writer because he has a membership card but because he writes. How do you know what bright ideas may not be swarming in my head? Or in his head?' And he pointed at Behemoth's head. The cat removed its cap to give the woman a better look at its head.

' Stand back, please,' she said, irritated.

Koroviev and Behemoth stood aside and made way for a writer in a grey suit and a white summer shirt with the collar turned out over his jacket collar, no tie and a newspaper under his arm. The writer nodded to the woman and scribbled a flourish in the book as he passed through to the verandah.

' We can't,' said Koroviev sadly, ' but he can have that mug of cold beer which you and I, poor wanderers, were so longing for. We are in an unhappy position and I see no way out.'

Behemoth only spread his paws bitterly and put his cap back on his thick head of hair that much resembled cat's fur.

At that moment a quiet but authoritative voice said to the woman :

' Let them in, Sofia Pavlovna.'

The woman with the ledger looked up in astonishment. From behind the trellis foliage loomed the pirate's white shirt-front and wedge-shaped beard. He greeted the two ruffians with a welcoming look and even went so far as to beckon them on. Archibald Archibaldovich made his authority felt in this restaurant and Sofia Pavlovna obediently asked Koroviev :

' What is your name ? '

' Panayev,' was the polite reply. The woman wrote down the name and raised her questioning glance to Behemoth.

' Skabichevsky,' squeaked the cat, for some reason pointing to his Primus. Sofia Pavlovna inscribed this name too and pushed the ledger forward for the two visitors to sign. Koroviev wrote ' Skabichevsky ' opposite the name ' Panayev ' and Behemoth wrote ' Panayev ' opposite ' Skabichevsky '.

To Sofia Pavlovna's utter surprise Archibald Archibaldovich gave her a seductive smile, led his guests to the best table on the far side of the verandah where there was the most shade, where the sunlight danced round the table through one of the gaps in the trellis. Blinking with perplexity, Sofia Pavlovna stared for a long time at the two curious signatures.

The waiters were no less surprised. Archibald Archibaldovich personally moved the chairs back from the table, invited Koroviev to be seated, winked at one, whispered to the other, while two waiters fussed around the new arrivals, one of whom put his Primus on the floor beside his reddish-brown boot.

The old stained tablecloth vanished instantly from the table and another, whiter than a bedouin's burnous, flashed through the air in a crackle of starch as Archibald Archibaldovich whispered, softly, but most expressively, into Koroviev's ear:

'What can I offer you? I've a rather special fillet of smoked sturgeon ... I managed to save it from the architectural congress banquet ...'

'Er ... just bring us some hors d'oeuvres ...' boomed Koroviev patronisingly, sprawling in his chair.

'Of course,' replied Archibald Archibaldovich, closing his eyes in exquisite comprehension.

Seeing how the maître d'hôtel was treating these two dubious guests, the waiters abandoned their suspicions and set about their work seriously. One offered a match to Behemoth, who had taken a butt-end out of his pocket and stuck it in his mouth, another advanced in a tinkle of green glass and laid out tumblers, claret-glasses and those tall-stemmed white wine glasses which are so perfect for drinking a sparkling wine under the awning—or rather, moving on in time, which *used* to be so perfect for drinking sparkling wine under the verandah awning at Griboyedov.

'A little breast of grouse, perhaps?' said Archibald Archibaldovich in a musical purr. The guest in the shaky pince-nez thoroughly approved the pirate captain's suggestion and beamed at him through his one useless lens.

Petrakov-Sukhovei, the essayist, was dining at the next table with his wife and had just finished eating a pork chop. With typical writer's curiosity he had noticed the fuss that Archibald Archibaldovich was making and was extremely surprised. His wife, a most dignified lady, felt jealous of the pirate's attention to Koroviev and tapped her glass with a spoon as a sign of impatience ... where's my ice-cream? What's happened to the service?

With a flattering smile at Madame Petrakov, Archibald Archibaldovich sent a waiter to her and stayed with his two special customers. Archibald Archibaldovich was not only intelligent; he was at least as observant as any writer. He knew all about the show at the Variety and much else besides; he had heard, and unlike most people he had not forgotten, the words ' checks ' and ' cat '. Archibald Archibaldovich had immediately guessed who his clients were and realising this, he was not going to risk having an argument with them. And Sofia Pavlovna had tried to stop them coming on to the verandah ! Still, what else could you expect from her. . . .

Haughtily spooning up her melting ice-cream, Madame Petrakov watched disagreeably as the table, occupied by what appeared to be a couple of scarecrows, was loaded with food as if by magic. A bowl of fresh caviar, garnished with sparkling lettuce leaves . . . another moment, and a silver ice-bucket appeared on a special little side-table . . .

Only when he had made sure that all was properly in hand and when the waiters had brought a simmering chafing-dish, did Archibald Archibaldovich allow himself to leave his two mysterious guests, and then only after whispering to them :

' Please excuse me—I must go and attend to the grouse ! '

He fled from the table and disappeared inside the restaurant. If anyone had observed what Archibald Archibaldovich did next, they might have thought it rather strange.

The maître d'hôtel did not make for the kitchen to attend to the grouse, but instead went straight to the larder. Opening it with his key, he locked himself in, lifted two heavy fillets of smoked sturgeon out of the ice box, taking care not to dirty his shirt-cuffs, wrapped them in newspaper, carefully tied them up with string and put them to one side. Then he went next door to check whether his silk-lined overcoat and hat were there, and only then did he pass on to the kitchen, where the chef was carefully slicing the breast of grouse.

Odd though Archibald Archibaldovich's movements may have seemed, they were not, and would only have seemed so to a superficial observer. His actions were really quite logical. His knowledge of recent events and above all his phenomenal sixth sense told the Griboyedov maitre d'hotel that although his two guests' meal would be plentiful and delicious, it would be extremely short. And this ex-buccaneer's sixth sense, which had never yet played him false, did not let him down this time, either.

Just as Koroviev and Behemoth were clinking their second glass of delicious, chilled, double-filtered Moscow vodka, a journalist called Boba Kandalupsky, famous in Moscow for knowing everything that was going on, arrived on the verandah sweating with excitement and immediately sat down at the Petrakovs' table. Dropping his bulging briefcase on the table, Boba put his lips to Petrakov's ear and whispered some obviously fascinating piece of news. Dying with curiosity, madame Petrakov leaned her ear towards Boba's thick, fleshy lips. With furtive glances the journalist whispered on and on, just loud enough for occasional words to be heard :

' I promise you ! . . . Here, on Sadovaya Street . . . ! ' Boba lowered his voice again. ' . . . the bullets couldn't hit it . . . bullets . . . paraffin . . . fire . . . bullets . . .'

' Well, as for liars who spread rumours like that,' came madame Petrakov's contralto boom, a shade too loud for Boba's liking, ' they're the ones who should be shot ! And they would be if I had my way. What a lot of dangerous rubbish ! '

' It's not rubbish Antonia Porfiryevna,' exclaimed Boba, piqued at her disbelief. He began hissing again : ' I tell you, bullets couldn't touch it ! . . . And now the building's on fire . . . they floated out through the air . . . through the air ! ' whispered Boba, never suspecting that the people he was talking about were sitting alongside him and thoroughly enjoying the situation.

However, their enjoyment was soon cut short. Three men, tightly belted, booted and armed with revolvers, dashed out of the indoor restaurant and on to the verandah. The man in front roared :

' Don't move ! ' and instantly all three opened fire at the

heads of Koroviev and Behemoth. The two victims melted into the air and a sheet of flame leaped up from the Primus to the awning. A gaping mouth with burning edges appeared in the awning and began spreading in all directions. The fire raced across it and reached the roof of Griboyedov House. Some bundles of paper lying on the second-floor windowsill of the editor's office burst into flame, which spread to a blind and then, as though someone had blown on it, the fire was sucked, roaring, into the house.

A few seconds later the writers, their suppers abandoned, were streaming along the asphalted paths leading to the iron railings along the boulevard, where on Wednesday evening Ivan had climbed over to bring the first incomprehensible news of disaster.

Having left in good time by a side door, without running and in no hurry, like a captain forced to be the last to leave his flaming brig, Archibald Archibaldovich calmly stood and watched it all. He wore his silk-lined overcoat and two fillets of smoked sturgeon were tucked under his arm.

29. *The Fate of the Master and Margarita is Decided*

At sunset, high above the town, on the stone roof of one of the most beautiful buildings in Moscow, built about a century and a half ago, stood two figures—Woland and Azazello. They were invisible from the street below, hidden from the vulgar gaze by a balustrade adorned with stucco flowers in stucco urns, although they could see almost to the limits of the city.

Woland was sitting on a folding stool, dressed in his black soutane. His long, broad-bladed sword had been rammed vertically into the cleft between two flagstones, making a sundial. Slowly and inexorably the shadow of the sword was lengthening, creeping towards Satan's black slippers. Resting his sharp chin on his fist, hunched on the stool with one leg crossed over the other, Woland stared unwaveringly at the vast panorama of palaces, huge blocks of flats and condemned slum cottages.

Azazello, without his usual garb of jacket, bowler and patent-leather shoes and dressed instead like Woland in black, stood motionless at a short distance from his master, also staring at the city.

Woland remarked:

' An interesting city, Moscow, don't you think ? '

Azazello stirred and answered respectfully :

' I prefer Rome, messire.'

' Yes, it's a matter of taste,' replied Woland.

After a while his voice rang out again:

' What is that smoke over there—on the boulevard ? '

' That is Griboyedov burning,' said Azazello.

' I suppose that inseparable couple, Koroviev and Behemoth, have been there ? '

' Without a doubt, messire.'

There was silence again and both figures on the roof stood watching the setting sun reflected in all the westward-facing windows. Woland's eyes shone with the same fire, even though he sat with his back to the sunset.

Then something made Woland turn his attention to a round tower behind him on the roof. From its walls appeared a grim, ragged, mud-spattered man with a beard, dressed in a chiton and home-made sandals.

' Ha ! ' exclaimed Woland, with a sneer at the approaching figure. ' You are the last person I expected to see here. What brings you here, of all people ? '

' I have come to see you, spirit of evil and lord of the shadows,' the man replied with a hostile glare at Woland.

' Well, tax-gatherer, if you've come to see me, why don't you wish me well ? '

' Because I have no wish to see you well,' said the man impudently.

' Then I am afraid you will have to reconcile yourself to my good health,' retorted Woland, his mouth twisted into a grin. ' As soon as you appeared on this roof you made yourself ridiculous. It was your tone of voice. You spoke your words as though you denied the very existence of the shadows or of evil. Think, now : where would your good be if there were no evil and what would the world look like without shadow ? Shadows are thrown by people and things. There's the shadow of my sword, for instance. But shadows are also cast by trees and living things. Do you want to strip the whole globe by removing every tree and every creature to satisfy your fantasy of a bare world ? You're stupid.'

' I won't argue with you, old sophist,' replied Matthew the Levite.

' You are incapable of arguing with me for the reason I have just mentioned—you are too stupid,' answered Woland and enquired : ' Now tell me briefly and without boring me why you are here ? '

' He has sent me.'

' What message did he give you, slave ? '

' I am not a slave,' replied Matthew the Levite, growing angrier, ' I am his disciple.'

' You and I are speaking different languages, as always,' said Woland, ' but that does not alter the things we are talking about. Well ? '

' He has read the master's writings,' said Matthew the Levite, ' and asks you to take the master with you and reward him by granting him peace. Would that be hard for you to do, spirit of evil ? '

' Nothing is hard for me to do,' replied Woland, ' as you well know.' He paused for a while and then added : ' Why don't you take him yourself, to the light ? '

' He has not earned light, he has earned rest,' said the Levite sadly.

' Tell him it shall be done,' said Woland, adding with a flash in his eye : ' And leave me this instant.'

' He asks you also to take the woman who loved him and who has suffered for him,' Matthew said to Woland, a note of entreaty in his voice for the first time.

' Do you think that we needed you to make us think of that ? Go away.'

Matthew the Levite vanished and Woland called to Azazello : ' Go and see them and arrange it.'

Azazello flew off, leaving Woland alone.

He was not, however, alone for long. The sound of footsteps and animated voices were heard along the roof, and Koroviev and Behemoth appeared. This time the cat had no Primus but was loaded with other things. It was carrying a small gold-framed landscape under one arm, a half-burned cook's apron in its paw, and on its other arm was a whole salmon complete with skin and tail. Both Koroviev and Behemoth smelled of burning, Behemoth's face was covered in soot and his cap was badly burned.

'Greetings, messire,' cried the tireless pair, and Behemoth waved his salmon.

'You're a fine couple,' said Woland.

'Imagine, messire ! ' cried Behemoth excitedly : ' they thought I was looting ! '

'Judging by that stuff,' replied Woland with a glance at the painting, ' they were right.'

'Believe me, messire . . .' the cat began in an urgently sincere voice.

'No, I don't believe you,' was Woland's short answer.

'Messire, I swear I made heroic efforts to save everything I could, but this was all that was left.'

'It would be more interesting if you were to explain why Griboyedov caught fire in the first place.'

Simultaneously Koroviev and Behemoth spread their hands and raised their eyes to heaven. Behemoth exclaimed : ' It's a complete mystery ! There we were, harming no one, sitting quietly having a drink and a bite to eat when . . .'

' . . . Suddenly—bang, bang, bang ! We were being shot at ! Crazed with fright Behemoth and I started running for the street, our pursuers behind us, and we made for Timiryazev ! '

'But a sense of duty,' put in Behemoth, ' overcame our cowardice and we went back.'

'Ah, you went back did you ? ' said Woland. ' By then, of course, the whole house was burnt to a cinder.'

'To a cinder ! ' Koroviev nodded sadly. ' Literally to a cinder, as you so accurately put it. Nothing but smouldering ashes.'

'I rushed into the assembly hall,' said Behemoth, '—the colonnaded room, messire—in case I could save something valuable. Ah, messire, if I had a wife she would have been nearly widowed at least twenty times ! Luckily I'm not married and believe me

I'm glad. Who'd exchange a bachelor's life for a yoke round his neck?'

'More of his rubbish,' muttered Woland with a resigned glance upwards.

'Messire, I promise to keep to the point,' said the cat. 'As I was saying—I could only save this little landscape. There was no time to salvage anything else, the flames were singeing my fur. I ran to the larder and rescued this salmon, and into the kitchen where I found this chef's overall. I consider I did everything I could, messire, and I fail to understand the sceptical expression on your face.'

'And what was Koroviev doing while you were looting?' enquired Woland.

'I was helping the fire brigade, messire,' answered Koroviev, pointing to his torn trousers.

'In that case I suppose it was totally destroyed and they will have to put up a new building.'

'It will be built, messire,' said Koroviev, 'I can assure you of that.'

'Well, let us hope it will be better than the old one,' remarked Woland.

'It will, messire,' said Koroviev.

'Believe me, it will,' added the cat. 'My sixth sense tells me so.'

'Nevertheless here we are, messire,' Koroviev reported, 'and we await your instructions.'

Woland rose from his stool, walked over to the balustrade and turning his back on his retinue stared for a long time over the city in lonely silence. Then he turned back, sat down on his stool again and said :

'I have no instructions. You have done all you could and for the time being I no longer require your services. You may rest. A thunderstorm is coming and then we must be on our way.'

'Very good, messire,' replied the two buffoons and vanished behind the round tower in the centre of the roof.

The thunderstorm that Woland had predicted was already

gathering on the horizon. A black cloud was rising in the west; first a half and then all of the sun was blotted out. The wind on the terrace freshened. Soon it was quite dark.

The cloud from the west enveloped the vast city. Bridges, buildings, were all swallowed up. Everything vanished as though it had never been. A single whip-lash of fire cracked across the sky, then the city rocked to a clap of thunder. There came another; the storm had begun. In the driving rain Woland was no more to be seen.

30. Time to Go

' Do you know,' said Margarita, ' that just as you were going to sleep last night I was reading about the mist that came in from the Mediterranean . . . and those idols, ah, those golden idols ! Somehow I couldn't get them out of my mind. I think it's going to rain soon. Can you feel how it's freshening ? '

' That's all very fine,' replied the master, smoking and fanning the smoke away with his hand. ' Let's forget about the idols . . . but what's to become of us now, I'd like to know ? '

This conversation took place at sunset, just when Matthew the Levite appeared to Woland on the roof. The basement window was open and if anybody had looked into it he would have been struck by the odd appearance of the two people. Margarita had a plain black gown over her naked body and the master was in his hospital pyjamas. Margarita had nothing else to wear. She had left all her clothes at home and although her top-floor flat was not far away there was, of course, no question of her going there to collect her belongings. As for the master, all of whose suits were back in the wardrobe as though he had never left, he simply did not feel like getting dressed because, as he explained to Margarita, he had a premonition that some more nonsense might be on the way. He had, however, had his first proper shave since that autumn night, because the hospital staff had done no more than trim his beard with electric clippers.

The room, too, looked strange and it was hard to discern any order beneath the chaos. Manuscripts lay all over the floor and the divan. A book was lying, spine upwards, on the armchair. The round table was laid for supper, several bottles standing among the plates of food. Margarita and the master had no idea where all this food and drink had come from—it had simply been there on the table when they woke up.

Having slept until Saturday evening both the master and his love felt completely revived and only one symptom reminded them of their adventures of the night before—both of them felt a slight ache in the left temple. Psychologically both of them had changed considerably, as anyone would have realised who overheard their conversation. But there was no one to overhear them. The advantage of the little yard was that it was always empty. The lime tree and the maple, turning greener with every day, exhaled the perfume of spring and the rising breeze carried it into the basement.

' The devil ! ' the master suddenly exclaimed. ' Just think of it . . .' He stubbed out his cigarette in the ashtray and clasped his head in his hands. ' Listen—you're intelligent and you haven't been in the madhouse as I have . . . do you seriously believe that we spent last night with Satan ? '

' Quite seriously, I do . . .'

' Oh, of course, of course,' said the master ironically. ' There are obviously two lunatics in the family now—husband and wife ! ' He raised his arms to heaven and shouted : ' No, the devil knows what it was ! . . .'

Instead of replying Margarita collapsed onto the divan, burst into laughter, waved her bare legs in the air and practically shouted :

' Oh, I can't help it . . . I can't help it . . . If you could only see yourself ! '

When the master, embarrassed, had buttoned up his hospital pants, Margarita grew serious.

' Just now you unwittingly spoke the truth,' she said. ' The devil *does* know what it was and the devil believe me, will arrange everything ! ' Her eyes suddenly flashed, she jumped up, danced for joy and shouted : ' I'm so happy, so happy, happy, that I made that bargain with him ! Hurrah for the devil ! I'm afraid, my dear, that you're doomed to live with a witch ! ' She flung herself at the master, clasped him round the neck and began kissing his lips, his nose, his cheeks. Floods of unkempt black hair caressed the master's neck and shoulders while his face burned with kisses.

' You really are like a witch.'

' I don't deny it,' replied Margarita. ' I'm a witch and I'm very glad of it.'

' All right,' said the master, ' so you're a witch. Fine, splendid. They've abducted me from the hospital—equally splendid. And they've brought us back here, let us grant them that too. Let's even assume that neither of us will be caught . . . But what, in the name of all that's holy, are we supposed to live on ? Tell me that, will you ? You seem to care so little about the problem that it really worries me.'

Just then a pair of blunt-toed boots and the lower part of a pair of trousers appeared in the little basement window. Then the trousers bent at the knee and the daylight was shut out by a man's ample bottom.

' Aloysius—are you there, Aloysius ? ' asked a voice from slightly above the trousers.

' It's beginning,' said the master.

' Aloysius ? ' asked Margarita, moving closer to the window. ' He was arrested yesterday. Who wants him ? What's your name ? '

Instantly the knees and bottom vanished, there came the click of the gate and everything returned to normal. Again, Margarita collapsed on to the divan and laughed until tears started from her eyes. When the fit was over her expression changed completely, she grew serious, slid down from the divan and crawled over to the master's knees. Staring him in the eyes, she began to stroke his head.

' How you've suffered, my poor love ! I'm the only one who knows how much you've suffered. Look, there are grey and white threads in your hair and hard lines round your mouth. My sweetest love, forget everything and stop worrying. You've had to do too much thinking ; now I'm going to think for you. I swear to you that everything is going to be perfect ! '

'I'm not afraid of anything, Margot,' the master suddenly replied, raising his head and looking just as he had when he had created that world he had never seen yet knew to be true. 'I'm not afraid, simply because I have been through everything that a man can go through. I've been so frightened that nothing frightens me any longer. But I feel sorry for you, Margot, that's the point, that's why I keep coming back to the same question. Think, Margarita—why ruin your life for a sick pauper? Go back home. I feel sorry for you, that's why I say this.'

'Oh, dear, dear, dear,' whispered Margarita, shaking her tousled head, 'you weak, faithless, stupid man! Why do you think I spent the whole of last night prancing about naked, why do you think I sold my human nature and became a witch, why do you think I spent months in this dim, damp little hole thinking of nothing but the storm over Jerusalem, why do you think I cried my eyes out when you vanished? You know why—yet when happiness suddenly descends on us and gives us everything, you want to get rid of me! All right, I'll go. But you're a cruel, cruel man. You've become completely heartless.'

Bitter tenderness filled the master's heart and without knowing why he burst into tears as he fondled Margarita's hair. Crying too, she whispered to him as her fingers caressed his temple :

'There are more than just threads . . . your head is turning white under my eyes . . . my poor suffering head. Look at your eyes ! Empty . . . And your shoulders, bent with the weight they've borne . . . they've crippled you . . .' Margarita faded into delirium, sobbing helplessly.

Then the master dried his eyes, raised Margarita from her knees, stood up himself and said firmly :

'That will do. You've made me utterly ashamed. I'll never mention it again, I promise. I know that we are both suffering from some mental sickness which you have probably caught from me . . . Well, we must see it through together.'

Margarita put her lips close to the master's ear and whispered :

'I swear by your life, I swear by the astrologer's son you created that all will be well !'

' All right, I'll believe you,' answered the master with a smile, adding : ' Where else can such wrecks as you and I find help except from the supernatural ? So let's see what we can find in the other world.'

' There, now you're like you used to be, you're laughing,' said Margarita. ' To hell with all your long words ! Supernatural or not supernatural, what do I care ? I'm hungry ! ' And she dragged the master towards the table.

' I can't feel quite sure that this food isn't going to disappear through the floor in a puff of smoke or fly out of the window,' said the master.

' I promise you it won't.'

At that moment a nasal voice was heard at the window :

' Peace be with you.'

The master was startled but Margarita, accustomed to the unfamiliar, cried :

' It's Azazello ! Oh, how nice ! ' And whispering to the master : ' You see—they haven't abandoned us ! ' she ran to open the door.

' You should at least fasten the front of your dress,' the master shouted after her.

' I don't care,' replied Margarita from the passage.

His blind eye glistening, Azazello came in, bowed and greeted the master. Margarita cried :

' Oh, how glad I am ! I've never been so happy in my life ! Forgive me, Azazello, for meeting you naked like this.'

Azazello begged her not to let it worry her, assuring Margarita that he had not only seen plenty of naked women in his time but even women who had been skinned alive. First putting down a bundle wrapped in dark cloth, he took a seat at the table.

Margarita poured Azazello a brandy, which he drank with relish. The master, without staring at him, gently scratched his left wrist under the table, but it had no effect. Azazello did not vanish into thin air and there was no reason why he should. There was nothing terrible about this stocky little demon with red hair, except perhaps his wall eye, but that afflicts plenty of

quite unmagical people, and except for his slightly unusual dress
—a kind of cassock or cape—but ordinary people sometimes
wear clothes like that too. He drank his brandy like all good men
do, a whole glassful at a time and on an empty stomach. The
same brandy was already beginning to make the master's head
buzz and he said to himself:

' No, Margarita's right . . . of course this creature is an emissary
of the devil. After all only the day before yesterday I was
proving to Ivan that he had met Satan at Patriarch's Ponds, yet
now the thought seems to frighten me and I'm inventing excuses
like hypnosis and hallucinations . . . Hypnotism—hell ! '

He studied Azazello's face and was convinced that there was a
certain constraint in his look, some thought which he was holding
back. ' He's not just here on a visit, he has been sent here for a
purpose,' thought the master.

His powers of observation had not betrayed him. After his
third glass of brandy, which had no apparent effect on him,
Azazello said :

' I must say it's comfortable, this little basement of yours, isn't
it ? The only question is—what on earth are you going to do
with yourselves, now that you're here ? '

' That is just what I have been wondering,' said the master
with a smile.

' Why do you make me feel uneasy, Azazello ? ' asked Margarita.

' Oh, come now ! ' exclaimed Azazello, ' I wouldn't dream of
doing anything to upset you. Oh yes ! I nearly forgot . . .
messire sends his greetings and asks me to invite you to take a
little trip with him—if you'd like to, of course. What do you say
to that ? '

Margarita gently kicked the master's foot under the table.

' With great pleasure,' replied the master, studying Azazello,
who went on :

' We hope Margarita Nikolayevna won't refuse ? '

' Of course not,' said Margarita, again brushing the master's
foot with her own.

'Splendid!' cried Azazello. 'That's what I like to see—one, two and away! Not like the other day in the Alexander Gardens!'

'Oh, don't remind me of that, Azazello, I was so stupid then. But you can't really blame me—one doesn't meet the devil every day!'

'More's the pity,' said Azazello. 'Think what fun it would be if you did!'

'I love the speed,' said Margarita excitedly, 'I love the speed and I love being naked . . . just like a bullet from a gun—bang! Ah, how he can shoot!' cried Margarita turning to the master. 'He can hit any pip of a card—under a cushion too!' Margarita was beginning to get drunk and her eyes were sparkling.

'Oh—I nearly forgot something else, too,' exclaimed Azazello, slapping himself on the forehead. 'What a fool I am! Messire has sent you a present'—here he spoke to the master—'a bottle of wine. Please note that it is the same wine that the Procurator of Judaea drank. Falernian.'

This rarity aroused great interest in both Margarita and the master. Azazello drew a sealed wine jar, completely covered in mildew, out of a piece of an old winding-sheet. They sniffed the wine, then poured it into glasses and looked through it towards the window. The light was already fading with the approach of the storm. Filtered through the glass, the light turned everything to the colour of blood.

'To Woland!' exclaimed Margarita, raising her glass.

All three put their lips to the glasses and drank a large mouthful. Immediately the light began to fade before the master's eyes, his breath came in gasps and he felt the end coming. He could just see Margarita, deathly pale, helplessly stretch out her arms towards him, drop her head on to the table and then slide to the floor.

'Poisoner . . .' the master managed to croak. He tried to snatch the knife from the table to stab Azazello, but his hand slithered lifelessly from the tablecloth, everything in the basement seemed to turn black and then vanished altogether. He collapsed sideways, grazing his forehead on the edge of the bureau as he fell.

When he was certain that the poison had taken effect, Azazello started to act. First he flew out of the window and in a few moments he was in Margarita's flat. Precise and efficient as ever, Azazello wanted to check that everything necessary had been done. It had. Azazello saw a depressed-looking woman, waiting for her husband to return, come out of her bedroom and suddenly turn pale, clutch her heart and gasp helplessly :

' Natasha . . . somebody . . . help . . .' She fell to the drawing-room floor before she had time to reach the study.

' All in order,' said Azazello. A moment later he was back with the murdered lovers. Margarita lay face downward on the carpet. With his iron hands Azazello turned her over like a doll and looked at her. The woman's face changed before his eyes. Even in the twilight of the oncoming storm he could see how her temporary witch's squint and her look of cruelty and violence disappeared. Her expression relaxed and softened, her mouth lost its predatory sneer and simply became the mouth of a woman in her last agony. Then Azazello forced her white teeth apart and poured into her mouth a few drops of the same wine that had poisoned her. Margarita sighed, rose without Azazello's help, sat down and asked weakly :

' Why, Azazello, why ? What have you done to me ? '

She saw the master lying on the floor, shuddered and whispered :

' I didn't expect this . . . murderer ! '

' Don't worry,' replied Azazello. ' He'll get up again in a minute. Why must you be so nervous ! '

He sounded so convincing that Margarita believed him at once. She jumped up, alive and strong, and helped to give the master some of the wine. Opening his eyes he gave a stare of grim hatred and repeated his last word :

' Poisoner . . .'

' Oh well, insults are the usual reward for a job well done ! ' said Azazello. ' Are you blind ? You'll soon see sense.'

The master got up, looked round briskly and asked :

' Now what does all this mean ? '

' It means,' replied Azazello, ' that it's time for us to go. The thunderstorm has already begun—can you hear ? It's getting dark. The horses are pawing the ground and making your little garden shudder. You must say goodbye, quickly.'

' Ah, I understand,' said the master, gazing round, ' you have killed us. We are dead. How clever—and how timely. Now I see it all.'

' Oh come,' replied Azazello, ' what did I hear you say ? Your beloved calls you the master, you're an intelligent being—how can you be dead ? It's ridiculous . . .'

' I understand what you mean,' cried the master, ' don't go on ! You're right—a thousand times right ! '

' The great Woland ! ' Margarita said to him urgently, ' the great Woland ! His solution was much better than mine ! But the novel, the novel ! ' she shouted at the master, ' take the novel with you, wherever you may be going ! '

' No need,' replied the master, ' I can remember it all by heart.'

' But you . . . you won't forget a word ? ' asked Margarita, embracing her lover and wiping the blood from his bruised forehead.

' Don't worry. I shall never forget anything again,' he answered.

' Then the fire ! ' cried Azazello. ' The fire—where it all began and where we shall end it ! '

' The fire ! ' Margarita cried in a terrible voice. The basement windows were banging, the blind was blown aside by the wind. There was a short, cheerful clap of thunder. Azazello thrust his bony hand into the stove, pulled out a smouldering log and used it to light the tablecloth. Then he set fire to a pile of old newspapers on the divan, then the manuscript and the curtains.

The master, intoxicated in advance by the thought of the ride to come, threw a book from the bookcase on to the table, thrust its leaves into the burning tablecloth and the book burst merrily into flame.

' Burn away, past ! '

' Burn, suffering ! ' cried Margarita.

Crimson pillars of fire were swaying all over the room, when the three ran out of the smoking door, up the stone steps and out into the courtyard. The first thing they saw was the landlord's cook sitting on the ground surrounded by potato peelings and bunches of onions. Her position was hardly surprising—three black horses were standing in the yard, snorting, quivering and kicking up the ground in fountains. Margarita mounted the first, then Azazello and the master last. Groaning, the cook was about to raise her hand to make the sign of the cross when Azazello shouted threateningly from the saddle :

' If you do, I'll cut off your arm ! ' He whistled and the horses, smashing the branches of the lime tree, whinnied and plunged upwards into a low black cloud. From below came the cook's faint, pathetic cry :

' Fire . . .'

The horses were already galloping over the roofs of Moscow.

' I want to say goodbye to someone,' shouted the master to Azazello, who was cantering along in front of him. Thunder drowned the end of the master's sentence. Azazello nodded and urged his horse into a gallop. A cloud was rushing towards them, though it had not yet begun to spatter rain.

They flew over the boulevard, watching as the little figures ran in all directions to shelter from the rain. The first drops were falling. They flew over a pillar of smoke—all that was left of Griboyedov. On they flew over the city in the gathering darkness. Lightning flashed above them. Then the roofs changed to treetops. Only then did the rain begin to lash them and turned them into three great bubbles in the midst of endless water.

Margarita was already used to the sensation of flight, but the master was not and he was amazed how quickly they reached their destination, where he wished to say goodbye to the only other person who meant anything to him. Through the veil of rain he immediately recognised Stravinsky's clinic, the river and the pine-forest on the far bank that he had stared at for so long. They landed among a clump of trees in a meadow not far from the clinic.

'I'll wait for you here,' shouted Azazello, folding his arms. For a moment he was lit up by a flash of lightning then vanished again in the grey pall. 'You can say goodbye, but hurry!'

The master and Margarita dismounted and flew, like watery shadows, through the clinic garden. A moment later the master was pushing aside the balcony grille of No. 117 with a practised hand. Margarita followed him. They walked into Ivan's room, invisible and unnoticed, as the storm howled and thundered. The master stopped by the bed.

Ivan was lying motionless, as he had been when he had first watched the storm from his enforced rest-home. This time, however, he was not crying. After staring for a while at the dark shape that entered his room from the balcony, he sat up, stretched out his arms and said joyfully:

'Oh, it's you! I've been waiting for you! It's you, my neighbour!'

To this the master answered:

'Yes, it's me, but I'm afraid I shan't be your neighbour any longer. I am flying away for ever and I've only come to say goodbye.'

'I knew, I guessed,' replied Ivan quietly, then asked:

'Did you meet him?'

'Yes,' said the master, 'I have come to say goodbye to you because you're the only person I have been able to talk to in these last days.'

Ivan beamed and said:

'I'm so glad you came. You see, I'm going to keep my word, I shan't write any more stupid poetry. Something else interests me now—' Ivan smiled and stared crazily past the figure of the master—'I want to write something quite different. I have come to understand a lot of things since I've been lying here.'

The master grew excited at this and said as he sat down on the edge of Ivan's bed:

'That's good, that's good. You must write the sequel to it.'

Ivan's eyes sparkled.

'But won't you be writing it?' Then he looked down and added thoughtfully: 'Oh, yes, of course . . . what am I saying.' Ivan stared at the ground, frightened.

'No,' said the master, and his voice seemed to Ivan unfamiliar and hollow. 'I won't write about him any more. I shall be busy with other things.'

The roar of the storm was pierced by a distant whistle.

'Do you hear?' asked the master.

'The noise of the storm . . .'

'No, they're calling me, it's time for me to go,' explained the master and got up from the bed.

'Wait! One more thing,' begged Ivan. 'Did you find her? Had she been faithful to you?'

'Here she is,' replied the master, pointing to the wall. The dark figure of Margarita materialised from the wall and moved over to the bed. She looked at the young man in the bed and her eyes filled with sorrow.

'Poor, poor boy . . .' she whispered silently, and bent over the bed.

'How beautiful she is,' said Ivan, without envy but sadly and touchingly. 'Everything has worked out wonderfully for you, you lucky fellow. And here am I, sick . . .' He thought for a moment, then added thoughtfully: 'Or perhaps I'm not so sick after all . . .'

'That's right,' whispered Margarita, bending right down to Ivan. 'I'll kiss you and everything will be as it should be . . . believe me, I know . . .'

Ivan put his arms round her neck and she kissed him.

'Farewell, disciple,' said the master gently and began to melt into the air. He vanished, Margarita with him. The grille closed.

Ivan felt uneasy. He sat up in bed, gazing round anxiously, groaned, talked to himself, got up. The storm was raging with increasing violence and it was obviously upsetting him. It upset him so much that his hearing, lulled by the permanent silence, caught the sound of anxious footsteps, murmured voices outside his door. Trembling, he called out irritably :

' Praskovya Fyodorovna ! '

As the nurse came into the room, she gave Ivan a worried, enquiring look :

' What's the matter ? ' she asked. ' Is the storm frightening you ? Don't worry—I'll bring you something in a moment . . . I'll call the doctor right away . . .'

' No, Praskovya Fyodorovna, you needn't call the doctor,' said Ivan, staring anxiously not at her but at the wall, ' there's nothing particularly wrong with me. I'm in my right mind now, don't be afraid. But you might tell me,' asked Ivan confidentially, ' what has just happened next door in No. 118 ? '

' In 118 ? ' Praskovya Fyodorovna repeated hesitantly. Her eyes flickered in embarrassment. ' Nothing has happened there.' But her voice betrayed her. Ivan noticed this at once and said :

' Oh, Praskovya Fyodorovna ! You're such a truthful person . . . Are you afraid I'll get violent ? No, Praskovya Fyodorovna, I won't. You had better tell me, you see I can sense it all through that wall.'

' Your neighbour has just died,' whispered Praskovya Fyodorovna, unable to overcome her natural truthfulness and goodness, and she gave a frightened glance at Ivan, who was suddenly clothed in lightning. But nothing terrible happened. He only raised his finger and said :

' I knew it ! I am telling you, Praskovya Fyodorovna, that another person has just died in Moscow too. I even know who ' —here Ivan smiled mysteriously—' it is a woman ! '

31. On Sparrow Hills

The storm had passed and a rainbow had arched itself across the sky, its foot in the Moscow River. On top of a hill between two clumps of trees could be seen three dark silhouettes. Woland, Koroviev and Behemoth sat mounted on black horses, looking at the city spread out beyond the river with fragments of sun glittering from thousands of west-facing windows, and at the onion domes of the Novodevichy monastery.

There was a rustling in the air and Azazello, followed in a black cavalcade by the master and Margarita, landed by the group of waiting figures.

' I'm afraid we had to frighten you a little, Margarita Nikolay-evna, and you, master,' said Woland after a pause. 'But I don't think you will have cause to complain to me about it or regret it. Now,' he turned to the master, ' say goodbye to this city. It's time for us to go.' Woland pointed his hand in its black gauntlet to where countless glass suns glittered beyond the river, where above those suns the city exhaled the haze, smoke and steam of the day.

The master leaped from his saddle, left his companions and ran to the hillside, black cloak flapping over the ground behind him. He looked at the city. For the first few moments a tremor of sadness crept over his heart, but it soon changed to a delicious excitement, the gypsy's thrill of the open road.

' For ever . . . I must think what that means,' whispered the master, and locked his dry, cracked lips. He began to listen to what was happening in his heart. His excitement, it seemed to him, had given way to a profound and grievous sense of hurt. But it was only momentary and gave place to one of proud indifference and finally to a presentiment of eternal peace.

The party of riders waited for the master in silence. They watched the tall, black figure on the hillside gesticulate, then raise his head as though trying to cast his glance over the whole city and to look beyond its edge ; then he hung his head as if he were studying the sparse, trampled grass under his feet.

Behemoth, who was getting bored, broke the silence :

' Please, *mon maître*,' he said, ' let me give a farewell whistle-call.'

' You might frighten the lady,' replied Woland, ' besides, don't forget that you have done enough fooling about for one visit. Behave yourself now.'

' Oh no, messire,' cried Margarita, sitting her mount like an Amazon, one arm akimbo, her long black train reaching to the ground. ' Please let him whistle. I feel sad at the thought of the journey. It's quite a natural feeling, even when you know it will end in happiness. If you won't let him make us laugh, I shall cry, and the journey will be ruined before we start.'

Woland nodded to Behemoth. Delighted, the cat leaped to the ground, out its paws in its mouth, filled its cheeks and whistled.

Margarita's ears sang. Her horse roared, twigs snapped off nearby trees, a flock of rooks and crows flew up, a cloud of dust billowed towards the river and several passengers on a river steamer below had their hats blown off.

The whistle-blast made the master flinch ; he did not turn round, but began gesticulating even more violently, raising his fist skywards as though threatening the city. Behemoth looked proudly round.

' You whistled, I grant you,' said Koroviev condescendingly. ' But frankly it was a very mediocre whistle.'

' I'm not a choirmaster, though,' said Behemoth with dignity, puffing out his chest and suddenly winking at Margarita.

' Let me have a try, just for old time's sake,' said Koroviev. He rubbed his hands and blew on his fingers.

' Very well,' said Woland sternly, ' but without endangering life or limb, please.'

' Purely for fun, I promise you, messire,' Koroviev assured

him, hand on heart. He suddenly straightened up, seemed to stretch as though he were made of rubber, waved the fingers of his right hand, wound himself up like a spring and then, suddenly uncoiling, he whistled.

Margarita did not hear this whistle, but she felt it, as she and her horse were picked up and thrown twenty yards sideways. Beside her the bark was ripped off an oak tree and cracks opened in the ground as far as the river. The water in it boiled and heaved and a river steamer, with all its passengers unharmed, was grounded on the far bank by the blast. A jackdaw, killed by Faggot's whistle, fell at the feet of Margarita's snorting horse.

This time the master was thoroughly frightened and ran back to his waiting companions.

' Well,' said Woland to him from the saddle, ' have you made your farewell ? '

' Yes, I have,' said the master and boldly returned Woland's stare.

Then like the blast of a trumpet the terrible voice of Woland rang out over the hills :

' It is time ! '

As an echo came a piercing laugh and a whistle from Behemoth. The horses leaped into the air and the riders rose with them as they galloped upwards. Margarita could feel her fierce horse biting and tugging at the bit. Woland's cloak billowed out over the heads of the cavalcade and as evening drew on, his cloak began to cover the whole vault of the sky. When the black veil blew aside for a moment, Margarita turned round in flight and saw that not only the many-coloured towers but the whole city had long vanished from sight, swallowed by the earth, leaving only mist and smoke where it had been.

32. *Absolution and Eternal Refuge*

How sad, ye gods, how sad the world is at evening, how mysterious the mists over the swamps. You will know it when you have wandered astray in those mists, when you have suffered greatly before dying, when you have walked through the world carrying an unbearable burden. You know it too when you are weary and ready to leave this earth without regret; its mists, its swamps and its rivers; ready to give yourself into the arms of death with a light heart, knowing that death alone can comfort you.

The magic black horses were growing tired, carrying their riders more slowly as inexorable night began to overtake them. Sensing it behind him even the irrepressible Behemoth was hushed, and digging his claws into the saddle he flew on in silence, his tail streaming behind him.

Night laid its black cloth over forest and meadow, night lit a scattering of sad little lights far away below, lights that for Margarita and the master were now meaningless and alien. Night overtook the cavalcade, spread itself over them from above and began to seed the lowering sky with white specks of stars.

Night thickened, flew alongside, seized the riders' cloaks and pulling them from their shoulders, unmasked their disguises. When Margarita opened her eyes in the freshening wind she saw the features of all the galloping riders change, and when a full, purple moon rose towards them over the edge of a forest, all deception vanished and fell away into the marsh beneath as their magical, trumpery clothing faded into the mist.

It would have been hard now to recognise Koroviev-Faggot, self-styled interpreter to the mysterious professor who needed none, in the figure who now rode immediately alongside Woland at Margarita's right hand. In place of the person who had left Sparrow Hills in shabby circus clothes under the name of Koroviev-Faggot, there now galloped, the gold chain of his bridle chinking softly, a knight clad in dark violet with a grim and unsmiling face. He leaned his chin on his chest, looked neither at the moon nor the earth, thinking his own thoughts as he flew along beside Woland.

'Why has he changed so?' Margarita asked Woland above the hiss of the wind.

'That knight once made an ill-timed joke,' replied Woland, turning his fiery eye on Margarita. 'Once when we were talking of darkness and light he made a somewhat unfortunate pun. As a penance he was condemned to spend rather more time as a practical joker than he had bargained for. But tonight is one of those moments when accounts are settled. Our knight has paid his score and the account is closed.'

Night stripped away, too, Behemoth's fluffy tail and his fur and scattered it in handfuls. The creature who had been the pet of the prince of darkness was revealed as a slim youth, a page-demon, the greatest jester that there has ever been. He too was now silent and flew without a sound, holding up his young face towards the light that poured from the moon.

On the flank, gleaming in steel armour, rode Azazello, his face transformed by the moon. Gone was the idiotic wall eye, gone was his false squint. Both Azazello's eyes were alike, empty and black, his face white and cold. Azazello was now in his real guise, the demon of the waterless desert, the murderer-demon.

Margarita could not see herself but she could see the change that had come ove the master. His hair had whitened in the moonlight and had gathered behind him into a mane that flew in the wind. Whenever the wind blew the master's cloak away from his legs, Margarita could see the spurs that winked at the heels of his jackboots. Like the page-demon the master rode staring at the moon, though smiling at it as though it were a dear, familiar friend, and—a habit acquired in room No. 118—talking to himself.

Woland, too, rode in his true aspect. Margarita could not say what the reins of his horse were made of; she thought that they might be strings of moonlight and the horse itself only a blob of darkness, its mane a cloud and its rider's spurs glinting stars.

They rode for long in silence until the country beneath began to change. The grim forests slipped away into the gloom below, drawing with them the dull curved blades of rivers. The moonlight was now reflected from scattered boulders with dark gulleys between them.

Woland reined in his horse on the flat, grim top of a hill and the riders followed him at a walk, hearing the crunch of flints and pebbles under the horses' shoes. The moon flooded the ground with a harsh green light and soon Margarita noticed on the bare expanse a chair, with the vague figure of a man seated on it, apparently deaf or lost in thought. He seemed not to hear the stony ground shuddering beneath the weight of the horses and he remained unmoved as the riders approached.

In the brilliant moonlight, brighter than an arc-light, Margarita could see the seemingly blind man wringing his hands and staring at the moon with unseeing eyes. Then she saw that beside the massive stone chair, which sparkled fitfully in the moonlight, there lay a huge, grey dog with pointed ears, gazing like his master, at the moon. At the man's feet were the fragments of a jug and a reddish-black pool of liquid.

The riders halted.

'We have read your novel,' said Woland, turning to the master, ' and we can only say that unfortunately it is not finished. I would like to show you your hero. He has been sitting here and sleeping for nearly two thousand years, but when the full moon comes he is tortured, as you see, with insomnia. It plagues not only him, but his faithful guardian, his dog. If it is true that cowardice is the worst sin of all, then the dog at least is not guilty of it. The only thing that frightened this brave animal was a thunderstorm. But one who loves must share the fate of his loved one.'

' What is he saying ? ' asked Margarita, and her calm face was veiled with compassion.

' He always says ' said Woland, ' the same thing. He is saying that there is no peace for him by moonlight and that his duty is a hard one. He says it always, whether he is asleep or awake, and he always sees the same thing—a path of moonlight. He longs to walk along it and talk to his prisoner, Ha-Notsri, because he claims he had more to say to him on that distant fourteenth day of Nisan. But he never succeeds in reaching that path and no one ever comes near him. So it is not surprising that he talks to himself. For an occasional change he adds that most of all he detests his immortality and his incredible fame. He claims that he would gladly change places with that vagrant, Matthew the Levite.'

' Twenty-four thousand moons in penance for one moon long ago, isn't that too much ? ' asked Margarita.

' Are you going to repeat the business with Frieda again ? ' said Woland. ' But you needn't distress yourself, Margarita. All will be as it should ; that is how the world is made.'

' Let him go ! ' Margarita suddenly shouted in a piercing voice, as she had shouted when she was a witch. Her cry shattered a rock in the mountainside, sending it bouncing down into the abyss with a deafening crash, but Margarita could not tell if it was the falling rock or the sound of satanic laughter. Whether it was or not, Woland laughed and said to Margarita :

' Shouting at the mountains will do no good. Landslides are common here and he is used to them by now. There is no need for you to plead for him, Margarita, because his cause has already been pleaded by the man he longs to join.' Woland turned round to the master and went on : ' Now is your chance to complete your novel with a single sentence.'

The master seemed to be expecting this while he had been standing motionless, watching the seated Procurator. He cupped his hands to a trumpet and shouted with such force that the echo sprang back at him from the bare, treeless hills :

' You are free ! Free ! He is waiting for you ! '

The mountains turned the master's voice to thunder and the thunder destroyed them. The grim cliffsides crumbled and fell. Only the platform with the stone chair remained. Above the black abyss into which the mountains had vanished glowed a great city topped by glittering idols above a garden overgrown with the luxuriance of two thousand years. Into the garden stretched the Procurator's long-awaited path of moonlight and the first to bound along it was the dog with pointed ears. The man in the white cloak with the blood-red lining rose from his chair and shouted something in a hoarse, uneven voice. It was impossible to tell if he was laughing or crying, or what he was shouting. He could only be seen hurrying along the moonlight path after his faithful watchdog.

' Am I to follow him ? ' the master enquired uneasily, with a touch on his reins.

' No,' answered Woland, ' why try to pursue what is completed ? '

' That way, then ? ' asked the master, turning and pointing back to where rose the city they had just left, with its onion-domed monasteries, fragmented sunlight reflected in its windows.

' No, not that way either,' replied Woland, his voice rolling down the hillsides like a dense torrent. ' You are a romantic, master ! Your novel has been read by the man that your hero Pilate, whom you have just released, so longs to see.' Here Woland turned to Margarita : ' Margarita Nikolayevna ! I am convinced that you have done your utmost to devise the best possible future for the master, but believe me, what I am offering you and what Yeshua has begged to be given to you is even better ! Let us leave them alone with each other,' said Woland, leaning out of his saddle towards the master and pointing to the departing Procurator. ' Let's not disturb them. Who knows, perhaps they may agree on something.'

At this Woland waved his hand towards Jerusalem, which vanished.

' And there too,' Woland pointed backwards. ' What good is your little basement now ? ' The reflected sun faded from the windows. 'Why go back?' Woland continued, quietly and persuasively. 'O thrice romantic master, wouldn't you like to stroll under the cherry blossom with your love in the daytime and listen to Schubert in the evening? Won't you enjoy writing by candlelight with a goose quill? Don't you want, like Faust, to sit over a retort in the hope of fashioning a new homunculus? That's where you must go—where a house and an old servant are already waiting for you and the candles are lit—although they are soon to be put out because you will arrive at dawn. That is your way, master, that way! Farewell—I must go!'

'Farewell!' cried Margarita and the master together. Then the black Woland, taking none of the paths, dived into the abyss, followed with a roar by his retinue. The mountains, the platform, the moonbeam pathway, Jerusalem—all were gone. The black horses, too, had vanished. The master and Margarita saw the promised dawn, which rose in instant succession to the midnight moon. In the first rays of the morning the master and his beloved crossed a little moss-grown stone bridge. They left the stream behind them and followed a sandy path.

'Listen to the silence,' said Margarita to the master, the sand rustling under her bare feet. 'Listen to the silence and enjoy it. Here is the peace that you never knew in your lifetime. Look, there is your home for eternity, which is your reward. I can already see a Venetian window and a climbing vine which grows right up to the roof. It's your home, your home for ever. In the evenings people will come to see you—people who interest you, people who will never upset you. They will play to you and sing to you and you will see how beautiful the room is by candlelight. You shall go to sleep with your dirty old cap on, you shall go to sleep with a smile on your lips. Sleep will give you strength and make you wise. And you can never send me away— I shall watch over your sleep.'

So said Margarita as she walked with the master towards their everlasting home. Margarita's words seemed to him to flow like the whispering stream behind them, and the master's memory, his accursed, needling memory, began to fade. He had been freed, just as he had set free the character he had created. His hero had now vanished irretrievably into the abyss; on the night of Sunday, the day of the Resurrection, pardon had been granted to the astrologer's son, fifth Procurator of Judaea, the cruel Pontius Pilate.

Epilogue

But what happened in Moscow after sunset on that Saturday evening when Woland and his followers left the capital and vanished from Sparrow Hills?

There is no need to mention the flood of incredible rumours which buzzed round Moscow for long afterwards and even spread to the dimmest and most distant reaches of the provinces. The rumours are, in any case, too nauseating to repeat.

On a train journey to Theodosia, the honest narrator himself heard a story of how in Moscow two thousand people had rushed literally naked out of a theatre and were driven home in taxis.

The whispered words 'evil spirits' could be heard in milk queues and tram queues, in shops, flats and kitchens, in commuter trains and long-distance expresses, on stations and halts, in weekend cottages and on beaches.

Educated and cultured people, of course, took no part in all this gossip about evil spirits descending on Moscow, and even laughed at those who did, and tried to bring them to reason. But facts, as they say, are facts and they could not be brushed aside without some explanation : someone had come to Moscow. The few charred cinders which were all that was left of Griboyedov, and much more besides, were eloquent proof of it.

Cultured people took the viewpoint of the police : a gang of brilliantly skilful hypnotists and ventriloquists had been at work.

Immediate and energetic steps to arrest them in Moscow and beyond were naturally taken but unfortunately without the least result. The man calling himself Woland and all his followers had vanished from Moscow never to return there or anywhere else. He was of course suspected of having escaped abroad, but there was no sign of his being there either.

The investigation of his case lasted for a long time. It was certainly one of the strangest on record. Besides four gutted buildings and hundreds of people driven out of their minds, several people had been killed. At least, two of them were definitely known to have been killed—Berlioz, and that wretched guide to the sights of Moscow, ex-baron Maigel. His charred bones were found in flat No. 50 after the fire had been put out. Violence had been done and violence could not go unchecked.

But there were other victims who suffered as a result of Woland's stay in Moscow and these were, sad to say, black cats.

A good hundred of these peaceful, devoted and useful animals were shot or otherwise destroyed in various parts of the country. Thirty-odd cats, some in a cruelly mutilated condition, were handed in to police stations in various towns. In Armavir, for instance, one of these innocent creatures was brought to the police station with its forelegs tied up.

The man had ambushed the cat just as the animal, wearing a very furtive expression (how can cats help looking furtive? It is not because they are depraved but because they are afraid of being hurt by creatures stronger than they are, such as dogs and people. It is easy enough to hurt them but it is not something that anyone need be proud of)—well, with this furtive look the cat was just about to jump into some bushes.

Pouncing on the cat and pulling off his tie to pinion it, the man snarled threateningly :

' Aha ! So you've decided to come to Armavir, have you, you hypnotist ? No good pretending to be dumb ! We know all about you ! '

The man took the cat to the police station, dragging the wretched beast along by its front legs, which were bound with a green tie so that it was forced to walk on its hind legs.

' Stop playing the fool ! ' shouted the man, surrounded by a crowd of hooting boys, ' No good trying that trick—walk properly ! '

The black cat could only suffer in silence. Deprived by nature of the gift of speech, it had no means of justifying itself. The poor creature owed its salvation largely to the police and to its mistress, an old widow. As soon as the cat was delivered to the police station it was found that the man smelled violently of spirits, which made him a dubious witness. Meanwhile the old woman, hearing from her neighbour that her cat had been abducted, ran to the police station and arrived in time. She gave the cat a glowing reference, saying that she had had it for five years, since it was a kitten in fact, would vouch for it as she would for herself, proved that it had not been caught in any mischief and had never been to Moscow. It had been born in Armavir, had grown up there and learned to catch mice there.

The cat was untied and returned to its owner, though having learned by bitter experience the consequences of error and slander.

A few other people besides cats suffered minor inconvenience. Several arrests were made. Among those arrested for a short time were—in Leningrad one man called Wollman and one called Wolper, three Woldemars in Saratov, Kiev and Kharkhov, a Wallach in Kazan, and for some obscure reason a chemist in Penza by the name of Vetchinkevich. He was, it is true, a very tall man with a dark complexion and black hair.

Apart from that nine Korovins, four Korovkins and two Karavaevs were picked up in various places. One man was taken off the Sebastopol train in handcuffs at Belgorod station for having tried to amuse his fellow-passengers with card tricks.

One lunchtime at Yaroslavl a man walked into a restaurant carrying a Primus, which he had just had repaired. As soon as they caught sight of him the two cloak-room attendants abandoned their post and ran, followed by all the customers and staff. Afterwards the cashier found that all her day's takings had been stolen.

There was more, much more than anyone can remember. A shock-wave of disquiet ran through the country.

It cannot be said too often that the police did an admirable job, given the circumstances. Everything possible was done, not only to catch the criminals but to provide explanations for what they had done. A reason was found for everything and one must admit that the explanations were undeniably sensible.

Spokesmen for the police and a number of experienced psychiatrists established that the members of the gang, or perhaps one of them (suspicion fell chiefly on Koroviev) were hypnotists of incredible skill, capable of appearing to be in two or more places at once. Furthermore, they were frequently able to persuade people that things or people were where they weren't, or, vice-versa, they could remove objects or people from someone's field of vision that were really there all the time.

In the light of this information everything was explicable, even the extraordinary incident of the bullet-proof cat in flat No. 50. There had, of course, been no cat on the chandelier, no one had fired back at the detectives ; they had been firing at nothing while Koroviev, who had made them believe that there was a cat going berserk on the chandelier, had obviously been standing behind the detectives' backs and deploying his colossal though criminally misused powers of suggestion. It was he, of course, who had poured paraffin all over the room and set fire to it.

Stepa Likhodeyev, of course, had never been to Yalta at all (a trick like that was beyond even Koroviev) and had sent no telegram from Yalta. After fainting in the doorway of his bedroom, frightened by Koroviev's trick of producing a cat eating a pickled mushroom on a fork, he had lain there until Koroviev had rammed a sheepskin hat on his head and sent him to Moscow airport, suggesting to the reception committee of detectives that Stepa was really climbing out of an aeroplane that had flown from Sebastopol.

It is true that the Yalta police claimed to have seen Stepa and to have sent telegrams about him to Moscow, but not a single copy of these telegrams was to be found, which led to the sad but incontrovertible conclusion that the band of hypnotists had the power of hypnotising people at vast distances and then not only individuals but whole groups.

This being the case the criminals were obviously capable of sending even the sanest people mad, so that trivia like packs of cards in a man's pocket or vanishing ladies' dresses or a beret that turned into a cat and suchlike were scarcely worth mentioning. Tricks like that could be done by any mediocre hypnotist on any stage, including the old dodge of wrenching off the compère's head. The talking cat was child's play, too. To show people a talking cat one only had to know the first principles of ventriloquy, and clearly Koroviev's abilities went far beyond basic principles.

No, packs of cards and false letters in Nikanor Ivanovich's briefcase were mere trifles. It was he, Koroviev, who had pushed Berlioz to certain death under the tramcar. It was he who had driven the wretched poet Ivan Bezdomny out of his mind, he who had given him nightmares about ancient Jerusalem and parched, sun-baked Mount Golgotha with the three crucified men. It was he and his gang who had spirited Margarita Nikolayevna and her maid away from Moscow. The police, incidentally, paid special attention to this aspect of the case, trying to discover whether these women had been kidnapped by this gang of murderers and arsonists or whether they had voluntarily run away with the criminals. Basing their findings on the ridiculous and confused evidence provided by Nikolai Ivanovich, taking into account the insane note that Margarita Nikolayevna had left for her husband to say that she was becoming a witch, and considering the fact that Natasha had vanished leaving all her movables at home, the investigators came to the conclusion that both maid and mistress had been hypnotised like so many others and then kidnapped by the gang. There was always, of course, the likely consideration that the crooks had been attracted by two such pretty women.

However, one thing baffled the police completely—what could have been the gang's motive for abducting a mental patient, who called himself the master, from a psychiatric clinic? This completely eluded them, as did the abducted patient's real name. He was therefore filed away for ever under the pseudonym of ' No. 118, Block 1.'

Thus nearly everything was explained away and the investigation, as all good things must, came to an end.

Years passed and people began to forget about Woland, Koroviev and the rest. Many things changed in the lives of those who had suffered at the hands of Woland and his associates, and however minor these changes may have been they are still worth following up.

George Bengalsky, for example, after three months in hospital, recovered and was sent home, but he had to give up his job at the Variety at the busiest time of the season, when the public was storming the theatre for tickets : the memory of the black magic and its revelations was too unbearable. Bengalsky gave up the Variety because he realised that he could not stand the agony of standing up in front of two thousand people every evening, being inevitably recognised and endlessly subjected to jeering questions about how he preferred to be—with or without his head ? Apart from that the compère had lost a lot of the cheerfulness which is essential in his job. He developed a nasty, compulsive habit of falling into a depression every spring at the full moon, of suddenly grabbing his neck, staring round in terror and bursting into tears. These attacks did not last for long, but nevertheless since he did have them he could hardly go on doing his old job, and the compère retired and began living on his savings which, by his modest reckoning, were enough to keep him for fifty years.

He left and never again saw Varenukha, who had acquired universal love and popularity for his incredible charm and polite-ness, remarkable even for a theatre manager. The free-ticket hounds, for instance, regarded him as their patron saint. At whatever hour they rang the Variety, through the receiver would always come his soft, sad : ' Hello,' and if the caller asked for Varenukha to be brought to the telephone the same voice hastened to reply : ' Speaking—at your service.' But how Ivan Savyelich had suffered for his politeness !

You can no longer speak to Stepa Likhodeyev if you telephone the Variety. Immediately after his week's stay in hospital, Stepa was transferred to Rostov where he was made the manager of a large delicatessen store. There are rumours that he never touches port these days, that he only drinks vodka distilled from black-currants and is much healthier for it. They say, too, that he is very silent these days and avoids women.

Stepan Bogdanovich's removal from the Variety did not bring Rimsky the joy he had dreamed of for so many years. After hospital and a cure at Kislovodsk, the treasurer, now an old, old man with a shaking head, tendered his resignation. It was Rimsky's wife who brought his letter of resignation to the theatre : Grigory Danilovich himself could not find the strength, even in daytime, to revisit the building where he had seen the moonlit windowpane rattling and the long arm reaching down to grasp the catch.

Having retired from the Variety, Rimsky got a job at the children's marionette theatre on the far side of the Moscow River. Here he never even had to deal with Arkady Apollonich Sempleyarov on the subject of acoustics, because he in turn had been transferred to Bryansk and put in charge of a mushroom-canning plant. Now Muscovites eat his salted chanterelles and his pickled button-mushrooms and they are so delicious that everybody is delighted with Arkady Apollonich's change of job. It is all so long ago now that there is no harm in saying that Arkady Appollonich never had much success at improving the acoustics of Moscow's theatres anyway, and the situation is much the same today.

Apart from Arkady Apollonich, several other people have given up the theatre for good, among them Nikanor Ivanovich Bosoi, even though his only link with the theatre was a fondness for free tickets. Nowadays Nikanor Ivanovich not only refuses to accept free tickets : he wouldn't set foot inside a theatre if you paid him and he even turns pale if the subject crops up in conversation. More than the theatre he now loathes both Pushkin and that gifted artiste, Savva Potapovich Kurolesov ; in fact he detests that actor to such a degree that last year, catching sight of a black-bordered announcement in the newspaper that Savva Potapovich had been struck down in the prime of life by a heart attack, Nikanor Ivanovich turned such a violent shade of

purple that he almost joined Savva Potapovich, and he roared :
' Serve him right ! '

What is more, the actor's death stirred so many painful memories for Nikanor Ivanovich that he went out and, with the full moon for company, got blind drunk. With every glass that he drank the row of hated figures lengthened in front of him— there stood Sergei Gerardovich Dunchill, there stood the beautiful Ida Herkulanovna, there stood the red-bearded man and his herd of fearsome geese.

And what happened to them ? Nothing. Nothing could ever happen to them because they never existed, just as the compère, the theatre itself, the miserly old aunt hoarding currency in her cellar and the rude cooks never existed either. Nikanor Ivanovich had dreamed it all under the evil influence of the beastly Koroviev. The only real person in his dream was Savva Potapovich the actor, who got involved merely because Ivanor Ivanovich had so often heard him on the radio. Unlike all the others, he was real.

So perhaps Aloysius Mogarych did not exist either ? Far from it. Aloysius Mogarych is still with us, in the very job that Rimsky gave up—treasurer of the Variety Theatre.

About twenty-four hours after his call on Woland, Aloysius had regained consciousness in a train somewhere near Vyatka. Finding that he had absentmindedly left Moscow without his trousers but had somehow brought his landlord's rent-book with him, Aloysius had given the conductor a colossal tip, borrowed a pair of filthy old trousers from him and turned back to Moscow from Vyatka. But he failed to find his landlord's house. The ancient pile had been burnt to the ground. Aloysius, however, was extremely ingenious. Within a fortnight he had moved into an excellent room in Bryusov Street and a few months later he was installed in Rimsky's office. Just as Rimsky had suffered under Stepa, Varenukha's life was now made a misery by Aloysius. Ivan Savyelich's one and only wish is for Aloysius to be removed as far away from the Variety as possible because, as Varenukha sometimes whispers among his close friends, ' he has never met such a swine in his life as that Aloysius and he wouldn't be surprised at anything Aloysius might do '.

The house manager is perhaps biased. Aloysius is not known to have done anything suspicious—indeed he does not appear to have done anything at all, except of course to appoint another barman in place of Sokov. Andrei Fokich died of cancer of the liver nine months after Woland's visit to Moscow. . . .

More years passed and the events described in this truthful account have faded from most people's memories—with a few exceptions.

Every year, at the approach of the vernal full moon, a man of about thirty or a little more can be seen walking towards the lime trees of Patriarch's Ponds. A reddish-haired, green-eyed, modestly dressed man. He is Professor Ivan Nikolayich Poniryov of the Institute of History and Philosophy.

When he reaches the lime trees he always sits down on the same bench on which he sat that evening when Berlioz, now long forgotten by everybody, saw the moon shatter to fragments for the last time in his life. Now that moon, whole and in one piece, white in the early evening and later golden with its outline of a dragon-horse, floats over the erstwhile poet Ivan Nikolayich while seeming to stand still.

Ivan Nikolayich now knows and understands everything. He knows that as a young man he fell victim to some crooked hypnotists, went to hospital and was cured. But he knows that there is still something that is beyond his control. He cannot control what happens at the springtime full moon. As soon as it draws near, as soon as that heavenly body begins to reach that fullness it once had when it hung in the sky high above the two seven-branched candlesticks, Ivan Nikolayich grows uneasy and irritable, loses his appetite, cannot sleep and waits for the moon to wax. When full moon comes nothing can keep Ivan Nikolayich at home. Towards evening he leaves home and goes to Patriarch's Ponds.

As he sits on the bench Ivan Nikolayich openly talks to himself, smokes, peers at the moon or at the familiar turnstile.

Ivan Nikolayich spends an hour or two there, then gets up and walks, always following the same route, across Spiridonovka Street with unseeing eyes towards the side-streets near the Arbat.

He passes an oil-shop, turns by a crooked old gas lamp and creeps up to some railings through which he can see a garden that is splendid, though not yet in flower, and in it—lit on one side by moonlight, dark on the other, with an attic that has a triple-casement window—a house in the Gothic style.

The professor never knows what draws him to those railings or who lives in that house, but he knows that it is useless to fight his instinct at full moon. He knows, too, that in the garden beyond the railings he will inevitably see the same thing every time.

He sees a stout, elderly man sitting on a bench, a man with a beard, a pince-nez and very, very slightly piggish features. Ivan Nikolayich always finds that tenant of the Gothic house in the same dreamy attitude, his gaze turned towards the moon. Ivan Nikolayich knows that having stared at the moon the seated man will turn and look hard at the attic windows, as though expecting them to be flung open and something unusual to appear on the windowsill.

The rest, too, Ivan Nikolayich knows by heart. At this point he has to duck down behind the railings, because the man on the bench begins to twist his head anxiously, his wandering eyes seeking something in the air. He smiles in triumph, then suddenly clasps his hands in delicious agony and mutters quite distinctly :

' Venus ! Venus ! Oh, what a fool I was . . . ! '

' Oh God,' Ivan Nikolayich starts to whisper as he hides behind the railings with his burning gaze fixed on the mysterious stranger. ' Another victim of the moon . . . Another one like me . . . '

And the man goes on talking :

' Oh, what a fool I was ! Why, why didn't I fly away with her ? What was I afraid of, stupid old ass that I am ? I had to ask for that document ! . . . Well, you must just put up with it, you old cretin . . . ! '

So it goes on until a window opens on the dark side of the house, something white appears in it and an unpleasant female voice rings out :

'Where are you, Nikolai Ivanovich ? What the hell are you doing out there ? Do you want to catch malaria ? Come and drink your tea ! '

At this the man blinks and says in a lying voice :

'I'm just having a breath of fresh air, my dear ! The air out here is so nice ! '

Then he gets up from his bench, furtively shakes his fist at the window which has just closed and stumps indoors.

'He's lying, he's lying ! Oh God, how he's lying ! ' mumbles Ivan Nikolayich as he walks from the railings. 'He doesn't come down to the garden for the fresh air—he sees something in that springtime sky, something high above the garden ! What wouldn't I give to find out his secret, to know who the Venus is that he lost and now tries vainly to catch by waving his arms in the air.'

The professor returns home a sick man. His wife pretends not to notice it and hurries him into bed, but she stays up and sits by the lamp with a book, watching the sleeping man with a bitter look. She knows that at dawn Ivan Nikolayich will wake up with an agonised cry, will start to weep and rave. That is why she keeps in front of her on the tablecloth a hypodermic syringe ready in a dish of spirit and an ampoule of liquid the colour of strong tea.

Later the poor woman is free to go to sleep without misgiving. After his injection Ivan Nikolayich will sleep until morning with a calm expression and he will dream, unknown to her, dreams that are sublimely happy.

It is always the same thing that wakens the scholar and wrings that pitiful cry from him. He sees a strange, noseless executioner who, jumping up and uttering a grunt as he does so, pierces the heart of the maddened Hestas, lashed to a gibbet. But what makes the dream so horrible is not so much the executioner as the lurid, unnatural light that comes from a cloud, seething and drenching the earth, of the kind that only accompanies natural disasters.

After his injection the sleeper's vision changes. From the bed to the moon stretches a broad path of moonlight and up it is climbing a man in a white cloak with a blood-red lining. Beside him walks a young man in a torn chiton and with a disfigured face. The two are talking heatedly, arguing, trying to agree about something.

' Ye gods ! ' says the man in the cloak, turning his proud face to his companion. ' What a disgusting method of execution ! But please, tell me,'—here the pride in his face turns to supplication—' it did not take place, did it ? I beg you—tell me that it never took place ? '

' No, of course it never took place,' answers his companion in a husky voice. ' It was merely your imagination.'

' Can you swear to that ? ' begged the man in the cloak.

' I swear it ! ' answers his companion, his eyes smiling.

' That is all I need to know ! ' gasps the man in the cloak as he strides on towards the moon, beckoning his companion on. Behind them walks a magnificently calm, gigantic dog with pointed ears.

Then the moonbeam begins to shake, a river of moonlight floods out of it and pours in all directions. From the flood materialises a woman of incomparable beauty and leads towards Ivan a man with a stubble-grown face, gazing fearfully round him. Ivan Nikolayich recognises him at once. It is No. 118, his nocturnal visitor. In his dream Ivan stretches out his arms towards him and asks greedily :

' So was that how it ended ? '

' That is how it ended, disciple,' replies No. 118 as the woman approaches Ivan and says :

' Of course. It has ended ; and everything has an end . . . I'll kiss you on the forehead and everything will be as it should be . . .'

She leans over Ivan and kisses him on the forehead and Ivan strains towards her to look into her eyes, but she draws back,

444

draws back and walks away towards the moon with her companion. . . .

Then the moon goes mad, deluges Ivan with streams of light, sprays light everywhere, a moonlight flood invades the room, the light sways, rises, drowns the bed. It is then that Ivan sleeps with a look of happiness on his face.

In the morning he wakes silent, but quite calm and well. His bruised memory has subsided again and until the next full moon no one will trouble the professor—neither the noseless man who killed Hestas nor the cruel Procurator of Judaea, fifth in that office, the knight Pontius Pilate.

THE HISTORY OF VINTAGE

The famous American publisher Alfred A. Knopf (1892–1984) founded Vintage Books in the United States in 1954 as a paperback home for the authors published by his company. Vintage was launched in the United Kingdom in 1990 and works independently from the American imprint although both are part of the international publishing group, Random House.

Vintage in the United Kingdom was initially created to publish paperback editions of books bought by the prestigious literary hardback imprints in the Random House Group such as Jonathan Cape, Chatto & Windus, Hutchinson and later William Heinemann, Secker & Warburg and The Harvill Press. There are many Booker and Nobel Prize-winning authors on the Vintage list and the imprint publishes a huge variety of fiction and non-fiction. Over the years Vintage has expanded and the list now includes great authors of the past – who are published under the Vintage Classics imprint – as well as many of the most influential authors of the present. In 2012 Vintage Children's Classics was launched to include the much-loved authors of our youth.

For a full list of the books Vintage publishes,
please visit our website
www.vintage-books.co.uk

For book details and other information about the classic authors we publish, please visit the Vintage Classics website
www.vintage-classics.info

penguin.co.uk/vintage